WİLD
HUΠGER

Also by Suzanne Wright

From Rags

The Dark in You Series

Burn

Blaze

The Deep in Your Veins Series

Here Be Sexist Vampires

The Bite That Binds

Taste of Torment

Consumed

Fractured

The Phoenix Pack Series

Feral Sins

Wicked Cravings

Carnal Secrets

Dark Instincts

Savage Urges

Fierce Obsessions

The Mercury Pack Series

Spiral of Need

Force of Temptation

Lure of Oblivion

WILD HUNGER

THE PHOENIX PACK SERIES

SUZANNE WRIGHT

Montlake Romance

Published by Montlake Romance, Seattle

www.apub.com

Amazon, the Amazon logo, and Montlake Romance are trademarks of Amazon.com, Inc., or its affiliates.

ISBN-13: 9781503902169
ISBN-10: 1503902161

Cover design by Erin Dameron Hill

Printed in the United States of America

For Quentin Tarantino—
thank you for creating the masterpiece
that is Pulp Fiction

CHAPTER ONE

It was really a good thing that Frankie Newman had never needed a knight in shining armor, because she'd only ever come across complete idiots wrapped in tinfoil. The guy in front of her was no exception.

Vance studied her appearance, taking in her protective clothes and the goggles she'd pushed onto her forehead. "I, um, guess you were busy."

"Good guess." But he hadn't had to guess. The sound of rock music blasting would have told him she was working. But then, Vance didn't see her job as "work." He saw it as more of a cute hobby that she should have grown out of by now. It didn't matter that her sculptures were displayed in galleries or that she had an established reputation. Much like her grandparents, he didn't take her profession seriously.

Ordinarily she'd have ignored the incessant knocking, but she'd thought he was her agent, who was due to arrive any moment now.

He patted the cardboard box he was holding. "I found some of your stuff lying around. I thought you might want it back."

"Thanks," she said, tone flat. He stepped forward, clearly expecting her to move aside and let him pass. Not gonna happen. She grabbed the box and set it beside her on the hardwood floor.

He cleared his throat. "How are you?"

"Fine." She'd be a hell of a lot better when he left. The wolf within her stirred, raring to swipe her claws at the human to warn him away. She wasn't a forgiving animal.

He scrubbed a hand down his face. "Shit, Frankie, I . . ." He sighed. "You have every right to be mad at me for getting back together with Layla, and I don't—"

"I'm not mad that you went back to her." She'd liked Vance's company, and he was certainly good in bed, but Frankie didn't love him. And it wasn't like she hadn't guessed that he still cared for Layla—a guy didn't constantly trash-talk his ex unless she was on his mind a little too much. But Frankie hadn't been mad about it back then; she knew that getting over someone wasn't a simple thing and that feelings couldn't be switched on and off.

While Layla had messed with his head by sending bitchy texts, posting pics of herself on Facebook kissing other guys, and even sleeping with one of his friends, Frankie had been there for him. The moment he'd "healed," he'd gone right on back to Layla. It seemed that they both got off on the drama or something.

His brow creased a little. "You're not?"

"No. But I *am* pissed that you led me to believe that you *wouldn't* go back to her. I'm pissed that I spent time out of my life being there for you, worrying about you, supporting you while *she hurt you*, when you ultimately planned to go back to her."

He held up a hand. "I swear, Frankie, I didn't plan it. I didn't want to hurt you, and I hate that I did."

"If you want to prove it, tell her to stop stalking me online. Tell her to stop leaving stupid comments on my Facebook fan page. Every time I block her, she creates another profile and does it again."

He winced. "I know. I told her to stop. She . . . obsesses about you. She refuses to believe that I'm over you. The more I deny it, the more she seems to believe that she's right. I can't win here."

"Well, maybe if you stopped texting and calling me when you're hammered and explained to Layla that you and I aren't all that well suited, she'd simmer down."

He bristled. "We suited each other just fine." The sexual implication in his voice was clear.

"In bed, sure. Out of it? Not so much." Which had disappointed her grandparents, because they'd loved the idea of her and the attorney—particularly her grandmother, who was close friends with his mother. "But that doesn't matter now. Really, Vance, you should just go. I hope things work out for you and Layla, and I hope you'll make her see reason and stop bothering me." She tried to close the door, but his hand shot out to hold it open.

"I was hoping we could go back to being friends again. We were friends before we started dating, remember."

Frankie wouldn't have described them as "friends." Acquaintances who'd met through her grandparents? Yes. Actual friends? Nah. "Look, I have no intention of bad-mouthing you to my grandmother, if that's your worry, so the full story isn't going to reach your mother unless you tell her."

"I already told her, and she's pissed at me. Not that she said as much. My mother's a big believer of 'If you can't say something nice, don't say anything at all.' 'Silence is golden' is one of her favorite phrases."

The unnecessary use of a proverb made Frankie's frown deepen. She just didn't get the need for proverbs. Like "All good things come to those who wait." Really? Weird, because she hadn't won the lottery yet. Like "You can't have your cake and eat it too." Well, why not? She wasn't going to buy a cake for no good reason; it was stupid to think differently. Like "It's raining cats and dogs." Um, no it wasn't—and never had—rained cats and dogs.

Why use a proverb when you could just use a phrase that made sense?

Well, Frankie had news for Vance's mother: silence was silence. It was nothing—couldn't be heard, seen, or touched. It therefore did not physically exist, and couldn't be any color whatsoever, let alone golden.

But she didn't want to prolong her conversation with Vance, so she simply said, "I have to go. I hope things work out for you and Layla this time around." Just then a familiar Mercedes convertible parked behind Vance's car. Frankie smiled as a middle-aged redhead dressed in a tailored blouse and skirt hopped out of the car.

"Who's that?" asked Vance.

"My agent."

His brow creased. "You have an agent?"

"You don't need to sound so surprised. You may not approve of my job, but others do."

"It's not that I don't approve. It's that you could be so much more."

Like sculpting was easy and something to sniff haughtily at. "You take care now, Vance." The dismissal clearly rankled, and his jaw hardened. Yeah, well, his dismissal of her career rankled too.

Striding up the path, Abigail took in Frankie's appearance and said, "You've been working. Good."

Frankie smiled. "Well, hello to you too." She counted Abigail as a friend, which Frankie didn't have many of. She'd never been a particularly social person and often buried herself in her work.

"You know I'm not one for pleasantries." Abigail eyed Vance curiously. "And who might you be?"

"Vance Browne."

"Oh, the attorney who crawled back to his ex." Yeah, that was Abigail—she didn't spare anyone's feelings.

His eyes hardened. "I didn't crawl anywhere."

"He has fabulous cheekbones, Frankie. You should sculpt his face. Then we can shatter the nose, break the jaw. Maybe even scalp it."

Frankie saw some appeal in the idea, but . . . "It would be a waste of clay."

"True."

Frankie stepped aside to let Abigail pass. "See you around, Vance. Give Layla my best." She closed the door, headed down the hallway, turned right, and walked into the studio attached to the house. She'd had it built a few years ago to her specifications. The high ceiling, spotlights, large windows, and good ventilation system made it a perfect work space.

Sunlight streamed through the open roll-up door, outside which she'd sectioned off a part of her backyard to use for bigger, more challenging sculptures. Tools, materials, and other equipment lined the walls; some sat on benches or shelves, others on metal racks or the floor, ensuring she had plenty of space to work.

Abigail's high heel clicked on the cold concrete floor as she stood near the locked door of the display room, tapping her foot impatiently. Frankie kept all her finished sculptures inside, and she'd recently completed a commissioned piece for the owner of a New York art gallery. She fished the keys out of the pocket of her coveralls and unlocked the door.

Eyes alight with eagerness, Abigail walked inside and pointed to a veiled sculpture. "This it?"

"It is." Frankie gently removed the cover, and there it was. A life-size child sat on a rickety chair, her head drooping forward so that her long black hair covered her face. Her gray nightie was dirty and ragged and stopped just below the knees. Deep scratches covered her legs and arms.

"Jesus, Frankie, she almost looks alive. This is terrifying. Honestly, my nape's prickling—like someone's watching me. This sets off that same feeling of danger. You've never used synthetic hair in a sculpture before, have you?"

"No." Frankie made mixed-media sculptures, liking to combine different materials in her projects.

"She looks spooky, and it makes me wonder if she's a victim or a creepy evil kid. Makes me want to part her hair to see what her face looks like. At the same time, I don't want to know."

"That's the point. Pierre wanted something that reflects how often we're too scared to look close enough to see what could be a dark truth, how often we see what we want to see."

"He's going to *love* it."

Frankie had gained quite a rep for creating dark sculptures. She rarely set out to make something dark, but often the finished result looked like something she'd plucked right out of a hellish nightmare.

"What are you going to call it?"

"Child's Play."

"Shit, even that's spooky." Abigail shivered. "You must have extremely bleak dreams."

She'd had nightmares as a child, but she could only recall flashes of them now. Remembered the snarling. The crying. The scary shadows. The sheer terror that had seized her. But the images had never made sense, had never come together to create a clear picture.

"Really, Frankie, I wouldn't have thought I'd like this kind of work. Wouldn't have thought I could truly admire it, let alone properly represent someone who created it. But every piece is so powerful that it touches me on some level—and sometimes it's a level that I don't like."

Frankie's mouth curved. "Good. If they don't touch people—" She cut herself off as her phone beeped. "Hang on just a sec." She dug her phone out of her pocket and opened the e-mail she'd received. She read it. Then she read it again. Then she read it again. The words began to blur, and she realized her hand was shaking.

"Is everything all right?"

Unable to properly process what she'd read, Frankie burst out, "What the fuck is this?"

Lounging in an armchair, Trick Hardy twisted the small object in his hand this way and that, studying it from every angle . . . as if it could somehow answer the many questions he had. His pack mates were spread across the room—perched on the sofa, sprawled in the armchairs, and sitting on the floor. They'd waited until the children were in bed before meeting to discuss the issue.

Taryn, the Alpha female, gaped at Trick. "You're seriously telling me that four of the pack's vehicles had been tagged with GPS trackers like that one? Jesus."

"Someone obviously wants to monitor our movements," said her mate, Trey, his large form pacing in front of the sofa. "Why?"

Dominic, an enforcer, tapped his fingers on the arm of a plush chair. "Packs always have reasons to want to keep a close eye on others."

Makenna frowned. "Yeah, but using trackers isn't exactly normal, is it? It seems extreme." Her mate, Ryan, grunted in agreement. The gruff enforcer didn't talk much. Luckily—and weirdly—Makenna seemed to be able to translate his grunts.

"Could be that someone's trying to learn our patterns," mused Trick. "Or maybe they're waiting until the tagged vehicles are all gone at once."

Trey's arctic-blue gaze narrowed. "Waiting for a time when the pack might be vulnerable, you mean."

Trick shrugged. "It's a theory."

"By monitoring our movements, they're monitoring the kids' movements," said Tao, the Head Enforcer, golden-brown eyes flashing. Sitting on the floor with his mate between his legs, he lightly massaged her stiff shoulders. Riley, a raven shifter, was the pack's Guardian and watched over the five children.

"It would be a good idea to keep them on our territory as much as possible," said Ryan. He cast his mate a pointed look, since Makenna liked taking their baby girl to the homeless shelter for lone shifters where she worked.

Sniffing, Makenna flicked her long, multicolored, beach-layered waves over her shoulder.

"There's no way to tell how long the trackers have been here," said Riley. "That bugs me—no pun intended—because it means we have no idea just how much of our movements have been recorded."

"Whoever planted the trackers will know we found them—they switched off the moment they were removed," said Marcus, another enforcer. "They didn't look particularly high tech to me."

Rhett, their IT expert and hacker, said, "They weren't. You could easily buy a batch of them online."

Taryn eyed the one that Trick was fiddling with as she said, "Thank God the mechanic spotted it when he gave the SUV a tune-up, or we might never have known about them."

Dante, the Beta male, stretched out his long legs. "I doubt whoever did it will risk planting any more, but we should still be careful. If we leave our territory, we should check the vehicles afterward—it wouldn't be hard to plant a tracker while we're out and about."

Perched on Marcus's lap, Roni—his mate and another enforcer—took her strawberry-flavored lollipop out of her mouth and said, "We should also be on the lookout for people tailing us. If someone really wants to keep track of our movements, they'll find another way."

Trick pursed his lips. "Do you think Morelli might have something to do with it, Trey?" Nash Morelli had become a pain in their asses. The wolf had built his pack by recruiting lone shifters, many of whom were assassins. He called it the Mortelle Pack, the word being French for "deadly." Trick found the idea a little pathetic. The pack had grown over time as Morelli had targeted small packs, challenging and killing their Alphas before then giving the rest of the pack members the choice to join him or die. As such, Trick doubted the Mortelle wolves would be particularly loyal to their Alpha. The way Morelli formed a pack didn't really say "Alpha material." He was quite simply an asshole.

Morelli had recently called Trey to request a meeting, which would take place in a few days' time, and no one was looking forward to it. Trick didn't think Morelli would be dumb enough to fuck with

Trey—not given the Phoenix Alpha's dark reputation—but some people were simply . . . well . . . stupid.

"It's possible." Trey rolled back his wide shoulders and turned to Rhett. "Have you found anything on him yet?"

Rhett blew out a breath. "If Nash Morelli truly exists, his history has been wiped. I'm more inclined to think that the guy changed his name."

Jaime, the Beta female, tilted her head, making her long sable hair brush her mate's jean-clad thigh; Dante immediately began playing with it. "Should we really assume this was Morelli's work? We're in contact with a few packs and prides. Sure, they're all allies, but that doesn't mean they wouldn't have some reason to record our movements."

"Jaime's right," said Roni. "But since we have no way to find out who it was, the only thing we can do at this point is wait and see what happens next." She sighed, her green eyes glittering with frustration.

Greta, Trey's antisocial grandmother, patted Roni's shoulder soothingly. "Don't worry, sweetheart, my boys will find out one way or another." By "boys" she meant Trey, Dante, Tao, and the male enforcers. The old woman seemed to pretty much despise Taryn, Jaime, Makenna, and Riley purely because they were mated to "her boys." Roni had somehow tricked Greta into liking her.

"What I really don't get is why Morelli would look for trouble when the rest of our kind is trying to win favor with humans," said Gabe, Jaime's brother. "I wouldn't have thought all the PR work would pay off, but it is."

When the radical, increasingly violent anti-shifter extremists had resorted to acts of terrorism that caused many human casualties, the groups had lost a lot of credibility. Even prejudiced humans were no longer so willing to listen to them; instead they seemed to be practicing the "live and let live" ethic. A lot of packs, prides, and other groups had pounced on that and had independently begun doing PR work for shifters, hoping to counter the negative stereotypes floating around about them. The last thing shifters needed was one of their kind attracting negative attention.

"Speaking of PR, your video now has over seventy million views, Trick." Dante's mouth twitched. "Bet you never saw that coming."

Trick cast him a hard look. "It's not my video."

Dante grinned. "Well, you're the star."

When Trick had fought off a gang of human boys who were about to mug and possibly assault a human female, someone caught the incident on their cell phone. He'd become a YouTube sensation overnight, and he wasn't pleased about it. He'd carried the terrified female—who'd clung to him like a barnacle—out of the alley, and the whole thing had been romanticized.

He *wasn't* a hero. He *wasn't* a good guy human girls should crush on. And he was damn sick of people asking him if he was the shifter savior on YouTube.

"You should be glad, Trick," said Jaime, smoky-blue eyes dancing with mischief. "Other shifters are working hard to gain acceptance and popularity with humans by going on the radio and appearing on daytime talk shows. You accomplished that for our pack just by doing a good deed. Although I'm not so sure it would have had the same effect if you weren't so hot."

Each muscle in his powerful build tensing, Dante scowled at his mate. "You don't get to call another guy 'hot' unless you want to get your ass spanked."

"Maybe that's *why* I did it, Popeye," Jaime shot back with a saucy grin.

Their byplay made Trick's chest clench and caused his wolf's mood to sour. A deep loneliness had steadily crept up on Trick and his wolf as they'd watched their pack mates and allies find their true mates, one by one. Of the adult male wolves within his pack, only he and Dominic remained unmated. There was now a bitter edge to his wolf's loneliness.

Dante and Jaime had known each other since they were children, when they'd all belonged to the Bjorn Pack. Trick had been a teenager when it split, and he'd left with some other wolves to form the Phoenix Pack. Jaime had remained behind, too young to make the decision to leave. It wasn't until she'd transferred to the Phoenix Pack as an adult that she and Dante had realized they were true mates.

It wasn't uncommon for mates to fail to immediately recognize one another. Several things could jam the frequency of a mating bond, including doubts, fears, and secrets. In other words, people often let their personal shit get in the way. They didn't listen to their inner animals and sometimes even blinded themselves to the obvious out of fear.

Personally, Trick didn't get it. What was so bad about having a mate? Nothing. Sure, your life would change in many ways, but you'd also be whole and happy in a way that you could never otherwise be.

Unlike some, Trick had no reservations about mating. He didn't have any hang-ups about being bonded to someone, wasn't fearful of commitment, and wouldn't shy away from the sacrifices he'd have to make.

He'd always had a drive inside him to find his mate. He wasn't sure if that was normal, but that need to hunt and claim her had always been there. Like an itch that needed scratching.

Since he didn't have any hang-ups that could jam the frequency of the bond, Trick was positive that he'd recognize his mate on sight. Of course, the frequency might not be clear for her, and so he wouldn't necessarily feel the tug of the mating bond straightaway, but that wouldn't stop him from acting. He'd simply approach her, voice his belief, convince her that it was true, and then cleave himself to her. There was no reason for it to be complicated. Oh, sure, it was important for couples to get to know each other and build trust, but that could be done while they were mated as far as he was concerned.

From her position on the rug, Lydia cleared her throat to get everyone's attention. "Um . . . if we're finished talking about the trackers, there's something I need to add."

Trick frowned. Her anxiety was almost palpable. She was a submissive wolf who was usually laid-back and easy to be around. At that moment, though, she was strung up tight. "What's wrong?"

She licked her lips and then opened her mouth to speak, but nothing came out.

"What is it?" asked Trey.

Her mate, Cam, gently nudged her, and Lydia inhaled deeply. "You're probably going to be mad," she warned the Alphas.

Taryn gave her a gentle smile. "Lydia, tell us what's wrong."

"I won't lose my shit," Trey promised. "Whatever it is can't be that bad. Now tell us."

Lydia's shoulders lost a little of their stiffness. "Those of you who once belonged to my childhood pack will remember that my older brother died when I was young."

"Damn, I'm sorry," said Taryn. "I didn't even know you had a brother." Unlike most of the Phoenix Pack, Taryn hadn't been part of the Bjorn Pack.

Lydia licked her lips. "He, um . . . he shot himself. He killed his mate, and then he shot himself."

Taryn's mouth fell open. "Oh my God. Wait, I think I once heard something about a wolf who turned on his mate before ending his own life."

"Many packs got wind of the story."

Trick had been just a kid at the time, but he hadn't forgotten that night. Hadn't forgotten the sadness, shock, and grief that had weighed heavily on the pack. After all, it wasn't often that mates turned on each other like that.

"Christopher wasn't a bad person," Lydia insisted. "He worshipped the ground Caroline, his mate, walked on. They argued, sure, and he had a temper, but . . . it was just so out of character for him to harm her. There was no way to work out exactly what happened that night.

There was only one witness—their daughter, my niece. She was only three at the time."

Jaime smiled weakly. "She was my favorite playmate."

Trick remembered little Francesca well. She'd been the youngest of the pups, so they'd all been very protective of her. She'd been bright and full of life, and he'd teased her often by tugging on her curls and chasing her around.

Even though she'd been tiny and delicate looking, no one had thought of her as weak. She was born prematurely and had gone through such a complicated birth that the pack healer hadn't expected her to live more than forty-eight hours. But she'd pulled through and instantly earned a reputation as a fighter.

"Three?" Taryn echoed. She shoved a hand through her hair, pinning back the different shades of blonde. "Jesus, she must have been terrified."

"She was the prettiest, sweetest kid you've ever known," said Lydia, nostalgia in her voice. "I was only eight years older than Francesca. We were very close. Her mom was beautiful—tall and slender with blonde spiral curls. Francesca was a mini version of her, only she had Christopher's blue eyes and dimples."

Trick drummed his fingers on his thigh. "She's a sculptor now, right?"

Lydia's eyes snapped to him. "Right. How did you know that?"

He shrugged. "I looked her up a few times. I was curious about how she turned out. Her work's good." Very good. And very dark.

Sighing, Lydia rubbed at her nape. "I don't know how much she saw that night, or if she even really understood what happened. I didn't get a chance to find out."

Taryn's brow furrowed. "What do you mean?"

"Her maternal family is human. They were devastated by their daughter's death—blamed my brother, my family, the pack. They wanted to take Francesca, and they did. The pack would have fought to keep her, but she seemed so traumatized. Mom thought that being away from the territory for a little while would be good for her, but what Mom hadn't counted on was that the humans would refuse to allow us to even visit her. They wanted all shifters out of her life, regardless of the fact that Francesca was half shifter herself."

"Bastards," muttered Riley.

"Mom appealed to the human courts for access to her, but her grandparents are mega-rich and they hired an attorney that ran circles around ours. We lost the case and were cut out of Francesca's life. Once I was old enough, I started to watch over her from afar. I had Rhett check on her and keep me updated. I passed on that information to Mom, who was heartbroken about being parted from her grandchild. We just wanted to be sure that Francesca was happy, healthy, and safe."

"Is she?" asked Makenna.

"It seems so," replied Lydia. "The Newmans gave her a good life. So many times I thought about contacting her, but I was worried that she wouldn't want to hear from us. I mean, my brother did kill her mother. It was enough for us to know that she was okay. But Mom isn't going to last long."

Though Lydia's mother, Iris, was a proud woman who liked to look after herself, she'd agreed to transfer to their pack so that Lydia could help care for her. Having recently lost her mate, Iris was weakening fast—many shifters died after losing their mate. Trick suspected that Iris had agreed to move here mostly so she could spend what time she had left with her daughter.

"She'd like to see Francesca just once before she passes on," Lydia added.

"You've contacted Francesca already," Marcus guessed.

"I sent her an e-mail earlier today, asking if she'd agree to visit. It was an impulsive decision. I'm sorry I didn't run it by you first," Lydia told the Alphas. "To be honest, I wasn't expecting her to answer. But she did."

"And?" prodded Taryn.

"Well, it was weird."

Trick frowned. "Weird how?"

Lydia bit her lip. "She doesn't seem to have a clue who I am."

CHAPTER TWO ⊙

Tao opened and closed his mouth a few times. "How can she not know who you are?"

"I don't know." Lydia lifted a shaky hand to her face. "I wasn't mysterious in the e-mail; I was clear about who I was."

Riley leaned forward, but Tao pulled her back against him. "Read me the e-mail you sent her," she said to Lydia, digging her elbow into Tao's ribs—he only grunted.

Lydia's thumbs tapped at the screen of her cell phone a few times.

"'Dear Francesca,

I doubt you'll remember me well, if at all. But you knew me very well as a child, before you left the pack and went to live with your grandparents. Your father, Christopher, was my older brother. Given what happened all those years ago, I can understand if you don't wish to have anything to do with the paternal side of your family. But we would very much like to see you. My mother, your grandmother, has been given mere weeks to live. She loves you very much—we both do. If you could find it in your heart to see her just one time, it would mean everything to her. I hope to hear from you soon.

Best wishes,
Your Aunt Lydia'"

"And her response?" asked Trey.

"'I'm pretty sure you've got the wrong Francesca Newman. Good luck with finding who you're looking for.'"

Dante narrowed his eyes. "Is it possible that you have the wrong person?"

"No way." Lydia shook her head, adamant. "I'm sure this is her. I've been following her life for a long time. I've seen pictures of her online—she still looks like Caroline."

Trick scrubbed a hand over his jaw. "If she doesn't know who you are, I'd say her grandparents have fed her bullshit about her past."

"Crap." Lydia raked a hand through her hair. "Now I don't know what to do. If she doesn't know about me, if they've fed her a different story, my contacting her will upset her life. I don't want that. Maybe I should agree that I got the wrong person." She looked at Cam for advice, but he shrugged.

"This has to be your decision, sweetheart," Cam told her.

"I don't think that backtracking will work," said Trick. "There are enough facts in that e-mail to make her wonder. Her mother's dead, she lives with her grandparents, she doesn't have her father in her life. She's not going to ignore all that. She'll look into it, talk to her grandparents about it."

"Trick's right," said Marcus, rubbing at the dark stubble on his jaw. "There's little point in going back now. But if you want to drop this, that's your decision. We'll respect it."

Jaime nodded. "I can understand that you're reluctant to upset her, Lydia, but she has every right to know the truth. I'm mad as hell that they lied to her all this time."

Lydia swallowed. "But the truth is pretty harsh, isn't it?"

"She still has a right to know," Grace firmly stated. "And I'd like to see her again. She wasn't in my life for long, but I see her as one of us."

"She is ours," said Dominic. "Iris only stayed with the Bjorn Pack because she wanted to be near Christopher's grave. But I think that if she'd had custody of Francesca, she'd have joined our pack for her sake. Francesca would have been a Phoenix Pack wolf. She was taken from us, and she's been without a pack for long enough."

"Yeah," agreed Marcus. "It's time she reconnected with us."

Lydia stroked her throat. "She may wish she'd never found out the truth."

"You should send her another e-mail tomorrow that makes things a little clearer, Lydia," Dante advised. "But don't tell her too much. You want to make her curious enough to meet you."

"If she's strong, she'll face it and deal with it." Lips pursed, Trick shrugged. "Guess this will show us just how strong she is."

After pulling up outside her grandparents' home the next day, Frankie switched off the ignition. The white three-story building was beautiful, there was no doubt about it. Stylish. Classy. Elegant. But when she was growing up, it had also felt constricting at times. When she was inside that house, certain things were expected of her—even as a child. Extreme politeness. Complete composure. Absolute obedience.

She'd failed on all counts.

Not purposely or spitefully. But because there was a wildness in her that wouldn't allow for that sort of control. Her wolf had always bucked against her grandparents' strictness—not in defiance, but out of her protectiveness toward Frankie.

She walked between the white columns and dashed up the steps. The housekeeper, Edna, opened the door and smiled. "Hello, Frankie."

It was a very informal greeting for a housekeeper, but Edna had been good to Frankie over the years, encouraging and supporting her when her grandparents didn't. Usually Frankie would talk with her a little. Today she was too anxious to speak to her grandparents.

With only an absentminded greeting for Edna, Frankie headed inside. The house was as classy on the inside as it was on the outside. Bright and spacious, with chandeliers, antiques, and crown moldings. There was plenty of artistic decor throughout, but not even one of her sculptures—it was a statement that her grandparents didn't approve of her chosen profession.

Her grandparents loved her, but they'd never understood her. Never understood that there hadn't really been a choice for her. Sculpting wasn't something she did to pass the time or amuse herself. There was a drive inside her to create, to shut out the world while she disappeared into her own. It made her feel alive. Maybe they didn't understand because, though they were both ambitious, neither of them had a "passion."

She didn't expect them to understand. She just wished they'd accept it.

Her heels clicked along the marble floor as she headed down the wide hallway. She found her grandparents in the cool, airy sitting room. Geoffrey stood in front of the high window, talking on his cell phone, while Marcia sat on the upholstered sofa, sipping what was probably iced tea.

Marcia's mouth curled. "Francesca, this is a surprise. I'm glad you're here. Selma White will be coming for dinner tonight with her son. I hope you'll join us." She rose, clearly expecting Frankie to cross the room and kiss her cheek. But Frankie couldn't seem to move. She felt rooted to the spot as she stared at them, looking at them through new eyes. Could they really have lied to her all these years? Why?

Ending his call, Geoffrey turned to her. He smiled automatically at the sight of her, but that smile faltered as he took her in. "Is something wrong?"

Frankie balled her hands into fists. "Do I have an Aunt Lydia?"

There was a boom of silence, and her grandparents exchanged a brief look.

"You told me that my father was Dustin Turner, that he was a lone wolf and he didn't tell you what pack he came from—that all you knew was that the pack wanted nothing to do with him or me." She forced herself to take a few steps forward. "Was that story a lie?"

Geoffrey rested a hand on the back of an armchair. "Francesca—"

"Was it a lie?"

Marcia calmly took another sip of her drink. A top neurosurgeon, Marcia Newman was extremely intelligent, and always cool and composed no matter the situation. Sometimes she was a little too cool. Unfeeling, even. "Just why would you ask that?"

"Just why won't you answer?"

Geoffrey sighed. "You have an Aunt Lydia, yes."

Frankie's stomach plummeted. "Was my father's name really Dustin Turner?"

Geoffrey hesitated. "No."

A shaky breath left her lungs. She felt cold all over as several emotions rattled her. Confusion. Shock. Hurt. Betrayal. Her wolf curled her upper lip, eyeing them both with distrust. "I don't understand. Why didn't you tell me about her? Why give me a false name? Why all the lies?"

"Who mentioned Lydia to you?" he asked.

"She did. She contacted me. Referred to my father as Christopher. Was that his name? Was it?"

Geoffrey's mouth twisted slightly. "Yes."

Jaw clenched, Frankie blew a breath out of her nose. "Why lie to me? *Why?*"

"Be sure you want the answers to these questions, Francesca." Geoffrey crossed to the little bar. "You won't like what you hear."

"The truth can't be worse than any lie." Not for Frankie.

"Don't be so sure of that." He poured himself a brandy, and she knew he was stalling.

Impatient, Frankie pushed, "Who was my father?"

"His name was Christopher Brooks," said Geoffrey in that authoritative voice she'd heard him use in court more than once as he sat at his bench, cloaked in a black robe. "He shot himself. But not before strangling your mother to death after stabbing her several times. He killed both her and himself right in front of you."

Nothing he said could have shocked her more. Nothing. She stood there, frozen, struggling to process his matter-of-fact delivery of such a horrific event. Frankie had grown up believing that her parents—loving, attentive parents who'd been devoted to her and to each other—had died in a car accident. She needed to sit down, but she couldn't seem to move.

Marcia set her glass on the table. "You were three at the time. We expected to find you terrified when we arrived on pack territory. But you were quiet, subdued. In shock. Naturally we brought you here, away from those animals."

And she seemed to think that Frankie should applaud her for that.

"You didn't seem to remember what you saw—as if you'd blocked it out." Geoffrey took a swig of his brandy. "You'd have nightmares, but you'd never remember them. We let you forget. We gave you a different story. We did it to protect you."

Protect her? Lying to her all her life sure didn't feel like "protection." It wasn't that she couldn't understand why they thought they were protecting her when she was just a child; she was just pissed to all hell that she was only finding out *now*.

She also felt embarrassed. She'd easily believed their story, easily bought their lies. Never once questioned them. Shouldn't she have sensed the deception? Probably not. It was really only natural that she'd believed them. She'd had no reason to doubt them. Yet she felt disappointed with herself. Humiliated, even.

"What does Lydia want?" demanded Marcia, distaste in her tone. "Money, I'm guessing."

"To meet," said Frankie.

Marcia huffed. "Well, she'll be rather disappointed when you turn her down, won't she?"

"Her mother's dying. She's hoping I'll pay her a visit so she can see me just once before she passes."

"In other words, she's trying to manipulate you with a sob story." Marcia sniffed. "You will, of course, ignore her attempt to reconnect with you."

Frankie's spine snapped straight, and her wolf growled. "Will I?"

Marcia's eyes went diamond hard. "Yes, you will. They defended him, Francesca. He killed Caroline, but they defended him. Said he must have been drunk or had a moment of madness—like there could be any excuse for what was done to her. They kept questioning you, trying to put words into your mouth, wanting you to say something that would somehow vindicate him. Over and over, you kept saying in a zombielike voice, 'He hurt her.'"

Hearing footsteps, Frankie looked over her shoulder to see her uncle waltz in. As usual, the accountant was dressed in a tailored suit and wearing a charming smile.

"Frankie, sweetheart, it's great to see you." Brad kissed her cheek. "Too beautiful for words."

"You knew the truth, didn't you?" Frankie accused him. "You knew they lied about my parents."

His grin melted away and he swallowed. "How did you find out?"

It was Marcia who answered, each word curt and bitter as she explained the matter to her only son.

Brad rested a hand on Frankie's arm. "Keeping the truth from you was for the best."

Frankie shrugged him off. "Best? Best for who, Brad?"

"For who? For you, of course."

Frankie snorted. She wasn't a weak, fragile flower; she could have handled the truth. Turning back to her grandparents, she said, "Look, I get why you'd want a child to forget something so traumatic. I understand why you'd rather never speak of what happened. But I'm twenty-seven years old. I've been old enough to understand and deal with the truth for a long time. You could have told me at any point. You didn't. I have the right to know."

Geoffrey held her gaze steadily—there was no remorse there. "Why hurt you with the truth?"

"The lie hurts too. It makes me wonder what else you've lied to me about."

Geoffrey exhaled heavily. "You're angry. You have a right to be, I suppose, but I can't be sorry for doing what I did to spare you pain. Your life isn't based on a lie, Francesca. We simply didn't tell you who your real father was or how your mother really died. Would telling the truth have really made such a difference to your life or changed the person you are today?"

Maybe, maybe not. She looked at Marcia and said, "I get it now. I could never quite measure up to your expectations, no matter what I did. You love me, I know that. But you've always held a little something back. I'm half shifter. I'm half of the person who killed your daughter. You've never been able to truly see all the way past that, have you?"

Marcia's mouth hardened, but she didn't confirm or deny it. She didn't have to.

Brad put his hand on her shoulder and turned her to face him. "Look at me, Frankie. You're loved deeply and unconditionally by every one of us. You're hurt and angry and overthinking things. I can understand why—you've had one hell of a shock and it's knocked you off balance. But don't let that shake your confidence and trust in your family."

"The wolves want to meet with her," Marcia snippily announced.

Brad's eyebrows snapped together. "Why? They were perfectly happy to watch her come live with us. They didn't fight to keep you, Frankie. Didn't even try to see you. Contacting you now and messing with your life this way—that's not right."

"It doesn't seem as if Lydia knows that I was lied to," Frankie told him, stepping back, needing her space.

Brad gave a quick shake of his head. "Doesn't matter. Everyone knows that shifters are protective of their own, particularly their children. If they'd loved you, they would have fought tooth and nail to keep you. They didn't. They turned their backs on you. Now you get to do the same thing to them. They're not good for you, Frankie. You're better off without them."

Seething, Frankie clenched her fists. She needed some goddamn air. She spun on her heel and headed for the door.

"You will not meet with those wolves, Francesca. I forbid it." The whip in Marcia's voice made her wolf snarl, but Frankie didn't break stride. She just kept walking.

Outside she slid into her car and let out a long breath. She'd come here hoping her grandparents would assure her that the whole thing was a case of mistaken identity. Honestly, though, she'd have found any denials hard to believe. It just seemed way too coincidental that there would be *another* shifter called Francesca Newman who had lost her parents and been raised by her human grandparents.

So, yeah, she'd expected to hear that there were plenty of things they hadn't told her. She hadn't thought one of those things would be that her father had murdered her mother.

Noticing a blue light flashing in her peripheral vision, she saw that she'd left her cell phone in the cup holder and knew she'd received a notification of some kind. Swiping her thumb across the screen, she wasn't surprised to see she'd received yet another e-mail from Lydia.

> Dear Francesca,
>
> I'm quite sure that you're the Francesca Newman I'm looking for. I've kept myself updated on your life, watching over you in my way. I don't understand why you seem confused about who I am, but I hope you will meet with me tomorrow so we can discuss it and I can answer any questions you have.
>
> I will be at the coffeehouse on Cherry Avenue tomorrow at noon. I hope you will be there.
>
> Best regards,
> Lydia

Frankie slung her phone back in the cup holder and twisted her key in the ignition. She needed to do some damn research.

A little later she pulled up in her driveway. Inside the house she hooked her jacket over the banister before kicking off her shoes and heading down the hallway. The oak flooring was cool and smooth beneath her feet.

Her wolf was happy to be back in her territory, surrounded by the soothingly familiar scents of lavender, wood, and leather.

In the homey walnut kitchen, Frankie poured herself a glass of red wine. She had a feeling she was going to need it. She sure as hell could have done with one when she'd talked to her grandparents, she thought, as she made her way into the living area. Standing on the soft rug near the fireplace, she stared at the framed photo of her mother that stood on the mantel beside other pictures and keepsakes. *What happened that night? Why did it happen?*

Frankie took a long gulp of wine and then set the glass on the coffee table. Sinking into the plush sofa, she dragged her cushioned lap tray onto her thighs and then set her laptop on top of it.

Her nearest neighbor was half a mile away; thus she never received complaints about the amount of noise she made while working, and there were no sounds of kids playing, people talking, or loud music filtering through the open window. There was only the ticking of her laptop keys and the hum of the air conditioning.

There were many websites and blogs about shifters, which was how she'd learned so many things about her kind that she wouldn't have otherwise known. The information had helped her understand her wolf and identify herself as a dominant female. Hopefully, there would also be information to help her understand what happened the night her parents died.

Bringing up the Internet, she typed in "Caroline Newman murder." Several results popped up, most of which appeared to be articles. She clicked on the first result, which took her to a blog that catalogued crimes committed by shifters. Leaning forward, she read it.

> Caroline Newman, a 25-year-old human ex-school-teacher, was attacked and killed by her mate and wolf shifter, Christopher Brooks, on Bjorn Pack territory in California in May 1993. Brooks stabbed her eleven times in the chest with a Japanese chef knife on their kitchen floor before strangling her to death. Brooks, 30,

later shot himself in the temple. The noise alerted pack
mates, who raced to the scene. The only witness to the
murder was their three-year-old daughter, Francesca,
who was too traumatized to provide a statement.

A photo accompanied the article, of Frankie being huddled into
her grandparents' car mere days after the murder.

Below that was a picture of Caroline and Christopher together,
happy and smiling like loons. Frankie studied him, took in each of his
facial features. She had his eyes, she thought. Had the same slight dent
in her chin and the same dimples when she smiled. She wasn't sure how
to feel about that.

Frankie went on to read other articles. There were pictures of her
mother in each one—a graduation photo, a picture of her on vacation,
and a family shot of Caroline with her parents. There was even one of
Caroline and Frankie together.

There was nothing but speculation about what had happened.
Some stated that "sources" claimed Christopher had killed Caroline in
a jealous rage. Others stated that he'd been out of his mind on a drug
that shifters had produced but denied existed. There were those who
believed that he'd been mentally ill and suicidal, and he'd only killed
Caroline because he'd wanted them to die together.

Some bloggers expressed surprise that a shifter would hurt his mate,
while others felt it was only to be expected, considering that "shifters
are a few evolutionary steps away from animals."

Members of the Bjorn Pack had refused to comment. Marcia
was quoted several times in various articles, defaming shifters and
bad-mouthing the Bjorn Pack. One particular quote was included in
several articles: "My daughter was a beautiful person, inside and out.
Christopher Brooks took her from us and robbed her of her life—
stabbed her, strangled her, and then shot himself like a coward. He
robbed their daughter of a mother. He was evil, pure and simple."

Rubbing her nape, Frankie sank back into her seat. She'd hoped for answers, but now she had yet more questions.

Was it true that Christopher had taken drugs?

Was it possible that he had in fact been mentally unbalanced?

Why had he killed her mother?

And . . . why hadn't he killed Frankie too?

Wanting to know more about his pack, she punched "the Bjorn Pack California" into the search engine. Again there were plenty of results. Finding a site that seemed dedicated to recording information on wolf packs, she clicked on the link. There was only a brief history of the pack, which was hardly surprising since shifters were highly private and insular. Her mother's murder was briefly mentioned in connection with the pack. However, the writer of the article seemed more interested in an event that later led the pack to divide.

Allegedly the original Alpha, Rick Coleman, lost a duel to his teenage son, Trey. Instead of stepping aside to allow the teen to rule, Rick banished him. Many supported the banishment. Those who didn't support it then left with Trey, grouping together to form the Phoenix Pack.

Frankie clicked on the hyperlink that would take her to a page on the Phoenix Pack and found herself intrigued by what she read . . .

Battled with the Bjorn Pack after Trey's father died and the Beta took the position of Alpha.

Clashed with anti-shifter extremists several times.

Defended a shelter for lone shifters against a pack Alpha.

Suspected to be related to the disappearances of local mobsters.

Frankie wondered if Lydia had been one of the wolves to leave with Trey or if she'd stayed with the Bjorn Pack. Squinting, Frankie looked more closely at the pictures of Phoenix Pack members as they stood outside stores or diners—all had been taken from afar and most likely without the pack's knowledge. She didn't see any females who resembled Christopher, but that didn't really answer the question of whether Lydia was part of the pack.

Hell, nothing Frankie had read really answered any of her questions. Reading what her mother had endured . . . that had been hard. She *hated* that her mother's life had been snuffed out. *Hated* that she'd suffered such pain before she died.

Frankie should also hate Christopher, shouldn't she? She should despise this person who'd killed her mother and himself right in front of her. But she didn't. Maybe because none of it seemed real. Maybe because she wasn't sure how to hate someone she didn't remember. Maybe because she just couldn't make sense of it. From everything she knew about shifters, they were loyal, devoted, caring mates who were often irrationally overprotective.

The pieces of the story just didn't fit. But then, she didn't know enough about Christopher to really make any assessment about whether he was the sort of person who'd harm someone he loved. She needed to talk to people who had known him.

There would be no point in going back to her grandparents with her queries—they'd either tell her to drop it or feed her more lies. Frankie wanted facts. Even if they told her the truth, their answers would be colored by their own hatred of Christopher. Not that she was likely to get the truth from the wolves. It was highly possible that Lydia's answers would be colored by her *love* for Christopher, but there was really no way of knowing without giving the woman a chance. She'd offered to answer Frankie's questions, hadn't she? Maybe she'd be honest, maybe she wouldn't. And, okay, maybe Frankie was curious about her.

Downing the last of her wine, she switched off her laptop and once again stared at the framed photo of Caroline on her mantel. She wondered if her mother would be upset with Frankie for seeking answers—hell, Marcia and Geoffrey would, and they'd no doubt see her meeting with Lydia as a betrayal. But Frankie didn't view it as a betrayal. In her opinion it was perfectly natural that she'd want some answers and to know about her past.

This was *her* life; she was entitled to know every part of it. And if her maternal family couldn't accept that, well, it wouldn't be the first time that they'd disapproved of her choices. Still, she didn't relish the idea of going head-to-head with the people who'd raised her. Loved her.

But they never really accepted you, a little voice in her head whispered.

Frankie couldn't argue with it. And then another voice was playing in her head—a voice that wasn't her own.

"You will not meet with those wolves, Francesca. I forbid it."

Frankie scowled at Marcia's words. Forbid it, huh? That was *so* the wrong thing to say to a dominant female wolf.

CHAPTER THREE

Sitting in the coffeehouse, Trick set down his half-empty mug. Around him were the murmur of voices, the clattering of dishes, the whir of blenders, and the ding of the cash register. The place was nice. Cozy. It was also busy as hell.

He stared out the large glass window, keeping a lookout for Francesca. It was almost noon, but there was no sign of her.

Cam laid a hand over Lydia's, stilling her tapping fingers. "Breathe, you're going to be fine."

Leaning forward, Lydia braced her elbows on the round bistro table and took a centering breath. "I don't know why I'm so nervous."

"Of course you're nervous," said Trick. "You want it to go well. This is important to you."

"If she didn't initially know the truth about her paternal family, I'm guessing her grandparents will have told her everything by now." Lydia worried her lower lip. "She might not want anything at all to do with us."

"If that's the case, we'll find out soon enough," said Ryan. He and Trick had accompanied Lydia and Cam for their protection. And, yes, because Trick was curious to see how Frankie had turned out.

Massaging his mate's nape, Cam asked, "Do you think she'll bring someone along?"

Ryan leaned back in his seat. "In her position, I would. To her we're strangers. Shifters too. The fact that we were once all part of the same pack probably won't make her any less wary."

Lydia nodded. "If she doesn't remember me, she probably won't remember any of you."

"I don't know about that," joked Trick, rolling his shoulders. "I'm pretty memorable."

Lydia snorted. "I can't even deny that." After a moment the amusement faded from her eyes. "She's not coming, is she? Damn, I should have just left well enough alone."

"She'll come," said Trick.

Cam tilted his head. "You sound real sure of that, but I'll be surprised if she does. Maybe it's best if she doesn't, considering it's pretty likely that she'll be a snob. Her grandparents are serious snobs."

"Caroline wasn't," Lydia pointed out. "She was a total sweetheart. Fragile, though. And very pliant and eager to please. Caroline's parents have very strong personalities and insisted on compliance."

Ryan straightened in his seat, eyes on the view outside. "What are those little bastards doing?"

Following his gaze, Trick noticed a group of teenagers checking out their SUV. Admiring the new model, or gearing themselves up to plant a GPS tracker? Whoever had planted the trackers originally might want to replace the ones that had been removed.

"I'll deal with it." Trick chugged the last of his coffee and strode out of the coffeehouse. He didn't speak to the boys. Just stood near the hood of the SUV, arms crossed.

One of them spotted him and froze. That got the attention of the others, and they all looked at Trick.

He gave them a toothy smile. "There a reason why you're hanging around my vehicle?"

The tallest lifted his chin, belligerent. "We didn't do anything. We were just looking."

"Now you're finished looking. Move on."

Muttering harsh, derisive words under their breath, they swaggered away. Trick kept his eyes on them . . . right until a silver Audi whipped into the space beside the SUV. A female slid out, and Trick stilled. He knew instantly that it was Francesca—she just looked so much like her mother. Cute with her big eyes, round face, flawless skin, spiral curls, and the sprinkle of freckles across her nose.

He raked his gaze over her. Designer clothes. Healthy skin. Good posture. Aura of confidence. It wasn't hard to tell that she'd grown up in a family that had a housekeeper, skied once a year, ate at Michelin-starred restaurants, and sent its kids to private schools.

He'd bet she'd also strained against whatever confines that lifestyle put on her, because the signs of a rebel were all there—rose-gold hair dye, smoky-eye look, dream catcher tattoo on her upper arm, and multiple ear piercings. He liked the piercings; the tiny diamond studs dotted the outer edges of her ear. He wondered if she had them anywhere else.

As a kid she'd always looked so delicate. Not now, though. Cute and sweet, yeah, but not fragile. She was slender, but she had soft curves and an incredible rack that made his palms itch. There was a fierceness about her that would have caught his wolf's interest if the animal's focus hadn't already been locked on her like a laser beam.

Her Persian-blue gaze met Trick's, and his surroundings just seemed to fade away until there was only her. Something inside him roared to life, and a strange possessiveness began to viciously claw at his gut and tighten his chest. It was as primal and basic as the need that twisted his stomach. His cock twitched, thickened, hardened—until he was full and aching like a bitch. The word "mine" pounded around his skull over and over. And that could only mean one thing.

There you are, Trick thought with an inner smile.

33

His wolf froze the way a predator would as he eyed his prey, watching it closely, looking for weaknesses, raring to pounce. Raring to claim what was rightfully his.

Her gaze held Trick's with a boldness that surprised him, considering she was truly the most harmless-looking thing he'd ever seen in his life. Trick was highly dominant, but she didn't cower from his scrutiny. No, she returned his stare. Pride flared inside him and his wolf. Their mate was strong. A match for them.

Trick saw a raw need in her eyes, knew she'd felt the same powerful snap of elemental attraction, but he didn't think she knew what it meant. Not yet. Especially since he wasn't feeling the tug of the mating bond. No, something on her end was jamming the frequency.

Her head slanted, making her long, glossy curls slide over her shoulder. One brow imperiously arched. "Do I have something stuck between my teeth?" she asked drily.

Not quite as sweet as she looked, apparently. But that wasn't why he blinked in surprise. He just would never have suspected a voice like that could belong to someone who looked so innocent. It was . . . He didn't really know how to describe it. Smoky. Raspy. Gritty. Like she'd spent a night doing nothing but smoking cigars, chugging whiskey, and screaming in ecstasy. His cock jerked. Yeah, that voice packed a hell of a punch.

Trick gave her a lazy smile, like she hadn't just turned his world upside down and changed everything for him. "Actually, there does seem to be a little something wedged between your two front teeth."

"I'm saving it for later."

His smile widened at the wry response. "Been a long time, Francesca."

Her eyes narrowed. "Do I know you?"

"You did, once upon a time." Trick inhaled, taking her scent inside him. He inwardly groaned. She smelled like mango, lime, and lemon fucking sherbet. When they were kids, he'd found it comforting. Now there was a "zest" to her scent that hadn't been there before—the zest of a fully mature female. A low rumble of arousal trickled out of his pacing wolf, who wanted to surface and claim what belonged to him.

Trick was in no better state. All he himself could think of doing was pinning her to the nearest wall and driving deep inside her. He didn't just want to fuck her, he wanted to completely possess her. Wanted to keep and protect her.

Oh yeah, she was his all right. There wasn't a doubt in his mind.

She pointed a finger at him. "Wait . . . you're the guy on that video who saved a human girl from being mugged, right?"

His mouth flattened. "I'm Trick Hardy, one of Lydia's pack mates." *And your true mate, but we'll get to that later.* "You and I used to play together as kids."

"Huh." No, Frankie didn't remember him. His scent did prick at her memories, though. *Black pepper, charred pinewood, and smoky leather.* It was . . . reassuring, somehow. It was also making her nipples tingle—well, that was new. Her wolf stirred, intrigued by the rich scent and the darkly dominant air about him. The animal recognized his scent, thought of him as "pack."

Frankie took a good long look at him. He was, in a word, ripped. Not in a "someone obviously loves steroids" way where he'd have to turn sideways just to fit through a door—Frankie didn't go for that look. No, Trick Hardy was perfectly toned and spilled a raw animal energy. All that roped muscle, sleek skin, and the dips and lines of the six-pack beneath his shirt . . . Yeah, God was a seriously creative being.

Trick's dark-ringed mocha-brown eyes were as sharp as they were warm. His short hair was the color of deep-brown leather, but it wasn't so short that a girl couldn't get a firm grip on it. The angles of his face were hard and rough, and they gave him a dangerous look that was accentuated by the claw marks that scarred one side of his face. The black, tribal, warriorlike tattoo sleeve on his left arm only added to his badass image.

Basically he was a broad-shouldered tower of supreme masculinity that a girl could very happily feast on.

He was also a little unnerving. Not much ruffled Frankie, but something about the way he looked at her . . . it flustered her. Put her on edge. There was a determination there she didn't understand. A need that was fierce and wild and called to something inside her. Something that made her blood heat, her breasts ache, and her clit tingle.

What the fuck was that all about?

Frankie didn't ever have such elemental reactions to guys. Hell, it usually took a little foreplay to wrench those kinds of responses from her body. But just the sight and scent of this male had her system almost . . . *readying* itself for him. It had to be a shifter thing—like calling to like or something. Hopefully he wasn't much of a talker, because his lazy drawl played across her nerve endings, and that would *not* help cool her blood at all.

Frankie flicked a glance at the coffeehouse. "I take it Lydia's inside?"

"She is." He opened the door and gestured for her to enter first.

With a nod of thanks, Frankie did so. It was a busy place; most of the bistro tables were taken, and there was a hell of a queue. A hand landed on her back, and she almost jumped. Then Trick's mouth was at her ear.

"Lydia's waiting in the corner, near the window." Keeping his hand on her back, Trick led her to the table. The scents of coffee, spices, and baked goods didn't override Francesca's tantalizing scent—it was like it had embedded itself in his lungs. His wolf wanted to roll around in it like a pup and wear it on his fur.

As they approached, Lydia rose and rubbed her palms on her thighs. Her smile was small but genuine. "Francesca, hi. I'm Lydia. This is my mate, Cam. And these are two of our pack mates, Ryan and Trick."

Frankie gave a short nod of greeting, feeling awkward and a little dubious. Not because she was intimidated, though Trick and Ryan sure had that dauntless air going on. Lydia and the baby-faced Cam weren't in the least bit threatening, but the way they looked at her with such familiarity . . . Yeah, it was just awkward.

"Please sit down," invited Lydia.

Trick pulled out a chair for Francesca, and, flicking him a quick glance, she took it. He sank into the chair beside hers. When he'd first arrived, his concern had been for Lydia. He'd been prepared to step in if Francesca decided to dish out any attitude. Now Francesca's feelings were his primary concern. His protective streak was a live wire around her, and his pack mates now took a back seat. Funny how one little person could shift his priorities so quickly.

The situation shouldn't have felt strange for him, but it did. He'd been so ready and eager to find his true mate that he'd always figured he'd take it in his stride—that he'd just accept she was his and act on it. But Trick found himself . . . off balance. A little staggered. Like he'd been hit by a two-by-four. His mate was right there in front of him, close enough to touch. The moment seemed surreal.

"You want coffee or anything?" Trick asked her, but she gave a quick shake of her head without even looking his way. Trick's wolf growled, wanting her attention.

Lydia smiled. "You look really good, Francesca."

"Frankie," she offered.

"Your dad used to call you Frankie." Lydia winced, as if thinking it wasn't such a great idea to mention him.

Uncomfortable with the affection lighting Lydia's eyes, Frankie decided to be straight with her. "I don't remember you."

Lydia's smile shrank a little. "I didn't think you would."

Frankie skimmed her eyes over each of them as she said, "I don't remember any of you. Your scents are a little familiar, but that's all."

Just like that, Lydia's smile was back. "That's more than I'd hoped for." She licked her lower lip. "I got the impression from your e-mail that you didn't know about me."

"I didn't know about any of you. I was told that my father was a lone shifter and that I'd never met anyone from his pack, that they didn't wish to know him or me."

Trick ground his teeth against the urge to curse. The idea that she'd grown up believing none of them wanted her pissed him *the fuck* off. His wolf pushed closer to Trick's skin, wanting to be near her, urging Trick to reach out and touch her. Trick didn't move, but he kept his gaze on her. He couldn't *not* look at her.

"I can see why your grandparents would rather you believed something like that," said Lydia, though it was clear that she wasn't at all happy about it. "Well, Christopher was no lone shifter. We all once belonged to the Bjorn Pack. It later split, and a bunch of us left to form the Phoenix Pack."

Well, that answered the question of which pack Lydia belonged to, Frankie thought. She decided not to mention that she'd done some research. She also decided to ignore that Trick was staring at her, his gaze focused and unblinking like that of a predator.

"He met your mother at a karaoke bar," Lydia continued. "She was with some friends. He said he fell hard at just the sound of her voice. They didn't realize they were true mates straightaway. I have lots of pictures of them together, but I didn't bring them with me—I didn't want to overwhelm you. To be honest, I wasn't expecting you to come. I was just hoping like crazy that you would."

"Why the sudden interest in me?" Frankie asked. "I can understand why your mother would want to say her goodbyes before she passes, but I don't get why you yourself seem so interested. You've been out of my life for a very long time."

"Not by choice," Lydia firmly stated. "We tried to have contact with you. Tried long and hard. Your grandparents wanted us out of your life, and they made it happen."

Frankie wished she could deny that they'd do such a thing, but of course they would have done it. She'd seen how much they hated

Christopher, and they weren't the type of people who compromised. "You could have come to me when I was old enough to decide for myself if I wanted to see you."

"I was worried that you'd hate us the way your grandparents do. It was more comfortable to not know. But my father, Alfie, died of a heart attack recently—it was very sudden. My mother, Iris, has been deteriorating ever since. Mates usually don't survive long without the other. She wants to see you just once. Of course, she'd love more, love to know you, but she doesn't expect anything of you."

"Why did he kill my mother?"

Lydia swallowed. "I don't know. Christopher adored Caroline. He really did. What happened shocked everyone."

"Was he on drugs?"

"Drugs? No. But a human reporter started that rumor. Another claimed he had to have been mentally ill. Both were wrong. Christopher wasn't suicidal either." Lydia sighed. "I really wish I could tell you why he did it, but I just don't know. The only person who was there that night was you, but you weren't what anyone could really consider a witness."

"But you wanted me to say something that would vindicate him." Frankie's tone dared her to deny it, and Lydia looked . . . hurt.

"No one ever tried to brainwash you into believing or disbelieving anything. Our main concern was you—you were traumatized, you needed help and family."

"And yet none of you were there."

"We would have been if it were possible."

Knowing it was unreasonable to snap at Lydia for something that was beyond her control, Frankie sighed. "I'm not mad at you for not being around." Just disappointed and a little hurt. "And I don't blame you for what your brother did. Maybe that's because I haven't quite digested it yet. But I just found out yesterday that much of what I grew up believing was a lie. I wouldn't have thought my grandparents and uncle would lie to me like that, but they did. So I'm real wary on what and who I can believe right now."

Lydia slowly nodded. "Understandable. We'll probably never know what happened that night. But if you want to learn about your father, about the other half of your family and your pack mates, you have that chance now. I'm not going to put you on the spot and ask you to make that decision here and now. That wouldn't be fair."

Lydia pulled a pen out of her purse and scribbled on a napkin. She then slid it across the table. "Here's my number. If you can find it in you to come, just call and we can arrange something." With what looked like extreme reluctance, Lydia rose. "Bye, Frankie. I really hope you call."

On guard, Ryan took the lead as he, Lydia, and Cam crossed to the door. Trick lingered and twisted slightly in his seat to face Frankie as he asked, "You all right?"

Frankie sighed, resting her elbows on the table. "Fine."

Bullshit. Trick guessed she was probably feeling let down by both sides of her family—one side for deceiving her, and the other side for not being around. Helpless against the need to comfort her, Trick rested a hand on her nape and gave it a little squeeze. "You have every right to be mad at the pack—don't say you're not, of course you are. We should have been there for you every step of the way. We weren't. But we're here now. We want to know you. You're ours."

She frowned at the possessive statement, though a part of her liked the sense of belonging that it brought her. A part of her also liked the proprietary edge to his touch. Nonetheless, Frankie shifted in her seat, making his hand fall away. "I was born into the Bjorn Pack, not the Phoenix Pack."

"Doesn't matter. It's not like you supported Trey's banishment—you weren't even there. I get that you love your maternal family and you don't want to hurt them by getting to know us. But they've had you to themselves for the last twenty-four years. Can't we at least have a day of your life? Would that be so bad? None of us want you to turn your back on the Newmans. This is about you, not them."

Trick grabbed the napkin on which Lydia had written her number and pushed it into Frankie's hand. "Call her when you're ready."

The very last thing Trick wanted to do was leave Frankie. No, he wanted to do exactly as he'd always envisioned he'd do on finding his true mate—declare she was his, take her home, and claim her as his own. But with Frankie he needed to tread carefully.

Right then she was far from open to him. Announcing that she was his true mate would overwhelm and scare her off. In fact, it was unlikely that she'd believe him anyway; she'd probably think that he was simply playing her in the hope that it would lure her to the pack.

This situation was going to require patience, understanding, and finesse. While it would agonize him to walk away, her needs came first. So he forced himself to rise and said, "It was good to see you, Frankie. I'll talk to you again soon."

One brow rose at the sheer confidence in that statement. "Will you?"

"Yeah, I will." Allowing himself the small luxury of skimming his fingers over her hair, Trick headed for the door. His wolf snapped his teeth in anger, lunging for her hard. Trick fought his desperate attempts to surface, half-surprised he didn't sprout fur.

Soon, he promised his wolf. Soon she'd belong irrevocably to them. But his wolf wasn't placated. The animal didn't just covet and crave Frankie; he wanted to keep her close, where he could be sure she was safe.

His pack mates were already in the SUV when he hopped into the passenger seat. Ryan looked at him, face twisted into the scowl that seemed to be his default expression, and asked, "What was that about?"

"What?"

"The delay. What were you talking about?"

"I was just trying to convince her to take a chance on the pack." Trick glanced at Lydia in the rearview mirror. "You okay?"

41

Lydia inhaled deeply. "The meeting went better than I thought it would. There was no yelling or condemning."

Trick nodded. "She impressed me."

"Why?" asked Ryan, reversing out of the parking space.

"I'd already figured that her grandparents fed her some lies," Trick replied. "She didn't do the textbook 'I don't know who I am now that I know my past is a lie.' Apart from the odd snippy comment, she didn't throw accusations around or take out her anger at Christopher or the situation on Lydia." He met her gaze in the rearview mirror again. "I mean, you're the closest thing to him right now, Lydia, but she didn't lash out. She's a cool one."

"It would be a shock to find out that your parent killed someone," said Ryan. "Especially if that someone was your other parent. As Frankie said, she hasn't properly processed it all yet. Once she does, she might act differently."

Cam linked his fingers with Lydia's as he asked, "Do you think she'll call?"

Trick twisted his mouth. "Yeah, I do." Hell, she'd do more than call and visit their territory. Sooner or later she'd be living there. He didn't say that, though, because he already knew what would happen—Lydia would panic, thinking he might scare Frankie away, and ask him to keep his distance from her. He wouldn't even be able to blame Lydia for that, considering the situation was already complicated enough. But staying away from Frankie wasn't something he could do, so he'd keep quiet about his discovery for now.

Cam lifted a brow. "Even though it will upset the people who've raised her?"

"Even though," said Trick. "Her wolf is very dominant. I'll bet her grandparents have had a damn hard time trying to get any compliance out of her." His mate was no pushover, he thought proudly.

She was not at all what he'd expected his mate would be like, which just seemed typical of fate, really. It wasn't only that she was very different from his usual type, it was also that she was human in many ways. She might have spent the first few years of her life in a pack, but she had no memories of that time. She'd lived as a human. Probably didn't know much about the ways of shifters. In fact, it was unlikely that she knew much about true mates either. He hadn't been prepared for a mate who knew so little about their kind.

Even more shockingly, he knew her. He'd once had her so close to him, yet he hadn't known she belonged to him—or at least he hadn't consciously known it. Now he wondered if he had in fact sensed she was his on some level and if that was why he'd lived with a drive to find his mate all these years—it had been more of a need to recover what he'd lost. And he hated that he couldn't do exactly that. Hated that she wouldn't be receptive to him yet. Hated that his long-standing plan to quickly claim his mate as his own wouldn't work.

That didn't mean he'd back off. It just meant he'd have to revise his plan. He would slowly but surely insert himself into Frankie's life until she couldn't imagine not having him in it.

He knew himself well enough to know that he wouldn't be tactful about it. No, he'd be intrusive. Full of unwanted advice. He'd question her under cover of polite conversation. Insist on doing things for her. Turn up unexpectedly at her home. Yep, he'd be a pain in her ass. And that perversely made him smile.

CHAPTER FOUR

A s Led Zeppelin sang about the stairway to heaven on the radio, Frankie flexed her hand and winced. It was starting to go numb and stiff from all the metal grinding. She didn't want to stop working on her sculpture, though. She wasn't ready yet.

Grabbing her water bottle from the shelf, she unscrewed the cap and took a long swig. She heard someone knock on the front door, thanks to her enhanced shifter hearing, but she ignored it. She figured it was Brad, who'd tried calling her several times that morning. He'd left a voice mail saying he just wanted to talk about the Lydia matter before Frankie made any rash decisions.

In other words, he hoped to talk her out of meeting with Lydia.

That would be a pointless conversation, considering she'd already done so. He wouldn't be mad—he respected that she had her own mind and would make her own decisions—but he'd be disappointed in her. His lectures were long and boring, and she had no time or patience for one.

Besides, she hadn't yet decided whether to go see Iris, and she didn't want anyone else's opinions to influence her decision. Making said decision was proving hard while she was feeling emotionally off balance and as if she were being tugged in different directions.

Iris's deathbed request was fair. The old woman had lost her son and, if what Lydia claimed was true, had then also been denied access to her grandchild. Iris didn't deserve to be punished for another person's actions, even if that person was her son.

But stepping on pack territory could open a can of worms. Iris would no doubt be pissed at the people who had kept her grandchild from her, and Frankie didn't want to listen to someone bad-mouth her grandparents—people who'd be upset that she'd paid Iris a visit.

Would Frankie then be forced to choose between the two sides of her family? Would the pack expect answers from her about what had happened that night long ago? Did she have extended family within the Bjorn Pack that would want contact with her too?

Frankie could also admit to being hurt that no one from either the Bjorn Pack or the Phoenix Pack had tried hard to see her. Brad had made a good point when he'd said that shifters were protective of their young. If what Lydia said was true, they had tried when she was a kid. But Frankie hadn't been a child for a very long time, and she didn't feel that Lydia's "I was worried you'd hate us and it was more comfortable not to know" claim was really a valid excuse.

In fact, it seemed more likely to Frankie that Iris and Lydia saw her as a reminder of what Christopher had done and—on a level that could be subconscious—didn't want that reminder around. Maybe Iris and Lydia, just like Marcia and Geoffrey, had wanted to push the truth aside so that they could more easily move on.

Frankie couldn't even blame them for that, but it still hurt. And that hurt part of her resented the pack for walking back into her life when they'd avoided her for so long. What right did they have to request anything of her when they'd let her go and then stayed away? She owed them nothing.

Still, she couldn't help wanting to know about her father, her family, the people who would have been her pack mates. Was it bad that, despite everything, she was curious? Would her mother judge her for that and see it as a betrayal of her memory? Frankie didn't think so, but the guilt crept up on her all the same.

Yeah, well, that guilt could just add to the pile she was already carrying. Her mother had been murdered. She'd seen it happen. Yet she didn't remember a thing.

It was unsettling enough to know she'd witnessed her father kill her mother and then himself. But to have no recollection of it? How could a person forget something like that? Okay, yeah, she understood it was rare for people to recall early memories. Still, she'd witnessed a *murder* and a *suicide*. Yet nothing.

She wondered if those nightmares she'd had as a child were actually replays of the event—an event that her mind had seemed intent on burying for her own sake. She didn't remember the nightmares either. Only snippets of—

The music suddenly lowered, and Frankie spun. And there was Trick, who'd seemingly rounded the house and entered through the open side door of the studio. She shoved up her protective goggles, annoyed that—odd as it was—she was glad to see him. Her wolf sat up, instantly alert and pleased that he'd come.

Trick raised his hands in a gesture of innocence. "I knocked. You didn't hear me." His eyes cut to the sculpture. "Wow."

"I heard the knocking. I just ignored it, since I'm busy and all." She hoped that was a clear hint for him to leave, but he wasn't listening to her. His attention was on the sculpture. Standing on a workbench, it was taller than he. He circled it, studied it, and absorbed it, looking genuinely awed.

Frankie blushed, self-conscious all of a sudden. She wasn't used to people other than Abigail and those within her field taking such a close look at her work. It made her feel exposed.

"I've seen some of your pieces on the interactive gallery on your website, but it's a whole other thing to see one in person." Trick backed up a little. "I wouldn't have thought I could ever find anything scary about a horse. How can something look beautiful, powerful, yet scary as fuck at the same time?"

She put the cap back on the bottle and returned it to the shelf. "It's a hellhorse."

"It's fucking amazing, Frankie," said Trick honestly—he wasn't simply trying to please or flatter her. The sculpture was genuinely super impressive, and he found himself in awe of her.

It represented the front half of a horse's body, yet it didn't look incomplete. More like it was in the middle of leaping from another dimension or something like that. It was entirely black metal—some parts were thick and smooth and curled slightly, almost like ribbons. Other pieces were so thin they looked more like mesh or metal string.

The creature was in midlunge, legs extended, mouth open, eyes like angry slits, broken chains hanging from its ankles. The wings were huge yet ragged, as if the creature had been left alone to rot and wither. It had broken free of its restraints, but it wasn't lunging for freedom. It was lunging for its captor. Lunging for vengeance. Or at least that was how it seemed to him.

He turned to Frankie, enjoying the simple luxury of looking at his mate. She was wearing blue coveralls that did nothing for her slim figure. Yet there was still something sexy about the picture she made right then.

When Trick had walked in, his wolf had reacted instantly and fiercely to the sight of her; he'd leaped so hard and fast to the surface that Trick would have shifted if he hadn't had such iron control. Well, maybe not *iron* control, given that his cock was so painfully hard and heavy that it hurt to walk.

He'd never wanted anything as much as he wanted Frankie Newman. Just looking at her made his gut twist with a fierce sexual need. The sight of her also brought him a supreme joy that nothing else could equal.

47

He'd woken more than once during the night, his cock full and aching, the image of her face in his mind. He'd showered several times since first meeting her, but her scent still haunted him every moment of the day. It seemed to live inside him now, like it had sunk into his pores. He'd know it anywhere.

Trick's eyes involuntarily dropped to her lush mouth. He wanted it under his. Wanted to lick and taste and bite. "What made you decide to make a hellhorse?"

"I didn't. Sometimes I don't really know what I'm going to create until I actually start the piece."

That surprised him. "Is that a bad thing?"

"Not for me. If I spend a lot of time pondering what I'm going to do, I overthink it. The fun is in the creative process itself, watching it come together little by little. I guess it's like when you tell a story—there are stages to it. I'm not a writer, but I don't think I'd like to know the end of a story before I wrote it. Part of the buzz would come from watching what happens in my head and writing each part down as it comes."

He nodded. "So you shove your consciousness out of the way so you don't think too much and can just go with it and see what happens."

"Yeah. That's exactly it." Frankie wasn't used to people understanding her. She wasn't used to people *wanting* to understand. It took her off guard, but her wolf liked that he showed such interest in her.

"You're not going to make the rear of its body, are you? Because it looks amazing as it is."

"No, I'm not." She skimmed her finger over the creature's neck. "There isn't much left for me to do now. Shouldn't take me more than a few weeks to finish." Realizing he was staring at her, she asked, "What?"

"It just amazes me that a person can make something like that. Really. I mean, it's one thing to see a picture of a sculpture. It's another thing to stand next to one, see it from every angle, and realize that someone actually made it by hand. Are all your sculptures so dark?"

"Most." She shifted uncomfortably. "Look, if you're here for Lydia or Iris—"

"I'm here to see you."

Her pulse skittered. "Why?"

He'd just needed to be around her, check on her, and breathe her in. Also . . . "I was curious about you." About where she lived and what kind of space she'd need for a studio, because Trick would have to make sure she had one on pack territory. He intended to make sure she had everything she needed to be happy there.

"Well, I'm pretty busy."

"You can take a break, right? All work and no play makes Jack a dull boy."

She sighed at the dumb phrase. "Who is this Jack? And why should I care if he's dull?"

Trick's mouth quirked. "It's just a turn of phrase."

"Yeah, but I don't understand the point in using proverbs when you have the option of saying something that makes perfect sense."

He supposed she had a point, though he didn't see why they annoyed her so much. "Okay, I'll rephrase. Working too much isn't good for you—you need to make time for fun." Glimpsing a door ajar behind her, he asked, "What's through there?"

"It's my display room. I keep all my finished pieces in there."

"Can I see?"

Since he was already heading right for it, Frankie grumbled, "I guess so."

Trick pushed the door open and stalked inside. What could only be described as nightmarish sculptures filled the space. Among them was a gargoyle, a large face scrunched up in agony, a nun wearing an evil smile, and a creepy-looking kid on a chair. "Wow."

While he studied her sculptures, Frankie studied him. Trick Hardy was something of a mystery to her. Why? Because she could sense that he did his best to downplay his dominance around her. It was a futile effort. He had a powerful presence. The air in the studio seemed charged with the compelling intensity that practically bounced off his skin like tiny little sparks. He could play the easygoing charmer all he wanted, but she wasn't buying it. Not even with his slow, lazy smiles and the sexy swaggering gait.

Trick turned to her, surprised to find her watching him. "Jesus, Frankie, how did you make this stuff? Every piece is both eerie and captivating at the same time." Her cheeks reddened at the compliment. Trick skimmed a knuckle over one of them, felt the heat of her blush. "Not used to people admiring your work, are you?" It made him wonder . . . "Do your grandparents approve of what you do?"

"Why wouldn't they?"

"Neither of them are arty people, from what I remember. I just wondered if they'd find it hard to understand that you have a passion." As her mouth clamped shut, Trick nodded and trailed the tip of his finger over the row of piercings on her ear. "Okay, I get it, you don't want to bad-mouth them to someone you barely know. Loyalty is good." He wanted some of that loyalty for himself.

Frankie stepped back, a little uncomfortable with how casually he touched her. No, a little uncomfortable that it didn't bother her wolf the way it should. The animal generally didn't like having her personal space invaded, but she didn't seem to mind sharing it with Trick. "You're pretty tactile, even for a shifter."

"You'll get used to it. Your wolf will let you know if I'm taking it too far. Has she ever surfaced?"

"Sure."

"How old were you when it first happened?"

"Thirteen." And she'd been scared out of her mind, because she hadn't known what to do.

Trick's eyes narrowed. "Tell me you didn't do it alone." Her eyes slid away, and he growled. "No one should be alone during their first shift. I'm sorry you were." And he felt like shit about it. He was her mate; he should have been there. If she hadn't gone to live with the Newmans, he *would* have been there. Those humans had a lot to fucking answer for. "So you're not used to being around shifters?"

"Nope."

"How does your wolf feel around me? Threatened? Edgy?"

"She likes you."

He smiled, since he'd half expected her to claim that her wolf didn't want him around. "I like that you're honest, Frankie. Far too many people aren't." Closing the distance between them in one fluid stride, Trick traced her cheekbones with his thumbs, all the while drinking in every curve, every line, every dent, every freckle on her face. "I'd like to sketch you."

"Is that what they're calling it these days?"

Trick laughed. His wolf was delighted with her. She was unexpected in the best ways. "I'm serious. I like sketching. It relaxes me. The same way I'm thinking that sculpting relaxes you."

Her nose wrinkled. "It's not relaxing in a way that makes me feel peaceful."

"Then how?"

Since he sounded genuinely interested, she replied, "I can disappear in it. It's energizing and tiring and rewarding."

Noticing she was flexing and wiggling her fingers, he frowned. "What's wrong with your hand?"

"It just gets stiff." She dismissed it with a flick of her wrist, but he took her hand and began massaging it. Damn if it didn't feel good. Still . . . "I'm not going to sleep with you."

His mouth slowly curled on one side. "That's all right. I'm not going to sleep with you either."

"So why are you here, flirting with me and stuff, if you don't want me?"

"I didn't say that I don't want you. I said I'm not going to sleep with you. That's just too light a term for what I'm going to do to you."

A blush crept up her neck. "Oh really?"

"Really." Using his grip on her hand, he pulled her closer and spoke in a low voice. "I'm going to take you. Possess you. Fuck you so hard you'll never want anyone else. And when we're done, I'll do it again."

Damn if her pussy didn't clench at that. Frankie narrowed her eyes. "Cocky."

Trick put his finger to her mouth. "Don't say it won't happen, or when you *do* give in to me—and you will, Frankie—you'll think it makes you weak. You're not weak. I wouldn't want you if you were." He shrugged, adding, "Some things are simply inevitable. Me taking you is just one of those things."

Her stomach fluttered. Not just at his declaration, but at the way those brown eyes drifted over her face, warm and possessive. It made her wolf release a low growl of contentment, which was out of the norm. Frustrated and horny, Frankie jutted out her chin. "I have work to do."

Sensing her arousal, Trick smiled, satisfied. "All right." He pressed a kiss to her palm and then released it. "I told you I'm not here for Lydia or Iris, and I'm not. But I want to say one thing about it. I know this situation is fucked up and you're not sure what to think, feel, or believe. But I get the sense that if Iris died tomorrow before you had the chance to meet her, you'd regret that you didn't. Am I right?"

"Maybe."

"Then I'd say the decision you have to make isn't whether you want to give your paternal family a chance; it's whether you want to live with the regret that you didn't." He cupped her chin and stroked her jaw with his thumb. "Take care, Frankie, yeah?" It was a soft demand. He needed to be sure that she'd be fine.

"Always do," she said. He lightly brushed his mouth over her temple, and then he was gone. Frankie took in a centering breath. Damn, the wolf was potent. Nothing like the guys she was used to—they were strong and self-assured, yeah, but none of them carried that air of supreme, unshakable confidence that came with knowing you could handle any situation with total ease. It was hot and admirable and her wolf absolutely loved it.

The animal wasn't at all happy that he'd left. She lay down, sulking. It was odd. Her wolf had liked Frankie's past partners well enough, but not like this. She hadn't wanted their company, hadn't particularly enjoyed having them around. Really, it was more like she'd tolerated them for Frankie's sake.

For the first time, her wolf *wanted* a male. Strangely, she also wanted to hold back from him a little. Not out of wariness, but to . . . test him. To see what he was made of and if he was worthy of . . . something.

Deciding it was pointless to try to understand it, Frankie turned back to her sculpture.

The following day, Trick accompanied Trey, Dante, and Dominic as they ventured to the local park for their meeting with Nash Morelli. It was a hot day, so there were many people around—sunbathers, cyclists, dog walkers, families, kids playing ball. Trick hoped the meeting didn't go to shit, because there would be a hell of a lot of witnesses if it did.

Morelli was already sitting at the picnic table when they arrived; five wolves stood behind him, on guard. Without a word Trey sat opposite Morelli. Dante stood solidly behind Trey while Trick and Dominic planted themselves on either side of their Beta. For a moment no one said anything. Just stayed still, sizing one another up.

Morelli was a big bastard. Thick neck, roped arms, thighs like tree trunks. He also had a wide grin that would have been charismatic if it weren't for its sly curve.

There was a similar grin on his Beta's face. Drake had a reputation for being . . . well, to be blunt, a fucking asshole. After being kicked out of his previous pack for slitting his sister's throat, Drake had earned protection and money as a gun for hire until Morelli took him into his sad excuse for a pack.

Taking the cigar from his mouth, Morelli shifted in his seat, making his leather vest creak. "Well, damn, if it isn't Trey Coleman. I've been wanting to meet you for a long time." He ran his gaze along Dante, Dominic, and Trick. His eyes lit up. "Ah, it's the YouTube hero. I've heard plenty about you. One of my wolves knows you. He says you can be brutal when the situation calls for it. That's why he found it so damn funny that the humans see you as a hunky hero."

The wolf was right, but Trick said nothing.

Morelli cut his gaze to Trey. "I always admired the way you challenged your old man. I heard enough to know he was a total prick and earned that beating you gave him. People don't always get what they deserve. It's refreshing when someone does."

Trey didn't react. Just watched the other Alpha, expression blank. It didn't seem to discourage Morelli at all. His wide grin remained in place.

"I sure do like your territory," said Morelli. "I mean, I haven't been able to see a lot of it, since you have that big fence and all. But it's vast and well protected. I heard you actually live inside one of the mountains. Is that true?"

"If you're planning on challenging me to take over my pack and seize my territory, it won't end well for you," Trey warned.

Morelli took a pull on his cigar and then blew out a puff of smoke, tainting the collective scents of sun-warmed grass and flowering trees. "I'll admit, the thought did cross my mind. But like I said, I admire how you dealt with your old man. Leaving the pack to create your own—that takes guts. Let's face it, it wouldn't be smart of me to take on a male whose wolf turns feral during battle. Not to mention that you're very well connected. The Mercury Pack in particular would seek revenge on anyone who brought harm to you or yours. I don't want them on my ass any more than I want a feral wolf chewing a chunk out of my wolf's ass."

"Why did you ask for a meeting?"

"Not real friendly, are you, Trey? Can I call you Trey?"

"No."

Morelli chuckled, seeming delighted. "Damn, I like you. As for why I wanted this meeting . . . It's quite simple, really. I'd like to propose an alliance."

"Would you," said Trey, his tone even.

"I feel it would benefit us both."

"Here's the thing. I don't like your methods of expanding your pack. I don't like the rumors I've heard about how your Beta here"—Trey tipped his chin at Drake—"deals with people. Your enforcers are constantly causing disruptions at bars and clubs and pool halls. That means either you don't have control of your pack, or you don't care what they do. Either way, that's not the kind of Alpha I want to ally myself with."

Morelli heaved a sigh. "That's disappointing, Trey. Really. I'd hoped we could be friends. It's good to have friends." He stubbed out his cigar on the table. "It's true that I don't police my pack much. But if I wanted a flock of sheep, I'd have bought a farm. We're shifters, Trey. We have a wildness inside us that humans will never understand. Why should we tone it down and pretend to be what we're not? Don't you see that it makes us seem weak to the humans? It's the same principle as when you're dealing with a spoiled kid. If you don't ignore their little outbursts and just carry on as normal, they'll keep on having them. You can't show them mercy or give in; if you do, they'll see you as weak, and they won't respect you."

"You're saying you don't police your pack because you think letting them do what they like will earn you people's respect?" asked Trey. "Let's go back to the spoiled kid analogy. You got this spoiled kid—let's call him Drake—who has some serious issues. If his parents don't guide or temper or insist on his respect, he'll do whatever the fuck he wants and they won't have his respect."

Morelli looked at his Beta. "You respect me, don't you, Drake?"

Still grinning, Drake said, "Of course I do, Alpha."

Morelli nodded at Trey, satisfied. "There you go." He rubbed at his jaw. "This PR work . . . there's no point to it. Humans will never fully accept us. Never. There will be a war between us and them sooner or later. No matter what we do or how cuddly we try to look, it will come. Maybe the extremists will lead it, maybe the government will lead it. Shit, maybe our own kind will start it—I don't know. But it will come. And you know what, Trey? We'll be easy pickings, and I'll tell you why that is. It's because we won't unite. We won't go out and fight as one. We'll hang back and defend our territories and our vulnerable members—it's instinct. That's why we'll lose."

Trey lifted a brow. "You're saying we should all band together?"

"Yes. I don't just mean wolf packs allying with each other. I'm talking all the local packs, prides, flocks, clans, herds, and whatever else there might be. We need to be ready. In order to be ready, we need to have a plan in place."

"And I'm guessing you have a plan."

"Like I said, hanging back to defend our territories will be our downfall. But we can't leave our vulnerable members. No, they'd die. What we need is somewhere for them to go. A sanctuary, if you will. Your territory would be the perfect place for the young and those unable to fight. They'd be inside a freaking mountain. I don't know how spacious it is, but I have the funds and resources to make that dwelling bigger and better if it's necessary. They could all hole up there, and you can do what you do best, Trey. Protect. Defend."

Trey's eyes narrowed slightly. "That's what I do best?"

"You're not an Alpha who looks for trouble or goes around challenging people. You protect your pack, defend your territory, aid your allies, and retaliate where necessary. You're a hell of a fighter, but you don't fight for fighting's sake. Not many would take lone shifters into their pack, but you do. Just like you helped defend a shelter for lone shifters. Recently your pack even helped a human who was being targeted by her own kind purely for speaking up for one of ours. These are the actions of someone I can respect. The actions of someone who is a protector at his core."

"And where will you be when me and my pack are protecting the vulnerable?"

Morelli shrugged. "Someone has to lead the fight."

For a long moment Trey said nothing. "I underestimated you, Morelli. You're smarter than I gave you credit for. You know just what to say. Just how to twist something to appeal to someone. But here's the thing: you underestimated me too. You thought you could meet with me, appeal to my protective streak, and get what you want—which isn't an alliance. Not really. You're not collecting alliances. You're building an army." Trey pushed to his feet and stepped over the bench seat. "My pack won't be a squad within your army."

Eyes hardening, Morelli said, "The war will come. Your territory is the ideal place for the vulnerable to hide."

"And if other shifters knew I'd provide sanctuary for their members, they'd be much more inclined to listen to you, wouldn't they?" Trey snorted. "If you want people to join you, you need to get your shit together and act like an Alpha. No one will trust you to lead them in an army when you can't even lead your own damn pack. The fact that you've elected *that* twisted fucker to be your Beta speaks volumes about what kind of person you are."

Flushing, Drake tried launching himself at Trey. Before anyone had the chance to move, Trick struck, slamming his fist into Drake's jaw and delivering a body shot to the ribs that made the dumb asshole keel over and drop to his knees, winded.

Morelli laughed, clapping his hands as if he were watching a show. "Good reflexes, hero. It's not often people take Drake off guard." He sighed at his Beta, like the guy was an unruly kid in a classroom. "I'm trying to have a conversation here, Drake. Simmer down, will you?" Shaking his head, he turned back to Trey. "Take some time to think about my proposal. Talk it over with your mate. You'll see that I'm right. When you do, give me a call."

As the Mortelle wolves walked away, Trey called out, "One last thing. If you try planting any more GPS trackers on my property, I'll rip your fucking throat out."

Morelli's face split into a grin. "I love how you say that with no emotion whatsoever. Me? I'm an emotional guy. Which is why I'm quite hurt that you'd suspect me of planting trackers." Face lined with mock pain, he turned and strode away.

Heading back to the SUV with his pack mates, Trick said with utter certainty, "It was definitely Morelli who planted the trackers."

"Yep," agreed Dante.

"You know what worries me more than anything he said?" asked Dominic. "He wants this war. You can see it in his eyes. I think if he gets enough people behind him, he might actually start it himself."

Trey nodded. "And he could just as easily turn that army on his own kind as he could on humans."

"He wants our territory," said Trick. "It's not just about using it as a sanctuary, though I think he'd like to do that. No, he wants it." Trick looked at Trey. "He just doesn't want to fight you for it."

"I agree," said Dante. "He knows he won't win a fight against you, Trey, and he knows that he'll earn himself plenty of enemies even if he did miraculously win. For that reason, it's a losing situation for him. He's smart enough to know that."

"He won't drop this, though," warned Dominic. "He has a plan. We're part of it. I don't think he'll let anything mess with it. No, I think he'll try and get us on his side."

"How?" asked Trey.

Dominic shrugged. "I don't know. And that bugs me."

CHAPTER FIVE

The tall gates swung open slowly, and Frankie drove across the border of Phoenix Pack territory. She paused at a security shack just as a male strode out. When she lowered the window, he bent forward. He was kind of cute, especially with the dimpled smile. He was also mated—she could smell it. "Hi, I'm—"

"Frankie Newman," he finished. "Lydia told me you'd be here at noon."

She'd called Lydia the previous night and arranged to come, because Trick had been right. The situation *was* fucked up and she *wasn't* sure what to think, feel, or believe, but she *would* in fact regret not meeting Iris.

"I'm Gabe Farrow. You won't remember me. You were good friends with my sister, Jaime. She's inside, looking forward to seeing you again."

Frankie's smile was a little nervous. "Great. What route do I take to—" Her head whipped to the side as her passenger door was pulled open. Trick slid into the car. His smile was lazy and languid and made her wolf sit up in interest.

"Hello, Frankie." Trick tipped his chin at Gabe and said, "See you at dinner, if not before." He then turned back to her. "You can give me a ride."

She slowly lifted a brow. "Can I?"

"Sure. Just follow the road."

Her tires crunched as they started up the rocky trail. She didn't drive fast, wanting to take in her surroundings. The territory was massive. Full of tall regal trees, lush grass, and steep, craggy mountains. Beautiful.

Feeling the weight of Trick's gaze on her skin, she threw him a sideways frown. "Stop staring."

"But you're such a pretty view." Trick loved looking at her. Loved absorbing every inch of her, knowing deep down to his soul that she was his.

He'd never in his life felt possessive of a partner, but the emotion roared through him whenever he saw her, thought of her, inhaled her scent. He was doing his best to hide it, tone down his intensity, and come across as easygoing so she didn't slam up her guard. It was hard; he wasn't used to subtlety. By nature he was forward and outspoken. But he didn't want to fuck this up. So far she'd been relatively relaxed around him, though he doubted she knew why.

His wolf was currently feeling rather self-satisfied, content to have his mate on his territory. The animal wanted to bite and claim her, and he was becoming increasingly pissed off at Trick for failing to do so. "Nervous?"

"Not really," said Frankie. God, she was *such* a liar. Her muscles were twitchy, her stomach kept rolling, and her mouth was dry as a bone. Yeah, well, it wasn't every day that a girl went to visit a grandmother and bunch of pack mates she couldn't remember. Honestly, she was glad Trick was there; he had a way of settling her. "I don't know what to expect. I don't like that."

"Iris and Lydia are more nervous than you are. Once upon a time, you were a little girl who adored them unconditionally. It's hard for them that you don't remember them."

"I can't help that," she said defensively.

"No, you can't. No one's expecting you to," Trick assured her. And if anyone made her feel bad about it, he'd give them a ration of shit. "How's the hellhorse coming along?"

"Good." She brought the car to an abrupt halt as something caught her attention. "Is that . . . Are there windows and balconies on that mountain?"

Trick grinned, proud of how observant his mate was. "You've got a good eye. Very few people notice until we point them out."

Frankie stared at it openmouthed, taking in the small windows, the pretty arched balconies, and the narrow stairways that had been carved into the face of the mountain. "Now that's art."

"Yeah, I guess it is." Trick hadn't really thought of it that way before. "My Alpha female, Taryn, calls it Bedrock."

"So you live inside the mountain?"

"Yeah. The large cave system was once an ancient dwelling. Don't worry—we have electricity and running water. It's become increasingly modernized over the years."

"It's a big place." Throwing the car into gear, she continued up the trail. "How many wolves are there in your pack?"

"We don't just have wolves. We also have a raven, a viper, and a cheetah. In total there are twenty-six of us—that's twenty adults, one juvenile, and five young ones."

"Young ones?"

"Why do you sound freaked by that?"

"Kids scare me."

Trick felt his brow crease even as he smiled. "How could kids possibly scare you?"

"I don't know. They just do." They always acted weird around her. Plus she didn't have any younger siblings or cousins, so she wasn't used to being around kids. "How many of you were part of the first generation, if you don't mind me asking?"

"Of course I don't mind you asking. It's pack business, but you are pack. Of the original seventeen, thirteen of us are left. Two died, two transferred to another pack."

"And one of those who died was Iris's mate, my . . . um, grandfather?"

"No. Alfie and Iris stayed with the Bjorn Pack. I'm guessing you did your research on the pack and you know why it split?" He would have in her position. At her nod, Trick went on. "They didn't stay behind because they agreed with Rick Coleman's decision; it was because they were worried that he'd stop them from visiting Christopher's grave if they left. Rick *would* have done that. He was an asshole that way. I thought they might move here when another Alpha took Rick's place, but they didn't. Iris recently joined the Phoenix Pack to spend what time she has left with Lydia." Trick spotted the iPhone in the cup holder. "That your cell?"

Frankie blinked at the abrupt change of subject. "Um, yeah. Hey, don't play with it," she said as he grabbed it, but it was too late.

"There. Done."

She frowned. "What's done?"

"My number is programmed in your phone." Trick then called his own cell using hers. "And now I have your number."

"Don't you think maybe you should *ask* before you do shit like that?"

"Would you have told me your number?"

"Sure. It's 911—but only dial it in an emergency."

He chuckled. "I do enjoy your sense of humor, Frankie." It surprised him that she had a playful side, since her maternal family had always seemed so serious. Even her mother, though gentle and kind, had never really been playful, from what he could remember. He pointed to an opening in the base of the mountain. "Go in there."

She drove through the opening in the cliff and found herself inside a cleverly concealed parking lot. Impressed, she lifted her brows. "Where do I park?"

"Anywhere."

She whipped her Audi into a spot and switched off the engine. "So is there anything I need to know? I mean, are there rituals to this sort of thing? I don't have to kneel before the Alphas, do I? Because that won't happen."

He smiled. "No, you don't need to kneel before anyone. Just listen to your wolf; she'll know what to do."

Hopping out of the car, Frankie looked at the collection of vehicles. The pack sure did like SUVs. She should have objected when Trick linked his fingers with hers and tugged her outside, but she didn't. And she couldn't have said why.

At the foot of the narrow stairway, Trick said, "After you." Then he could stare at her ass as they climbed. Happy days. Halfway up, she stopped to look around. He frowned and asked, "You all right?"

"Yeah. I've just never been to a place like this. Never seen anything like it. My wolf wants out. She wants to roam and explore. I don't blame her—it's really amazing."

It was good that she thought so, Trick mused, because it would be her home soon enough. "Later, after you've spoken to the pack and seen Iris, I'll give you a tour." He splayed his hand on her lower back and gently urged her on, and they started walking again. "Do your grandparents know you're here?"

"No." Frankie hadn't told Brad either. She'd called him this morning, tiptoed around the subject of Lydia, and agreed to meet with him later that day. "They won't be happy about it."

"There's no point in living to make other people happy, Frankie. We're all responsible for own happiness anyway." Finally they reached the main entrance to the caves. He carefully shouldered past her and rested a hand on the door. "Ready?"

Frankie rolled back her shoulders. "As I'll ever be." He opened the door, gesturing for her to enter first, and she suddenly found herself inside a large tunnel. It wasn't dark and dull, as she might have expected.

The smooth walls were light-cream sandstone that seemed to illuminate the tunnels, and she briefly skimmed her fingers along them.

"Everyone's waiting in the living area." Trick led her through the network of tunnels, keeping his pace slow so she could get a good look around.

As he guided her into the living area, everyone stood. It reminded him of the time when the juvenile of the pack, Zac, had first arrived. Ryan's young cousin had been staying at the shelter where Makenna worked until they brought him into the pack. Maybe Zac was remembering it too, because his voice cut through the awkward silence.

"They weren't kidding when they said you look harmless."

Casting Zac an affectionate hushing look, Taryn stepped forward and smiled at Frankie. "I'm Taryn, Alpha female. This is my mate, Trey, and he's holding our son, Kye. Welcome to Phoenix Pack territory."

Frankie nodded at the dainty female. "Thanks."

Trey inclined his head at her. "I doubt you'll remember me. I really didn't like girls much back then—I used to shove daisies down the back of your dress."

Frankie's mouth twitched. "I hope I didn't take that lying down."

"No, you didn't. You used to charge at me like a bull."

"I remember that," said Lydia, looking like she wanted to embrace Frankie. She refrained. "I'm so glad you came."

Taryn quickly went on. "Let me introduce you to everyone. Obviously you know Lydia and Cam. Standing next to them are Grace, Rhett, and their little girl, Lilah. Over there near the back wall are the Beta pair, Jaime and Dante, and some of our enforcers, Marcus, Roni, and Dominic. There's Ryan, who you met at the coffeehouse, standing with his mate, Makenna, and his cousin, Zac. The sleeping pup in Makenna's arms is Sienna Rose. The woman over there looking miserable and disapproving is Trey's grandmother, Greta—an accident of nature.

"Last but not least, we have this little cluster of people near the sofa. Hope is Gabe's mate, Tao is the Head Enforcer, and Riley is the pack's Guardian. The little girl with the pigtails is Savannah, and the little blond boy with the bulging pockets is Dexter—they belong to Tao and Riley, who are mates."

Feeling awkward and a little overwhelmed by the overflow of information, Frankie did a slow nod. "It's nice to meet all of you." Some of them looked at her with a familiarity that made her uncomfortable. Others just looked curious, particularly the kids, who stared at her. Greta, though, was eyeing Frankie with suspicion.

Dominic stepped forward, a weird grin on his face, but Dante fisted the guy's shirt and pulled him back with a firm shake of his head.

"Iris wanted to be here to greet you," began Trey, "but she can't leave her bed much."

"She's super excited to see you," said Lydia. "I'm under strict orders to take you straight to her. That okay with you?"

Frankie gave an easy shrug. "Sure."

As Lydia started to lead her out of the room, Trick quietly asked Frankie, "You'll be all right?"

"Of course."

Satisfied, he nodded. "If you need anything, call." He didn't turn back to the pack until she'd disappeared down the tunnels.

"She really doesn't remember any of us, does she?" said Jaime, sounding sad.

Dante draped his arm around his mate's shoulders. "Maybe it's better that way. If she remembered us, she'd likely also remember her father killing her mother."

Jaime, who'd witnessed the death of her own parents, said, "You're totally right. It's better for her this way. Still, it's hard. As kids, we played together and tormented the boys together, but she only sees a stranger when she looks at me."

"Doesn't mean you can't be friends now, does it?" Dante nuzzled his mate. "I'm sure she could do with a friend right now."

"I think Trick's already filled that position," said Trey.

Ignoring the speculation in the Alpha's eyes, Trick said, "You can never have too many friends."

Stopping outside a thick oak door, Lydia spoke quietly to Frankie. "Don't be nervous. She knows you don't remember her. No one's expecting an emotional response from you that you can't give. She'd just like to talk to you and—"

"Stop muttering outside the room and let me get a look at the girl," a croaky voice called out.

Lydia rolled her eyes and opened the door. Frankie followed her inside, quite surprised to see that the space looked like a luxury hotel suite. It had all the basics—bed, TV, plush chair, table, bedside cabinet, triple wardrobe with mirrored doors. There was even a balcony and a private bathroom.

Frankie's attention was drawn to the woman in the bed, who was propped up on pillows. She studied Frankie through blue eyes that seemed to have dulled slightly with age. She looked pale and weak, but not defeated. Her gray hair was pulled into a tidy bun, and its shade made Frankie think of doves. Then the woman smiled, and her whole face seemed to light up.

"Well, I'll be damned. You look just like me when I was your age."

Mouth curved, Lydia sighed at her mother. "She does not. You have the same eyes—that's pretty much it."

Iris sent her daughter a mock glare. "Are you saying I wasn't beautiful?"

"Don't try to talk me in circles."

Iris turned back to Frankie and gestured at the armchair beside her bed. "Come sit." Once Frankie was seated, Iris clasped her hands and prompted, "So tell me about yourself."

Frankie felt her brow furrow. "I'm pretty sure, from what Lydia told me, that you already know quite a lot."

"I know some basic facts. I know where you live, where you went to school, what you do for a living, and I'm guessing you've left a trail of broken hearts wherever you've gone—I did the same."

Lydia sighed again. "You did not."

Iris ignored her. "Favorite color?"

"Yellow," said Frankie.

"Favorite food?"

"Chocolate."

"Favorite movie?"

"Role Models."

"Favorite sex position?"

Frankie's mouth curved. "There are too many to choose from."

Iris let out a croaky laugh. "I like you. I was always partial to the reverse cowgirl."

Lydia gasped. "Mother!"

"Although my mate liked the scissors—"

"Mom, stop, *I'm begging you.*"

Iris threw an impatient look at her daughter. "Really, Lydia, it's not as if you're new to sex."

"I'm pretty sure that Frankie didn't come all the way here to discuss the *Kama Sutra.*"

"It was simply a question," Iris defended herself. Sliding her gaze back to Frankie, she said, "Tell me more." She asked lots of questions, but they were casual and even funny at times. She wanted to know all about sculpting, Frankie's time at school, and what her wolf's personality was like. Basically—just as Lydia had said—Iris simply wanted to know her.

After a while Iris said, "Your head is probably pounding from all my questions. Feel free to ask me some, if there's anything you want to know."

Although Iris hadn't once touched the subject of her parents, Frankie said, "I want to know about *him*. And yet I don't."

"I understand. Christopher was a pain in my ass." Frankie's surprise must have shown on her face, because Iris asked, "Oh, you thought I'd paint him as a misunderstood saint? No, I won't do that. He wasn't a bad person, but he could be damn irritating because he was stubborn, anal, and saw things in black and white. There were no gray areas for him. If you made a mistake, if you did him wrong, you were the bad guy. He wasn't unforgiving, just slow to let any slights go. He was also temperamental, though I'm told that's normal for artists."

"He was an artist?"

"Liked to paint. He was pretty good. Not art gallery–worthy, but he had a lot of talent. He had many good qualities. He was loyal. Protective. Strong willed. Honorable. He loved you. Used to carry you around on his shoulders, called you his princess. And he loved Caroline." Iris took a shaky breath. "I don't know what went wrong. I truly can't imagine what it could have been. They seemed so happy."

"I can't give you answers about what happened that night," Frankie said gently. "I understand why you'd want them, but if you're hoping I can tell you, I can't. I don't remember."

Iris patted her hand. "I won't deny that I'd like closure, but I'm not under the illusion that you're able to give it to me."

"You don't think I saw anything?"

"You were a smart kid. You would have known to hide if there were trouble. But you were also bold as brass even then. Much too curious for your own good. You'd have come out of hiding to see what was happening, so yes, I believe you saw something.

"I've seen pictures of your sculptures, Frankie. They're captivating, even though they're also like something from a nightmare. They make me wonder if your subconscious keeps that event locked up tight. But I wouldn't dream of asking you to drag it all back up—no good could come of that for you. And finding out the whole story wouldn't change anything."

Noting the slight slur in Iris's voice, Frankie shot Lydia a concerned look.

"She's tired herself out," Lydia told Frankie. "Mom, you need to rest now."

Iris huffed. "Fine, fine. I'm grateful that you came, Frankie. More grateful than you can ever know. I hope you'll come back, but I'll understand if you don't."

Stepping outside the room, Frankie blinked in surprise at Trick leaning against the wall. "Iris needs to rest, so Lydia's just getting her settled."

"You were in there for a while," he observed. "Not as bad as you'd thought it would be?"

Far from it. "Iris made it easy."

"Good. Time for that tour."

"Aren't you busy?"

"I'm off duty. Come on."

Too curious to turn down such an offer, Frankie followed him. He showed her around the caves first, taking her to the different levels and letting her peek inside the game room, the infirmary, and even the laundry room.

Afterward he took her outside. There was so much to see. Not just the forest and the mountains, but the river, the wildlife, and his favorite spots. He told her lots of stories about the pack, making her laugh again and again.

At her request they hiked to the top of one of the mountains. The view was outstanding, and it was relaxing to listen to the wind whistling along the cliff and making the trees below creak as they rocked slightly.

Her wolf loved it. Loved the wild scents of cold rock, pine needles, and the earthy moss beneath Frankie's feet.

"Is it hard?" he asked.

Sweeping her gaze over the valley below—admiring the ravine, the frothy waterfall, and the birds she could see perched in high treetops— she asked, "Is what hard?"

"Living off pack territory?"

Frankie felt her nose wrinkle. "I was about to say I don't know any different. I don't *remember* things being any different. My wolf's kind of edgy, and I often wonder if it's because she's without a pack and a territory. I guess she gets lonely."

Trick pinned her gaze with his. "You're not without a pack."

Being considered part of a pack and actually feeling as though she belonged to it—yeah, they were two different things. "Do you remember much about my parents?"

"Yeah. Your father used to chase me and the other boys away, tell us to stay away from his princess. It was just play, and you used to laugh your little head off. Your mother always had cookies, and she'd hand them out to everyone if they promised not to get into mischief. You were a lively, happy kid. Full of energy. Sweet too." His mouth twitched. "Not so sweet now."

"No, I can be kind of mean. Why does that make you smile?"

"I like mean."

"Then you'll fucking adore me."

He chuckled, thinking that, yeah, he would. "We should head back. It's time for dinner. You're welcome to stay the night. As you've already seen, we have lots of guest rooms."

She walked toward the slope, almost wincing as a bumpy rock prodded the sole of her foot. "I'm meeting someone later, but thanks." She halted abruptly as he suddenly appeared in front of her.

"Who are you meeting?"

The rumbled demand surprised her. "Sorry?"

"*Who* are you meeting?"

"What's with the tone?" Because she didn't like it *at all*. His easygoing charm was gone, and the dark predatory streak that he hid seemed to take over.

"Answer the question, Frankie."

"And just why would you think it had a damn thing to do with you?"

70

He growled. "It has everything to do with me." He went nose to nose with her and whispered, "I don't share."

She narrowed her eyes. "I'm not yours *to* share."

"You will be."

Frankie really wished those words pissed her off. Instead the possessive statement made her a little tingly. Her wolf liked it. "Is that a fact?"

"It is." He cupped her chin. "When I'm sure that you're ready, I'll come for you. You should probably know that." Softening his voice, he coaxed, "Tell me who you're meeting. I need time to look them up, find their address, and beat the shit out of them so they can't make it to the meeting. Really, time is of the essence here."

She wouldn't smile, Frankie promised herself. She wouldn't. But she did. "My uncle. I'm meeting my uncle. And I would prefer it if you didn't beat him up." Like that, his face went all soft, and the menacing glint receded from his eyes.

"There. Was that so hard?" Trick brushed his mouth over hers. "Don't worry; your uncle's safe from me." Unless the human hurt her in any way, that was. Trick wouldn't tolerate that. Releasing her, he stepped back. "Come on, time to eat."

Back inside the caves, Trick escorted her to the kitchen and seated her beside him at the long table. Frankie noticed that he didn't look happy when Dominic sat opposite her, and he even tossed the blond enforcer a warning look that made him blink innocently.

As she piled food on her plate, she glanced around the table. People were talking, laughing, teasing, and—in the case of Dexter—stuffing food in their pockets. Frankie hadn't grown up in a house full of laughter. Meal times were stiff, dignified affairs; there would be light conversation, but no funny stories or mirth.

Being around the pack was, well, odd. Not bad odd, but different. The way they all lived together, ate together, held different roles, constantly touched each other . . . Maybe it should have been off-putting, since it was so unfamiliar, but she liked it. At the same time, it was kind of sad. Like being on the outskirts of a secret club, having a peek of what went on inside, but only being an observer. Not that they ignored her or anything. No, they included her in their conversations and told her things about themselves—particularly Jaime, who also shared some funny stories from their childhood.

One such story made Frankie's head jerk back. "I would never eat a beetle."

"You didn't eat it, but you did chew it. So did I. Then we both spat the mashed-up insects at the girl who happened to be Dante's girlfriend at the time."

Dante winced. "Yeah, I remember that. She screamed like a banshee." His eyes dropped to the oversize, odd-looking ginger cat that suddenly sprang onto his mate's lap. He glared hard at the feline, who glared right back—like they were engaged in some kind of dominance battle. Then the cat hissed, and Dante snapped his teeth.

Jaime cuddled the cat close to her. "Popeye, leave him alone. Frankie, this is Hunk."

Frankie's brows lifted. "Really? He's . . . cute." *Lie.*

"So, Frankie . . . ," began Dominic, leaning forward. "What time do you have to be back in heaven?"

"Oh, for God's sake," Lydia burst out. "No, Dominic, you will not do this to my niece."

He looked the image of innocence. "What?"

"Don't mind Dominic," Taryn told Frankie. "He says cheesy lines to just about everyone."

"I mean it, Dominic," Lydia said sternly. "Leave her alone."

He smiled. "Oh, I see, you're jealous. Ah, Lydia, you know I adore you. I especially love those long legs. What time do they open?"

Taryn sighed, raising a brow at Frankie. "See what I mean?"

As a chuckling Dominic turned back to Frankie, Trick softly but firmly said, "No."

The enforcer frowned. "But—"

"No," Trick repeated. "Unless you're curious about what your balls taste like."

Dominic exhaled in frustration. "You're no fun."

"How do we know you're telling the truth?" Greta asked Frankie, her mouth tight as she stared at her.

Blinking, Frankie said, "I'm sorry?"

"You say the Newmans lied to you all these years." Greta lifted her chin in challenge. "But how do we know that's true?"

Frankie felt her brows lower. "Why would I lie about it?"

"That's what I'm wondering."

Trick draped his arm over the back of Frankie's chair. "Greta, just don't."

"It's a valid question," Greta insisted.

"It's you looking for reasons not to like or trust Frankie," he corrected her.

Makenna leaned into Frankie and said quietly, "Don't take it personally. Greta doesn't like unmated females around her precious boys. She's very possessive of Trey, Dante, Tao, and the male enforcers. Doesn't like any of their mates, other than Roni. She hates me most of all." The last was said with pride.

Greta's focus snapped back to Frankie. "I never liked your grandparents. They're hoity-toity. Think they're better than everyone else, especially shifters. Your grandmother has a coldness about her. When I look at you, I see that same coldness."

Frankie licked her fork. "When I look at you, I see someone so ancient she probably has an autographed Bible."

Taryn burst out laughing, leaning into Trey, whose shoulders were shaking with silent laughter.

Greta glowered at the Alpha female, griping, "Oh, you would find that amusing." Greta sneered in disgust and marched out of the kitchen, her head held high.

A little while later, Frankie thanked Grace for the meal and—since it seemed kind of rude that she was immediately leaving—apologized for having to eat and run. She politely refused Lydia's offer for her to stay the night, but she did go and say goodbye to Iris before leaving.

Trick walked her to the parking lot and over to her Audi. His fingers combed through her hair. "I'm glad you came, Frankie."

Surprisingly . . . "Yeah, so am I."

"Good."

She should have seen it coming. She'd just gotten so used to him touching her without taking it too far that she'd lowered her guard, so she hadn't been braced for the hand that slid up the back of her neck, gripped a fistful of her hair, and held her head still as he pinned her against the car.

Her heart leaped and her breath left her in a rush. He didn't slam his mouth on hers as she'd expected. No, he skimmed his nose down her neck and breathed her in. His low growl reverberated up his chest and made her nipples bead.

"Fucking love your scent, Frankie."

She gripped his arms as his teeth scraped over her pulse just hard enough to make her pussy clench. His tongue swirled over her skin to soothe the sting, and then he was kissing his way up her neck and over to her mouth. His tongue sank inside and lashed hers. He didn't rush. He lingered. Explored. Savored. Devoured. Left her without any defenses.

Feel-good chemicals swam through her brain and flooded her body. The whole thing was so delicious and intoxicating that her head spun and her pussy grew unbelievably wet.

Sliding a hand under her thigh, Trick hooked her leg over his hip as he crushed her against the car, letting her feel how hard he was for her. Fuck, she tasted as sweet and tangy and perfect as she smelled. Her soft, incredibly responsive body curved into his, fitting against him just right.

He possessively closed his hand over her breast, and her hard nipple brushed his palm. He felt her raspy moan all the way down to his balls. Growling into her mouth, he slanted his head, deepening the kiss, needing more. Knowing he'd never get enough.

He'd never experienced this depth of raw need in his life. Never needed something so badly that he felt like he'd go insane without it. It was getting harder and harder to tone down his urge to claim her. He'd waited so damn long for her, needed her so fucking badly. But he wouldn't take her right then.

Trick pulled back, panting a little, and rubbed his nose against hers. "I will have you, Frankie. But it won't be up against a car. Not the first time, anyway. I want to lick and savor every inch of you. Can't do that here."

Striving to find some composure after that kiss that had all but destroyed her, Frankie licked her lower lip. The way he was looking at her, the way he spoke—so serious, so determined, so resolved—was unnerving as hell. To lighten the moment, she teased, "What if I don't like casual sex?"

He pursed his lips. "I suppose I could dress up. Put on my best shirt."

She chuckled. "You know what I mean." She liked their back and forth. Everything in her life was so serious right then, and he was like a long, cool glass of water—calming and refreshing. And he kissed like a fucking master.

"Your laugh could stop traffic." Raspy and gritty, like her voice, it never failed to make Trick's cock twitch. And since he was currently pressed up against her, there was no way she hadn't felt it. He kissed her once more. "I needed that." Stepping back, he opened the car door for her. As she slipped inside, he said, "Stay safe, Frankie."

"You too."

He let the door swing shut and watched her drive away. It was hard. Painful, even. Every instinct he had badgered him to keep her close.

His wolf lunged after her, but Trick kept a tight hold on him. It had to be this way. For now.

Once his wolf settled, Trick returned to the caves and headed to the living area. Most of the pack were gathered there, and they all looked at him oddly as he entered.

Dante arched a brow. "Something you want to tell us?"

"You've already figured it out." Trick had suspected they would. It wasn't like he'd be able to hide his possessiveness from them—they knew him too well.

"When did *you* figure it out?" asked Lydia.

"Day one," Trick replied.

Marcus rubbed at his nape. "Well, this complicates things, but I'm happy for you."

The others nodded . . . except for Lydia, who sighed and began, "Trick—"

"You don't want anything to rock the boat and scare her off," said Trick. "I know. Neither do I. But don't ask me to keep my distance from her. I can't do that. I *won't* do that. She's mine, and I've lived without her for long enough. I'll hold off on telling her we're mates, though it's possible she'll figure it out for herself." His mate was smart. "She's in tune with her wolf."

"In the long run," began Taryn, "it will work to our advantage that you're her true mate. It means she'll move here at some point. But for now, well, if she knew the truth, I think it would make her feel pressured."

"Like I said, I'll hold off on telling her. I want her here more than any of you do."

Lydia gave him a soft smile. "I'm glad you're her mate, Trick. You'll be there for her, look out for her. If the Newmans turn on her over this—and I'm pretty sure they will—she's going to need whatever support she can get."

CHAPTER SIX

The bar wasn't far from Brad's workplace, and they'd met there a few times in the past. Despite the dim lighting, Frankie spotted him easily enough—her being half shifter meant she could see well in the dark.

She shouldered her way through the patrons, most of whom seemed to be focused on the football game that was playing on the wide-screen TV. Her wolf released a disgruntled growl at the scents of beer, cigarette smoke, and cologne.

Reaching the long bar, Frankie slid onto the wooden stool beside Brad's and said, "Hey."

He smiled. "There she is." He kissed her cheek. "You look tired."

"It was a long day." And she hadn't slept well the night before, nervous about her trip to Phoenix Pack territory. "How are you?"

"Fine, sweetheart. What are you drinking?"

"Beer."

"No girly neon drinks for you. I like that." He called to the bartender, who handed her a beer and replaced Brad's empty one with a fresh bottle. Brad turned back to her. "You've been dodging my calls."

"I've genuinely been busy." She took a swig of her beer before continuing. "Plus, you want to express an opinion that I've already heard. I don't need to hear it again."

"I stand by what I said, Frankie. The wolves are not good for you, and you're better off without them in your life. I know it, you know it." He paused as dismayed shouts burst from a bunch of guys in the corner who were watching the game. "It's best all around if you forget you ever received that e-mail and forget all about the wolves."

"I met with Lydia."

He stilled with his bottle halfway to his mouth. "What?"

"I met with her."

He took a deep breath. "Okay, you were curious. I can understand that. If I found out I had relatives I'd never met, I'd be interested in meeting them too."

She was about to point out that she actually *had* met Lydia before, she just didn't remember her, but he forged on.

"If you had questions, you could have come to me. I would have told you whatever you wanted to know."

"And you'd have told me the truth?"

He frowned, affronted by the doubtful note in her voice. "Of course."

"Like you told me the 'truth' about my parents dying in a car crash?"

He looked away. "That was different. You know the full story now. I would have told you the rest."

"Like how they never wanted or tried to see me? You said I should turn my back on them like they turned their backs on me. But they didn't do that, did they, Brad? You, Marcia, and Geoffrey blocked them all the way. As shit as it is, I can't trust any of you to give me the truth. You twist the answers to suit your agenda—which is to keep me away from my paternal family."

"And *they* no doubt twist the truth to suit *their* agenda, which is to steal you away from us."

"They haven't tried to do that."

"Give it time. They will." Brad chugged down more of his beer. "Shifters are cunning like that." He grabbed a handful of nuts from the complimentary bowl and shoved them in his mouth. "Deviousness is in their very nature."

"I'm *half* shifter," she reminded him.

He waved that away. "You're not like them. They're hostile and uncivilized and animalistic. I agree with Dad, packs aren't much different from cults—hell, I wouldn't be surprised if some of them are Satanic."

"I went to Phoenix Pack territory today."

"You did *what*?" He thumped his bottle down on the bar. "Frankie, what the fuck were you thinking?"

Shocked at his outburst, she blinked. "Brad—"

"One of theirs *killed* your mom, my sister. How can you let them into your life? I warned Caroline that mating with a shifter was a bad idea. I warned her that they weren't like us, that she wouldn't fit there. She wouldn't listen. She got caught up in the fantasy of being surrounded by a pack and having someone completely devoted to her who'd never betray or harm her. Well, that was a load of shit, wasn't it?"

"Brad—"

"Now *you're* going to get caught up in that same fantasy? I thought you had more fucking sense." He bowed his head and pinched the bridge of his nose. Finally he looked up. "I love you, Frankie. You're more like a daughter to me than a niece. I respect that you're a big girl who can make her own decisions. But this?" He shook his head. "I can't condone this."

Well, that got her back up. "I'm not asking you to condone it," she said stiffly. "I don't need you to."

His jaw hardened. "Well, that puts me in my place, doesn't it?"

She sighed, tired. She didn't want to hurt him, but she would not be made to feel that she—a grown woman—had to justify what she did and seek permission for her actions.

"Doesn't it matter to you that this will kill Marcia and Geoffrey?"

"Brad, I've never been able to please them. I learned a long time ago that it was pointless to try. But you go run to them with tales of my treachery if you feel you have to. It's not like they won't find some other reason to complain about me."

He said nothing for a long moment. "I won't tell them. I'm happy for them to never, ever know. I won't breathe a word about it, but you have to promise me that you'll stay away from those wolves. This has to be as far as it goes, Frankie."

Her wolf snarled at that. "Does it?" she asked evenly.

"You don't need them in your life," he insisted, his face hard. "They're no good for you. Now *promise* me you'll stay away from them."

She didn't. She couldn't.

He shook his head with a sigh. "You've let me down here, Frankie. What's more, you've let your mom down." With that parting shot he shoved his beer aside and stalked out. So, yeah, she went home feeling *pissed off*.

Her sleep was short and restless, so she didn't wake up in the best mood. And since her hand was so stiff and sore from metal grinding that she was forced to take a break from sculpting, Frankie's mood turned even more sour.

As such, it really was not the best time for her to have lunch with Marcia and Geoffrey, especially since she might well get the cold shoulder, but it seemed cowardly to make excuses and stay home. So Frankie went along, braced for the cold shoulder. Oddly, they acted normal, as if their heated conversation with her had never occurred. Brad seemed to be no longer angry, because he was also his usual self.

It should have been a relief. It wasn't. It was irritating, because it felt like they'd dismissed the conversation as if it were unimportant. As if her *pain* were unimportant.

They ate at the long table in the impressive dining room while classical music played low in the background. Talk was light and shallow—mostly tales about recent happenings at work. Of course, Frankie wasn't classed as "employed" in their book, so it wasn't a conversation she could really join.

The lunch was nothing like her meal with the Phoenix Pack. No fun, no teasing, no laughing, no *life* to the occasion. And that was kind of sad.

Once they'd eaten dessert and moved to the parlor, Brad pulled her aside and whispered, "I'm sorry I yelled at you last night. I was upset."

She gave a slight shrug. "Forget it." But she wasn't truly feeling so forgiving.

"Really, I'm sorry. The last thing I want to do is upset my girl. I just want what's best for you and—"

"What are you two whispering about?" Marcia called out from the sofa.

Brad blanked his expression and turned to her. "Nothing."

Marcia's perceptive eyes narrowed at Frankie. "Did Lydia try to contact you again?"

"Can we not talk about the shifters?" Brad asked.

Marcia's face went hard. "I'll take that as a yes. You should give me her contact details, Francesca. I'll hand them to our attorney—he can deal with the matter."

Geoffrey nodded in agreement, taking the armchair. "He'll ensure she understands that continuing to contact you will be classed as harassment."

Brad spoke before Frankie could get a word in. "Mom, Dad, let's just talk about something else."

"Fine." Marcia's gaze cut to Frankie. "Selma's son was disappointed that you didn't stay for dinner the other day. His parents are throwing a charity ball in two weeks. He'd love to escort you there."

Frankie raised a brow. "He'd love it so much that he's asking through you?"

Brad chuckled, though the sound was strained. "She has a point, Mom. He's not much of a man if he can't, or won't, take the time to ask her himself."

Mouth twitching, Geoffrey inclined his head. "I share Brad's disappointment in this," he told his wife. "Our granddaughter is worth the effort."

But Marcia huffed. "He's a busy man. Oh, Francesca, Selma informed me that there's a vacancy within her department for a—"

"I have a job."

"Well, yes, but I'm sure it doesn't take up much of your time and attention."

"Building six-foot-tall sculptures really couldn't be simpler," Frankie said drily.

Marcia looked at her as though she were being dramatic. "Francesca, you know I dislike sarcasm."

Brad cupped Frankie's elbow and said quietly, "She means well."

Did she? Right then, Frankie couldn't have cared less. She was tired and frustrated and didn't have the patience to *yet again* defend her chosen profession. As such, she didn't stay long.

Just as she was saying her goodbyes to Geoffrey, Marcia spoke words that made Frankie grind her teeth.

"Before you leave, I'd like Lydia's details."

Mentally readying herself for battle, Frankie said, "No."

"Francesca—"

"It's too late anyway."

Marcia went stiff as a board. "You met with her?" Anger blazed in her eyes. "You defied me?"

Frankie sighed wearily. "It's really such a big drama that I wanted to meet these relatives that I don't remember? You don't think it's natural that I had questions? Honestly?"

"Those wolves—"

"Aren't asking for the world. What if it had been the other way around? What if it were *you* on the deathbed and you wanted to see me just once, would that have been such a crime?"

"You went to see that woman too, didn't you? *Iris.* You went to see her. How could you do this to me?"

"I didn't do it *to* you. Nor did I do it to *spite* you or to *hurt* you. This doesn't have anything to do with you." But Marcia sure liked to make it about her.

"Doesn't it matter to you that your mother is *dead* because of her son? If she hadn't mated with him—"

"I wouldn't have been born. Does that not matter to you?"

Geoffrey intervened then. "Francesca, you know we love you. You may not wish to hurt us, but this situation *does* cause us pain."

Frankie looked at him. "I'm sorry if that's the case."

"I don't think you really are," clipped Marcia. "Don't you see that they're beasts? They're barbaric. Pitiless. Vile."

"They're people," said Frankie. "They drink coffee, play video games, make cookies, and watch TV." They just also happened to shift into animals—no biggie.

"You will not see them again, Francesca, I won't have it."

Again with this shit? Frankie sighed. "I'm going home. You all enjoy the rest of your day." She strode out of the room and down the hallway.

Brad jogged after her and caught her by the arm. "Frankie, wait. You have to see why they're hurting."

"It doesn't have to hurt them. I'm not shoving it in their faces. I'm not living on pack territory or denouncing the family. And I won't be made to feel guilty for this. Not by them, and not by you."

"I'm not trying to make you feel guilty. I just can't approve of it. They'll *never* approve of it."

"That's the thing, Brad. I'm not asking for their blessing. I understand that this is hard for them, so I'd never dream of expecting them to be okay with it—that truly wouldn't be fair. I just want them to let me be. But they won't—not about this, not about any decision I make that they don't like. After all, they know best. I live in a fantasyland where I'm a sculptor."

"Frankie—"

"I have to go, I'll see you later." She pulled her arm free and left.

Anger kept her muscles tight throughout the drive home. But by the time she got there, the anger had fizzled out. She was no longer pissed. She was tired. Weary. Sad. It seemed that no matter what move she made, there was someone she disappointed.

Any other time, she'd have shut herself in her studio and disappeared into her own world as she worked on her sculpture. While her hand was still sore, that wasn't going to happen.

So instead she poured herself a glass of red wine and headed through the patio door, out onto the deck. The breeze was slightly chilly, so she flung some logs into the fire pit and then settled on one of the rocking chairs. She sighed at the feel of the sun-warmed wood at her back and the scents of woodsmoke, herbs, and fragrant flowers.

Yes, this was what she needed.

It was a pretty garden. Stepping-stone path, patches of colorful flowers, and plants growing in cute little planters. But she couldn't take credit for it. The only real contributions she'd made were the sculptures and the mermaid fountain. It was Marcia who'd done the rest. Marcia who'd bought the magnolia tree, the wisteria on the trellis, and the flower boxes of mock orange, roses, and lily of the valley.

"Every woman needs a little sanctuary where she can relax," Marcia had said.

Frankie had refrained from saying that her studio was her sanctuary, because she'd known that Marcia was trying to be nice. Known that Marcia *wanted* good things for her, wanted her to be happy, and wanted to find ways to connect with her.

She'd heard enough stories about her mother to know that Caroline and Marcia had shared some hobbies, like gardening, playing the piano, and listening to classical music. Marcia had no doubt hoped that her granddaughter would be much the same. Instead she'd ended up with someone who barely remembered to *water* plants (hence the sprinklers), who would rather play with metal and clay than a piano, and who enjoyed blasting rock music as she worked.

Really, Frankie felt bad that they didn't share any interests. Just as she felt bad that she was at odds with Brad and her grandparents. They might not particularly understand her, but they did care for her. They did want her to be happy. They just wanted to be in control of what made her happy. And that made her wolf crazy.

Currently her wolf was in a shitty mood, which meant it probably wasn't the best time for Frankie to be having negative thoughts. She needed to relax.

She cast a glance at the hot tub at the end of the deck. A dip in that might help . . . Maybe later.

Letting her head fall back, she closed her eyes and soaked in her surroundings. All she could hear was the chirping of the birds, the gurgle of the fountain, the wood snapping in the pit, and the rhythmic creak of the chair as she rocked. Little by little, the tension in her body slipped away, and—

Frankie snapped awake at the knock on the front door. She blinked, surprised to realize she'd dozed off. She wasn't sure how long she'd been asleep, but the sky had darkened a little.

Knuckles again rapped on the door. Sighing, she pushed to her feet. It was probably Geoffrey, she thought. When Marcia was unsuccessful in getting Frankie's cooperation, he would often later come and try to "reason" with her. In other words, he'd try persuading her to back down.

But as Frankie swung open the front door, she found that it wasn't Geoffrey. No. It was Trick, leaning one hip against the rail of her porch. Her wolf instantly perked up. As for Frankie . . . it was like her system took a long, relieved breath. "Why are you here?" she asked, though not unkindly.

He gave her a pitiful look. "I'm hungry. Feed me."

"You're not even kidding, are you?"

He pushed away from the rail and stalked forward. "I never joke about food."

"I'm positive that if you went home, Grace would make you something."

"But then I wouldn't have your stimulating company or access to this amazing mouth." Trick planted a long, lingering kiss on her lips. Tasting. Teasing. Possessing. He'd missed her. Barely knew her, really, but he'd missed her sultry voice, her secret smile, her quick humor, and her little mean streak.

Ending the kiss with a nip to her lip, Trick framed her face with his hands, drinking her in. That was when he noticed the lines of strain there. His hackles rose. "What's wrong?"

"Nothing. It's just been one of those days."

Trick gently backed her into the house, kicking the door closed behind him. "Tell me what's wrong. Don't say 'Nothing.' Tell me. Get it out."

She sighed. "I had lunch with my uncle and grandparents. It didn't go so well."

Pissed that the fuckers had upset her *again*, Trick felt his jaw harden. He didn't voice his anger—she didn't need to deal with his shit on top of theirs. He rubbed his nose against hers and skimmed one hand down her hair. "Want my wolf to go piss on their tires?" As he'd hoped, she laughed. It was a quiet, tired sound, but still.

"Nah, but I appreciate the offer." Frankie released a sigh of pleasure as his fingers feathered over her nape. "I really don't think I'll make good company, but if you want to take your chances you can grab a beer and join me on the deck." His face went all warm and lazy, and she figured it had pleased him that he hadn't had to coax his way farther inside. Well, she wasn't going to pretend she didn't want him there. That would just be stupid.

"I'll take my chances." Trick grabbed a beer from her stainless steel double-door fridge. Outside he settled on the rocking chair beside hers. "Sweet setup you've got here." Especially with the hot tub and the monster grill.

He was guessing she'd made the sculptures. One was a black, twisted, rickety, evil-looking tree that contradictorily had beautiful white blooms dangling from the branches. The second was a large black chess piece that was peppered with moths and had six crows perched on top. Neither sculpture should have looked right in such a beautiful garden, but they gave it an edge and made it look better. Balanced out the natural perfection of the flowers.

"How's your day been so far?" she asked.

"Dull, really." Trick tossed her a smile. "Much better now." He drank some of his beer. "What was the first sculpture you ever made?"

Thinking back, Frankie smiled. "It wasn't very good. Or very big. It was a volcano. Someone with severe burns was crawling out of the top. You can imagine how horrified my grandparents were. They even sent me to a therapist."

"A therapist?"

"Yeah. I remember feeling really frustrated that he asked why I'd chosen to make it. I tried explaining that I didn't realize I was making it until it started to come together. He seemed to understand. Anyway, he told Marcia that using art as a form of expression was healthy, and that she should encourage the hobby. In that sense he did me a favor. You said you like to sketch. Is it something you've always done?"

Trick used the heel of one foot to gently rock his chair. "It was my mom who encouraged me to try it. I was a restless kid. Liked having something to do with my hands. She thought sketching might help relax me, and it did. Still does. But I can't say I have a drive to create art. I can't even call it a hobby. It's just something I do sometimes." He paused to sip at his beer. "The first time I saw one of your sculptures online was a few years back. I wondered if you made them to purposely disturb people. But I can see now that it's more than that."

Frankie frowned. "You saw one of mine years ago?"

"I looked you up, curious about what you were doing with your life."

"Why?"

"I'm a curious guy. I was surprised by how well you've integrated yourself in the human world. I wondered why you hadn't ever contacted the pack. In your position I'd have wanted to talk to the other half of my family and hear their side of things. I didn't think for one second that you'd been fed lies. What exactly did the Newmans say happened to your parents?"

"That they both died in a car crash. They said my father's name was Dustin Turner. Said he was loving and loyal and devoted to my mother. I know why my family lied, I just can't help being pissed that they lied for so long." She rubbed at her temple. "They're not happy about me having contact with the pack. The way they see it, shifters stole Caroline from them."

"That so? Well, they stole you from me, your paternal family, and the rest of your pack mates. I don't think this will ever be a situation that works for everyone. You just have to do what you feel is best for you. So what do you want?"

Frankie took a long breath. "Pizza. I want pizza."

His mouth curved. "Then we get pizza."

Pulling out her cell phone, she asked, "What do you like on yours?"

"Anything except anchovies." He waited until she'd finished the call to the pizza place before he spoke again. "I know a thing or two about feeling like you've disappointed the people who raised you."

"Yeah?"

"My parents were loud supporters of Trey's banishment. They hadn't suspected I'd leave with him. Oh, they knew I was close to Trey and that I didn't respect Rick, but they never anticipated that I'd go against their wishes. That was the way they saw it—that I was choosing Trey over them. I wasn't. I was choosing what was right for me. They were so angry with me, but they were positive I'd run back there with my tail tucked between my legs."

Noticing her flexing her fingers, Trick took her hand and massaged it as he continued. "But I didn't. I made a place for myself in a new pack. It was a small group, but we built something good and strong. I contacted my parents a few times, invited them to Phoenix Pack territory. I wanted them to see what we'd built, wanted them to see what a pack *could* be like. They just kept insisting that I go back. I wouldn't say it didn't matter to them that I was happy. I think it did—and does still—matter. They just wanted me to find happiness *their* way."

That sounded familiar, thought Frankie as she drank the last of her wine.

"They've missed so much of my life. They don't think that's their fault. Dad blames me. Mom blames Trey. And that ate at our relationship. The point? Some people expect others to fall in line with what they want. They reject anyone who doesn't, including those they love, for reasons only they can justify. And they won't see that it's wrong."

"Marcia and Geoffrey aren't bad people, Trick. Really, they're not. They want everything on their terms, but I think that partly comes from having jobs with such high positions. They're used to making the decisions and taking the lead. Brad mostly goes along with what they want."

"It's not bad that you don't. I know what it's like to have people who *expect* things from you. You have to do what's best for you, because when it comes to people like that, there'll always be *something* that they expect. You can never really please them."

Frankie exhaled heavily. "I know. I frequently disappoint my grand-parents. I used to feel guilty that I couldn't be a lawyer or a doctor like they wanted. Sculpting isn't a skill to them. It's a wasteful hobby. I can't give it up, though. Not even for them."

"They shouldn't want you to give it up. It should be enough that it makes you happy. But they're waiting for you to 'come to your senses.' It would have suited them if you'd failed at what you do, but you didn't. Yet they won't admit that they were wrong. Probably never will." He kissed the palm of her hand. "You don't have to be alone anymore, Frankie."

Her brow furrowed. "I haven't been alone."

"Yes, you have. You might have had the Newmans, but you've always felt like you didn't quite measure up and fit in with them, haven't you?"

Yeah, she had.

"You didn't have your pack; you lived with the feeling that some-thing was missing. And as much as I'm grateful that your grandparents took care of you, I'm pissed at them for what you missed. Pissed that you didn't have all your family, that you were alone for your first shift, and that they made you believe we didn't want you." And that he'd missed so many years with her. If she hadn't been kept from him, they could have been happily mated by now.

"They were protecting me."

"Were they? Or is that their excuse for keeping you away from us?" He nipped the heel of her hand. "Maybe they did want to protect you, but that wasn't the only reason they cut us out of your life. You know that."

Yeah, she did know that. They'd wanted some measure of revenge against the people they blamed for their daughter's death, and they'd used her to hurt Iris and the rest of the pack because . . . well, because they could.

A knock sounded at the door. "Pizza's here." She plonked her glass on the table as she rose. "I'll get it."

They settled at the island in the middle of her kitchen and demolished the pizza. No dishes or cutlery. Just the box and their hands. Trick entertained her with random tales of things that had happened on pack territory, and she knew he was hoping to lure her into going back for another visit. She also knew she'd probably go back at some point.

By the time they'd eaten the last of the pizza, her gray cloud had lifted and she felt lighter. She had no idea how just having him around could ease her mind and calm her system, but she was glad for it.

After they'd cleaned up, Trick pulled her to him. "As shit as it is, I have to go. My shift starts soon."

Hiding her disappointment, Frankie smoothed a hand down his arm. "Okay." She sighed into his mouth as he kissed her senseless with one hand collaring her throat. Her wolf bucked a little at the dominant move, but she also kind of liked it. The animal didn't want him to leave; she wanted him to stay, wanted to bite and mark him. *Not good.*

Trick growled into her mouth. Her mouthwatering scent had warmed and ripened with arousal, and all he wanted was to bend her over the kitchen island and fuck her hard. Instead he eased back and brushed her nose with his. "Now, why do you look freaked out?"

"My wolf likes you a little too much."

"So do you," he teased. "You're not ready for me yet. But you will be." She walked him to the front door, where he gave her one last, thorough kiss. "I'll pick you up at six tomorrow."

SUZANNE WRIGHT

Frankie frowned at his back as he walked away. "Wait, what?"

He turned, but he didn't stop walking. "I'll be here at six. Be ready."

"For what?"

He looked at her like she was simple. "To go see a movie."

"I never said I was going to see a movie with you."

"Yes, you did. While we were eating pizza. I said, '*We should go see a movie tomorrow.*' You said, '*Trick, how did you know I wanted to go see a movie? It's like we have one mind.*'"

Frankie laughed. "I did not say that."

"Sure you did." He pointed at her. "Six. Be ready."

CHAPTER SEVEN

S omeone dropped their popcorn all over the patterned carpet, and Frankie winced in sympathy. Waiting in the long queue for the concession counter, she rested her hand on the rope and looked at the pricing boards for the snacks and drinks. The foyer of the movie theater was well lit and cheerful with all the framed posters and cardboard cutouts for new and upcoming releases.

Trick's front was pressed against her back, and he'd slung one arm over her shoulder so that he could breeze his fingers along her collarbone. He was a little tense, which wasn't surprising. A group of girls in the line parallel to theirs kept glancing at him with knowing looks, talking quietly to one another about the YouTube video he was featured in. One girl even subtly snapped a picture of him with her cell phone. It was clear that he despised the attention and the heroic image that people had of him. Just remembering the look on his face when a kid in the parking lot outside had pleaded for an autograph made her smile. And now those girls had him tense as a bow.

Feeling her shake with silent laughter, Trick spoke into her ear. "What's funny?"

"The big, bad enforcer is scared of some giggling teenage girls."

He nipped her earlobe in punishment for teasing him. "The last set of teenage girls that came asking for an autograph also wanted a photo of me holding each of them just like I'd held the girl on the video. Stop laughing, it's not funny. It's whacked."

"What did you do?"

"Grunted at them and walked away. What else was I going to do?"

"And now you're snuggling up to me so those girls don't get any ideas—effectively you're using me as a shield."

"I'm snuggling up to you because you smell good and I like having you close." His wolf pushed up against his skin for the same reasons, truly content at that moment. Nuzzling her neck, Trick took in her scent, letting it override the smells of popcorn, nachos, spices, and fruity slushes. He was on a date with his mate. Life was good.

It would be fair to say he'd tricked her into going on the date, but only because he'd known that she wouldn't fuss about it. One thing he really liked about Frankie was that there were no games. No playing hard to get. No acting like she was there under protest. No lies or bullshit. No playing it cool. It was fucking refreshing, and it made her easy to be around.

She was complex in that she had lots of facets—all of which fascinated him—but she was otherwise straightforward and uncomplicated. He loved that. Loved that he could trust her to say what she truly thought and felt, that he didn't have to waste time reading between the lines.

He was snapped out of his musings as a kid playing on a token machine whooped with joy. Trick slipped his free arm around Frankie's waist, holding her to him even as they stepped forward with the slow-moving queue. That was another thing he loved: he knew it was strange for her to have someone she barely knew touching her so often, but she didn't pull away. She let herself relax with him, even though she had to be confused about just why it was so easy for her.

"You should stop nuzzling and nipping my neck," said Frankie.

"Why?"

Quietly she replied, "Because it's making you hard, and it's making me all flustered." Frankie felt his lips curve against her neck.

"I know. I can smell that you're wet."

And she could feel that he was hard. Considering his body was practically folded around hers, Frankie figured she probably should have felt a little claustrophobic. But she didn't. She felt safe. Protected. Cosseted, even. Her wolf liked having him so close, liked the possessiveness in his touch.

He didn't release her until, finally, they arrived at the counter. As the cashier rang up their order, Frankie grabbed straws and napkins from the dispensers. Just as they were walking away with their popcorn and sodas in hand, Frankie spotted none other than Vance and Layla heading toward the concession lines. And sadly, they spotted her. *Well, hell.*

She'd bumped into them once shortly after she and Vance broke up. Layla had clung to him, sending her smug looks. He'd been civil yet stiff toward Frankie, eager to get away. The next day he'd called Frankie to apologize for being unfriendly, explained that he just hadn't wanted to "set Layla off."

Today, well, Layla was too busy staring at Trick to care about sending superior looks at Frankie. And her wolf did *not* like the female appreciation in Layla's eyes whatsoever. Vance's gaze, hard and unreadable, danced from Trick to Frankie.

It was Trick who broke the awkward silence. "There a problem here?"

Layla almost jolted. "No, not at all. Frankie's decided to be rude, so I'll introduce us. I'm Layla, and this is Vance. We're . . . distant friends of Frankie's."

Unconvinced, Trick drawled, "Right." He could sense his mate's discomfort, just as he could sense that there had once been something between her and Vance. It was clear to see in the way the human male looked at her with an intimate familiarity—something that pissed Trick the fuck off. It was also clear by Vance's pinched expression and tight muscles that he didn't like seeing Frankie with another male. Tough fucking shit.

Anger flashed through his wolf, who urged Trick to rake his claws down the human's chest and warn him away from his mate. It was an idea he'd consider.

Layla's eyes narrowed a little. "I know you."

Trick tensed. "No, you don't." And he was done here. He arched a brow at Frankie. "Ready, baby?"

Layla clicked her fingers. "Wait, you're the shifter from that YouTube video—you helped that girl. It was so sweet and brave of you to intervene like that." Her eyes cut to Frankie. "Well, it's good to see you're moving on."

Frankie almost snorted. Yeah? Layla didn't really seem happy for her at all. Her eyes had been all dreamy and covetous when they'd stared at Trick. Once they sliced to Frankie, they'd darkened in envy and resentment. Layla had loved the idea that she had the guy Frankie wanted, loved that she'd "won." Seeing Frankie with a male who was a billion times hotter than Vance apparently ticked her off. Good.

"Your grandparents didn't mention that you were dating someone," Vance said to Frankie, his voice flat. "I'm guessing they don't know about him."

"Not liking how close you're standing to Frankie," said Trick, glaring hard at him.

Vance's brows snapped together and he blinked, as if he only then realized that he'd taken a step toward her. He backed up and moved aside to let them pass, pulling an irritated Layla out of the way.

Trick turned to Frankie. "Let's go, baby." As they strode off, Trick raised a brow. "So that asshole's an ex of yours?"

Frankie sighed. "Sadly, yes. Layla was *his* ex. He ran back to her, but she hates me."

"*He* doesn't hate you. He's pissed that you're with me. I'm thinking he'll make it his business to be sure your grandparents know that you were on a date with a shifter."

"I wish I could disagree with you."

"Well, we're not going to think about them," Trick declared. "We're going to watch this movie, enjoy it, and stuff our faces with popcorn."

Frankie's mouth curved. "Your plan has merit."

After they'd had their tickets checked, they were directed to the theater. Soon they were heading down the dimly lit hallway and into the dark theater. As they climbed up the carpeted stairs, she noticed that there weren't many people there.

Trick led her down the empty row at the very top. "I always sit at the back so I don't have to deal with people kicking the back of my chair."

"And here was me thinking you'd done it so we could make out in peace." Her wolf liked his somewhat devilish chuckle. Sitting down, Frankie placed her soda in the cup holder and settled the extra-large popcorn on her lap. Curtains hung on either side of the big screen that was currently displaying overly loud previews. Still, she could hear people talking and munching on popcorn and nachos.

Trick's cell glowed in the dark as he took it out of his pocket to switch it off. "So tell me, what do you wear for bed?"

A chuckle burst out of her. "What?"

He shrugged. "It's a simple question. What do you wear for bed?"

Frankie delved into her popcorn. "Who says I wear anything?" She couldn't help smiling at the low growl that rumbled out of him.

"Such a tease." Since they were sharing the popcorn, he grabbed some and chucked it into his mouth. "But that's okay, because so am I." It was both a warning and a promise.

As they watched the movie, he massaged her free hand—the same one that often seized up. It might have relaxed her if he didn't occasionally nip at her fingers or rake his teeth down her palm.

About halfway through the movie, he took the box of popcorn from her and put it on the floor. Ready to complain, Frankie looked at him. And her stomach clenched. There was no playful grin there. There was heat and need and hunger.

He spoke against her mouth. "Undo your jeans."

Wait, what?

His hand curved around her throat and he gave it a light squeeze. "Do it."

The idea of him touching her that way in public probably shouldn't have revved her engines, but damn if it didn't. She was particularly curious about just how far he'd take it. So she snapped open the buttons of her fly and waited to see what he'd do. His eyes went languid with satisfaction, and his hand released her neck.

"Good girl. Now watch the movie."

Like her attention would be on anything other than what he was doing. Still, Frankie turned her face to the screen. He sucked on her earlobe just as his hand slid into her jeans and panties. Not far, just far enough for him to reach her clit. She liked the direction things were heading in.

Trick spoke into her ear. "I want you to stay still for me while I play with this pretty little clit. Don't make a sound, Frankie."

He didn't play with her clit. He *worked* her clit. Tormented her until she wanted to cry.

Her pussy throbbed and clenched as his finger circled, rubbed, flicked, pressed, and stroked her clit. Her eyelids flickered as they fell shut. God, she was so wet it wasn't even funny. Occasionally he'd dip his finger inside her, but only enough to scoop out some cream so he could lubricate her clit. She bucked her hips slightly, wanting that finger to slide between her folds and slip all the way inside her. But his hand stilled and he bit her earlobe.

"Do that again and I'll stop." Trick rubbed the side of her clit again, watching as she sank her teeth into her plush lower lip to hold back her moans. She wasn't shy about her sexuality, and he loved that. Loved how responsive she was to him. Loved that she hadn't bristled at his orders, that she'd trusted him to give her what she needed. Oh, he didn't doubt that there would be times when he pushed her too hard and she told him to shove his orders up his ass. She was a dominant female, after all. But for now she was letting him lead, and he liked that a fuck of a lot.

"You're close, aren't you?" he whispered. "Good. Mouth, Frankie, give me your mouth." She turned her face to his, and he kissed her hard and deep as he stroked the side of her clit just the way he'd learned she liked it. When he sensed that she was on the very edge, he thumbed her clit and swallowed her groan as she came.

Cheeks flushed, eyes glazed over, she panted against his lips. He wanted nothing more than to drive his cock inside her and take what belonged to him. *Not yet.* "Next time, you'll come when I'm inside you." He withdrew his hand and shoved his wet finger into her mouth. "Suck it clean. I'd do it myself, but I want to have my first taste of you when my head is buried between your thighs." She did as he told her, holding his gaze. "That's it, good girl."

Frankie expected him to grab her hand and drag her outside so he could get her home fast and take care of the hard-on she could see straining against his zipper. He didn't. He just deftly fixed her fly, returned the popcorn to her lap, and turned back to the screen. She hissed. The orgasm had been great and all, but it only made her want more.

She wasn't sure how she got through the rest of the movie without slapping him for getting her in such a state. As they were leaving, she shot him a look that called him an asshole. He just grinned.

Back in the foyer, he asked, "You need to use the restrooms before we go?"

"Yes," she clipped, still annoyed with him. That got her yet another grin.

"If you're out before me, wait here." Trick kissed her, tasting popcorn and salt. "Go." He waited until she was inside the ladies' room before he turned to the men's. He quickly did his business, eager to get back to her.

He was zipping his fly when he felt it. A presence. He wasn't alone. And then a scent drifted to him—dark and familiar. His wolf's upper lip peeled back.

There was no time to twirl and confront the fucker, because he heard the slight whistle of air. Trick ducked, barely avoiding the steel bar that then slammed into the tiled wall.

Trick rammed back his elbow, connected with a hard gut. There was a pained grunt as the body behind him staggered back. Twisting, Trick stood upright and jerked to the side as Drake then tried bringing the bar crashing down on his head. *Son of a bitch.*

Anger and adrenaline surging through him, Trick grabbed the wrist holding the bar and pressed his thumb hard on a pressure point, making Drake drop the bar with a curse. Grunting and snarling, they collided with a fury of fists.

It wasn't combat. It was a brawl. Fast, furious, and bloodthirsty.

Drake was no easy target, and he got some good shots in. A punch to the temple. A strike to the solar plexus. A hard blow to his ribs that sent ripples of agony through Trick and made his stomach roll.

Trick got plenty of his own shots in. A ram of his elbow to the throat. A solid uppercut to the chin. A hard punch to the cheekbone that made Drake's head whip to the side. Trick topped that off by ramming his forehead into Drake's nose, smiling grimly at the resulting crack and spray of blood.

The prick didn't back off, though. He kept on coming, eyes cold and flinty, face flushed and contorted into a scowl. And when he crouched, grabbed the bar, and swung it at Trick's leg—*motherfucker*—Trick rammed the sole of his foot into the bastard's face. Drake fell back, dazed, and the bar slipped from his fingers.

Seething with a rage that bubbled in his veins, Trick fisted Drake's collar and dragged him along the bloodstained tiles into a stall. He forced Drake's face into the toilet and flushed. He let him struggle. Let him feel the panic. Let him feel the burn of the fluid in his lungs.

With what little mercy he had left in him right then, Trick yanked the wolf's head up out of the toilet. Drake didn't fight back. He sucked in deep, loud breaths, coughing and hacking like a guy who'd just run out of a smoking building. Still, Trick might have dunked the asshole again if he hadn't looked up to see Frankie leaning casually against the doorjamb of the stall.

Fuck. Shifters fought brutally, sure, and they solved a lot of shit through violence. But Frankie hadn't been raised with that culture. She'd likely been taught that if shit went down you defended yourself, got out of harm's way, and called the police for help.

Trick dumped a coughing Drake on the floor and strode out of the stall. She backed up to give him room, simply watching him. Trick stood there, chest heaving, muscles quivering, waiting for her to say something. Anything.

She sighed. "I leave you alone for five minutes . . ." She shook her head sadly, but there was a glint of humor in her eyes.

Relief blew through him, and he pulled in a deep breath through his nose. He couldn't quite stop grinding his teeth, though. Rage still had a tight grip on him.

"Are you okay?" she asked, the humor in her eyes now replaced with concern. He just nodded. She tipped her chin toward Drake. "Friend of yours?"

Trick forced his jaw to unlock. "Let's go. I'll tell you about it when we get out of here."

But he didn't tell her. He fell silent the moment they slid into his SUV. Despite his slow, steady breaths and relaxed body language, Frankie could sense that he was still fuming. Giving him the time he seemed to need, she stayed quiet, looking through the window and watching the scenery pass by.

Thanks to the sounds of music, girls' laughter, and the deafening hand dryer, Frankie hadn't heard the struggle coming from the other restroom at first. She'd barged in and simply stared as she took in the blood spatter on the floor, the cracks in the tiles, the long steel bar, the kicking legs in the doorway of a stall, and—finally—Trick stuffing some guy's head down the toilet.

Not a scene a girl expected to find while on a date.

Although she'd love an explanation, she kept her mouth shut. Soon enough he pulled up behind her Audi and switched off the ignition, but he didn't move to get out. His hands were clenched around the wheel, and he was staring straight ahead. She noticed that his knuckles were no longer swollen or scuffed—God bless shifters' enhanced healing. "You calm yet?"

"Calm? Let's see. I took my woman out so she could relax, have fun, and forget about all the shit going on in her life. Then some motherfucker comes at me from behind with a steel fucking bar when I'm taking a piss, and totally fucks it up. So no, baby, I'm not calm."

"I wouldn't say he fucked it up. I did relax, have fun, and forget about the other stuff."

"I would never hurt you."

The words made her blink. "What?"

"I know I might have seemed out of control back there, and I won't deny that I can be brutal in a fight. But I'm not someone who flies off the handle and beats the shit out of people. That guy back there is part of a messed-up pack that wants an alliance with Trey. The Alpha, Nash Morelli, isn't happy that Trey won't give it to him. Drake is Morelli's Beta. He charged at Trey during a meeting, and I dealt with it. That back there was retaliation."

"And since you just kicked his ass, he'll probably retaliate again," she mused.

"Probably. Which means I should stay away from you for a while."

Her stomach bottomed out. "Stay away?"

"I should. But I won't." Trick held her eyes, willing her to believe him as he repeated, "I would never hurt you. You never have to fear me. Never."

"Trick, if I feared you or I believed you'd harm me, I wouldn't have gotten into the SUV with you. I certainly wouldn't be thinking about having you in my bed tonight." She opened the door, hopped out, and walked up her driveway.

Trailing behind her, Trick said, "Say that again." Because it really was the very last thing he'd have expected her to say.

"You heard me. I already knew that you have a dark streak. You think I bought your laid-back act?" Snorting, Frankie opened the front door and entered the house. "That easygoing charm hasn't fooled me. I know you tone down your dominance around me. What I don't know is *why* you do it."

Trick closed the door behind him. On the one hand, he liked that he didn't have to pretend. On the other, she'd have questions he didn't want to answer. "I didn't want you feeling overwhelmed or intimidated. You might be half shifter, but you're not used to our intensity, our ways, or just how possessive we can be."

That made both her and her wolf bristle. "I'm not made of fine bone china, Trick. You don't need to protect me from you." She narrowed her eyes. "Is this what you meant when you kept saying I wasn't ready for you? You don't think I can handle you the way you are?"

"I don't think you can handle just how much I'll want from you. Not yet."

"Elaborate."

"And scare you off?" He shook his head. "That's not on my list of things to do."

"Why would it scare me? You're not making sense. Are you trying to say that you're a sadist or something? If so, that is going to be a problem."

"I'm not a sadist."

"Then I don't understand what you're getting at. Given that you're very dominant, assertive, and you have a forceful personality, I've already figured out that a relationship with you wouldn't be easy. Am I wrong?" It was a dare to lie to her.

He shrugged. "I don't know. I've never been in a relationship."

"Never?"

"There've been flings, but they were short and shallow. I never let my partners get too close." Not even Marcus. Before the enforcer mated, he and Trick had scratched each other's itches occasionally. Trick had let him close as a friend, but not as a partner.

"So that's all you want with me—a fling?"

Trick shook his head and gently tapped her nose. "You're different."

Frankie frowned. "You mean you see me as yours, since we're part of the same pack?"

"Something like that." He pulled his cell out of his pocket. "I need to call Trey."

Frankie watched him closely as he swiped his thumb over the screen and tapped it a few times. "*Something like that,*" he'd said, an odd glint in his eyes. And then her heartbeat kicked up as it all seemed to thread together. The way her body reacted to him, that fierce determination in his eyes, the possessiveness he displayed, the way her wolf tested him to see if he was worthy. Worthy as a mate, Frankie now realized. Her wolf didn't fight her assumption. *Oh hell.*

She wasn't quite as shocked as she should have been, so maybe she'd subconsciously suspected they were mates. Or maybe she'd just had so many shocks lately that she was immune to them at this point. Her primary emotion right then was unease. Not because she didn't want it to be true, but because she did. She wanted Trick to be hers. She just didn't want the shit-storm that could follow.

"Trey, we got a problem," he said. "Or we had a problem until I shoved its face down a fucking toilet . . . Drake . . . I was at the movies with Frankie. He came at me in the restroom. Tried to bash my head in with a steel bar . . . No, I'm fine. I don't know if Morelli sent him, but I'm more inclined to think that the motherfucker was retaliating for what happened at the meeting . . . Yeah . . . No, I'm with Frankie . . . Yeah. All right. Later." Ending the call, Trick turned to Frankie. Whatever he saw on her face made his brows snap together. "You okay?"

She swallowed hard. "Are we mates?"

Trick stilled. Really, he wasn't all that surprised that she'd figured it out. As he'd told the pack, she was smart and open-minded. He crossed to her, pleased when she didn't back up. "Yes, baby, we are." He curved his hand around the side of her neck. "At first I thought this was shit timing for you, what with everything else that's going on. But I was wrong. If there's one thing you need right now, it's support, someone who's all about you. Someone who's on *your* side—not the Newmans' side, not the pack's side, just yours."

Frankie raked a hand through her hair. "This is . . ."

"Going to make things a lot harder for you with the Newmans. I get that. And it wouldn't surprise me if you're not quite sure that true mate bonds are such great things, given what happened with your parents. But I'm not going anywhere, Frankie." He skimmed his thumb over her jaw. "It eats me up inside that I missed so much of your life. Eats me up that I didn't realize who you were to me when we were kids. I've been waiting to find you—or, as it seems, to get you back—for so fucking long . . . I'm not going to give you up. Not to spare the Newmans' feelings, and not because you're scared."

"I'm not scared, I just . . . Look, I watched the mated pairs when I visited your territory. I saw how devoted they are to each other. I don't think, just because something went wrong for my parents, that having a mate is a bad thing. But I feel so torn right now. I'm still struggling to find a way to make everyone happy—"

"You can't," he said softly. "I wish you could, baby, but you can't." His pack would be happy as long as they had contact with her, but she couldn't give them that without hurting her maternal family.

"I have to try."

"Then you try. But the Newmans will expect you to give me up and cut contact with the pack, just like they expect you to give up sculpting—like it isn't part of who you are." Trick draped an arm over her shoulders, hating how vulnerable she looked right then. "Come on. You need to sit. We'll talk this out." He led her to the kitchen, where she slid onto one of the stools at the island. "Wine or beer?"

"Beer." Frankie waited until she'd had a long drink from the bottle before she asked, "How long have you believed we're mates?" She thought back to the way he'd behaved at the coffeehouse, how he'd watched her like a hawk, touched her with so much possessiveness. "It's been since that first day, hasn't it?"

Trick planted a hand on the island on either side of her, caging her in. "I knew the moment our eyes met outside the coffeehouse and my world tilted that you're mine."

"You were so sure so quickly?"

He gently brushed her nose with his. "How much do you know about mating bonds?"

Being half shifter, she'd made a point of learning about mating bonds by reading blogs written by shifters. "They're metaphysical. Once they're fully formed, they're only breakable by death. They join the couple so closely that it's rare that one can live without the other."

"That's right. Some pairs recognize each other as their true mates instantly—not often, but it does happen. Then the mating urge kicks in, and it literally drives the couple to claim each other."

She'd read about that, read that it was like a fever in the bloodstream that sent the person's arousal soaring, and the arousal wouldn't go away until the couple bonded. "I haven't felt any mating urge."

"Because something's blocking the bond. It's like a frequency; the way needs to be clear for the couple to pick it up. Fears, secrets, and doubts can block a bond. I don't have to wonder what's blocking ours. You're struggling to balance everything. You're trying to find a way to belong to both worlds—in doing that, you're splitting yourself in half. *All* of you has to accept your shifter side."

Frankie bristled, pausing with the bottle halfway to her mouth. "I *do* accept my wolf. Always have."

"Not talking about your wolf. I'm talking about what comes with her: your heritage, your past, your pack—especially since mating with me will mean moving to pack territory. In case you're wondering, no, you are not expected to give up your job. You're not the only pack member who has one. The only thing you would be giving up is this house." But accepting all that would mean the Newmans would likely turn on her.

Frankie tossed back a mouthful of beer. "If there was no mating urge, how were you so sure we were mates so fast?"

"Because nothing's blocking the bond on my end. I have no doubts or fears about mating. I have plenty of personal issues, but none that would get in the way of mating." He dabbed a kiss on first one corner of her mouth and then the other, needing the contact. "It's commonly believed that our inner animals know their mate at first sight. I trust my wolf's instincts and I listen to him, so I always believed that I'd recognize my true mate at the same time as he did. To be honest, though, a part of me started to doubt that he'd recognize her so easily."

"Why?"

"Tao's wolf didn't like Riley at first, so I started to wonder if maybe our animals don't always know instantly. I told myself that just because Tao's wolf didn't initially like her didn't mean that he didn't recognize her as his. Riley loved to drive Tao insane, so I supposed it was possible that his wolf just felt disrespected and dismissed by her." Trick cupped the side of her neck and began lightly breezing his thumb up and down the column of her throat. "If my wolf recognized you as mine when we were kids, he didn't communicate it to me."

"Maybe you just weren't as in tune with him back then."

"I should have known."

Frankie didn't like the self-condemnation in his tone. "Why? Did you have the same mentality about mating that you do now?"

"No. I was a kid, so my priorities were much simpler. But I was protective of you, though I just figured it was because you were the youngest pup. I was even a little possessive, now that I think about it. When you left, I kept asking Iris when you were coming back. I was angry when you didn't. Not at you, just at the situation. My wolf was just as angry."

"How did your wolf react to me when we met outside the coffeehouse?"

"He went perfectly still. Searched for a weakness. Ready to pounce and claim. He sensed you were his instantly. He was pissed the hell off when I left you at the coffeehouse. Wanted to take you home and keep you safe." He paused as something occurred to him, something that made his pulse quicken and gave him hope. "You haven't said we might not be mates. Why?"

"I haven't slept with a lot of guys, but I have enough experience to know that my body's instant reaction to you wasn't normal. At first I figured it was just because you were an unmated shifter—that it was like calling to like. But I didn't react that way to Dominic, and he's unmated.

"Plus I'm not a touchy-feely person and I like my personal space, but it doesn't bother me or my wolf that you're very tactile or that you eat up all that space. And you have this way of putting me at ease just by being there, even though I barely know you. I'm a lot of things, but I'm not willfully blind. None of that is normal, is it?"

"No, it's not. And I'm glad that you're so open-minded and you don't turn a blind eye to things that you don't understand." He snaked his hand around to cup her nape. "You are mine, Frankie. And I'm yours. You were made for me. And I was made for you. Are you going to fight that?"

She swallowed. "I'm not going to deny that you're right. I think you are. But I don't know if I'm ready for the bond yet."

"Baby," he began softly, "didn't you hear what I was telling you earlier? I *know* you're not ready. You're still adjusting to being part of a pack and facing the truth about your parents. The bond will demand everything from you, and you've got enough things demanding stuff of you right now. I can wait. I'm here, and I will continue to be here through all the shit that's going on. I know you're feeling like you're being pulled in different directions, but I'm the one person you don't have to try to please, because you please me by just existing. You're my priority. You get me?"

Frankie licked her bottom lip. "I don't think I've ever been anyone's priority."

That just about broke his heart. "You can trust that you come first to me. There isn't one single damn thing that's more important to me than you." He took the bottle from her and placed it on the island. "Kiss me, Frankie."

Tired of thinking, she shoved everything out of her head. Everything but him and how much she wanted him. Frankie pressed her mouth to his, but she didn't kiss him. She traced his lips with her tongue, hands sliding up his chest to fist his shirt. Teasingly, she briefly slid her tongue into his mouth just enough to glide it against the tip of his own. And apparently that was all Trick could take.

With a growl he slammed his mouth on hers and plunged his tongue inside. It wasn't a kiss. It was an explosion of need. An earth-shattering devastation of her senses.

He shoved his hands up the back of her shirt and yanked her forward so she was flush against him. Sensations bombarded her. His tongue licking into her mouth. His teeth biting her lip. Calloused fingertips digging into her waist. His dark scent swirling around her, flavored with need.

His growls poured down her throat and rumbled in his chest, vibrating against her nipples. Claws raked at her back just hard enough to feel good. And when he shoved his hand under her bra and splayed it possessively on her breast, she tugged on his hair, demanding more. Always more.

Trick cupped and squeezed her breast as he kissed his way down to her pulse. He sucked it into his mouth, felt it beating there, and decided right then that he'd one day leave his claiming mark on that very spot. He couldn't claim her yet—not officially—but he would sure as hell make her *feel* thoroughly claimed. He wouldn't take his mate for the first time on a kitchen island, though.

He slid his hands under her thighs and lifted her, and she locked her legs around him. As he carried her up the stairs, she licked, bit, and sucked at his neck—branding him as hers, and sending his need soaring. The demanding prick of her claws on his back made him growl.

Reaching the landing, he fisted her hair, snatched her head back, and took her mouth. Possessing and dominating, ensuring she knew exactly who was in control. When she went pliant, he spoke. "Bedroom?"

"On your left," Frankie rasped.

Carrying her inside, he slid her down his body. There was no finesse in the way they stripped. Clothes were tugged, clawed, and yanked until they were both finally naked.

Frankie swallowed at the deliciously masculine view before her. He was all hard muscle and sleek skin and untamed power. She skimmed her hands over his solid shoulders and down his tanned, totally ripped chest, heading right for the long, thick, hard cock that—

He tossed her on the bed, and Frankie surprised herself by chuckling. When he didn't move to join her, she said, "You going to stand there all night or are you going to fuck me?"

"I'll fuck you when I'm ready to fuck you," Trick said simply, raking his gaze over her. Fuck, she was gorgeous. Her breasts were round and full, topped with rosy nipples that tightened even further under his scrutiny. The diamond anchor belly button ring was hot as fuck, especially with the black, delicate vine tattoo that started on her left hip, diagonally swirled its way across her ribs, and then disappeared up her side.

"You *look* ready to me," she said, flicking his hard cock a meaningful glance.

Trick fisted his hands as she spread her thighs a little, tempting him, inviting him. Her pussy was pink and glistening, and he needed to taste it. He snapped his eyes to hers. "Grab the headboard, Frankie." Her brow slowly lifted, but she curled her hands around the iron rungs of the headboard. "Good. Keep those hands right there. Do not let go."

"But—"

"Do not let go." He knelt on the bed and tapped her thigh. "Wider, Frankie. Offer me what's mine." Agonizingly slowly, her thighs fell open. Her scent rushed into his lungs. Yes, this was what he wanted, her all spread out for him like a feast. "I'm not going to claim you yet, but I am going to leave my brand on you. Here. Now. As many times as I want."

Frankie gripped the headboard tight as Trick began to torture her neck with his tongue and teeth, leaving several marks. Not bites that were hard enough to draw blood or scar like a claiming mark, but hard enough to make a statement that she was his. As those possessive hands roamed and explored and squeezed, they also branded her as his just as surely as any bite.

A gasp flew out of her as he suckled on her nipple. Each rhythmic tug seemed to shoot sparks of need straight to her clit. "Trick—" She jolted as he left a suckling bite on the swell of her breast. "I get it! Consider me branded and fuck me!"

"Not done with you yet." Trick kissed his way from her breast to the vine on her ribs and then trailed his tongue along the tattoo, following it all the way down to her hip. He bit hard, leaving yet another mark, and soothingly laved it with his tongue. He *needed* her to be all marked up. It galled him to know that she'd been with others. If things had been different, he could have claimed her long ago. He'd have been the only male to ever kiss her, ever touch her, ever sink inside her.

A growl rattled his chest. "No one else should ever have had you." He curved his hand around her chin, his grip tight. "No one but me will ever again have you, Frankie. No other mouth will taste you. No other cock will fuck you. No other hands will touch you. Why is that?"

She licked her lips. "Because I'm yours."

Loosening his grip on her chin, he stroked his thumb along her jaw. "That's right. Mine. And you won't forget that, will you?"

"You wouldn't let me."

Trick smiled. "You're right, I wouldn't." Sliding down her body, he settled himself between her thighs and inhaled deeply. "I swear I could get drunk off your scent." He swiped his tongue between her slick folds and groaned at her sweet and spicy taste. "Fuck, yeah, I like that."

Keeping a tight grip on her quivering thighs, Trick pretty much devoured her. Every raspy, gritty moan stroked his cock. Every buck of her hips spurred him on. Every rain of honey on his tongue shoved him that much closer to losing his control.

He'd held back with every one of his past partners. Always held a part of himself in check. With Frankie he didn't have to hold back a damn thing. He could lose himself in her, give her everything, because *she* was everything.

Trick carefully dipped his thumb into the tight bud of her ass. "Did you save this for me, baby?" She nodded, and his wolf growled in contentment. Trick gave her pussy a long rewarding lick. "My good girl tastes so good." He draped himself over her and slammed home just as his hands closed around hers, keeping them locked around the iron rungs. He groaned as her inferno-hot pussy squeezed and rippled around him.

She curved into him. "Move."

"I'll keep to my word and not claim you, Frankie, but there's no going back after this. None." He needed her to understand and accept it. "Mating bond or not, you're mine. Are we clear on that?"

"Crystal," she rasped. "Now fuck me."

"Oh, I'll fuck you." He flexed his cock inside her. "I'll fuck you until your hot little pussy clamps around my cock and milks me dry. You want to feel my come shoot inside you?" Her pussy rippled again. "Good. Because you're gonna." And then he began ramming into her.

Frankie had always liked her sex rough, and she'd never been ashamed of it. *This* was beyond rough. Each hard punch of his hips was aggressive and ruthless. His cock stretched her until it stung and battered at her womb. Yet this wasn't just fucking. She knew it. Felt it. Saw it in the dark eyes that stared at her with a gut-twisting naked possessiveness.

She struggled to pull her hands free, wanting to touch him, but his hands kept hers pinned. And she had to admit, a part of her liked it. Liked that all she could do was take the hard pounding he gave her. "Trick, I'm close."

"I know." He growled into her ear. "Can you hear your pussy greedily sucking my cock back inside you?" Trick ground his teeth as her pussy heated and fluttered around his dick. "Fucking love that sound." He slammed harder, faster, pushing her closer to the edge.

Frankie tightened her legs around him. "I'm going to come."

"You're going to come *for me*, Frankie. You're going to make me come inside you." He sank his teeth into her neck with a growl. Her spine snapped straight as she screamed, her pussy squeezing and contracting around him. His own release swallowed him whole and, keeping his teeth locked on her neck, he brutally thrust his cock deep and exploded—the white-hot pleasure went on and on and on.

When his brain finally switched back on, he rolled onto his back, taking her with him and keeping his cock snug inside her. A strange kind of peace settled over him, leaving him more sated and content than he'd ever been in his life. And he knew it would be ten times better when he finally claimed her. For now, this was enough.

As she lay over him, boneless, he trailed his fingers over her back. Feeling slight grooves, he lifted his head to see fresh claw marks. He didn't remember leaving the brands, but he sure as hell liked the look of them. He saw something else there too. Between her shoulder blades was a weeping willow tattoo, its low branches whipping in the breeze. He traced it with his finger as he guessed, "You had this done for your mom."

"How did you know?" she asked, her voice dreamy.

"She planted a weeping willow tree near your cabin on pack territory. You used to dance around it."

Propping her chin up on his chest, Frankie frowned. "I don't remember that. She planted one in Marcia's flower garden too. Apparently she used to sit under it and read or write in her journal. It was her favorite spot."

He smoothed his hand over the tattoo on her upper arm. "Why a dream catcher?" She just shrugged. Trick hazarded a guess. "So that you can catch and hold on to your dream of being a sculptor, no matter what others say?"

Her eyes narrowed a little. "I'm not sure I like how well you understand me."

"Learn to like it." Bunching her hair in his hand, he kissed her. Tasted. Teased. Savored.

"Speaking of tattoos," began Frankie, "I like yours." The tribal tattoo sleeve on his left arm also bled onto the left side of his chest and abs. On the right side of his upper chest was the quote "Hell is empty and all the devils are here." It was a Shakespeare quote, if she remembered rightly. She was just about to ask what had prompted him to choose those tattoos when his thumb breezed over a mark he'd left in the crook of her neck, making her shiver just a little.

"I've been wanting to leave my mark on you since first I saw you at the coffeehouse," he said. "You can't imagine how hard it was to walk away from you that day. It never gets easier." And Trick was done with it. "No more nights apart, Frankie. I won't pressure you to give me what you're not ready for, but I need something. I need what you *can* give. And now that you know we're mates and that this is heading somewhere, I don't need to tread so carefully around you. You're not going to be confused or weirded out by me turning up here whenever I want and spending whatever time I can get with you. We're both busy people, but we can at least spend our nights together. Yeah?"

Frankie swallowed and said softly, "Yeah."

His face smoothed out and went all lazy with satisfaction. "That's my girl." He gave her a light kiss. "Now sleep."

CHAPTER EIGHT

There was no rational reason why four kids could so easily freak her out, but Frankie found herself fighting the desire to squirm in the armchair as they sat on the rug, staring at her. They weren't snarling or anything, but their expressions were weirdly blank. It was a good thing that Trick was currently in a meeting with Trey and some other males from the pack, because he'd probably laugh his ass off at her discomfort—then she'd have to hurt him.

Trick's tongue lapping at her pussy had certainly been a hell of a wake-up call. Just as she'd been on the verge of coming, he'd thrust his cock inside and fucked her hard and deep. He'd also been sure to leave a very visible brand on her neck. When she'd called him on it, he'd just smiled and said, *"But it looks so pretty there."*

It hadn't been long after their shower this morning that he'd received a call from Trey, summoning him home. Trick had persuaded her to come with him. Honestly, it hadn't taken a lot of effort on his part. She'd liked her last visit with Iris, and she thought it would be good to see her again.

At the moment, though, Iris was enjoying a visit from some relatives who were part of the Bjorn Pack. Well, *honorary* relatives. Apparently

Clara had been Iris's best friend since childhood and they considered each other family.

Frankie wasn't quite ready for a big reunion with others from her old pack, so she'd decided to wait in the living area with Lydia, Taryn, Jaime, and Makenna.

Her wolf was pushing her to track Trick down. It was odd. Now that he'd branded her, her wolf wanted to be around him more. As though the bite had linked them. Not mentally, but metaphorically. Like the wolf had half accepted his claim on her. Maybe. Probably. Frankie couldn't really make sense of it.

Cuddling a sleeping Sienna, Makenna cleared her throat. "Kids, why don't you pick a DVD to watch?" At that, they scrambled over to the large rack of DVDs.

Jaime eyed the bite on Frankie's neck. "That's quite a brand you have there. Nice and visible."

"I was clear that his claiming mark better not be so damn obvious," said Frankie, but she wasn't holding her breath.

Lydia stilled. "Claiming mark?"

Frankie felt her brow furrow. "He hasn't told you that we're mates?"

"He didn't need to," said Taryn. "We know him well; we could see that he was incredibly protective and possessive of you. That kind of thing is unusual for Trick." Her mouth twisted. "He said he'd hold off on telling you, though."

"He didn't tell me." Frankie shrugged. "I guessed."

Jaime's brows lifted. "You guessed?"

"It wasn't really that hard to figure it out," said Frankie. "My body's reaction, my wolf's reaction, the way he settles my nerves, his possessiveness, how much more tactile he is with me than I've seen him be with you guys . . . It just made sense that we could be mates. He confirmed that I was right."

Jaime looked at Taryn. "Don't you just love the way she put the pieces together and just accepted it? She didn't stew on it, didn't worry on it, didn't leap into a pit of denial. That's just awesome."

Taryn nodded in agreement. "I didn't guess that Trey was my mate, because I'd believed that I lost mine when I was a kid."

"I've had a crush on Dante for as long as I could remember," began Jaime, "so my strong reaction to him didn't seem weird or anything to overthink. I was used to it."

Makenna spoke. "I knew Ryan was right when he said we were mates. I did, but I didn't want to fully believe it in case I was wrong. The way you put it together reminds me a little of Ryan. He just added the facts, looked at it logically, and decided we were mates."

Frankie didn't believe it was logic that had helped her work it out. She had a creative mind and lived in a world full of possibilities, and that made her open to things.

"And you accept his claim on you?" Lydia asked.

"I'm not ready for the bond yet—Trick agrees with me on that— but I do accept that we're mates," said Frankie.

Lydia smiled, but then that smile faded as she asked, "Have you told the Newmans yet?"

"No." And that was not a conversation that Frankie was looking forward to having. She didn't have the slightest idea how she was going to break it to them that not only would she mate with a wolf, she would move to Phoenix Pack territory one day. They'd see it as abandonment, as her choosing a side, no matter what she said.

"Let's face it, they'll probably never accept Trick," said Lydia. "But he won't be the only one around here who has problems getting along with their mate's family."

"That's true," agreed Taryn. She flicked the kids—who were currently arguing over what DVD to watch—a quick glance before lowering her voice to add, "Trey would happily rip out my father's throat."

"And I'd eagerly beat the shit out of Dante's brothers," said Jaime, her voice just as low.

Makenna's mouth flattened. "Ryan's parents are total assholes—I let them know exactly what I thought of them."

"And we'd all kick Greta's ass if there wasn't a risk that her brittle old bones would shatter," said Taryn, at which the other females nodded firmly.

"Not that one!" shouted Kye, who was trying to snatch a DVD from Savannah. The little girl opened her mouth and screamed in his face. Kye howled at her.

Shaking with repressed laughter, Taryn clapped her hands to get their attention. "Kids, enough." They hushed, shoulders slumping.

Stifling a smile, Frankie asked, "Don't they spend their time with Riley?"

"She's taking a shower, since Dexter got jam in her hair," explained Makenna.

"Ah." Frankie started to speak again, but then she noticed that all four kids were staring at her yet again. "Someone make them stop."

"Have you chosen a DVD?" Taryn asked them. Like that, they turned back to the rack.

Hearing voices in the tunnels, Lydia spoke. "Seems like Iris is done talking with her visitors."

Moments later, a plump, gray-haired woman walked in with three identical adult males. Spotting Lydia, the woman smiled. "There you are. We have to leave, I'm afraid." As she caught sight of Frankie, her face lit up. "Oh, you must be Francesca. Iris has just been jabbering on about you."

Lydia spoke. "Frankie, this is Clara—my godmother and honorary aunt. And these are her sons, Cruz, Eke, and Wendel. If you need to tell the triplets apart, just remember that Cruz is the one with an earring, Eke is the one with shoulder-length hair, and Wendel is the one with the scar on his forehead."

Frankie forced a smile and said a quick greeting, hoping she was hiding that she was shockingly locked in an inner battle with her wolf. The moment the strangers walked in and the scent of rain, brine, and burned wood hit her nose, the animal had gone *crazy*. Snarled, growled, and swiped out with her claws. Her wolf wanted to surface and lunge. The scent had set her off—a scent that belonged to all three of them, since the triplets were identical.

Clara clasped her hands together. "You look so much like your mother it's uncanny. Doesn't she, boys?"

"It's good that you've reconnected with the family," said Eke.

Cruz nodded. "We've wanted that for a long time."

"I have one of your sculptures in my cabin," Wendel told her. "I bought it a few years back. *Rosa.*"

Eke looked at Wendel and tilted his head. "You mean the clay woman's head? Her face is beautiful, but it's rotting in places?"

"That's the one," said Wendel. His gaze returned to Frankie as he added, "The eyes—I don't know how you did it, but whatever angle I stand at, I feel like its eyes are on me. Always feel like it's looking right at me."

"Oh, I've seen that piece," said Clara. "I have to say, it scared me. I hope you'll come for dinner sometime, Francesca. It would be lovely to get to know you."

Frankie just smiled, thankful that Clara didn't notice how strained the smile was. Wendel noticed, though. His eyes narrowed slightly, but he didn't comment. Only once the four Bjorn wolves disappeared down the tunnel with Jaime as their escort did Frankie's wolf settle down.

Taking a centering breath, Frankie rubbed at her chest. Her wolf had never had such a visceral, violent reaction to a scent. Frankie could only conclude that the animal didn't have good memories of one—if not all three—of the people it belonged to.

"You okay, Frankie?" asked Lydia, concerned.

Frankie blanked her expression. "Sure."

120

Lydia didn't appear convinced, but she smiled. "Good. How about we go see Iris now?"

"Won't she be too tired to stand another visit?"

"Clara and the triplets weren't in there very long, and seeing you will lift her spirits." As Lydia led Frankie through the tunnels, she said, "I have to be honest with you, Frankie, this may be the last time you're able to speak with her. She's weakening fast. I'd give it two days at most before she's gone."

In that case Frankie was glad she'd come. "I won't keep her too long."

Finally they reached Iris's room. Lydia entered first. "Hey, Mom. You up to seeing another visitor?" She opened the door wide, revealing Frankie.

Iris beamed. "I was hoping you'd come back."

Frankie smiled, veiling her shock at just how much Iris had weakened. Her face was pale and haggard, and her voice was weak and hoarse.

"How are you?" Iris asked.

Frankie sat in the armchair near the bed. "Good, thanks."

"You smell like Trick. Do I detect a romance? Going by the mark on your neck, I certainly should."

"We're mates."

Iris swallowed. "I'm relieved that I was here long enough to see you find him. Now I don't have to worry about you. Trick's a good boy. My favorite of the Phoenix boys, but don't tell the others I said that. He'll take care of you. And you'll let him," she insisted. "Now, you've had some time to think since we last spoke. You said you were curious about your father. I have some photo albums I'd like to show you, but there's no pressure. If you're not ready for that yet or would rather not see them, that's fine too."

Kind of curious, Frankie said, "Show me."

At Iris's request, Lydia dug them out of the closet and placed them on the bed. She then perched herself on the side of the mattress.

Iris selected the first album and opened it. "As you can probably tell by the Christmas tree in the corner, this was the first Christmas they spent together. They hadn't realized they were mates, but I think they may have suspected it. That sack Christopher is carrying was full of gifts for her. The handsome hunk in the background is my Alfie."

Frankie leaned forward in the armchair as she studied the photos of her parents, which showed them opening their gifts, eating turkey, drinking wine, feeding each other pudding, having a snow fight, and celebrating New Year's Eve. They looked so happy and infatuated with each other.

There were pictures of other people too, such as Iris, Lydia, Clara, Clara's sons, and someone Iris told her was Clara's mate, Cesar. They truly looked like one big happy family.

Opening another album, Iris said, "Ah, these are of the mating ceremony. It was simple but beautiful. Not sure how much you know about the ceremonies, but I'll tell you because you'll be having your own soon enough. You'll get all dressed up, and then someone will escort you to a clearing on the territory. The others will already be there, gathered in a circle around Trey and Trick. Once you've been escorted into the circle, Trey will recite some words. They don't have any true power, they're just ceremonial, but it's a public way of saying you accept and love each other."

Lydia stroked a finger over a photo of a younger version of herself holding Caroline's hand. "Her dress was so beautiful. She looked perfect."

She really did, thought Frankie. Caroline's diamond-studded dress of lilac silk was long and hugged her body just right.

"Christopher was so nervous," said Iris. "But he instantly settled once she walked into the circle." Turning a page, she added, "These are shots of the after-party."

Frankie blinked in surprise at seeing Brad and her grandparents in the pictures. "They attended the ceremony?"

"Oh yes," confirmed Iris. "I don't think they were very comfortable, though we did our best to make them feel welcome."

In one picture Frankie noticed Brad in the background, glaring at Christopher. "Brad didn't like him much, huh?"

"No, he didn't," said Lydia. "He took an instant dislike to him. It didn't seem to be prejudice. Maybe he just felt that his sister could do better, or maybe he just wanted her to live among humans. Marcia and Geoffrey were cordial enough, though I don't think a shifter would have been their preferred choice of partner for Caroline. The hate they feel for us now didn't come until after the murder. And who could blame them for that hatred?"

As Iris slowly flicked through the album, Frankie couldn't help but observe that . . . "Wendel watched my mother a lot."

Iris looked amused. "So did his brothers and most of the unmated males in the pack. She had such a fragility about her that it made everyone want to sweep her up and protect her."

The fact that the other males seemed to covet his mate didn't appear to bother Christopher. He was always laughing and joking with them in the photos, especially Cruz, whom he was pictured with often. "Looks like Christopher and Cruz were close."

Iris nodded, sighing sadly. "They were. Cruz took his death harder than the others did. He was the first to arrive on the scene. You can imagine how devastated he was to find his best friend dead."

Frankie couldn't help but feel a pang of sympathy for him. As she looked through photos of Brad and Caroline, she noticed Cruz glaring in the background. "I see that Cruz didn't like Brad."

"It was more that he didn't like Brad's attitude toward Christopher," said Iris.

They went through another album of random photos, some of which showed Caroline pregnant. Christopher always seemed to be close by, and his hand was often splayed protectively over her round belly.

Selecting yet another album, Iris said, "These pictures are mostly of you, Frankie. I'm not sure if your grandparents told you, but you were born early and the pack healer didn't think you'd survive. You proved her wrong."

Actually, Frankie hadn't known that. *More secrets.*

"You can see just how proud as punch Caroline and Christopher were of you."

They did indeed look proud, thought Frankie. Tears even glittered in his eyes at one point as he stared at her, stroking her cheek. "My grandparents have pictures of me with my mother, but none with my father. I should have questioned that, shouldn't I? I mean, she showed me pictures of some random guy and claimed he was my father, but shouldn't I have found it weird that he wasn't in any of the photos with me or my mother?

"I did *ask* if there were any. Marcia would always say, oh, they're probably in the attic, and she'd get someone to pull them down for me when she had a chance. And then I'd forget that I asked for them, or I'd drop the subject because speaking of my parents always put her in a bad mood. I should have pushed her."

Lydia reached over the bed to pat her hand. "You had no reason to question her because you had no reason to believe she'd lie."

Frankie swallowed as she gazed at one particular photo of Christopher smiling down at Caroline while holding Frankie in his arms. "He loved her."

"Worshipped her," said Iris. "Worshipped you."

The last album showed yet more photos—some were taken on Christmases, others on birthdays or Halloweens—and Frankie could see herself changing as she aged. There were many of her cuddling with Iris and Lydia, and it was clear that they had indeed loved her, just as she'd clearly loved them in return.

"This picture here was taken at your third birthday party," said Iris. "The little boy tying balloons on your wrists is Trick. You asked him to do it, hoping they'd lift you into the air."

Lydia pointed to one of Frankie and her parents at her party. The three of them were huddled around a cake, smiling. "That's one of my favorite photos. You should take it."

Iris nodded. "I'd offer you one of the albums, Frankie, but I know you won't take any. Still, you should have at least one photo of the three of you together. One of a happy time."

Frankie didn't want to take it, worried she'd squash or lose it. "I'll snap a picture of it with my cell phone."

"You should take a snap of the one of you and Trick too," suggested Lydia. "He'll get a kick out of seeing that."

Having taken a picture of both photos, Frankie looked at Iris. "You're tired."

Iris sighed. "Always am these days. Even if I hadn't had the mating bond, Alfie's death would have broken me. I couldn't have survived long without him, whatever the case." She placed her hand over Frankie's. "You take care now, you hear? You grab every bit of happiness out of life that you can get. Don't let anyone steal that happiness from you. Take care of Trick, and let him take care of you. Even a strong woman needs to lean on her man sometimes. I miss mine. I'm okay with dying, because it means I'll see him again."

Swallowing hard, Frankie squeezed her hand. She wished she could have told Iris that she loved her and would miss her, but it would have been a lie. Iris was still too much of a stranger. Instead Frankie said, "I'm glad I got the chance to know you." That earned her a wide smile. "Rest now."

"Couldn't stay awake if I tried."

Outside the room, Frankie asked Lydia, "How are you doing?"

Face pained, Lydia exhaled heavily. "Okay."

"Must be hard losing both your parents in such a short time. I can't say I can relate to that, since I can't remember losing mine."

"Dad's death was a shock. Mom's won't be, but it will still be hard. Thank you for seeing her. She'll rest easier now when she passes."

"You don't need to thank me. Like I told Iris, I'm glad I got the chance to know her. So thank you for taking a chance on me and sending me that e-mail."

Lydia gave her a watery smile. "Thank you for responding to the e-mail and giving *us* a chance."

A croaky voice called out from inside the room, "Are you going to keep thanking each other for stuff, or are you going to leave so I can sleep?"

That got an eye roll out of Lydia. "We're going, we're going."

Standing in his Alpha's office, Trick had just finished listening to Trey's account of the call he'd made to Morelli the previous night. Anger flooded him. "He laughed?"

Trey nodded, hands planted on his desk. "Said he thought I was joking. Said he's quite aware that Drake's a wild card, but he didn't figure him for an idiot. I insisted that Drake is a *total* fucking idiot. Morelli said he'd talk to him and call me back today at noon. That's why I summoned you home. I figured you'd want to be here when he called."

Dante scratched his chin. "We can't really blame Morelli for wanting to check out your story, Trey. You'd do the same, in his position."

"That doesn't mean I like that he doubted my word or the word of one of my wolves. I definitely don't like that he found what I had to say fucking amusing. I asked Nick if Morelli had called him, asking for a meet," said Trey, referring to the Alpha of the Mercury Pack, which was so closely allied with theirs that they shared both Roni and Marcus. "He said no."

"On another note, how's Bracken doing?" Trick asked, referring to one of the Mercury enforcers. Bracken and his parents, sisters, brother-in-law, and baby nephew had been at a shifter-owned drive-in cinema when all hell broke loose. Anti-shifter extremists had not only thrown grenades and detonated several bombs, they'd had snipers picking off the people who tried to flee. Only Bracken, his mother, and one of his sisters got out alive. Neither female tried to survive the breaking of her mating bond. Within days they too died.

Trey's expression was grim. "According to Nick, not good. It was bad enough that he lost his whole family just like that. The worst of it is . . . Bracken was holding the baby when he died. The bullet hit Bracken in the back and went right through him into the three-month-old's head. He had the baby's blood and brains splattered all over him."

"Jesus," Trick breathed, rubbing his nape. "No wonder the guy looked like the living dead the last time I saw him."

Just then, Trey's cell phone rang. The Alpha tapped the screen, putting the call on speakerphone, and clipped, "Hello."

"Coleman, it's Nash. How are you doing on this fine afternoon?"

Trey's jaw hardened. "How's Drake?"

"He was doing better until I beat his ass for attacking your wolf. He knows I want an alliance with your pack—such behavior does not help my cause. It is in fact counterproductive, and I don't suppose it's helped convince you to accept me as an ally, has it?"

"No."

"Maybe this will help. Drake has been punished. Severely. He has also been suspended as Beta. When I'm ready to reinstate his position, I will. But only if he proves himself."

Trick exchanged a grim look with Dante. Suspending a Beta never worked out well. To lose his position even temporarily would lose Drake the respect of his pack mates. They would no longer consider him an authority, and at least one of them would decide to challenge him for the position. In other words, it created discord and resentment and it made the hierarchy unstable.

In past instances of a Beta being suspended, they often did the only thing that would regain the rest of the pack's respect and obedience— they challenged their Alpha. If Morelli were a true Alpha, he'd have known that instinctively. Of course, there was no saying he truly had suspended Drake. Morelli could just be feeding Trey shit to placate him.

"Pass on my apologies to Trick," Morelli continued. "He can be assured that Drake won't bother him again."

"You positive of that?" asked Trey.

"One hundred percent. You have my word on that."

"If Drake does attack again, I'll hold you responsible." With that, Trey ended the call.

Dominic pursed his lips. "Do you think he's really suspended him?"

"I don't know," said Marcus. "He'll be pissed at Drake for what he did. And if he's dumb enough to claim he suspended him thinking it would impress Trey, he's also dumb enough to have actually done it."

"Whatever the case, he'll order Drake to stay away from you," Trey told Trick.

Tao nodded. "The question is, can Morelli keep that dog on a leash?"

"No," said Trick. "But Morelli believes he can, so he won't watch him close enough. We need to be prepared for Drake to make another move."

Once the meeting was over, Trick left the office in search of Frankie. He found her in the living area, curled up on an armchair. Careful not to spill her coffee, he gently picked her up and sat down, settling her on his lap. "Hey, baby. You have a good talk with Iris?"

"Yeah. We looked at some photos. Check these out." She pulled out her cell phone and showed him the pictures she'd taken.

Trick laughed at the one of them at her birthday party. "I remember that. I kept telling you the balloons wouldn't make you fly, but you were determined to try." He looked at the photo of her and her parents, wondering how the fuck a family that looked *that* happy together could possibly go to shit.

"Iris said she thought I should have one of me with them."

"It's okay to want it, Frankie." But he sensed she felt some guilt. "There's nothing bad about treasuring a happy moment." Even if that happiness had later evaporated.

"I kind of hoped that looking through the albums would jog my memories, that I might remember something, which is just stupid, since people rarely recall any memories from that age. But I hate that there are so many holes in the story."

Trick kissed her forehead. "I know you do. But you have to stop being mad at yourself," he said quietly, "because it's pissing me off."

"Excuse me?" She kept her voice low, so it didn't carry to the others.

"You're angry with yourself because you think you could solve the mystery so easily if you hadn't buried the memories when you were a kid. But it's not your fault, Frankie. You hear me? It's not your fault. We'll probably never have the answers. You need to learn to be okay with that or you'll torment yourself, and then I'll have to paddle your ass because *no one* hurts my mate—not even her."

While part of her bristled at his words, Frankie found herself snorting in amusement. "Paddle my ass, huh?"

"Paddle your ass, yes. I'll make no bones about it—do not test me on this."

She frowned. "You can't make bones at all."

He rolled his eyes. "It's a figure of speech, and you know what I mean," he said impatiently. He smoothed his hand down her back. "I'll bet your ass would turn a very pretty shade of pink." Trick was getting hard just thinking about it. "In fact, fuck the paddle. I'd use my hands. Yeah, seeing my handprints on your ass would be seriously fucking hot."

"You don't really have a paddle, do you?" His wicked smile was all the answer she needed. And it made her blush. She was about to declare, in no uncertain terms, that *no* paddle would get anywhere near her ass, but then his eyes cut to something over her shoulder. "What is it?" she asked.

"Why are the kids staring at you?"

She sighed. "I don't know. I'm thinking they like the smell of my fear."

Chuckling, Trick tucked his face in the crook of her neck.

"It's really not funny." But he just laughed harder. Asshole.

Frankie rubbed her arms. She was inside her display room. It was cold. Dark. She heard sniffling. She turned. It was her sculpture of the girl in the chair, her head plopped forward. She was sniveling and—

The sound abruptly cut off. There was a deathly chill to the silence. And Frankie was suddenly very afraid. The girl's head began to lift, the movement stiff and jerky. Oh sweet Jesus, no. The synthetic hair parted. The face . . . it was Frankie. A much younger Frankie. "He hurt her," she whispered.

"Who?" Frankie asked, her voice cracking. "Who hurt her?"

The child's head slowly turned. She stiffly lifted her hand. Pointed.

Turning her head just as slowly, Frankie looked. Gasped. There was a black, frothy blur bobbing in the air. There were no eyes, but it saw her. She felt its eyes on her.

The scent of rain, brine, and burned wood swirled around her as a grating voice said, "You're supposed to be in bed, Frankie."

Frankie's eyes snapped open, and she sucked in a breath and gripped the coverlet. Her heart was pounding like a drum, slamming against her ribs. She sucked in another breath, feeling like she couldn't get enough air.

A warm, calloused hand cupped her cheek. "Shh, baby, it was just a nightmare." Trick gathered her close and kissed her hair. "Want to talk about it?"

She shook her head, burrowing into him, absorbing his warmth and inhaling his scent. She supposed it wasn't surprising that she'd have a nightmare, given that her mind was full of dark questions to which she had no answers. Still, it had been damn disturbing. "Sorry. Didn't mean to wake you." Shit, her voice actually trembled.

"Shh," he soothed, kissing her hair again. "Sleep. I've got you."

She snuggled closer and shut her eyes, but it was a long time before she fell back to sleep.

CHAPTER NINE

The knock at the front door snapped Frankie out of her zone. *Dammit.* Any other time, she'd have ignored it, but she was waiting on a delivery and needed the materials for her next project.

She put down her tools, lowered the music, and then pushed up her goggles as she made her way to the front door. As she swung it open, Frankie silently cursed.

"Hello, Francesca."

She forced a smile for Geoffrey. He didn't return it. His expression was grave, and there was a grim twist to his mouth. No prizes for guessing what had brought him here. Vance had obviously called him about Trick. *Weasel.*

Stepping aside, Frankie invited him in with a sweep of her arm. "Can I get you coffee?"

"Please."

Frankie headed to the kitchen, knowing he'd follow. She pulled the goggles off her head and placed them on a stool. As she handled the coffee machine, she flicked him surreptitious glances. Her wolf watched him carefully, distrustful of this man who'd lied to Frankie.

"It's been a while since I've been here." He glanced out the window. "Your backyard is still in good shape. Do you spend much time out there?"

Crossing her arms, she leaned against the counter. "Some."

"It occurs to me that I'm not quite sure how you spend your time these days. You used to enjoy surfing and diving."

"I still do, when my time's free."

"What have you been doing with your free time lately?" he asked, and it was obvious what he was getting at. Oh, that was Geoffrey. He'd ask inane questions, lead the conversation exactly where he wanted it, and then pounce.

Well, she wasn't interested in playing games with him. "Why don't you say what you really came to say?"

His chest puffed up. "I got a call from Vance. He said he saw you at the movie theater."

Her wolf snarled at the mention of the asshole. Frankie grabbed a mug from the cupboard and placed it on the countertop. "He did."

"He also said you were on a date."

"I was."

"Vance claims that the man you were with at the movie theater is a shifter."

"Trick is a shifter." Having poured coffee into the mug, she set it on the island between her and Geoffrey. "And I noticed that you didn't come here to ask me if it was true. You took Vance's word for it. So why *have* you come?"

Geoffrey's mouth flattened. "Your grandmother is distraught. So much so that she wouldn't even come with me to see you."

Which hurt, but . . . "It's not the first time she's given me the cold shoulder. It won't be the last." That only added to the hurt.

"We lost Caroline to one of those savages. We will not lose you to one too."

Irritation tightened her muscles. "I'm sure Vance told you *how* he knows that Trick is a shifter, which means you know that Trick recently defended a woman who was being mugged. But I see that you're going to overlook that and paint him as a bad guy."

"One good deed does not make someone a good person. For all we know, it was a setup, a publicity stunt."

"You don't truly think that."

"I want your word that you'll end this relationship. It's not as if it has a future." He dismissed the very idea of it with a flick of his hand and adjusted his tie. "Shifters will only commit to their predestined mates."

He was wrong about that, but she wasn't sure whether he was ignorant as to how things worked or he hoped to shake her faith in Trick and what was growing between them. "If you don't think it has a future, why does it bother you?"

"You know why," he snapped. "Have you been back to Phoenix Pack territory?"

"Yes. I wasn't going to tell you about it, because I know it's not something you'd want to hear and I don't wish to hurt you. But if you're going to ask me about it, I won't lie."

He shook his head in disbelief. "Why would you allow people into your life who are blood relations of that piece of filth who killed your mother?"

She felt her eyes flash wolf as the animal reached for the surface to make her anger clear. "*I'm* his blood relation," Frankie pointed out. "So if being his relation makes them filth, it makes *me* filth."

Geoffrey appeared to flounder. "The word will soon spread that you're dating a shifter, now that Vance's mother knows. That woman can't keep anything to herself. Do you have any idea how hard it will be for Marcia to listen to talk of how her granddaughter has repaid everything she's ever done for her by turning to the people responsible for Caroline's death?" His nostrils flared. "I don't understand why you want them in your life. Are you doing it to punish us for lying to you about your past?"

That rubbed her the wrong way. "Why do you think this is about you and Marcia? I gotta say, it's a little narcissistic of you. Or maybe it's guilt. Maybe some part of you knows you did wrong by lying to me."

His chin lifted. "We did what was best for you. We always have."

Okay, now that pissed her off. Because it was a total lie. "Always? Really? I was terrified when I shifted for the first time. *Terrified.* Because I was alone, and I didn't know what to do. I'd known it was coming for weeks because I felt my wolf trying to rise. You *knew* how frightened I was, because I told you. And you said that there was no one to help me. But there was, wasn't there?"

"They had no place in your life."

"You made sure of that. You didn't think of how it might have felt if the situation were reversed; you just cut them off. I would have expected better of a judge. Aren't you supposed to consider all sides of a situation? Aren't you supposed to deal with others with sensitivity and have no bias?"

"They didn't deserve our sensitivity!"

"Did I? Because I don't think you once considered me in your decision to remove them from my life. You knew I was half shifter. Knew it would be hard for me to be away from other wolves and have no territory. Knew I'd have to one day shift and that someone should be there with me to make sure it went smoothly. You made a decision that worked for you, not for me. You made a decision that allowed you to hurt them, so don't say you did what was best for me. Maybe you and Marcia kidded yourselves into thinking it was for my benefit, but you won't kid me."

His cheeks reddened. "We did what we thought was right."

"I know you too well to believe that lie." She sighed. "So, what, you're holding your love hostage? I can't have it back until I do what you want?" Frankie shook her head. "Unreal. *I* make my decisions. I'm a full-grown woman—"

"Then act like one. Grow up. Get a real job."

"You did *not* just fucking say that."

They both turned at the sound of Trick's voice. He stood in the doorway, eyes flinty, jaw hard. Frankie bit her lip. Maybe it hadn't been such a great idea to give him a key to the house.

When he'd pulled up outside the house, Trick had guessed that the Lexus at the end of her driveway belonged to either Frankie's uncle or her grandparents. He'd also figured that there was a good chance that her ex had called them about her date with Trick. So the sound of raised voices had come as no surprise to him.

He'd been ready to step in and defend his mate whether she needed it or not. What he hadn't been prepared for was the pain in her voice as she'd spoken of how terrified she'd been during her first shift. The words rang with the sense of isolation and loneliness she'd felt back then. It had gutted Trick and his wolf. Absolutely gutted them.

What made it worse was that her maternal family had *known* how frightened she'd been. They'd done *nothing*. One phone call. They could have made one fucking phone call, and Lydia would have been at her side to help her through it. But they didn't. And then for Geoffrey to so coldly and scornfully snipe that she should get a "real job" was the icing on the fucking cake.

Anger surged through Trick, heating his blood. He stalked into the kitchen, fisted Geoffrey's collar, and literally hauled the flailing human down the hallway and through to Frankie's studio. There Trick shoved him toward the hellhorse sculpture. "Look. *Look.*"

Geoffrey looked at it, and he actually did a double take.

"Frankie made that. Not just physically. She created it up here." Trick tapped his temple. "Tell me that's nothing. Tell me you've ever made something like that in your life. Tell me you *could* ever create something like that with not only your own two hands, but with your brain. You can't, can you? That's not a simple hobby. It's a gift. A skill. One that's appreciated worldwide by galleries, artists, critics, and art lovers. But her biggest fans should have been you, your wife, and your son. If nothing else, she should have had your support and respect. Because *that* kind of creativity and skill is worth a hell of a lot of respect. Am I wrong?"

"You're not wrong," conceded Geoffrey, but his voice was void of emotion.

"Then why doesn't she have it?" Trick demanded. "Why won't you give her the credit she's due?"

Geoffrey didn't answer. Just stared at him.

"Is it because Christopher used to paint?" Trick asked. The human's eyes flashed, and Trick knew he'd hit the nail on the head. "He was arty, wasn't he? You see that trait in her, and you don't like it. But see, that's *your* problem. And it should have been a problem you ignored out of love for her and because you want her to be happy. But you didn't. For that, you should be ashamed of yourself."

Jutting out his chin, Geoffrey sniffed. "I don't have to listen to this."

"But you will. It's been a long time coming." Trick tilted his head. "I don't know why you'd link this 'hobby' with Christopher since, when you think about it, she probably got the sculpting skill from you and your wife. Isn't that what you've always tried to do to Frankie? Shape and mold her into what you want?" Upper lip curling back in contempt, Trick loomed over him. "You're not going to do that to her anymore. I won't let you."

Geoffrey sneered. "You've got a lot of nerve standing there, judging me, when your pack is responsible for my daughter's death."

"That's a weak argument. And an attempt to shift the focus from you."

"Your pack took my daughter from me and my family. I won't let you take my granddaughter from us too."

Trick growled, and his wolf snapped his teeth. "*You* took her from *me*. She's mine. Always was."

The raw possessiveness in his voice took Geoffrey off guard. He looked from Trick to Frankie, and realization flashed in his eyes. He shook his head in denial. "No."

"Yes," Trick bit out. "She's my mate. I missed twenty-four years of her life because you wanted to punish her paternal family and pack mates for what happened to Caroline. But you didn't only hurt us, you hurt Frankie. You won't take her from me again."

"See, you're trying to steal her from us—you and your pack."

"We don't need to try to steal her. You're pushing her to us with the way you're acting. In your efforts to bring her to heel, you're driving her away." Trick had no idea how the guy couldn't see it. "And you know what? We hate that. We're not gloating. We hate that she's hurting. If you truly love her, you'll stop and let this be. There's no reason why she can't have both sides of her family in her life. Don't make her choose."

"You think she'll choose you?" Geoffrey smirked, as if the idea were ridiculous.

"Yeah, I do. Don't test that."

The smirk on Geoffrey's face died. He turned to Frankie, who was standing off to the side, watching the exchange with a blank expression. But Geoffrey didn't say a word to her. He straightened the lapels of his jacket as he stormed out of the studio and then out of the house, slamming the front door behind him.

Trick rubbed a hand down his face. "I'm sorry that you had to be here for that, because it put you in an awkward position," he told her. "But I'm not sorry for any of what I said. He needed to hear it."

Face softening, Frankie uncrossed her arms. "Trick, I'm not going to get upset because my boyfriend stood up for me." She wasn't convinced that anything he'd said to Geoffrey had done any good, but Trick was right—her grandfather had needed to hear it.

Trick crossed to her and cupped her face. "I'm not your boyfriend. I'm a fuck of a lot more than that."

She laid a hand on his chest. "It doesn't seem fair of me to call you my mate when I haven't let you claim me. I can't have it both ways, can I?"

He gave her a slow grin and whispered, "Sure you can." He kissed her, lashing her tongue with his, sipping from her mouth. He slid his hands over her, soothing and gentling her. "I'm guessing that Vance told your grandparents about us."

"Yep. But we'd expected that."

"Did Vance know what kind of trouble his news would cause?"

"He knew they'd be upset, but not like that."

Maybe not, thought Trick, but still . . . "He had to know that they'd expect you to end it. And I'll bet that's exactly what the bastard wanted."

"It might seem like he wants me back, Trick, but he doesn't. What he wants is to keep his options open, to have me waiting on the sidelines in case things mess up with Layla."

Trick clenched his jaw. "He needs to get it out of his head that you're an option. And he should know that you have more self-respect than to pause your love life on the off chance that he might come knocking on your door."

Liking that comment, Frankie melted against him and smoothed her hands up his back. "No one's ever gone to bat for me before. Not that I needed them to, but still . . ." It had been kind of nice.

Trick kissed her. "Get used to it. No one gets to harm you by word or deed."

The protective growl made her skin tingle. "My agent will like you."

His mouth curled on one side. "Yeah?"

"Yeah." Abigail was protective and constantly tried to set Frankie up with "good guys." She'd very much approve of how well Trick treated Frankie.

"You know what I think would be good right now?" he asked.

"What?"

"A dip in the hot tub."

Frankie smiled. "I like that idea. But I have a delivery coming soon."

He tucked a loose strand of her hair around her ear. "We'll hear it arrive."

"Okay then." Upstairs, she quickly changed into a neon-orange bikini and scooped her hair up into a high ponytail. Walking into the backyard a few minutes later, she was surprised to find him wearing trunks.

Seeing the question in her eyes, Trick said, "I stuffed them in my overnight bag in case we used the tub." He drew her to him, skimming his hands down her body, shaping and caressing. Possessiveness pounded through his veins. She was his. All fucking his. He tugged on her lower lip with his teeth and bit down. "It's tempting to forget the tub and strip you naked so I can have my way with you now."

"Later," she promised with a wicked smile.

It didn't take long to get the tub ready. As she sank into the curved seat, she let out a contented sigh. Trick sat opposite her, bracketing her legs with his, and curled his hands possessively around her calves. The tub was big enough for four people, so they had plenty of room to stretch out.

Goosebumps rose on her arms as she draped them over the back of the tub. The bubbling pressure from the jets deliciously hammered at her muscles. She closed her eyes and leaned her head back as she listened to the splosh and burble of the water and enjoyed the rising of the steam as it warmed her face.

Trick gave her calf a light squeeze. "Listen, I'm going to tell you something that I should have told you before. I wasn't deliberately keeping it from you, but it occurred to me earlier that you might want to know."

Unease crept over Frankie. Lifting her head, she opened her eyes. "Okay."

"I told you I've never been in a relationship. That's true. My past has been nothing but flings and one-night stands." He paused. "I had the occasional one-nighter with Marcus."

All right, well, that was a shocker. Frankie sat up straighter. "Just to be clear, you mean your pack mate, Marcus? The enforcer who's mated to Roni?"

He nodded. "We're close friends, but we were never close as partners. We didn't have a fling. We just scratched each other's itches from time to time."

Frankie's brow furrowed. It was just hard to imagine them together, since she'd never detected any attraction there. "So you're bisexual."

He grimaced. "I'm not really into labels. For me it's not about gender. It's about the person."

Maybe so, but it occurred to her that he likely enjoyed the kind of fun she couldn't physically provide, considering she didn't have a cock. Was that going to be an issue? Would he miss that kind of fun? If so, it was possible that she wouldn't be enough for him sexually, that she couldn't fully satisfy him.

Trick growled. "Get it out of your head that this could mean you won't be enough for me."

Frankie gaped. "How did you—?"

"I know how your brain works. I knew your mind would go there. It's a whacked place to go. Look, I get that your maternal family made you feel that you're not enough. That's bullshit. I don't have needs that you can't fulfill or anything stupid like that. The only thing I need is you."

His voice rang with truth, but she couldn't quite relax. "So there was nothing serious between you and Marcus?"

"Not at all," he said.

"You were more like friends with benefits?"

"Not even that, because there was nothing regular about it. They were random encounters. To me this isn't significant. It has no bearing on what's between you and me. But I didn't want you to find out another way." Leaning forward, he slid his hands up to her thighs. "Tao once wanted to imprint on Taryn."

Her mouth fell open. "No."

"Yes. This was before Taryn and Trey knew they were true mates. Initially they were faking it so that Taryn could escape an arranged mating and Trey could then have access to her father's alliances."

Wow, thought Frankie. Having seen how tight the Alphas were, she found it hard to believe that they were originally brought together by nothing more than a deal.

"The plan was that she'd leave after a few months, and Tao made it clear that he was willing to leave with her. He didn't love her, which was probably why that willingness died pretty quickly. There was never any lingering jealousy or a yearning that he tried to hide. It was just one weird, very short period in his life that none of us ever even thought about—it just faded to the backs of our minds. It was so insignificant to him that he didn't think to mention it to Riley. But Greta did."

Frankie winced. The old woman was *such* a bitch.

"She blindsided Riley to hurt her. I don't want Greta blindsiding you with anything from my past, so I'm telling you straight up about Marcus. In your position I'd want to know anyway."

"I'm glad you told me." Even if it did pluck at her jealous streak. Her wolf didn't like hearing about his past either.

"And you believe that it doesn't mean I have needs you can't fulfill," Trick pushed, stroking his thumb down her cheek, which was pink and warm.

Frankie inhaled deeply, breathing in the moist air. "I believe you when you say I'm enough for you." He'd never given her any reason to think differently. "But if it turns out that you lied about that . . . well, there's a good chance I'll stomp on your spine until I hear something crack."

Trick smiled, perversely finding the threatening glitter in her eyes kind of hot. He cupped her nape. She'd tied her hair up into a high ponytail, but curly tendrils hung around her neck. "You're not only enough for me. You're everything."

She really didn't know how to handle it when he said stuff like that. He didn't say it shyly or with any hesitation. He spoke boldly yet casually, holding her eyes the entire time. As if he sensed her discomfort, he gave her a lopsided grin that made the claw marks on his cheek darken. She tilted her head. "Can I ask you a question?"

"You just did, baby. Not really giving me a choice here, are you?"

Frankie gave him a droll look. "Funny." She bit her lip. "You can tell me to mind my own business if you want—"

"I'm yours. My business is your business. What do you want to know?"

"How did you get the scars on your face?"

"I'm surprised you didn't ask about them sooner." He'd sensed that she was curious about them. "It's not a pretty story," he warned her, slowly smoothing his hands up and down her legs. "When I was fourteen and still part of the Bjorn Pack, a twelve-year-old girl declared to me that we were true mates."

She blinked. "Wow. Just wow."

"Jana was adamant that she was right. She truly believed it, but I didn't. There was no doubt in my mind that she wasn't mine. The moment was awkward as fuck, and I felt like a bastard when I refuted it, but I had to make her see that it was just a crush. She wasn't hearing me, though. She believed I was hers. Said she knew her own mind and her own feelings. She accused me of denying it out of fear of mating."

"Which is something you've never feared."

He exhaled a heavy sigh. "I'll admit I lost my temper. I didn't want to hurt her, but I knew that being firm about it was the only way to shut that shit down. I wouldn't have in a million years suspected that she'd attempt suicide."

Frankie's eyes bulged. "She *what?*"

"She wrote a note and said she didn't want to live a life without me in it. Then she slit her wrists in the bathtub."

"Jesus." Frankie loosely hooked her arms around his neck and studied his expression as she said, "It wasn't your fault, Trick. You know that, right? It was tragic that she tried to commit suicide, but it was *her* choice. You don't hold any blame for it."

"I know that." But he'd still been hit hard by regret, shame, and guilt back then. "She was a nice kid, you know. Fun and bright and upbeat. She had really bad lows, though. Could bounce from happy

143

to sad to angry in an instant. Being around her had been like walking on a minefield. But she had a spark; it made people like her, made her seem strong. I realized later that the spark was just that—a spark. Not a sign of strength."

"And you felt like you'd snuffed out that spark," Frankie realized.

"At first, yeah. Not by saying that it was a crush, but by losing my temper and hurting her."

"To be fair, Trick, I don't think there is a sensitive way of telling a young girl that the guy she's crushing so hard on isn't really her mate. Not if she truly believed it. If you hadn't been firm about it, she might have interpreted it as indecision on your part—purely because it would have been what she *wanted* to believe."

"Maybe." Trick's eyes drifted almost shut as Frankie's fingers soothingly traced patterns on his back. "Anyway, her family was understandably upset. Her parents agreed with me that it was just a crush that she mistook for something more. They didn't blame me, but her older brother sure did. He went for my throat."

Bastard. Her wolf growled at the idea. "How old was he?"

"Seventeen. He was angry and looking for someone to take it out on. The fight was brutal. I was younger than him, but I was equally dominant, and I was big for my age. I won the duel and he submitted, which meant I didn't have to kill him. But he dug his claws in deep enough for that strike to scar me. For a while that scar felt like a reminder of what an insensitive bastard I'd been to Jana. But intellectually I knew that I wasn't responsible for her choices. I eventually came to believe that."

"Good, because you did nothing wrong. Sounds to me like she wasn't emotionally stable. Is she better now?"

"I have no idea. Her family left the pack shortly after that." He rested his forehead on hers. "No one outside my childhood pack mates knows that story."

"It's safe with me."

"I know." He snaked a hand around her throat and kissed her, slow and wet and deep. He got lost in it. Lost in her. And now his cock was full and aching. He growled. "I love this mouth."

"Yeah?"

"Yeah. I think about it a lot. I think about tasting it. Then I think about fucking it. Then I think about fucking you. Then I think about you fucking me. You see the pattern."

"You think too much." Her mouth twisted. "This might seem like a stupid question . . ."

"It probably is. Ask anyway."

She gave him a mock glare for that comment. "Did you ever think there was a chance that your true mate was a guy?"

Trick narrowed his eyes, wondering if the real question was *Did you hope your true mate was a guy?* "I always thought my mate would be female."

She slanted her head. "Why?"

"It was just a feeling. Now, though, I think maybe a part of my subconscious had already recognized you and so I *knew* my mate was female. Frankie, when I was with someone in the past, it wasn't about whether they had a pussy or a cock. I didn't prefer one over the other." He gripped her neck. "Hear me when I say this because it's important— I don't need cock, I don't need pussy, I need *you*. Just you."

Frankie bit the inside of her cheek. They might not have been poetic words, but they got to her. "I'm not like you."

His brow lifted. "In what way, baby?"

"I don't find it easy to say nice stuff. I'm outspoken, I'll say what I'm thinking or feeling, but I find it awkward when it comes to talking about personal feelings. And I'm annoyed at myself for that. You don't hold anything back, and you deserve to hear what I'm feeling."

Trick's chest clenched. He scooped her up and brought her close to straddle him. "I know what you're feeling. It's written all over your face."

She couldn't help bristling. "What am I feeling?"

"You're so madly, deeply, irreversibly in love with me that you find yourself bursting into happy tears at random times, thanking fate for sending me your way and letting you get caught up in my sexual web."

Frankie stifled a smile and said, deadpan, "Yeah, that's exactly what I'm feeling."

"See, it's like one mind."

"Uh-huh."

He curved his hand around her chin. "I don't need pretty words from you, Frankie. I find it cute that you struggle with them. But I can see that this really bothers you, so let's do this another way. Do you want me here?"

"If I didn't want you here, I'd have kicked your ass out."

She'd have *tried*, thought Trick. It wouldn't have worked. "Am I enough for you the way I am?"

She swallowed. "Yes."

"Do you think you could ever love me?"

"I'm kind of halfway there," she whispered.

Satisfied, Trick smiled. "That's all I need to know."

CHAPTER TEN

The next morning, Frankie was cursing at her cell phone when she sensed Trick enter the kitchen. "Brad's still not answering my calls," she told him without looking up. Apparently her uncle was taking a page from Marcia's book and giving Frankie the cold shoulder. "Well, I'm not calling again so he can keep blowing me off. He knows I want to speak to him. I'm not giving him the satisfaction of chasing after him." When Trick said nothing, she lifted her head and met his eyes. The sober look on his face made her tense. "Something wrong?"

He crossed to her stool and took her hands in his. "Baby, it's Iris. She passed away in her sleep last night."

The words stabbed Frankie right in the stomach. She took in a huge gulp of air. "Oh."

"Come here." Trick drew her to him, curling his arms tight around her. He kissed her hair. "I'm sorry, baby."

The gentleness in his voice made her chest tighten. "I didn't really know her."

Trick framed her face with his hands. "She was your grandmother, and she loved you. She was a good woman, and I'm sorry that you didn't get more time with her. And I'm sorry for all the years that you missed with her. If nothing else, you can mourn what you missed."

Frankie rested her forehead on his chest. She hadn't expected to feel such deep sorrow about the news. Iris was her grandmother, sure, but she was also a virtual stranger. Still, Frankie remembered those pictures she'd seen in the albums of Iris hugging her tight, kissing her cheek, holding her hand, or carrying her around. Iris had loved her, and the child that Frankie had once been had loved her right back.

Realizing she was clinging to Trick, Frankie loosened her grip on him. "Will there be a funeral?"

"It'll be held on Bjorn Pack territory in a few days."

She frowned. "Bjorn territory?"

"Iris wanted to be buried near her mate and son." Which meant that if Frankie went, she'd see Christopher's grave. Trick wasn't sure if that was something she was ready for. "You don't have to go to the funeral, Frankie. Iris would have wanted you to be there, but she would also have perfectly understood if you didn't go."

"I'll be there." She wanted to pay her respects. His eyes searched hers, uncertain, so she assured him, "I'll be fine."

"Okay. The graveyard is near the border of Bjorn Pack territory, so there'll be no need for us to drive through the heart of it."

That was a relief. She wasn't ready to revisit the place yet. Wasn't sure if it was something she'd ever want to do.

"Don't know if you're one of those people who like to be alone when you're sad or grieving, but I'm telling you now that that won't be happening. I'm staying at your side. We don't have to talk about this anymore if you don't want to, but I'm not leaving you."

"I wasn't going to ask you to go." Her chest felt tight, and she rubbed the heel of her hand over it. Her stomach was churning, and she was surprised she hadn't retched.

"We need to go check on Lydia. She'll want to see you. Think you're up to that?"

"I thought we'd established that I'm not made of fine bone china, Trick."

He cupped her face. "I know you're not fragile. But you are mine. That means I intend to take care of you, no matter how strong you are."

"Even a strong woman needs to lean on her man sometimes."

Hearing Iris's voice in her head made her swallow hard. Frankie went pliant against him, and he wrapped his arms tight around her once more. She said nothing as he gently rocked her from side to side; she allowed herself to take comfort from him. Her wolf pushed up against him, letting out a whine of grief. "You're right, she was a good woman. She didn't deserve to have her granddaughter taken from her life."

Trick kissed her temple. "No, she didn't. But she got to see the woman you'd become. That made up for a lot." He squeezed her nape. "Come on, let's go home." He was glad when she didn't argue that Phoenix Pack territory wasn't her home. They both knew she wouldn't be living in the house much longer. "We'll see Lydia, and then we'll let our wolves out so they can run together."

"Sounds good."

An hour later, they were walking through the caves of pack territory. As they entered the living area, Frankie saw that most of the pack were gathered around, all looking grief-stricken to varying degrees.

Lydia's lips trembled as she saw Frankie. Her eyes were red rimmed, and her face was puffy and splotchy. She stood and crossed to Frankie.

Not good with grieving people, Frankie shifted from foot to foot. She opened her mouth, intending to say the typical "I'm sorry for your loss," but the words just seemed so formal and distant. All that came out was, "Hey."

"Frankie," was all Lydia said. Then she wrapped her arms around Frankie. It wasn't a hug that offered comfort, it was one that begged for it. Frankie awkwardly returned the hug.

"I really can't thank you enough for coming to see her," Lydia whispered, as if her voice lacked strength. "She'd wanted it for so long . . ."

Frankie swallowed. Her throat felt sore and scratchy from the sob that she couldn't seem to let go. "I'm glad I was able to see her. As Trick said, she was a good woman." Hell, they weren't exactly comforting words, but she was truly at a loss for what to say.

"I knew it was coming. Even though I was prepared, it still hit me hard when I went to check on her and realized she was gone." Lydia shuddered, and then it was like she just crumpled. Her sobs were heartbreaking. Cam gently pulled her to him, murmuring in her ear as Lydia cried, clutching his arms.

Trick draped an arm over Frankie's shoulders, holding her close, as people offered her sympathetic looks and words of comfort. He knew his mate. Knew she'd feel that she didn't deserve that support, considering it felt to her as if she'd only met Iris twice. But he also knew that Frankie was hurting. Mourning the years that she'd lost with her grandmother, and imagining how different things would have been if they hadn't been separated from each other all those years ago.

Taking a shaky breath, Lydia raked a hand through her hair. "Clara will be here soon. She wants to help with the funeral arrangements. She'll probably bring her sons with her."

He felt Frankie tense in his arms and wondered why. Figuring she felt overwhelmed, he spoke into her ear. "Come on, let's go for that run."

Taking possession of her hand, he led her out of the caves and down to a clearing near the river. He grimaced at the thick gray cloud that smeared the sky. "Rain's coming, but I think our wolves will have enough time to play before it starts."

As they began to strip, she asked, "Are you sure this is a good idea? I mean, our wolves could claim each other."

Trick chuckled. "I can't promise that my wolf won't try his luck, but I know your wolf won't let him claim her. Not yet. She's still testing me."

"You're winning her over. Fast."

"Good. Now let her free," he coaxed. Bones snapped and popped as his Frankie withdrew and a creamy blonde wolf with a patch of silver fur between her ears stood in her place. The female stretched, scrabbling her claws on the ground. Trick crouched down to her and patted her neck while she licked his jaw. "Beautiful," he said. Then he shifted.

The male wolf shook fur that was a mix of gray, brown, and gold. He sniffed his mate. She backed away with a playful snarl. Then she ran. He chased her through the woods, paws padding over fallen leaves, pine needles, flowers, and mushrooms. Gaining on her, he pounced.

The female barked as he wrestled her to the ground. She twisted. Playfully bit and swatted him. Back on her feet, she ran again.

For hours they explored, leaping over crumbling logs, lapping at the stream, and chasing forest creatures into the underbrush or up the trees.

Random drops of water wet their fur, but they kept playing. It wasn't until the rain picked up that they turned to head back to the river. It was too late. The rain was soon pounding down on them. The male wolf herded his female into a small building for shelter. Then he pulled back, allowing his human half to surface.

Trick scratched the she-wolf's ear. "Shift, baby." He waited, muscles coiled, ready to pounce.

Standing, Frankie blinked rain out of her eyes, surprised to see a row of SUVs. Realizing it was a small garage, she said, "Why do you have—" A mouth closed over hers, hot and hard. For a second she froze, startled. Then she gave herself over to him.

He backed her against an SUV, his growl vibrating with pure power. His hands roughly fisted her wet hair, angling her head. Yes, this was what she needed. His heat. His strength. The ferocity of what he felt for her. And he'd known that, she realized. Known that soft and gentle would do nothing for her while so many emotions were putting her through the wringer. She didn't want to be gentled, she wanted to be fucked. Taken. Used.

She shivered, but it wasn't from the cool air or the rain that dripped from her hair down her back. No, it was her body instantly responding to Trick—heating, melting, shaking, readying itself.

She probably looked like a drowned rat—her skin was wet and clammy, and her hair was plastered to her head. Trick didn't seem to care. He ravaged her mouth, aggressively shoving his cock against her. A moan slipped out of her as he licked his way down to her pulse. She winced at the hard bite of his teeth.

Trick laved the mark with his tongue to soothe the sting. "Just a little reminder that you belong to me." He slid his finger between her folds, groaning at how slick she was. His cock twitched, so full and heavy that he ached.

He sank two fingers inside her and hooked them just right. "All mine. Yeah, my pussy is so hot and tight." Her inner muscles spasmed, and he knew she loved it when he talked that way. So, as he slowly fucked her with his fingers, Trick whispered into her ear—telling her how much he loved being inside her, how thoroughly he intended to fuck her, how he'd one day claim her ass just as surely as he'd claimed her pussy.

He didn't want her thinking about Iris, the Newmans, or anything else that hurt her. He wanted to sweep her away from it all, wanted her priority right then to be simply how bad she needed to come. At that moment she needed it so bad, she was quivering.

Outside, the rain drummed at the roof of the small building and pounded the ground. He could smell the fresh scent of rain and ozone. More, he could smell her need, and the sweet and spicy scent drove him out of his mind.

Sensing she wouldn't last much longer, he spoke into her ear. "I want you to come on my hand. Come on, give it to me, Frankie." He picked up the pace, thrusting hard, stroking her sweet spot. Her head fell back as her release hit and she let out a raspy, choked moan that was like a fist around his cock.

Frankie was still recovering from her orgasm when he yanked her forward and twirled her to face the SUV. She swayed, taken off guard. His hands snaked around to cup her breasts, squeezing roughly and tugging on her nipples. She relaxed against him, her pussy throbbing, needing him. "Trick—"

"Tell me how bad you want me to fuck you," he rumbled into her ear.

Part of her balked at admitting it, but she knew he'd wait all damn day for her to answer. "I need it."

"You need it?" Trick raked his teeth over her shoulder. "Well then, I'd best give my baby what she needs. Bend over." No sooner had she leaned forward and placed her palms on the hood than he slammed home, burying himself balls deep. Her pussy clamped around him so tight he had to grit his teeth against the urge to come. Trick let his arms fall to his sides. "Fuck me."

Frankie braced her hands on the SUV as she slammed herself on his cock over and over. God, he was so thick inside her. Stretched her just a little too much. But she didn't mind the bite of pain. Right then, she even welcomed it.

"Harder, Frankie. Yeah, that's it."

She fucked herself on him like she was caught in a frenzy, wanting him as deep as he could possibly go. She needed to feel his cock possessing her, filling every inch of her pussy. Her world had gone tits up and her mind was a whirl of chaos. Trick was the one solid thing in her life.

Everybody seemed to want something from her. The Newmans wanted her complete obedience; the pack wanted her in their life, Newmans be damned; Trick wanted her body, heart, and soul. Compared to the others, he wanted a hell of a lot more from her—and rightfully so, given that they were true mates. But he was the only person who wasn't *demanding* anything of her when he was probably the one person who had the right to do so.

He wasn't pressuring her. Wasn't becoming impatient with her. He was allowing things to move at her pace, and, as he'd promised, he was on *her* side. For that alone she fucking adored him.

Feeling his release creeping up on him, Trick gripped her shoulders and took over. He pounded into her, slamming so deep that he hit her cervix with every brutal thrust. She didn't wince, didn't ask him to stop. Instead she threw her hips back harder, as if needing that little bit of pain.

Her pussy began to flutter around him, becoming hotter and tighter. "Wait for me."

"I can't," she rasped.

"You want to give me what I want, don't you? So wait for me." He powered into her, eyes locked on a spot on her shoulder. He itched to bite her there, to brand her flesh once more.

"Trick, I—"

"*Wait.*" Gripping her hips, he leaned over her and licked the little spot he'd chosen. "Come." He sank his teeth down hard, growling as her pussy contracted around him and she exploded with a throaty scream. Trick's cock swelled inside her, and he rammed himself deep as his release tore through him and he growled out her name.

As they both quivered with aftershocks, he lapped at the new mark. His wolf loved the sight of his brand on her skin. Wanted to leave another. And another. And another.

Once his cock slipped out of her, Trick curled an arm around her waist and straightened so they were both upright. Nuzzling her, he pressed a kiss to her neck. She was like melted wax in his arms. "You okay?"

"Better than okay." She glanced around. "What is this place?"

"A garage. We keep some vehicles here in case we need to use the concealed exit nearby."

"Ah. Gotcha."

He turned her to face him and shoved back the hair that was stuck to her forehead. "Sounds like the rain has eased off."

"Then I say we head back and take a hot shower."

He gave her a soft, lazy kiss. "Sounds like a plan."

Once again in their animal forms, they trotted through the forest to the spot where they'd left their clothes. They shifted shape and wrapped up the rest of their clothes in their T-shirts so that their wolves could easily carry the bundles inside the caves.

They didn't shift back into their human forms until they were in Trick's room. While they showered, he fucked her again against the cold tiles, leaving yet more marks on her body. She didn't complain. Never did, unless it was to playfully tease him, as if she sensed that he *needed* to mark her so thoroughly while the urge to claim what belonged to him hounded him day and night.

Later, when it was time for dinner, they made their way through the tunnels toward the kitchen. Hearing his cell beep, Trick fished it out of his pocket. It was a text message from his Alpha. "Trey wants to see me in his office," Trick told her. "You remember the way to the kitchen, right?" At her nod, he said, "I'll meet you there in ten minutes."

Frankie watched him go and then headed down the tunnel that she was *pretty* sure would take her to the kitchen, but she couldn't be absolutely certain. Soon the scents of food drifted to her, and she knew she'd taken the right route.

She heard footsteps approaching just before a male wolf rounded the corner. *Marcus.* Her wolf stilled, watching him. Knowing he had history with Trick made Frankie feel a little awkward. And slightly jealous, yeah, even though she knew it was ridiculous. Something in her expression must have given her away, because realization dawned on his face and he halted.

Marcus scratched his chin. "Trick told you, huh?"

Slowing to a stop, she nodded and then gave a slight shrug, going for nonchalant. She didn't want him to see that the whole thing bothered her on any level, particularly since she knew it was senseless. "He didn't want Greta to blindside me with it."

"I think Roni found it a little weird at first. Maybe even felt a little threatened by it, like Trick would be competition. She couldn't have been more wrong." Marcus rubbed his jaw. "He's probably already told you this, but maybe it will help if you hear the same from me. Trick and I were never a couple. Never wanted to be. We were close friends and trusted each other, so that made it . . . comfortable, I guess you could say, to indulge in random one-night stands. Uncomplicated and undemanding. There was nothing more than that between us."

Not really comfortable with the conversation, she simply said, "Okay." She hoped he'd end it there. He didn't.

"Even if I had wanted more—which I hadn't—he wouldn't have given it to me. He's always been so very sure that he'll recognize his mate on sight that he held his sexual partners at a distance, reasoning that letting them close could lead them into thinking he wanted more. He did it out of loyalty to a mate he hadn't yet found—or, as it turns out, who he hadn't consciously known he'd found. For Trick, there's only ever been you. No one else counted."

Warmed a little by his seeming determination to reassure her, she nodded. "Thank you for telling me that."

"You're good for him. For a long time, Trick has made a point of taunting the fuck out of others. But it's been at least four months since he last teased anyone. I knew something was wrong, wondered if maybe he and his wolf were becoming restless and sour by watching others find their mates while he remained alone. He wouldn't talk about it. Wouldn't even admit that he was losing hope of finding you. See, Trick comes across as someone who's easy to read, but he's not. A lot of stuff goes on in his head; he just keeps it to himself. He does that for the same reason that he pushes—or *did* push—people's hot buttons and deliberately stirs things up."

"To keep a part of himself separate from others." She tilted her head as something occurred to her. "Is it because of Jana?"

Marcus rocked back on his heels. "He told you about her? Good. It shows he's holding nothing back from you."

He did seem to be genuinely pleased by it. This wasn't someone who was at all jealous or even slightly discomfited by her connection to Trick, she mused. The tension that had stilled her muscles began to ebb. Even her wolf began to relax a little.

"To answer your question, yes, I think it is because of Jana. No one's going to crush hard on a person who goads them, taunts them, and deliberately makes them feel uncomfortable—even though he's not malicious about it. He wasn't like that until the Jana incident."

"What was he like?" she asked, curious.

"More empathetic, sensitive, and unguarded. Oh, he still teased people, but he did it in a lighthearted way. He did it to lift the mood or make them laugh, not to piss them off. I've seen him act that way with you. I wondered if there was anything of the old Trick left in him. It's good to know that there is; it's good to watch it resurface. I'm glad he has you back."

Frankie felt a smile curve her mouth. This wolf was easy to like. "I can't really blame him for scratching your itches." Especially since Marcus was hot.

Marcus laughed. "Thanks. So things aren't going to be weird between you and me? Because I really don't want that."

"Things aren't going to be weird," she assured him truthfully.

"Good. See you at dinner after I go see what Trey's called a meeting for."

They parted ways, and Frankie soon arrived at the kitchen. It was kind of odd walking inside on her own. Sure, this was *technically* her pack, but she still felt like a visitor at times. Grief marred the air, but there was an unexpected hint of warmth there too.

Jaime smiled the moment she spotted her. "Hey, Frankie." She patted the chair beside her in invitation. "Lydia was just telling us about all the crazy shit that Iris did whenever she was drunk. Lydia, tell her about the time your mom wrote the poem for a badger."

Lydia did, and Frankie couldn't help but chuckle. As she listened to each of Iris's drunken incidents, she felt the grief's tight grip loosen.

Sniffling, Greta rubbed at her nose with a tissue. "I'll miss Iris. She was a lovely woman."

Riley's brows drew together. "You called her fit to burn a week ago."

"I did not," stated Greta, affronted.

Behind the old woman, Grace mouthed "She totally did," and then placed another platter of food on the table.

"I had a lot of respect for her," Greta claimed. "She was like me. Family oriented. Fair. Supportive. A survivor. She'd been through a lot, but she didn't let any of it beat her. No."

Taryn shook her head in what looked like amazement. "You have a glossy opinion of yourself that is massively undeserved."

Makenna nodded in agreement. "Some find ignorance to be bliss, I suppose."

"My boys are the ones living in ignorance," sniped Greta. "For some reason, they don't see their mates as unworthy of them. Marcus did me proud finding Roni. But the rest of them . . ." Greta grimaced. "They let me down, and they let themselves down." Her eyes slid to Frankie. "I had high hopes for Trick and Dominic, but there you sit with my Trick's mark on your neck—bold as brass, like the hussy you are. That wouldn't have happened back in my day. *Nooooo.* I never let anyone but my Arthur leave a brand on me."

Frankie snickered. "You also took your driver's test on a dinosaur."

Clapping, Riley threw back her head and laughed. The kids didn't seem to have any clue what she found so funny, but they started clapping along.

Jaime bumped Frankie's shoulder with her own. "Iris would have loved that one."

At that moment Trey, Dante, Tao, and the enforcers filed into the room. Trick sank into the seat beside Frankie and kissed her temple. "What's so funny that has Riley doubled over with laughter?"

158

Frankie just shook her head. "Is everything okay? Did the meeting have anything to do with Drake?"

Piling food on his plate, Trick explained, "Trey wanted to let me know that Morelli called him with a warning."

She frowned. "What kind of warning?"

"Drake's gone missing. Or, more likely, he's gone AWOL."

"Meaning he could come after you again." Her wolf's upper lip curled. "I'd say it was good of Morelli to warn you, but he's probably done it so he can deny blame for whatever Drake does or doesn't do next."

"That was my thought. We'll find out soon enough. For now, let's eat."

CHAPTER ELEVEN

Frankie had never been to a shifter funeral before. It wasn't much different from those held for humans, except that there were no clergy members reading out scriptures. Instead the Bjorn Alpha, Josh—who was also one of Dante's older brothers—had spoken of what a warm, supportive pack member Iris had been and then voiced his wishes that she rested well. After that, other Bjorn wolves and relatives began to take turns speaking, sharing funny or touching stories.

Frankie listened intently to the stories, eager to hear more about her grandmother. Focusing on them also helped her ignore the curious glances and whispers coming from the Bjorn wolves.

People sniffled and sobbed, even as they chuckled at the anecdotes. One thing was clear—Iris had been well loved by these people. It wasn't surprising; the woman had won Frankie's affection quickly. Right then her heart felt heavy, and there was a huge lump in her throat. Yeah, the tears were building. Hoping to ward them off, she took a deep breath and drew in Trick's scent and the smells of earth, fresh flowers, and sun-warmed stone.

Right then, his warm hand supportively engulfed hers. He never strayed far from her side. He was always touching, kissing, and soothing her. When he wasn't holding her hand, he was massaging her nape, cupping her elbow, splaying his hand on her back, or resting it on her shoulder. Frankie soaked in his support, needing his strength.

His presence also reassured her wolf, who didn't like being on Bjorn territory, which surprised Frankie. She had been born there. She'd spent the first three years of her life there. But her wolf wasn't moved by that. Nor was she comforted by some of the scents that she vaguely recognized. Then again, graveyards weren't exactly comforting places.

All in all, this particular graveyard seemed to be pretty well maintained. There were several rows of carved headstones, some granite, some marble, some concrete. Most were well kept and had decorative flower beds and framed portraits. Others were cracked and discolored, with patches of overgrown grass and dead wreaths. She wondered if the neglect signified that the people buried there hadn't been well liked by the other members.

Frankie hadn't failed to notice the marble headstone beside Iris's: "CHRISTOPHER BROOKS, BELOVED SON AND BROTHER." His grave showed no signs of neglect and wasn't covered in graffiti, as she might have expected. He'd killed his mate and himself, after all. Maybe the headstone had been left alone out of respect for Iris, Alfie, and Lydia.

Speaking of Lydia . . . Frankie briefly glanced at her. The female was leaning into Cam, shoulders bowed, eyes raw, silent tears coursing down her face. She'd insisted that Frankie stand at the front of the mourners, among the other people who'd been close to Iris. Honestly, it made Frankie feel like a gawker, since she hadn't known Iris well enough to grieve as deeply as they were, but Lydia had refused to budge on it.

Considering the two packs had once been one and there was some *serious* history there, Frankie would have thought that there would be some glaring or posturing going on. Instead everybody was reasonably civil. For the most part, though, the packs remained divided even at the graveside. The Phoenix wolves stood on the left, and the Bjorn wolves stood on the right. Only a few wolves had breached that invisible line and—

The whispering of her name snapped Frankie out of her thoughts. She didn't look to see who was murmuring about her now. Instead she stared straight ahead and squeezed Trick's hand. His thumb brushed over her knuckles. She wanted to force a cough to clear the thick lump in her throat, but she didn't want to make any noise or draw more attention her way.

When the service finally reached its end, Lydia tossed some dirt on top of the smooth casket. Uttering something under her breath, she gave a quick, watery smile. Then she walked into her mate's open arms. Others followed suit, throwing soil on the casket and whispering things. Frankie . . . well, she kind of just stood there, feeling lost.

As if sensing that, Trick pulled her to him, carefully brushing her hair out of her face. "Let's go wait for the others in the SUV so you can privately let go of that sob that's stuck in your throat."

God, he read her so well it was frightening at times. "I'm okay." Hell, her voice cracked. He kissed her; it was a mere brush of lips, but that gentleness made her feel treasured.

"No one expects you to be okay, least of all me." Placing one hand on her back, he began to guide her toward the SUV, but they both halted at the sound of someone calling her name.

Frankie turned to see Clara fast approaching, dabbing her eyes with a crumpled tissue. "Frankie, I'm so glad you came." The woman enfolded her in a massive hug. Pulling back, she said, "I shouldn't be such a mess. Iris is with Alfie now, and that was what she wanted. But I'll miss her. This is my mate, Cesar."

The white-haired, jowly male behind Clara gave Frankie a gentle smile and shook Trick's hand. "It's good to see you both, but I wish it could have been under better circumstances."

"Do you think Iris would have liked the service?" Clara asked her.

Frankie nodded. "I think she would have liked that people told funny stories."

"Yes. She wouldn't have wanted everyone to be in a dark mood. Oh, Josh is signaling me. I'll see you at the reception," she added as she and Cesar walked away.

Frankie's heart stuttered. She'd originally assumed that the reception would be held on Phoenix Pack territory, but Trick had told her on the way here that it was instead being held at Iris and Alfie's old home. A place from Frankie's childhood. A place where her father had grown up, that her mother had visited frequently, and where Frankie had played as a child.

According to Lydia, it was also the closest cabin to Frankie's childhood home. She didn't feel ready to go back. Wasn't sure she ever wanted to.

Having a pretty good idea of why his mate had just gone stiff as a board, Trick ate up her personal space, cupping her face as he spoke quietly. "Baby, we don't have to go to the reception. Iris wouldn't give a flying fuck that you didn't go to her cabin, eat finger food, and all that shit. She'd just be happy that you went to the burial."

Frankie so badly wanted to grasp that out and just leave. But it would be disrespectful, selfish, and cowardly to miss the reception, wouldn't it?

"We don't have to go," Trick repeated. "Honestly, my wolf would rather be home anyway. He doesn't like it here. Too many shitty memories. And my mom's pissing him off, because she keeps scowling at Trey."

Yeah, Frankie had noticed that. She'd known Trick's mother instantly because she'd seen him wear that same scowl. He'd inherited her brown eyes, high cheekbones, and full mouth. Frankie wasn't sure where he got his height and burly build from, but it sure hadn't come from his father. The guy was built like a rake and was a foot shorter than Trick.

"Aren't you going to talk to them?" she asked.

"There's no point when Trey's around. Uma's not so bad if I'm on my own or with Marcus, but she feels the need to maintain a bitchy demeanor when Trey's around. Right now, my concern is you. I can't guarantee she'd resist taking potshots at him right here at the graveside, even though she liked and respected Iris. I don't want you exposed to that."

"This day is about Iris." Frankie licked her lips. "That's why I'm going to the reception."

Trick's eyes narrowed a little. "It's okay if you can't handle it. It doesn't make you weak."

"No, but it would make me a self-centered coward." She gripped his arms. "I've had my self-centered moments in the past, but I've never been a coward. I'm not going to start that shit now."

He sighed. "That both irritates me and fills me with pride." Trick didn't want her in a place where she felt even remotely uncomfortable, but he respected why she felt she needed to be there, and he admired her for being able to push past that anxiety. His gaze pinned hers, all seriousness now. "An hour. We'll stay for no longer than an hour. If you feel uncomfortable or want to leave for any reason at all before then, you tell me. I'll claim that I received a call and I need to leave. Okay?"

She smiled. "You're awesome. You know that?"

"Of course I know that."

"It saddens me that you have such self-esteem issues," she said drily.

Jaime appeared then, using her knuckle to wipe away a tear. "You guys ready to go back?"

Trick rested his hand in the crook of Frankie's neck. "Actually, we're going to the reception."

Jaime's eyes cut to her, glinting with concern. "Are you sure about this?"

No, thought Frankie, but she nodded. "It's just something I have to do. We won't be staying long."

Jaime sighed. "All right. But I'm sure you've noticed that a lot of people are curious about you. I doubt that anyone will be rude, but they'll have plenty of questions, and if they can get you alone they might take the chance to say some shitty stuff about the Newmans, considering that the humans were a big source of Iris's unhappiness over the years. Stay close to Trick and the rest of our pack at all times."

"I'm planning to." Many Phoenix Pack members had attended. Since they all couldn't leave their territory at the same time and no one wanted to bring the kids to the funeral, the pack had agreed that half would go to the burial and then go home so that the other half could attend the reception. That way everyone got to pay their respects to Iris, and the kids would stay home and be well protected.

Jaime looked at Trick. "I'd say, 'Take care of her,' but I know you will." With that, she crossed to Dante.

Ignoring the weight of his mother's glare, Trick guided Frankie to the SUV and opened the door. Once they were both inside, he twisted in his seat to face her. "Let it out." She'd been holding her grief in all damn morning, and it was driving him and his wolf crazy.

"I can't yet. Not until after the reception."

"Frankie—"

"I *can't* yet."

He sighed. "All right. But later, you have to let it all go."

"I will." It was a promise.

Minutes later, Lydia and Cam joined them in the SUV. Trick drove them through the territory toward Iris's cabin. The whole time, Frankie stared out the window, taking everything in. Of course, nothing sparked memories to surface, nothing seemed familiar. It was both frustrating and a relief.

As they pulled up near the cabin and she hopped out of the vehicle, Frankie resisted glancing at the cabin that was a few kilometers down the way. That resistance didn't last long. The cabin seemed a little bigger than Iris's. It was also boarded up. Apparently no one wanted to live in a place where one person had been murdered and another had committed suicide. Understandable. She was surprised the pack hadn't just knocked the building down.

Trick held his hand out. "Ready?"

Slipping her hand into his, she nodded. Lydia and Cam entered first, which gave Frankie cover. Her sensitive stomach churned at the smells of coffee, lasagna, finger foods, and perfume. Despite the bright decor and the flower arrangements, the cabin seemed dull—probably because everyone was dressed in black and the mood was mostly bleak.

The den, dining area, and kitchen was all one open space, so it was easy to see that some people were gathered around the buffet while others bustled around the kitchen. Most, however, were seated around the den on the sofa, armchairs, and folding chairs.

She could hear people speaking in hushed tones, cutlery clinking and clattering, and the subdued laughter from those exchanging yet more funny stories.

Trick spoke into her ear. "Want me to get you a plate?"

She grimaced. "I don't have a much of an appetite right now."

With Trick at her side, Frankie wandered from room to room, looking at mementos, knickknacks, and framed photographs. Lydia had already boxed up the things that Iris had kept at Phoenix Pack territory, saying it had felt cathartic. Frankie wasn't sure if she personally would have been able to handle something like that so quickly in Lydia's situation, but she knew everyone handled grief in different ways.

She pretended she was oblivious to the stares and avoided making eye contact with any of the Bjorn wolves. In her current mood, she had no patience for small talk or probing questions. She was there for Iris, not—

Frankie came to an abrupt stop as something caught her eye. "That's mine."

Trick looked at the clay sculpture of a cloaked, hooded figure that was propped up on a shelf near the staircase. There was nothing but a pit of black where its face should be, making him think of a grim reaper.

But that wasn't what creeped Trick out. It was that those bony fingers were gripping the handle of a baby stroller. "You made that?"

"She never told me she had one of my pieces. She just said she saw them online."

Trick's brow furrowed. "It is odd that she didn't tell you. It's even stranger that she left it here when she moved to our territory, considering she took her most prized possessions with her." He pursed his lips. "Maybe she didn't know it was your work. If she had, it would have had pride of place in the den."

"So someone bought it for her but didn't tell her that I made it?"

He shrugged. "Seems like it." Such an act was both kind and cruel, in his opinion. "But there's—" He cut off when he noticed the Bjorn Alpha headed their way. Josh wasn't a bad guy but, honestly, Trick had never liked any of Dante's brothers. Mostly because they'd been absolute assholes to their baby brother, treating him like the runt of the pack. Well, said runt was now bigger, faster, and more dominant than all of them. Funny how things worked out.

He gave Trick a brief nod before turning to Frankie with a smile. "I'm Josh, the Alpha. But you don't remember me, I see."

She shook her head. "Sorry." And she was finding it kind of annoying that some people thought they were so special that they'd somehow stick out in her memory.

He shrugged. "It's not your fault."

Well, obviously not, thought Frankie.

A small, plump woman sidled up to the Alpha and said, "Josh, I was hoping to—oh, you're little Francesca, all grown up." It was obvious that the woman had pretended she wanted to speak with Josh just so she could talk with Frankie.

Trick inwardly sighed in annoyance. She didn't hesitate to pelt Frankie with questions, and others quickly came over and followed the woman's lead. His pack mates realized what was happening and came over just as Trick held up his arms and interrupted.

"Frankie's here to pay her respects to Iris. Not to answer questions. I understand why you're curious, but you'll have to put that aside." Trick looked at Josh. "That includes you."

At that moment, Clara shouldered her way through the crowd and shooed all the Bjorn wolves away, even Josh. The Alpha took pity on the grieving woman and didn't reprimand her for the insubordinate behavior.

With a heavy sigh, Clara said, "I'm sorry, Frankie. They shouldn't have crowded you that way. They didn't mean any harm, but it wasn't fair of them. How are you doing?"

Frankie swallowed. "Fine. You?"

"I'm holding up. It's hard. She was the best friend a girl could ever have."

Keeping her voice casual, Frankie asked, "Clara, did Iris buy this?"

Clara squinted at the sculpture. "No, she didn't. I asked her once why she'd have such a frightening piece in her home. She said she'd never give away a gift. She was good like that." Her chin trembled, and she dug a tissue out of her pocket. "Excuse me. I need to use the bathroom."

Frankie blew out a breath and turned to Trick. "Can we go now?" She was tired and edgy, and her face felt stiff from how long she'd been fighting the urge to cry.

He squeezed her nape. "Yeah, baby, we can go." He signaled to Trey, who tipped his chin. Trusting his Alpha to gather the rest of their pack mates together, Trick slid an arm around Frankie's shoulders and led her outside. The moment they stepped on the porch, those shoulders stiffened. He frowned. "You okay?"

No, Frankie wasn't. When she'd stepped out onto the porch, a familiar scent of rain, brine, and burned wood had reached her nostrils. That was when her wolf went ape-shit—snarling, snapping her teeth, and raking Frankie's insides with her claws.

Frankie stiffly turned to face Cruz, Eke, and Wendel. While they exchanged greetings with her and Trick, she worked hard to soothe her wolf.

"It was good of you to come, Frankie," said Eke, face lined with grief. "My mother appreciates it."

Cruz nodded. "She needs family around her right now."

Wendel opened his mouth to speak, but then he shook his head. "Sorry, it's just . . . you look so much like Caroline that it's like having her standing in front of me."

The affection with which he said her mother's name unsettled Frankie. She lifted a brow. "You knew her well?"

"Not *well*, but I'd like to think we were friends. Some humans find it hard to adjust to being within a pack. Not Caroline. She took to pack life as if she were a shifter."

Mouth curving into a nostalgic smile, Cruz nodded again. "Christopher was so proud of that. He'd have been so proud of your success too. He'd have liked that you were an artist, like him." Hearing the shake in his voice, Frankie thought he might cry. Instead he gave her a wobbly smile.

As if eager to change the subject and rescue Cruz's mood, Eke quickly said, "You were always in Iris's thoughts, Frankie. I'm sure you've noticed there were many pictures of you around her cabin."

"There was one of my sculptures too," she told him.

Wendel blinked. "She didn't tell me she had one of your pieces."

Before Frankie could tell him that she suspected Iris hadn't known it was one of hers, a dark-skinned female popped her head through the doorway and shouted, "Boys, your mom is looking for you!"

Sighing, Cruz shrugged a little helplessly. "We have to go. You take care now, Frankie." He tipped his chin at Trick and then headed inside the cabin. Muttering their goodbyes, Wendel and Eke followed their brother.

Relief scuttled down Frankie's spine, and she rolled back her stiff shoulders. It wasn't until she was inside the SUV, though, that her wolf finally simmered down. Breathing deeply, she clicked on her seat belt, hoping that Lydia and Cam would hurry their asses up.

Trick rested one hand on the wheel. "Okay, baby, here's where you tell me why the triplets make you so uncomfortable."

Agitated, Frankie threw her hands up. "It's not me. It's my wolf."

His brow creased. "Your wolf?"

"She loses her shit around them. The scent they all share sets her off every time. I don't know why, but she despises them."

Trick's frown deepened. "Really?" He glanced at the cabin, thoughtful. "I don't recall them ever doing anything to upset you when we were kids. But if your wolf behaves that way, there must be a good reason." He was about to say something else, but then he noticed that his parents were nearing Iris's cabin. It appeared that they'd walked from the graveyard instead of driving, and he wondered if his father had insisted on it out of respect for Iris—hoping that Trey would be gone by the time they got there so that any awkward scenes could be avoided.

Noticing him, they stopped at the driver's side of the vehicle. Trick wound down the window and inclined his head.

Michael nodded, face drawn. "Son." He looked past him and said with a strained smile, "You must be Francesca. I'm Michael, Trick's father. This is Uma, his mother."

Uma smiled. "It's nice to see you again, Francesca, though it would have been much better if it had happened under other circumstances. I'm sorry about your grandmother. Iris was an amazing woman."

Unsure what to say, Frankie simply agreed. "Yeah, she was."

Uma turned her smile on Trick. "You look good."

"I feel it," said Trick.

"Will you be moving back to Bjorn Pack territory?" Uma asked Frankie.

"No," replied Frankie. "I, um, I'll be moving to Phoenix Pack territory at some point."

Satisfaction flooded Trick at that, and he rested a hand on her thigh.

"I see." Uma looked from her to Trick. "You're mates." She slanted her head, eyes on Trick. "I remember how protective you were of her. I didn't think anything of it. I should have." She raised a brow. "You don't think it would be best for Francesca if she were to return to her childhood—"

"Do not try to use this situation to meet your own needs," Trick snapped.

Michael lifted a placating hand. "Let's drop this, yes?"

Uma's mouth tightened. "Fine. I hope you'll at least make time to visit us soon. And grandchildren would be nice, by the way." The cabin door creaked open, and Trey stepped out. Uma's face went rock hard.

"Mom, leave it," Trick bit out. "Your anger is pointless."

Uma turned back to him. "You lost years of your mate's life because her grandparents took her from you. Are you not angry with them for that?"

He knew what she was getting at. "Trey didn't take me from you. I made the decision to leave. I made the choice that was right for me. Dad knows that, which is why he's mad at me, not Trey."

Michael exhaled a weary sigh. "I lost that anger years ago, Trick."

Trick shook his head. "I see it in your eyes."

"That anger isn't directed at you. I'm angry that the strain between us went on too long for the damage to ever be completely repaired." Michael looked at Frankie. "We're sorry for your loss, Francesca." At that, he guided Uma away. Whatever he whispered into her ear stopped her from spewing any harsh words at Trey as they passed him.

Trick's shoulders lost their tension as Lydia and Cam finally appeared. "Now we can get the fuck out of here."

When they all finally returned to Phoenix Pack territory, Trick took Frankie to his room and lay her on the bed beside him. "Let it go," he gently ordered. And she did. The entire time she cried, he held her close, whispering soothing words and planting light kisses on her face and hair. Once she was all cried out, she drifted off, still in his arms. He tightened his hold on her and watched over her while she slept.

CHAPTER TWELVE

H er foot caught on something, and Frankie cursed as she stumbled. Only Trick's hold on her arm kept her upright. She hissed.
"Will you take this damn blindfold off me now!"

"Nearly there," he assured her.

"You said that twenty minutes ago."

"Baby, we've only been walking for five."

She snarled at him, though she had no idea if he noticed. When
he'd said that he had a surprise for her, she hadn't expected that they'd
need to go stomping through the woods to reach it. Well, *she* was
stomping, causing leaves to crackle and twigs to snap beneath her feet.
Trick didn't make a sound. If it weren't for his hand on her skin and his
scent surrounding her, she wouldn't even know he was there.

For days she'd been very aware that he was hiding something from
her—he'd occasionally shot her a little secret smile that had a slight
taunt to it. But no amount of bugging on her part had made him even
admit to *having* a secret, let alone made him tell her what it was.

Busy working on her sculpture, she'd let it go, especially since
immersing herself in her work stopped her from thinking about the
messes in her life. It had been almost two weeks since Iris's funeral.

Though the grief had lost its cutting edge, it still hurt to think of her and—

Frankie nearly tripped again. "Fuck, Trick, you need to take this thing off before I fall flat on my face." Her wolf was embarrassed on Frankie's behalf.

"Not yet," he said, words vibrating with humor.

"Asshole." Grinding her teeth, she kept walking—well, stomping. It felt like forever before he finally brought her to a halt.

"Don't move from this spot, and *do not* take off the blindfold."

Planting her hands on her hips, she impatiently drummed her fingers. "Fine." There was the sound of metal screeching, like a roll-up door was being lifted. Then Trick was behind her, gently guiding her forward and inside . . . something. Before she could wonder at the slight draft or investigate the scents, the blindfold fell away.

"Surprise," Trick whispered into her ear.

Frankie's mouth dropped open, and her arms slipped to her sides. The building was pretty much a replica of the studio attached to her house—same layout, same amount of space, same high ceiling and ventilation system. He'd even ensured that there was a patch outside for her to work on. And she feared she was going to cry.

She turned to him, knowing she had to look dazed. Words failed her, and all that came out of her mouth was, "How?"

"The Mercury Pack Alpha, Nick, has a lot of contacts. One is an architect who runs a firm—they revamped the Mercury Pack's main lodge, built all the lodges that are scattered around Nick's territory, and then recently constructed his pack's motel. I told them what I wanted, and they built the studio. I was impressed by how fast they did it."

"That's why you haven't been pushing me to come here during the daytime lately," she realized. "You said it was so that I could work on my sculpture, but it was because you didn't want me to hear the construction work."

He nodded. "That was also why we didn't go on any more runs in our wolf forms around here." They'd done it near her house instead. Trick stood back, mouth curved, as she wandered around the large space, touching things with a proprietary edge and leaving her scent everywhere. "So are you happy with it?"

A short, spontaneous laugh popped out of her. "How can I not be?" She crossed to him and looped her arms around his neck. "I really didn't expect you to do this." Her voice cracked. "I figured I'd just keep using the studio at my house."

Trick smoothed his hands up and down her back. "This territory is your home. I want you to have everything you need for when you officially move here."

She bit her lip. "Thank you."

Smiling at the way her eyes sparkled, he said, "You're welcome."

Struggling to explain how fucking amazed and grateful she was, Frankie said, "I feel all warm and fuzzy inside." Like she'd had a few too many glasses of wine. "You're the shit, Trick Hardy."

He laughed, pleased to see her happy. His wolf was smug about their being the cause of that happiness. "How long before the hellhorse is complete?"

"Another couple of days."

Good, thought Trick. Once it was done and it could be safely moved, he intended to press the matter of her moving to pack territory. "I take it you'll be working on it some more today." Which he fully supported. The sooner it was done the better.

"I have to head down to the salvage yard first. It's a great place to get scrap metal. Before that, though, I'll need to go to the house and get the van I keep parked at the back of the studio."

If he didn't have an important meeting to attend, he'd go with her. Hearing her talk about sculpting, Trick had become unexpectedly fascinated by it. He was interested in every step of her process, but he couldn't be there for this one. "I want to sketch you while you work one day."

Her nose wrinkled. "I don't let people watch me while I work."

"Which is why I'll come up with a clever bribe."

"Bribe?"

"I know what my baby likes."

"Oh yeah?"

"Yeah." Wrapping his arms tight around her, he lifted her off her feet and kissed her. The taste of her swam through him, invigorating and marking him and filling every empty space. They were her spaces to fill. She was born for him. His other half. Better half.

"Well, I don't respond to bribes."

"That's okay. I'm good at getting what I want. There's more than one way to skin a cat."

Frankie's brows snapped together. "Why would you want to learn even *one* way to skin a cat?"

With a tired sigh, he just shook his head. "Forget it."

A few hours later, Trick was leaning against the SUV, watching as a red Chevy Camaro convertible pulled up. Why the guy had asked to meet in the parking lot outside a construction site, Trick had no idea. But he didn't trust the fucker as far as he could throw him, which meant he hadn't come alone. Marcus was in the SUV, concealed by the tinted windows.

Within Trick, his wolf paced. He didn't like the scents of metal, cement, sawdust, and burning plastic. Didn't like the hammering, pounding, drilling, metal clanging on metal, or whir of a forklift. And he *really* didn't want to be near the human who stepped out of the Camaro.

Said human took two confident strides toward Trick, studying him from head to toe. He probably would have looked down his nose at Trick if he weren't a good five inches shorter. The human might seem composed, but there was an unnatural stillness about him that told Trick he was fighting the urge to fidget.

"You're Patrick Hardy." It was a statement that held a small note of accusation.

Trick just looked at him blankly, letting the moment stretch out. He didn't push away from the SUV; he just continued leaning against it, keeping his shoulders loose and his stance casual. "Yeah."

"I'm Brad Newman."

"I know." Trick had met him several times as a child. Apart from the lines of age on his face, the guy hadn't changed much. He'd e-mailed Trick the previous evening, wanting to arrange a meeting. It was mostly curiosity that had made Trick agree.

Brad smoothed his tie. "Does Frankie know about this?" The question was posed casually, but it was clear that he was hoping the answer was no.

Trick shook his head. "I didn't see the need to bother her with it." Not until he'd gotten it over with, anyway.

"My father told me about the conversation you had with him at her house."

"Did he?"

"He was raging. Even threw his glass across the room. My father doesn't rage. Then he crumpled. Honestly crumpled—another thing he doesn't do. I knew then that he wasn't just angry about her having a relationship with a shifter, that there was something else. So I badgered him to tell me the rest." Brad licked his lower lip. "He was upset because you made him face a few things. You made him see that both he and my mother let Frankie down in a number of ways. From what he told me, you seem to get her, which is something they never did."

"But he still won't accept my place in her life," Trick guessed.

"No, he won't. He's as pissed at you as he is at himself. My mother doesn't agree that they did anything wrong, so she's giving *him* the cold shoulder now too." Brad sighed. "Look, I love my niece. I want her to be happy. I do. However, given how the true mate thing worked out for my sister, I'm not convinced you will make Frankie happy. Especially when the whole situation is ripping my family apart."

"Your parents are *choosing* to let it rip the family apart. They could just let it be, for Frankie's sake. They won't."

"No, they won't. That's why I'm here." Brad briefly averted his eyes. "I don't agree that this is the right thing to do, but if I don't do this for my mother, she'll find another way to ensure that it's done." He pulled something out of his pocket and held it out.

Taking the small sheet of paper from him, Trick barely held back a growl.

"That's a check for fifty thousand dollars."

"I can read."

"It's all yours . . . if you walk out of Frankie's life and never return to it."

Seething, Trick stared the human right in the eyes as he carefully tore the check into tiny pieces. Some landed on the ground, others fluttered away with the cool breeze.

Brad's jaw hardened. "Then maybe this will change your mind." He crossed to his car, reached into the open window, and pulled out a manila envelope.

Trick took it with a bored sigh and slid out the thin file. Anger flared inside him as he read it. Apparently Brad had done a little fishing.

"It wasn't easy to find that information," said Brad, the smugness in his voice making Trick's wolf snap his teeth. "Once Frankie learns that, she'll hate your ass. She'll be long gone. If you walk away now, she never has to know. She'll be upset with you for dumping her, sure, but at least she won't hate you."

Trick returned the file to the envelope and tossed it at Brad's feet. "Your source either didn't know the entire story or decided to spice it up a little with some fiction. Either way, it makes no difference."

"It would make a difference to Frankie, if she found out."

"She already knows."

Brad paused, nostrils flaring. "Knows that she's not your true mate? That you walked away from your true mate years ago and that she tried to kill herself because of it?"

"I don't explain myself to people, but I'll give you a little info, since you're Frankie's uncle. Jana wasn't my true mate; she was an emotionally unbalanced juvenile with a crush. Nothing more, nothing less. If you want to believe differently, that's on you. But Frankie knows the truth; that's all that matters to me." Trick flicked a dismissive look at the manila envelope. "All this was a waste of my time and yours."

"Do you care for her? Because if you do, you owe my parents."

Trick couldn't believe his fucking ears. "Say that again," he rumbled.

Brad drew back. "You should be thankful to them. They raised her to be the person she is today. They cared for her, kept her safe, ensured she got a good education, and—"

"Lied to her all her life," Trick finished. "They also made her feel like she didn't quite measure up to their expectations. And considering they ripped Frankie's paternal family apart by cutting them from her life, you could say they had this coming."

Brad's eyes narrowed. "You're loving this, aren't you?"

"That's where you're wrong. I don't like that sides have formed. I want Frankie to have all the people she cares for in her life. You and your parents are the ones who are stopping that from happening, not me. And for what? It's not like we'll expect any of you to step on our territory or welcome the pack into your lives. But if you and your parents want to be in *her* life, you all need to jump down from your high horses. So fuck them, fuck you, *and* fuck your bribe."

Brad's eyes flickered. "It was my mother who—"

"Your mother might know you're here, but she didn't ask you to write that check. You're laying the blame on her in case I tell Frankie what happened here today."

"If you tell her, she'll be pissed that you came without her."

"Yes, she will. But there will be no lies between me and my mate. I won't keep this from her, even though I know it will hurt her. Like I told your father, you're all driving her away with the shit you're pulling. I think she'd have expected this kind of thing from your parents, but not from you. You've just sincerely fucked yourself over." With that, Trick hopped into the SUV and sharply twisted the keys in the ignition. "Motherfucking motherfucker."

Marcus blew out a breath. "Hell, Trick, I don't know how you didn't kick the shit out of the bastard."

Trick reversed out of the space and drove out of the lot. "It was hard not to, but it'll hurt Frankie bad enough to hear that her uncle tried bribing me. It would hurt her even more to hear that her mate and her uncle then came to blows."

Marcus inclined his head. "You did the right thing. If you'd left a single blemish on him, he'd have gone crying to her with a bullshit story that made *him* a victim and *you* the villain."

"I'd have left more than a blemish on him," Trick rumbled. He'd have delivered some serious pain on the asshole.

After a long moment, Marcus said, "Hey, did she tell you that she and I had a little talk?"

Although Trick knew that his friend was changing the subject to help Trick cool his anger, he went with it. "She mentioned it. Reassured me that there'd be no awkwardness between you and her."

"Some females wouldn't accept our past so easy. They'd let jealousy eat them up. She obviously has enough confidence in you and what you feel for her to not worry about whoever came before her. That's good. And it means you've done the right thing by not pushing her. Winning her trust and moving at her pace was what she needed. But I'm sensing that it's getting harder for you *not* to push."

"If you're sensing it, she'll be sensing it too." She hadn't said a word about it, though.

"Probably. You won't have to hold out much longer, Trick. I've watched her with you. Watched her gradually soften. She used to frown at the way you constantly touched her. Now she leans into it. She never used to touch you back, but now she does. She's also started to relax around the rest of the pack, but she doesn't smile at us or talk as openly with us as she does with you. And if you're not in the room with her, she's uncomfortable."

While the latter made Trick feel kind of smug, it also saddened him that she hadn't yet fully relaxed with the pack. He understood it would take a little time, though.

"I like the way you are with her," said Marcus. "And I have to say, I'm surprised, relieved, and impressed that she leans on you. A lot of females see that as a weakness. She seems to respect your need to take care of her, and she's happy to let you do it—maybe because she's never had anyone to lean on before and she's not afraid to try it on for size. These are all good things that indicate that she's happy with you and accepts that you're her mate. She just needs to face whatever's getting in the way of the bond, which I'm guessing is connected to the Newmans."

Trick's hands clenched around the wheel. "She's still hoping she can find a way to make them accept her decision to have the pack in her life."

"I don't foresee that happening."

"Neither do I, but they won't think that they should feel guilty about that. They've always made *her* feel like the bad guy, and I fucking hate that. Oh, she sees that she's not the one being unreasonable, but it still makes her feel like shit."

"All you can do is exactly what you've been doing since you found her again—be there for her." Marcus twisted his mouth. "We're not far from her house. Why don't we stop by and see her? I get that she's busy, but it's probably the only thing that will calm your ass down."

Totally true. "She might not be back from the salvage yard yet."

"Call her and find out."

Frankie had just finished hauling the scrap metal out of the van and into the studio when her cell phone rang. She lowered the music and snatched the phone from the shelf. Trick's name flashed on the screen. "Yup?" she answered simply.

"Hey, baby. You done at the salvage yard?"

She frowned at the strained note in his voice. "Yeah, I'm back at the house. Where are you?"

"About ten minutes away. I'll be there soon to help you unload the stuff out of the van."

Damn, he was too sweet. "I'm already done with that. But you're still welcome to come."

"I'll be there soon," he said, his voice a little warmer this time.

"Okay, I'll—" The sound of a car engine made her turn. Seeing a blue Chevy Tahoe, she sighed. "Crap."

"What?"

"Looks like Vance has decided to pay me a visit."

Trick swore. "*Do not* let him in the house. Pull down the fucking studio door and ignore the bastard. I'll deal with him."

"I can handle him just fine myself." She slowly walked out the side door as the car turned up the driveway that led to the studio. No way was she letting the bastard in her—"Wait, it's not Vance," she realized as she saw the license plate. Vance's ended in "VCE." "*Motherfucker,*" she spat, because the driver slammed their foot on the pedal and the tires screeched as the car zoomed right at her.

"Frankie? *Frankie!*" yelled Trick.

Without a thought she fled to the side door and turned into the studio, but the car followed her inside and screeched to a halt, clipping her leg hard enough to send her sprawling onto the concrete floor. Pain pounded up her leg and burned the heels of her hands. Grinding her teeth, she rolled onto her back. That was when the driver smoothly exited the car.

He looked vaguely familiar. She hadn't gotten a good look at the guy who'd attacked Trick in the restroom, but she suspected that this was him. *Drake.* Well, fuck.

She clenched her fist. Where the hell was her phone? She'd dropped it when she fell, and she couldn't see it anywhere. Dread hit her square in the chest.

In retrospect, it had been stupid to run into the studio—she would never have been able to shut the metal door in time to keep the fucker out, but she hadn't been thinking. She'd been too busy *panicking.* That panic flooded her now, pumping adrenaline through her veins. She braced herself on her elbows, wondering if he could hear the frantic beat of her heart—it thrashed in her ears, just as her wolf thrashed inside her with rage.

He came toward her, whistling. "Hey, sweet girl. Fast runner, ain't you? Just not fast enough. Now, why don't I help you up?"

Her claws sliced out and she swiped at him, slashing his face and drawing blood. He jerked back, as if shocked by the sight of her claws. Taking advantage of that, she slashed at him again.

Laughing, he jerked back and dodged the move. Yes, he *laughed.* "I did not know you were a shifter. You live out here, no pack, no mate. It's a good thing I like surprises."

She struggled to her feet—bad idea. Her leg still throbbed with pain. Sensing he was ready to lunge, she snarled. "Don't even try it, motherfucker." She might not know the type of combat that shifters often learned, but she could still cause him pain.

"Sorry, sweetheart, but you need to come with me."

"Not gonna happen."

He moved fast. *Wicked* fast. His fist slammed into her jaw, dazing her. "Shame I had to mess up that pretty face," he said. Whistling again, he dragged her toward the vehicle, but her bad leg crumpled and went out from underneath her. It caught him off guard, and he stumbled as she fell onto her back. Leaning over her, he sighed. "Do you have to be awkward?"

She thrust her claws into his abs, stabbing deep, scraping bone. "Yes." He let her go so abruptly that the back of her head hit the concrete with an awful crack. Her head swam and nausea curdled in her stomach.

"Fucking *bitch*."

A boot slammed into her stomach, knocking the breath right out of her. She curled up, hissing. Her wolf went ape-shit and lunged for the surface, but then sharp claws pressed against Frankie's throat hard enough to break the skin. Both she and her wolf froze.

"I'm done playing," he said. "Now, we're going to get into the fucking car and go somewhere quiet. Somewhere where we can have some privacy. Won't that be nice?"

Um, no. She knew deep down to her bones that if she left with him, she'd be dead within the hour. But there was no way of fighting back without getting her throat slit open. She forced her voice to shake as she said, "I'll go with you. I won't struggle. Just don't kill me. Please."

He beamed at her. "So polite. I like it when they beg. Wait until I tell your boyfriend how you begged for me. Ooh, he'll sure as shit hate that. Now, sheathe those claws for me. That's it. See, following orders isn't so hard." He dropped his claws from her throat and yanked her to her feet by her arm—*fuck* if that didn't hurt. That was when she slammed her forehead into his nose. The animalistic sound that came out of his throat was a mix of anger and pain.

Even as her head pounded, she pulled free of his hold and snatched the hammer from the peg on the wall. She swung it at his head. A slight vibration shot up her arm as the hammer connected with his skull. He staggered with a pained grunt, hand flying to his head.

Knowing there was no sense in running, Frankie slowly took jerky backward steps, careful not to lose her footing. Hammer still in one hand, she unsheathed the claws of her other, waiting.

He glared at her, eyes cold, mouth twisted, blood running from his broken nose. "You'll pay for—" He stiffened. They could both hear the mad rumbling of a car engine and the squealing of tires.

She smiled. "Here comes Trick."

His eyes widened as he peeked outside. "Fuck!" He looked like he might make another grab for her, so she swung the hammer once more. She missed. But he swore and—clearly deciding she was more trouble than she was worth—scrambled into his car and reversed out of the studio fast. Then he sped away, out of sight, leaving a cloud of dirt in his wake.

Letting the hammer drop to the floor with a clang, she hobbled to the doorway and watched his car disappear down the road mere moments before an SUV paused just long enough for Trick to jump out. Then the SUV was gone, chasing the other vehicle.

Maybe it was the adrenaline crash or maybe it was the relief at seeing him, but both her legs gave out, and her ass hit the floor. Trick crouched in front of her and cupped her face. Even though his eyes were hard and his face was set into a mask of fury, she'd never felt safer.

Trick's heart slammed against his ribs as he got a good look at her. Her jaw was bruised, pain was etched into every line of her worryingly pale face, there was blood spatter on her clothes, and . . . "Fuck, why is blood dripping down your neck?"

She lifted her chin slightly so he could better see the puncture wounds. "His claws pricked my throat; the cuts aren't deep."

Trick saw that she was right, but it didn't calm him whatsofuckingever. His wolf predictably lost his shit and charged at Trick, demanding the freedom to stalk his mate's attacker. Trick fought him, focusing on Frankie. Vengeance could come later. "Where else are you hurt?"

"Leg. Ribs. Back of my head. I don't think I'm bleeding anywhere other than my neck."

"You're wrong," he growled as his hand gently probed the back of her skull and he felt a sticky warmth and one hell of a lump.

She winced. "Fucking ow."

Hating that he'd hurt her, he kissed her forehead. "I need to get a look at your stomach." He gently peeled up her T-shirt and spit a curse at the black-and-purple bruise that was starting to form. A growl vibrated his chest. "I'll kill him. I'll fucking kill him."

"It was Drake."

"I know. I can smell him." The scent of the bastard was driving his wolf almost as crazy as the scent of her blood. "Marcus is chasing his ass."

"He wanted to take me with him."

It struck Trick that if he'd been even a minute later, Drake would probably have had her in his grasp right then. That thought was enough to make his breath catch in his throat. "You said your leg was hurt. Which one?"

She gently touched her calf. "I don't know what's wrong with it. He clipped it with the car." She almost jerked in surprise as his claw sliced open the leg of her jeans without even grazing her skin. Damn, her calf was swollen and bruised, and she thought it was possible that the hit had fractured something. "Shit. Well, at least the sculptures are okay."

Trick did a slow blink. "What did you just say?"

"He drove his car in here—he came close to knocking over the hellhorse. That would have been bad."

He glared at her in pure disbelief. "Your *wounds* are bad." She was more important than any damn sculpture.

"Don't growl at me."

Closing his eyes, Trick inhaled through his nose. "Woman, you drive me insane." He straightened, and her hand shot out and grabbed his wrist. He cupped her chin. "Hey, I'm not going anywhere."

Frankie swallowed and let him go. "I know. I'm sorry. I don't know why I did that."

"You did it because some asshole just scared you out of your mind." Standing, he carefully scooped her up. "We're getting the fuck out of here. Taryn's a healer. She can help with your wounds."

"I need to lock up."

"I'll do that; let's just get you in the car first."

Frankie sighed. "Okay." She melted against him, shaking as the adrenaline drained from her system. As he cradled her close to his chest, he buried his face in her hair and inhaled her scent as they headed to her Audi. She felt light-headed and dizzy. Dammit, she would *not* faint. Newmans didn't faint. "You must have broken all kinds of laws to get here so fast."

"I didn't know what was happening; I just knew someone had come for you. I swear my fucking heart stopped—then it was pounding like crazy." It still hadn't calmed. "I heard you shout, I heard the car engine getting closer, and then the line went dead."

"That guy's not altogether sane, you know."

"Yeah, I know. He won't hurt you again. Never again." Trick settled her in the passenger seat of her Audi and, careful of her wounds, clicked on her seat belt. "Wait here." He quickly locked up the studio, found her phone, and secured the house. He was just adjusting the driver's seat to give himself more legroom when his cell rang. "That'll be Marcus." Trick dug out his phone and answered, "Tell me you have him."

A sigh. "I wish I could," said Marcus. "I lost him."

Trick growled, and his wolf lashed out in anger, raking Trick's insides with his claws. "How could you possibly have lost him?"

"He pulled up outside a big fucking building and ran inside," said Marcus. "I followed him in there and searched for him, but he'd just disappeared in the crowd. There were too many scents for me to find him."

"Smart," said Frankie, her shifter hearing picking up Marcus's words.

"I'll search his car before it gets towed and see if I can find anything that will tell us where he's staying—if Morelli's telling the truth that Drake split, that is."

Trick closed his eyes, seeking calm. "I have to go, Marcus, I'll talk to you later." Ending the call, he slipped his cell back into his pocket.

Hearing his teeth grinding, she patted his thigh with a shaky hand. "I'm okay." She couldn't quite stop trembling. "Really, I'm okay."

"No, you're not. But you will be." He switched on the ignition. "We're going home. Taryn will heal you."

Frankie sure hoped his Alpha female was good at what she did, because now that the adrenaline had faded from her system, the pain was starting to kick in. Her head throbbed like a bitch, her leg pulsed with pain, and the puncture marks on her neck stung like hell. Worse, every single breath hurt, thanks to what she suspected was a cracked rib. "Stop growling."

Trick couldn't. When they hit a road bump and she gasped in pain, he swore viciously. "Sorry, baby." As he drove, fury pulsed through his veins, threatening to steal the rationality that he was holding on to by a very thin thread.

He forced himself not to think of what had happened, to simply concentrate on the road so they didn't end up in a fucking car accident. But it was damn hard while the scent of her blood filled the small space.

Finally back on their territory, he carried her up the face of the cliff, hating every step he took because he knew each jostle hurt her. She didn't make a sound, though. She squeezed her eyes shut and shoved her face in his chest as one hand bunched up his T-shirt.

When he barged into the living area, everyone jumped to their feet like they'd been given a fucking electric shock.

"Shit, what happened?" demanded Jaime, her eyes wide.

"I'll explain everything once Frankie's healed," said Trick. "Her leg is fucked up, she has a cracked rib, and there's a goose egg on the back of her head with a slash that only just stopped bleeding. The puncture wounds on her neck have stopped bleeding as well. The bruise on her jaw has faded, but it's still a little swollen."

Lydia knotted her hand in her hair, eyes wide. "Oh my God."

"Trick, lay her on the floor," said Taryn, all business. "Ryan, open the window."

Trick carefully set Frankie down. "Just stay still, baby."

"Can't really go far on this leg anyway," she pointed out.

Taryn rested a hand on Frankie's forehead, and each of her wounds glowed through her skin.

Trick frowned at his mate. "You didn't tell me your shoulder was hurt."

"He yanked hard on my arm to pull me off the ground, but I'm pretty sure my shoulder isn't dislocated or anything."

"It was close," Taryn told her. Then she put her mouth to Frankie's, inhaled deeply, and turned to the window as she exhaled. A stream of black particles zoomed through the air and out the window. Then she did it again and again.

As Taryn healed his mate, Trick quickly and succinctly explained to the pack what had happened. "Call Morelli," he told Trey. "If I do it, there'll be nothing diplomatic about what comes out of my mouth, and I'll end up challenging the son of a bitch." And he didn't want to leave Frankie's side.

"Morelli said Drake's gone AWOL," Tao reminded them. "He might not have had anything to do with it."

Trick looked at the Head Enforcer. "But I'd settle for ripping out Morelli's throat in lieu of Drake's, which is why Trey needs to be the one who makes the call."

Their Alpha male nodded. "It'll be done."

"You know what will happen," said Dante. "Morelli will offer to find Drake, bring him in, and then hand him over to us, but only if you agree to an alliance."

"Fuck him." Taryn coughed and, done healing Frankie, sat back as she accepted a bottle of water from Grace. "He'll get nothing from us."

Trick helped his mate sit upright and checked her over, even though he knew each of her wounds would be gone. Until he saw for himself that she was fine, he couldn't relax.

"We can get to Drake without his help," said Ryan. "Besides, the guy's insane, but he's not completely stupid. He'll know that Morelli might make that kind of offer, so he'll keep his distance from him."

"I agree," said Trey. His gaze slid back to Trick as he vowed, "We'll find him. And we'll do it before he gets the chance to harm Frankie or anyone else."

Frankie blew out a breath. "I really wish the hammer had connected with his skull both times."

Trick blinked at his mate. "What?"

"After I broke his nose—"

"You broke his nose?"

"—I grabbed my hammer. But only the first hit connected. It hurt him, though, which fills me with glee. Still, it would have been more satisfying to have caved in the side of his skull." Realizing that everyone was staring at her, Frankie frowned. "What?"

Jaime gaped down at her. "You really broke his nose and hit him with a blunt instrument?"

"Clawed his face and stabbed him in the lower stomach too," said Frankie.

Lydia looked down at her niece in disbelief. "You look so sweet, it's just hard imagining you swinging a hammer at someone's head."

Frankie opened her mouth to speak, but then Trick took her off guard by suddenly scooping her off the floor and stalking out of the room. "I can walk," she said. His response was a low growl—the sound seemed to come from both the man and the animal. She rubbed his chest, hoping to pet the anger out of him. His muscles were so tight with tension, she wondered if they ached. His blood pressure was probably through the roof.

He didn't put her down until they were inside his room. She grimaced as she said, "I badly need a shower." She was covered in dried blood, which was no one's definition of fun, and she knew that Trick had no chance of calming while the scent of her blood was in the air. He seemed to be barely holding on to his control.

He didn't respond to her announcement other than by giving a short nod. It hurt her to see him standing there, muscles stiff and eyes fevered, caught up in a mood so dark that she wasn't sure anyone could reach him right then—not even her. She knew all about needing space when you were angry, so, figuring that time on his own might help, she took a quick shower and scrubbed all the blood off her skin and out of her hair.

Afterward she wrapped a fluffy towel around herself and headed back into the bedroom . . . only to find Trick pacing up and down like a caged animal, neck corded, stare unblinking. His muscles weren't quite so rigid, but it was clear that he was still far from calm.

He didn't even look her way as she pulled on a T-shirt, panties, and shorts. She was just done brushing the tangles out of her wet hair when, still pacing, he finally spoke.

"Later we'll go back to your place, pack your shit, and bring it all here."

Frankie's head snapped up. She figured she should have seen that coming. "Trick, I—"

"You're moving here." His tone left no room for negotiation. "It's time, Frankie."

"You know I can't until—"

Trick rounded on her. *"That asshole knows where you live,"* he ground out, fists clenched. "What's to stop him going back for you? It's not enough that you're here most nights. He could still do something cruel like set fire to the fucking house."

Horror struck her at the thought. "Oh my God, he'd destroy my sculptures."

Trick's eyes blazed at her. "Could we forget about them for one damn second?"

"No, they're important—"

"I know." Trick cupped her face with hands that trembled slightly with rage. "I know that a piece of your soul went into every single one of them. That is all the more reason to bring them here, where he can't get to them. Most importantly, *you* need to be here, where he can't get to *you*."

He should have killed Drake when he'd had the chance, Trick thought. Should have bludgeoned him with the steel bar. No, too quick. He should have held his head in the toilet until his lungs filled with fluid and the life left his body. "Your moving here is going to happen at some point, Frankie. There's no reason why it can't be sooner rather than later." He made an effort to soften his voice as he asked, "Would it really be so bad?"

She sighed. "No. Look, I understand that it must be driving you crazy that you haven't claimed me yet; I know I'm not giving you what you need."

"You're all I need."

"But I'm not giving you the level of commitment that you rightfully want. And I know the urge to claim me has to be riding you hard, but—"

"I can wait to claim you. But while I do, I want you here, with me. Here, where you and your wolf are happy. Here, where the Newmans can't turn up and give you shit. Here, *where Drake can't reach you*."

She jutted out her chin. "I'm not moving until the hellhorse is finished. I can't. It's not stable enough to be moved yet."

Hating that he had to respect that, Trick inhaled deeply and took a moment to think. "You said it would take a couple of days to finish the sculpture. While you work on that, the pack will help me move whatever you want to take with you, including the sculptures that can already be moved. I'll put them in your studio here."

"But—"

"I know you're still hoping that you can fix things with your uncle and grandparents," he said, striving to sound sensitive. "I know you're worried that if you move here, they'll see it as you choosing a side. But they're not stupid, Frankie. They're well aware that you'll come to live on pack territory for the simple reason that we're mates. You can't win with them, no matter what you do. I learned that for myself today."

She narrowed her eyes. "What does that mean?"

He slid his hands from her face down to her shoulders. "I met with Brad earlier."

"Brad as in my uncle?"

"He sent me an e-mail, asking to meet me alone." Trick raised a hand when her eyes flared with anger. "I didn't tell you because you would have insisted on coming, and then I wouldn't have found out whatever it was that he wanted to say because he'd have minded his words in front of you."

"And what *did* he want to say?" She clenched her hands when he hesitated. "Trick, tell me." So he told her. And she gawked. "He offered you fifty thousand dollars to walk away from me?" Her wolf went stock-still.

"He said he was doing it at Marcia's request, but he was lying. That was all him. She might have known about it—if she did, she'd probably even approved of it—but bribing me was his idea." Trick rubbed at his jaw. The damn thing ached from how hard he'd ground his teeth. "He also did a background check on me. He found out about Jana—though he'd been told that she was truly my mate—and he threatened to tell you, thinking it would make me walk away so that you'd never have to know."

Frankie should have been angry at the news. Instead the swell of emotions inside her just . . . deflated, leaving only the ache of betrayal. She wouldn't have thought that Brad would ever do something so sly and devious—it seemed so out of character for him. But then, he'd lied to her all these years, hadn't he? So maybe she shouldn't be so surprised.

Trick tugged her closer. "I didn't want to tell you about this, because I knew how much it would hurt you. But there shouldn't be lies between mates. I won't keep things from you."

"You kept it from me until *now*. Yes, I know why. I also can't disagree that you made a valid point: I would have insisted on going. He would never have said any of that shit in front of me."

The pain in her eyes gutted Trick. He rested his forehead on hers. "I hate that they do this to you."

Yeah, so did Frankie. She backed away, swallowing hard. "I'm going to sit out on the balcony for a while." He moved so silently that she didn't even realize he'd followed her until he took the patio chair beside hers.

At the impatient look she tossed at him, Trick raised his hands. "I won't touch you, I won't speak to you, but I also won't leave you on your own. I'm here if you want to talk. If you don't, that's fine. But I don't want you to be alone, so don't ask me to move."

She turned her gaze to the scenery. "Awkward fucker."

"I've been called worse." As he'd promised, Trick didn't say a word as she simply sat there, facing the view, her gaze focused inward. That promise became harder to keep the longer she didn't move. He didn't know what was going on in her pretty little head, and he worried that it was something he wasn't going to like.

Still, he kept his mouth shut and didn't reach out to touch her as he so badly wanted to. No, not wanted. *Needed.* Not just to calm and reassure himself that she was physically fine, but because the drive to soothe pounded through him. He hated that she was hurting, hated that he couldn't avenge that hurt.

His wolf wanted the freedom to hunt, mangle, and kill. Wanted to see and smell and taste Drake's blood. Not even his mate's presence was calming him or—

She straightened in her chair and twisted to face him. "Get ready."

Trick blinked. "For what?"

"It should hit us any minute now."

"What do you—?" Red-hot arousal slammed into him and flooded his system. Just like that, his blood thickened, his body tightened, and his cock filled to bursting. And then the drive to soothe her disappeared, completely drowned out by the urge to take and claim and *mate*. He double-blinked. "Fuck."

She swallowed, her mouth suddenly bone-dry. "Yeah, we need to fuck."

CHAPTER THIRTEEN

They collided. Frankie didn't remember getting to her feet. One second she'd been sitting on the chair, needing him so badly it hurt; the next thing she knew they were both standing upright and he was kissing the breath from her lungs.

Growling and groaning, they clawed off each other's clothes. She fisted his cock—it was long and thick and warm—and began to pump. He thrust into her grip, sucking on her pulse and grunting into her neck.

She wanted his cock in her mouth. Needed him to feel her mouth around him. It was a primal thing she couldn't quite explain, but it was all tied up in this undying need to brand him as hers.

Not much took Trick off guard, but he'd been so caught up in Frankie's taste that he almost stumbled when she suddenly dropped to her knees. Her lips closed around the head of his cock, and her tongue licked and danced. "Suck," he rumbled. But she didn't. She ran her tongue along his length and lapped up the drop of pre-come. He growled. "I said suck it, not play with it."

She finally took him in her mouth, and Trick fisted her hair. "Perfect for bunching in my hands while I fuck your mouth." He pumped his hips, mesmerized by the sight of his cock disappearing between her lips over and over. "You still look so innocent, even with your mouth wrapped around my dick." She swallowed, and her throat contracted around him. "Jesus. You're going to make me come. I'm not ready yet." He stilled his hips and tugged on her hair. "Get up." The moment she was upright, he propped her on the patio table. "Lay back and spread your legs. My turn."

Frankie shook her head. She loved his fingers and his tongue, but she didn't have the patience for foreplay. Her pussy throbbed and ached. She wanted him in her, fucking her, claiming her.

Trick arched a brow. "I want the taste of you in my mouth. You can give it to me or I can take it." Her eyes narrowed, but she lay back and spread her thighs. "Good girl." He sank two fingers inside her. "Soaking wet."

Frankie gripped the edges of the table as he lifted her hips and swiped his tongue through her folds. He growled, and his fingers bit into her as he feasted. He didn't just lick and nip, he sucked at her folds, swirled the tip of his tongue around her clit, and repeatedly stabbed his tongue inside her. The friction built, wound her tighter and tighter, until she just couldn't take any more. "Trick . . ." It was a warning. She was going to come.

Trick hooked her legs over his shoulders, sucked a nipple into his mouth, and plunged deep into her pussy. And she came. He ground his teeth, fighting the urge to explode along with her. His cock throbbed inside her, as if objecting to him holding back.

Panting, Frankie practically melted against the table. That had been one hell of an orgasm, but her pussy still ached. She got the feeling that the mating urge wouldn't cool until he'd come deep inside her. "Fuck me."

"Oh, I'll fuck you all right." He drew back until only the head of his cock was inside her, and then he slammed home. Her pussy clamped around him, so wet and tight it was sheer fucking heaven. And Trick lost all pretense of control. He brutally hammered into her. And that was no exaggeration. He'd been fighting the drive to claim her for weeks, and all that frustration poured out of him in a frenzy of violent thrusts. "Tell me to stop." Hearing her say it would be the only thing that could ease that frenzy.

She shook her head, eyes glinting with panic. "No, don't stop. God, don't stop."

Fuck. He kept on powering into her, branding her with every possessive stroke, driven by the need to claim and his wolf's determination to take and own. "You looked so fucking good with my cock in your mouth. You'll take it again. But next time, I'll come down your throat." Her pussy squeezed and fluttered around him.

As he stared down at her—taking in the gorgeous tattoos, the hot little piercing, the way her tits jiggled with each thrust, and the way her eyes glazed over—he felt his own release closing in on him.

He leaned over her. "Bite me," he growled. "Mark me, Frankie." He knew that the moment he sank his own teeth into her skin, the moment he finally claimed what belonged to him, his cock would fucking detonate. He didn't want to be midorgasm and half out of his mind when she claimed him; he wanted to feel every second of it. "Do it," he growled.

Needing it as badly as he did, Frankie reared up and bit down hard on the crook of his neck, drawing blood—she sucked and licked, branding him, just as her wolf demanded.

"Fuck, baby." He sucked her pulse into his mouth, felt it beating there hard and fast, and he sank his teeth down hard enough to break the skin. His release slammed into him, and he roughly rammed his cock deep as he exploded. Her pussy contracted around him as a scream tore from her throat and she came. All the while, he sucked and licked to leave that definite mark that would never fade, that would declare to the world that she belonged to him.

He collapsed over her, shuddering and gasping for breath. "Baby—" White-hot pain stabbed his head and pierced his chest. His breath seemed to stutter, and his vision dimmed. Beneath him, her back briefly arched, and then a gasp of wonder flew out of her. He knew why—because the pain quickly smoothed away as the mating bond now pulsed between them.

Satisfaction. Relief. Awe. Each emotion ballooned inside him. He'd known that the bond would make him feel utterly complete—she was the other half of his soul. But nothing could have prepared him for just how powerful the bond truly was. It soothed and anchored him. Gave him a sense of home that even his pack had never given him.

Trick cupped her face, stroking his thumb along her cheekbone and enjoying the soul-deep knowledge that this creature was and would always be his. No one would ever take her from him. No one. Never again. "You okay?"

"Uh-huh." Frankie didn't need to ask how he was feeling; masculine satisfaction and contentment buzzed down the bond, touching her mind as clearly as the pads of his fingers touched her face.

She hadn't expected to be able to feel the bond so strongly, but it was as much a part of her as her limbs. She felt Trick everywhere, as if she now wore him as a second skin—it was hard to explain. She felt . . . centered. Balanced. Whole. Knew this bond would settle and steady her in a way that nothing else ever could have. Equally happy and tranquil, her wolf stretched out, lazy with utter contentment.

As his cock slipped out of her, Trick lifted her in his arms and carried her inside the room. Gently he lay her on the bed, keeping her close. "Now you're irrevocably mine."

He sounded so smug about it, but she was way too relaxed to care. She snuggled into him and doodled on his chest with her fingers. "I didn't intend to leave you, bond or no bond."

Trick almost snorted. He wouldn't have let her leave him. He kissed her gently, sipping from her mouth. He liked her this way, muscles loose and limp, eyes heavy lidded and languid. "What brought that on? What made you reach for the bond?" he asked.

"It was a couple of things."

Realizing she was tracing her name on his skin with her finger, he smiled. "Such as?"

"Well, I was sitting there, thinking of everything you told me, and I had to face that you were right. I wouldn't find a way to make everyone happy. I had to do what was right for me and my wolf. I knew she was testing you to see if you were worthy, but I didn't really understand it. Not until I realized she was ready to be claimed."

"She was ready?"

"Not until today. You see, growing up, I didn't have other shifters in my life. My maternal family didn't fully accept me, and they sure as hell didn't accept my wolf. She and I only really had each other. I was her protector, and she was mine. I guess she wasn't prepared to give up that job unless it was to someone she felt could and would truly protect me. You did it when my grandfather came to my house. You did it at the funeral, when people were crowding me and I needed to get away. And you did it again today, when you scared Drake away and stayed with me. The whole staying-with-me part seemed to mean more to her."

"It was important to her that you were my priority," said Trick, understanding. "She needed to know that I'd put you first—including before my own anger and my own thirst for vengeance." Because no one had put Frankie first in a very long time. He appreciated that her wolf was so protective of her, and it humbled him that the animal trusted him with Frankie.

"Although all those things you did meant something to me too, I was still holding on to the hope that I could make each side of my family accept the other. But then you told me what Brad did, and I realized that I was going to have to choose." She rubbed her thumb over the brand she'd left on his neck, but she kept her eyes locked with his. "I chose you and whatever comes with you."

Curving his hand around her nape, Trick kissed her. Consumed her. Relished the knowledge that she'd chosen him. He rested his forehead against hers. "I'm going to be hell to live with until the mating bond snaps fully into place. Even more ridiculously possessive and hyperprotective than I was before. I won't like other males getting too close to you, especially if they're unmated. My wolf will be just as intense about all this. Be patient with us."

"I can't promise that." Frankie wasn't known for her patience. "When will the bond fully snap into place?"

"When you let go of whatever's blocking it."

She frowned. "I'm not holding back from you."

"No, but you're holding back slightly from the bond."

Frankie's frown deepened as she thought on it. "I'm not doing it on purpose." She tried to undo it, tried to figure why it was happening, but she couldn't. "Seriously, Trick, I don't mean to hold back. I don't know how to fix it."

"Shh, don't panic." Trick kissed her. "Give it time. We'll work out what it is, and we'll take care of it. But this isn't something that can be rushed." He lapped at his mark. There was a world of difference between knowing she was his and having that assurance that she was irreversibly his. That assurance both steadied and energized him. It was better than any drug. "I say we go outside and let our wolves run together."

Frankie smiled. "She likes that idea." As his hand slid from her nape to the back of her head where the wound had been, Frankie said, "It's gone."

"I know." But Trick would never let it go. "I'll make him pay," he promised her.

"Okay. But can you fuck me again first?"

He smiled. "I don't see why not." He rolled on top of her, hiked her leg up, and smoothly drove inside his mate.

It took three days for Frankie to finish the hellhorse sculpture, but it was a further two days before she was willing to move it; she needed to be sure that the glue was dry. Trick hadn't been happy about the delay, but he'd surprised her by not voicing his frustration. During that time he and some of the other Phoenix wolves had gradually moved her things to pack territory, including her completed sculptures.

She'd originally planned to sell the house, but Makenna asked if she would be willing to rent it out to a female from the shelter. Frankie agreed and intended to leave much of the furniture for her new tenant, who wouldn't be moving into the house until the Drake situation had been taken care of.

According to Trey, Morelli had sounded pissed on hearing that Drake had harmed her. So pissed, in fact, that he'd cut the asshole completely loose. Once again, Drake was a lone shifter. Or so Morelli said, anyway. Neither Frankie nor Trick was convinced of that.

When the day finally arrived that the sculpture could be moved, Trick and some of the Phoenix wolves came to help Frankie pack up the last of her things and take her equipment from the studio. That was no doubt why Abigail looked completely perplexed when Marcus escorted her into the garden, where Frankie was supervising Ryan and Tao as they disassembled the hot tub—Trick wanted that for their balcony.

Frankie smiled at her agent. "Hey."

Abigail glanced at the males taking apart the tub. "You're moving, Frankie?"

"Yeah. I forgot to mention it on the phone." More accurately, she'd been a little distracted by Trick's tongue stabbing into her pussy. "This is Ryan and Tao, by the way."

The antisocial Ryan did no more than grunt. Tao, not a fan of humans or anyone outside his pack, merely inclined his head.

"Where are you moving to?" Abigail asked her. "Please say New York, because it will mean I don't need to keep flying over here to see you. And who is that guy who just escorted me out here?"

Frankie led her into the kitchen as she explained. "Marcus is a friend of mine. I'm not moving to New York, sorry. I'm staying in California. I'm actually moving to shifter territory."

Abigail's mouth fell open. "Shifter territory?"

"Yes. I found my mate. We've claimed each other. A lot of stuff has gone on and, um, well, it's a long story."

Abigail settled on a stool. "I have time." After Frankie told her everything, her agent shook her head. "Wow. Do your grandparents know that the wolf claimed you?"

"Not yet. But they'll know it's pretty much inevitable. I haven't heard or seen anything of them for a while now."

"And this guy, Trick, is good to you?"

Frankie nodded. "Very. He badly wanted to claim me from the start, just like any shifter would do if they found their mate. But he was so patient with me. Didn't push. Didn't try to make me pick a side. I sensed he was getting impatient, but he never showed it."

"You love him," Abigail whispered.

"Maybe."

Abigail lightly tapped a hand on the table. "Well, I'd like to meet him before you show me your latest sculpture. Is he here?"

"Yep. He's in the studio." Frankie walked ahead of her as they made their way into the studio, where he and a few others were moving the last of her equipment. "Trick?"

He turned to her, and his eyes softened. "Hey, baby, what do you need?"

"This is Abigail, my agent." An agent who was currently looking a little tongue-tied. Frankie could hardly blame her, given that Trick had whipped off his shirt and there was a whole lot of muscle to admire.

Draping his arm around Frankie's shoulders, Trick gave the human a nod. "Frankie speaks highly of you."

Shaking off her stupor, Abigail said, "Well, she's just spoken very highly of you."

His mouth curved. "Good to know." He moved aside so he was no longer blocking her view of the sculpture. "Impressive, right?"

Abigail's brows lifted. "Well." She crossed to the hellhorse and slowly circled it, taking in every detail. "It's fantastic, Frankie. Really, I don't know whether to feel happy for the creature for escaping its chains, or whether I should be worried about what it will do to avenge itself. It makes you wonder if it was chained for a good reason." She twirled to face Frankie, eyes alight. "You never fail to astonish me. I love it. It will fit in perfectly with the theme of the art show."

Just like that, Trick decided he liked Abigail a fuck of a lot. The fervor of her praise and admiration was genuine. It was also exactly what Frankie deserved. Her appreciation and relief hummed down their bond, and he knew that her agent's opinion didn't just matter to her on a professional level. She considered Abigail her friend, and the human's judgment meant something to her.

Packing up the sculpture wasn't a quick or easy process, but they all pitched in so that both the creepy kid and the hellhorse could be transported to New York at the same time.

Later, as Frankie unpacked the last of her things in their room on pack territory, Trick came up behind her and slid his arms around her waist. He dabbed a kiss on her claiming mark, breathing her in. He fucking loved her scent; he wanted it mixed with his own.

"That's me all moved in," she told him, closing the drawer that he'd cleared out for her. "Happy now?"

"Ecstatic." He sucked on her earlobe, splaying his hand possessively on her stomach. "Now you're exactly where you belong." Her head tipped back as he licked, kissed, and nipped at her neck, paying particular attention to his claiming mark. He snaked his hand under her shirt and traced the tattoo he knew as well as the back of his hand. "You're damn distracting." He tapped her ass and stepped back. "Come on, time for dinner."

Breathing a little hard, she scowled as she pivoted to face him. "Hey, you can't get a girl all revved up and then not follow through."

"I'm hungry."

"So am I." But not for food.

Trick smiled and sucked her bottom lip into his mouth. "Later, I'll be doing all kinds of very dirty things to you. Right now, we eat."

She groaned, dragging her heels as he led her out of the room. "You can't say shit like that when I'm horny."

"Of course I can, baby."

"Asshole." She slammed the door behind them, giving emphasis to her insult.

"So you often say." Keeping his fingers linked with hers, he kept her close as they walked through the tunnels. A few days ago, when he'd announced to the pack that he and Frankie were officially mated, they had all been overjoyed. He'd sensed Frankie's surprise at just how happy they'd been. He'd realized then that although she'd known they wanted her living on their territory, she hadn't realized just how much they'd all come to like and respect her. Probably because she simply didn't expect people to like her much.

He blamed her grandparents for that. In making her feel that she lacked, they'd left her with some self-esteem issues. He was proud that, despite all that, she was a confident female who went after what she wanted in life. Was proud that she was his mate.

"Okay, now that I can smell food, my appetite is building," said Frankie. "But I still think a quickie wouldn't have been a bad idea."

"We don't have quickies, Frankie. We try, but it never quite works out." He always got too carried away in her, always needed to taste and touch as much of her as he could.

"I can't really deny that." She'd taken one step into the kitchen when she jumped out of her freaking skin as a bunch of voices shouted, "Surprise!"

The whole pack was gathered there, smiling, raising glasses, and blowing party poppers. Behind them on the wall was a large banner that read "Welcome Home, Frankie!" There was a huge cake on the table in the center of an impressive spread of food. And damn if a lump of emotion didn't build in her throat.

Trick draped his arm over her shoulders and kissed her temple. "It's an official welcome to the pack."

Frankie bit her lip. "I don't know what to say, except . . . wow."

Laughing, Taryn came forward, shoved a glass of something bubbly in Frankie's hand, and said, "Come on, let's get absolutely hammered and torment Greta."

CHAPTER FOURTEEN

I t was the soft murmurs that tugged Frankie out of sleep. Or maybe it was the mouth pressing light kisses to the palm of her hand. Both of those things would have been fine if she hadn't woken with the hangover from hell.

Her eyes throbbed, her stomach churned, her body seemed drained of energy, and her head—oh God, her head. Apparently she'd chugged down cosmos like they would grant her the gift of eternal life.

Her mouth was dry as a damn bone. She licked her lower lip. Tasted something. Toothpaste crust. Awesome.

"Time to wake up, baby," Trick whispered, one hand smoothing the hair from her face.

"Turn the light off," she slurred. Because it made her feel like someone was stabbing the backs of her eyeballs with toothpicks.

"No lights are on."

"Then close the curtains." She tried tugging the covers over her head, but she only managed to flap her hand.

Trick softly chuckled. "You need to get up. It's past noon."

She wasn't moving from the bed. Ever. Nuh-uh. She wasn't fit to be seen anyway. She'd had enough killer hangovers to know that she probably looked like a reject from *The Walking Dead*. She *felt* like a reject.

Another light kiss to her palm. "I'd pegged you for a lightweight, but it took countless drinks before the alcohol seemed to actually hit you."

Why was he talking? Did she look like she was capable of conversation right then? Her wolf snapped her teeth at him, warning him to go away and leave her to recover. But the bastard didn't.

"Come on, baby. I'll help you up."

She moaned. "Dying. Get. Priest."

Trick's body shook, and his amusement buzzed down their bond. "Open your eyes for me, Frankie."

She tried, but the light stabbed her eyeballs. Rookie mistake. "Just let me die in peace," she begged. She didn't want him there, laughing at her. She wanted painkillers. Frankie + Tylenol = BFFs.

Trick kissed her bare shoulder, wondering if he should tell her that not only did she have supremely bad bedhead, but her makeup was smeared all over her face. It could motivate her to get into the shower, but it could just as easily motivate her into hiding under the covers.

He was surprised that she hadn't spent the night vomiting, given how many cosmos and beers she'd consumed. She'd only thrown up once, just before she tumbled into dreamland. "I almost had to tie you to the bed last night. After you yacked in the bathroom, you declared you wanted to go to Taco Bell. You were adamant about it, so I said that if you rested for ten minutes, I'd take you. Thankfully, you fell asleep."

Frankie squeezed her eyes shut. No, that hadn't happened. It hadn't. It couldn't have. Fuck, that had actually happened! Oh, she was 100 percent sad. Just. Sad. That much was totally without question.

Trick lifted the glass from the nightstand. "Here. Drink this."

"Will it help me die quicker?"

"It's water."

Water . . . Oh, that sounded good. She couldn't take the bitter taste in her mouth much longer. Carefully lifting her head, she waited until the urge to gag faded and then slowly sat upright. He put the glass to her lips, and she sipped at the water, almost tearing up with happiness when he placed two Tylenol in her hand.

She swallowed them, studying him through squinty eyes. He'd clearly showered and dressed. The bastard looked fresh and . . . *alert*. How was that even possible? Her memories were fuzzy, but she did remember him drinking several beers. "Why aren't you hungover?"

He shrugged. "I don't really get hangovers."

"I despise you right now."

His mouth curved. "You love me. You know it. You just feel awkward saying it."

Her spine would have snapped straight if her body didn't badly lack energy. "My, my, my, aren't we full of ourselves?" Not that he was wrong.

He just chuckled. "You need to get up, showered, and dressed."

That would require fine motor skills, which meant it was a no-go. "Later," she mumbled. He pressed his fingertips to her temples and began a light massage. That confirmed it. He was an angel sent directly from heaven. "My eyes are bloodshot, aren't they?"

"Yep. But they're still beautiful," he said gently.

She grunted. "I remember somebody crying. It wasn't me, was it?"

His mouth twitched into a smile. "No, it wasn't you. It was Greta. Roni managed to get her smashed, and—for just a few hours—the woman was almost well adjusted. You don't remember singing 'Greased Lightning' with her on the karaoke?"

"Now you're just lying."

"It's true," he said, chuckling.

"Another lie." But his words did tug at a memory she *never* wanted to access, for the sake of her own sanity. "I do remember Taryn and Jaime setting up the karaoke in the living area. And I remember Dominic sang 'Livin' on a Prayer' while all the females cheered him on like it was a concert."

Trick gave her a look filled with sympathy. "Baby, you were one of those females. In fact, you were leading the 'Dominic Brigade.'" He'd have been jealous if it hadn't been so damn ridiculous. Even his wolf had been amused.

"I was not. Why was Greta crying?"

"Because she was so happy that her boys had found themselves mates that were worthy of them. Or at least that's what she said."

Frankie gaped. "No!"

"Oh yeah. You don't remember wiping her tears with the bottom of your shirt?"

"No. For which I'm glad."

"You also took some selfies of you both, pouting like supermodels."

"Stop lying!"

Trick laughed. "It's not a lie. Check your cell phone."

"Later." Once she was in a state where she could handle the shame.

"Yes, later. Now you need to shower."

He helped her out of bed, but she still swayed. Bracing her hand on the wall, she said, "I'm okay. I've got this."

She showered and dressed, every movement clunky and lazy and *pitiful*. Then she was walking alongside him through the tunnels, her footsteps dragging, her arms hanging loose at her sides. Leaving her bed had truly been a mistake. At first she'd felt a little better. Now she was back to wanting to curl up on the floor and die.

As they neared the kitchen, the smell of greasy food made her stomach roll. But her attention was on the sound of someone crying. No, a *recording* of someone crying.

"I love you, Taryn," sobbed Greta. "I really do. I should have told you that before."

A loud voice overrode the recording. "*That* is not me."

"Greta, it's a *video*," said Taryn. "We can all see you on it, clear as day."

"It's not me," Greta insisted.

"*Woman, we know what you look like.*"

At that moment Frankie and Trick walked into the kitchen. Heads turned their way, and several pairs of bloodshot eyes met theirs. It made her feel slightly better to know that she wasn't the only one suffering . . . though she had to admit that none of them looked quite as bad as her.

Lydia winced. "Damn, sweetie, I thought *I* looked like shit."

Frankie wanted to speak, but all that came out was a grunt.

Trick sighed and spoke to Lydia. "Frankie's body is here. She is not."

Asshole.

A few hours later, Grace suggested a pack run. Everybody, including the kids, went along. The wolves all padded through the woods, ambushing one another and play fighting. Riley's raven repeatedly dive-bombed Greta and circled the kids to make them laugh.

After a while they all settled in a small clearing. Some rested on the ground or lapped at the river, while others pounced and wrestled each other to the ground. Savannah dangled from a tree branch and threw acorns at the other kids—Dexter then collected the acorns and either put them in his pocket or tossed them in the river.

Frankie's wolf sprawled on the ground, enjoying the heat of the sun. Her mate stayed close at all times, protective and possessive. Whenever he crowded her too much, she snapped her teeth. He either licked at her jaw in apology or growled in frustration.

Hours later, when she shifted back into her human form, Frankie was feeling a lot better. Which was a good thing, since she'd previously agreed to have dinner at Clara's house that evening. The invite had also been extended to Trick, Lydia, and Cam, so all four of them hopped into the SUV, and Trick drove them to Bjorn Pack territory.

Honestly, Frankie was a little nervous. Not just because she had no idea if Clara's sons would be there, but also because it still felt weird to be around relative strangers who treated her as though she were one of their family.

Clara's cabin wasn't far from Iris's. Neatly planted flowers surrounded it, some exotic, some common. The floral scents gave the place a restful, welcoming feel.

Clara eagerly ushered them inside and kissed their cheeks, chattering happily. Looking around, Frankie saw that the decor was earthy and rustic, full of antiques and knickknacks. Clara had good taste.

While the home was smaller than Iris's cabin, Frankie couldn't help but note that she didn't feel cramped, whereas the house she'd grown up in was three times this size, yet she'd felt more confined in that house than she had anywhere else.

Frankie couldn't have been more relieved to hear that Clara's sons wouldn't be there. The scents of lavender, lacquered wood, and sizzling-hot food also went a long way to putting her at ease. And when Clara and Cesar sensed that Frankie and Trick were mated, they were so delighted that more of her tension slipped away.

Everyone talked and laughed at the dining table. All the while, the TV played low in the background since, as Cesar told his mate, "If I can't watch the game, I can at least listen to it from here."

Trick was constantly touching Frankie—toying with the ends of her hair, rubbing his jaw against her temple, pressing light kisses to her cheek, skimming his fingers over the back of her hand—reassuring her that he was there, that she wasn't alone, and keeping her wolf steady.

Aside from the moment where she almost knocked her wine over, everything went pretty well. The food was *spectacular*. For their first course, they had tomato soup with hot, freshly baked rolls. The second course was steak, ribs, fried onions, and chunky fries with a side salad. For dessert Clara brought out a Mississippi mud pie in honor of Iris, as it had been a favorite of hers.

Before anyone could cut the pie, Lydia piped up. "Wait!" She pulled out her cell phone. "I have to snap a picture of this to show Grace. She'll think it's amazing."

The ice tinkled against the glass as Clara lifted her drink and said, "I noticed that you and Trick were close, Frankie, but I didn't think you were mates. I was so caught up with what was happening with Iris that I wasn't really paying much attention. Did she know?"

Frankie nodded. "I told her."

A smile curled Clara's mouth. "I'm glad. That will have eased her worries for you. We talked about you during her last few days, and she said how wonderful you were. She was proud of the person you've become. It broke her heart that you'd felt so alone all these years. I know you had your maternal relatives, but a wolf without a pack can often feel very lonely."

"I suppose they weren't happy to hear you've moved to pack territory," guessed Cesar.

Frankie bit her lower lip. "They don't know yet." Under the table, Trick rested his hand on her knee and gave it a comforting squeeze.

Cesar sighed. "I'm sorry that things have worked out this way, Frankie, and you've been forced to choose, but I can't be sorry for their sake. They caused Iris a lot of pain when they kept you from her."

Feeling unexpectedly defensive of them, she said, "They're not awful people."

"Of course they're not." Clara cut into the pie and began serving everyone pieces. "They love you, Frankie. Always have. I must admit, I was initially worried that they wouldn't accept you at all."

"Why?" asked Cam, taking the word right out of Frankie's mouth.

"We were overjoyed when we heard Caroline was pregnant," said Clara. "It never occurred to me that they might not be so pleased. But I found her sitting under her willow tree behind her cabin, crying. They were already upset with her for giving up her teacher's job, even though she'd been unhappy at the school, and she thought that hearing she was pregnant might appease them. It didn't."

Lydia sighed. "They'd hoped she'd one day leave Christopher."

Confused, Frankie said, "But my parents were *mated*."

"Yes, but I don't think the Newmans quite understand the concept of true mates." Cesar paused, stroking his mustache. "In fact, I don't think they want to understand."

Clara nodded, but she didn't speak until she'd swallowed the food she was chewing. "Iris once told me that she overheard Caroline telling her mother how amazing it was to find and bond with the other half of your soul—that she felt complete. Her mother told her not to be so adolescent and foolish, said there was no such thing as soul mates and that Caroline needed to wake up and see that she didn't belong here."

Sounds like something Marcia would say, Frankie thought as she forked up some pie.

"I don't believe that your grandmother is a bad person," Clara went on. "Not at all. But I think she felt like she was losing Caroline. Her daughter used to live quite close to her. Suddenly she was living on pack territory, surrounded by other people and madly in love with a male who had a bond with her that no other connection could ever surpass."

Trick draped his arm over the back of Frankie's chair and drew circles on her shoulder. "Marcia felt threatened by the mating bond."

"Brad seemed to feel the same way," said Cesar. "Christopher was an interloper in their eyes. I'm not sure how much Brad understood about true mates, but I know his parents didn't believe in any kind of metaphysical bond. They thought Caroline could walk away from Christopher if she ever chose to do so. They thought he'd brainwashed her into believing that she was stuck with him. Nothing Caroline said seemed to make any difference."

Clara caught Frankie's gaze as she said, "Although your grandparents weren't pleased about the pregnancy, they *doted* on you. Didn't they, Cesar?"

"Oh yes," he agreed. "They were so proud, especially as you looked the image of Caroline when she was a child. They even softened toward Christopher, after a while. Unfortunately, Brad didn't. He remained very hostile toward your father, but he loved you. 'My Frankie,' Brad called you."

Finished with her pie, Clara dabbed her mouth with a soft napkin. "The point I'm trying to make is that there were always sides, even before your parents left this world. Caroline often felt torn and sad that she'd disappointed her family. But she made her decision to be with

Christopher; she stuck to it. Eventually they softened. Not completely, but enough that they didn't leave her life. Maybe they'll soften for you, in time. It may seem highly unlikely now, but it is possible."

Frankie wasn't all that convinced of that, but she gave a short nod. "Wendel said that Caroline took to pack life like she was a shifter."

Clara's smile turned nostalgic. "Oh, she did. The day Christopher brought her here, he was the envy of the pack. All the males were sweet on her. She was just so bright and hopeful and fresh, like an ethereal fairy. None of them ever poached, of course, but they did envy your father. She only had eyes for him, and vice versa."

Tilting her head slightly, Frankie asked, "Did anyone ever give him trouble over it?"

"Oh no. If your parents hadn't been true mates, it's possible that someone would have challenged him for her. But nothing could be gained from challenging a male for his true mate—to break the bond would be to kill her, so there would be no prize." Exhaling heavily, Clara shook her head sadly. "Everyone was devastated by her death. They were even devastated by Christopher's, despite what he'd done. He was one of us. We all loved him."

Frankie poked her tongue into the inside of her cheek. "Is it usual for pack members to own a gun?"

Cesar blinked. "No. We were surprised to find out that he possessed one. Josh has a rifle, but it's a keepsake of some kind; he doesn't use it. Doesn't need it. Shifters fight with tooth and claw, so there was no need for Christopher to own a gun. I think that was why some believed he was suicidal. But I don't believe he bought a firearm contemplating ending his own life. He had no reason to want to die. It didn't make sense."

Many things made no sense, in Frankie's opinion. "Do you have any of his things?"

"No, why?" asked Clara.

"I have some of my mom's things. Marcia gave them to me. I have Caroline's scent. But I don't have his."

Her face softened with understanding. "I'm pretty sure Iris boxed up his belongings and put them in her attic." Clara got up, disappeared into the den, and then quickly returned. "Here. This is the key to her cabin. You're welcome to take anything of his as a keepsake. Iris would want that, and so would he."

Taking the key, Frankie nodded. "Thank you."

"Me and Cam will wait here," Lydia told her. "You should have privacy for something like that. Well, obviously, you won't have *total* privacy—Trick will be with you. But I think you'd rather have him there anyway."

Frankie smiled. "Well, how else am I going to reach the high shelves, chase off spiders, or pick up heavy boxes?"

Snorting, Trick threaded his fingers with hers and then tugged her to her feet. "Come on. Let's get it done."

Clara followed them to the front door. "Oh, Frankie, you asked about the sculpture. It only occurred to me later that you may have been interested about it because it was one of yours—especially with it being somewhat creepy. Is that why you asked?" At Frankie's nod, she said, "Thought so. Well, I asked around, tried to find out who bought it. No one seems to know."

Veiling her disappointment, Frankie gave her a grateful smile. "All right. Thanks." Outside, she spoke to Trick. "Maybe Abigail can track the buyer of the sculpture. I'll ask her."

"Good idea." Trick walked her to the SUV. "You sure you want to do this?"

"I'm sure."

"All right." He opened the passenger door for her. "Get in."

Minutes later, they pulled up outside Iris's cabin. Except for the birds chirping and the leaves rustling, it was eerily quiet. She spared her childhood cabin a brief glance before crossing to Iris's front door. She unlocked it, but Trick stepped inside first—the protective move made her smile.

As she walked inside, her brows lifted. "I'm surprised no one has started packing up her stuff." Nothing appeared to have been disturbed.

"Lydia wanted to start straightaway, but Clara's not ready yet—she wants to give it a few weeks," Trick explained. "Lydia agreed to give her time." He led the way up the stairs and searched the ceiling until he found the hatch door for the attic. "Here it is." He shoved it open and extended the fold-down staircase. "I'll go first and make sure the ladder's stable."

Frankie rolled her eyes. "I think I'll be fine."

"Indulge me," he said, climbing up the wooden rungs. The ladder wobbled only slightly. Reaching the top, Trick glanced around the attic. He ignored the pull-string light. As shifters, they could see just fine in the dark. "Quick warning: it doesn't smell great up here."

"I can handle it," Frankie assured him. But when she joined him, she put her sleeve to her nose, grimacing at the scents of mold, mothballs, stale air, and mildew. Her wolf curled her upper lip in distaste. "I don't think anyone's been up here in a while." Rays of moonlight speared through the single window, illuminating the dust motes in the air.

"My wolf doesn't like the tight space."

"Neither does mine."

Trick stepped forward but then paused as a loose floorboard almost gave beneath his feet. "Let's not stay up here too long."

"Works for me." The dusty floorboards creaked as they walked, passing trunks, sheet-covered furniture, an old record player, children's toys, and sealed, labeled boxes. The sight of the cradle in the corner tugged a smile out of her.

She stubbed her toe on something and hissed. "Motherfucker." Looking down, she realized she'd almost knocked over a painting propped up against a large chest.

Crouching down, Trick took a good look at it. "This could be one of Christopher's. He liked to paint landscapes."

"Maybe this chest could have his old stuff in it, then," mused Frankie.

"Maybe." Trick moved the painting out of her way. "Want to do the honors yourself?"

"Yes." Crouching beside him, she flicked open the metal hinge and shoved up the heavy lid, wincing at the loud creak. The chest shook, and dust clouded the air. She turned her face away, covering her nose. "Damn."

"Hey, looks like you were right."

Frankie turned back to the chest. At the top was a framed portrait of a teenage Christopher. She looked at it for a moment and then carefully placed it on the floor. She flipped through the other items—there were clothes, books, baseball cards, sports medals, and . . . "Nice." She lifted the chain. At first the pendants looked like military dog tags. But then she realized that one of the tags was thicker than the other. "I think it's a locket."

"Open it."

Using her nail, she pried it open. There was a photo on either side—one of Caroline and one of Frankie as a toddler. Swallowing hard, she closed the locket and looked at the thinner dog tag. Engraved on it was "To the best mate a woman could wish for. Happy birthday, Chris."

When she went to return it to the chest, Trick gently shackled her wrist and said, "You should take the locket."

Her brow creased. "But—"

"Your parents would want you to have that, just as you would if the situation were reversed. This meant something to them, just as you do. Clara said you were welcome to take something as a keepsake."

"Yeah, but this is jewelry. It looks expensive."

"When people come to pack Iris's things, they'll take all this stuff too. A lot of it will be thrown away or donated to charity. Lydia would probably see this and keep it, but she'd then give it to you anyway. No one would begrudge you taking it."

She twisted her mouth, torn. Maybe she should ask Lydia first and—

Trick took it from her and shoved it in his pocket. "There. Now I've taken it. Your conscience is clear."

Frankie softly snorted in amusement. "If I wasn't busy, I'd make a citizen's arrest." She lifted one of Christopher's shirts to her nose. Beneath the smell of stale cotton was . . . "Earthy musk, dark chocolate orange, and . . . Caroline. I remember this smell." For some reason her eyes filled. "I didn't remember hers as clearly as I do his. That makes no sense. I have some of her old things."

"Yes, but those things probably belonged to her before she mated with Christopher, so her scent would be slightly different on those. You only knew your parents when their scents were intertwined," he pointed out.

Damn, she hadn't thought of it that way.

"If you were to find something that belonged to her *after* she mated with Christopher, her scent would then be as memorable to you as his is." Trick flicked a look at the shirt. "How do you feel when you inhale his scent?"

"It makes me feel safe and happy," she admitted in a low voice.

"Until the end, you were safe, and you were happy."

"Some think Christopher killed himself because he didn't want to live without her, but wouldn't he have died from the severing of the bond anyway?"

"Right. But most believe he wasn't thinking clearly. He was acting on pure emotion. Emotion can make you do stupid things. I always thought it was more likely that he pulled that trigger because he hated himself for what he'd done to your mother and just couldn't live with it a moment longer—that he didn't think he *deserved* to live a moment longer."

"Maybe." Dust tickled the back of her throat, and she coughed.

"Ready to go?"

"Yeah. I'm ready." She returned everything to the chest, secured it shut, and then stood upright. Rubbing her hands together to shake loose the dust, she said, "I'm glad I did this."

He gave her nape a light squeeze. "Good." Turning, Trick ducked, careful not to knock his head on a wooden beam, and then crossed to the ladder.

"Wait."

He glanced over his shoulder. "What?" But she didn't answer. She was staring at a huge cardboard box. He stalked to her side and saw that "Caroline's things" had been scribbled on the side of the box with a black marker. He also saw that someone had clawed through the masking tape, leaving the top flaps open. Peeking inside, he frowned. "There's nothing in there."

"Nothing?" Frankie looked in the box. "Why would someone take her stuff?"

He shrugged. "Maybe Iris sent whatever was in here to your grandparents. Just because they didn't give you anything of Caroline's from *after* she was mated doesn't mean that they don't actually have anything."

"I guess you're right." It just seemed odd to Frankie that the empty box had been left behind.

"Come on." He led the way out of the attic, closed the hatch behind them, and then guided her down the stairs. As they were passing the shelves, Trick paused. "Want to take the sculpture? She'd rather you have it than anyone else. She'd have liked that it came full circle."

Frankie nodded. "Grab it." Outside she took a deep breath, breathing in the clean air. As they dusted off their clothes, her gaze was drawn to her childhood cabin. "I want to go in there."

Trick stiffened, and his wolf growled in objection. "Frankie, you've already put yourself through something emotionally taxing tonight."

"Actually, it wasn't taxing. I feel better for it." Which tremendously surprised her.

"I'm glad, but you won't feel better for walking through that place."

"Maybe not. But it's just something I feel I have to do."

"Is it something you really have to do right now? Because we're both covered in dust, and Lydia and Cam are waiting for us. You said that going through your father's things has helped you feel better. Take the time to enjoy that."

Frankie eyed him curiously. She could feel his anxiety through the bond. "Why don't you want me to go inside?"

Trick crossed to her and curved his hand around her neck. "Because I know you're hoping that something will jog your memory of that night, even though it's highly unlikely. Lots of things make no sense for you. You want answers. I get it, and I don't blame you for that. But it will only hurt you when it doesn't work. I've told you before, *no one* hurts my mate—not even her."

"I'm not expecting to have flashbacks. I was so young when it happened . . ."

"But you're hoping that you somehow miraculously will. You're still mad at yourself because you buried the memories and you can't seem to get them back."

Frankie ground her teeth. It really was annoying just how well he read her.

"Look, if you really feel you have to do this, I'll make it happen. I'll get permission from Josh to go through the place. But can we not do it tonight? Going through your father's things was huge for you— even though it turned out to be a good thing, it still wasn't easy. Let's take it one step at a time." He rested his forehead against hers. "Please. For me."

She took in a long breath. "Okay."

His face softened. "Okay."

Shivering, Frankie rubbed her upper arms. It was cold and dark and dusty in the display room. The eyes of her sculptures were closed. They were sleeping. She had to be quiet.

She tiptoed through the door that led to the studio. But when she walked through the door, she wasn't in the studio—no, the door had led her right back into the display room. She saw a hatch door above her head. She opened it, pulled down the staircase, and climbed the steps. And she found herself back in the display room.

Trick was there. He was staring at The Face. It wasn't twisted in pain, not while it was asleep. Trick looked at her. "I don't like it when you hurt yourself. You have to stop."

She closed her eyes and took a breath. When she opened them, Trick was gone. Iris was there, looking as hale and hearty as she did in her photos, and there were puzzle pieces all over the floor.

"Don't pick them up," Iris told her. "Leave them where they are. Let it lie, Frankie."

The pieces suddenly rose off the floor and began to orbit around Frankie. They moved too fast for her to really see any of them. She looked back at Iris, but she wasn't there anymore. "Where are—?"

The pieces froze in the air. Fell to the ground. She could smell gun oil and gunpowder and blood. Beneath those was his scent—rain, brine, and burned wood.

She noticed then that The Face had woken, and his eyes bore into hers—eyes that were now human and familiar, yet not. "You're supposed to be in bed, Frankie."

Her eyes snapped open, and she drew in a shuddering breath, clenching her hand around the coverlet. The arm that was curled around her from behind twisted her to face Trick, and she let him pull her flush against him.

He kissed the top of her head. "Another nightmare?"

She just nodded, keeping her face buried in his chest.

"Talk to me, Frankie. Your heart is pounding like crazy, and my wolf is raring to get out and hunt down whatever scared you. Tell me about the nightmare."

She swallowed. "I think someone other than my parents was there the night my mother was killed."

The hand stroking her back stilled. "Who?"

"He smelled like rain, brine, and burned wood. I smell that scent every time I'm around Clara's sons, but since they're triplets they all smell the same."

Trick resumed stroking her back, petting the anxiety out of her. He hated the tremor in her voice. His wolf rubbed up against her, trying to comfort her. "What makes you think he was there that night?" he asked softly.

"I smell that scent as well as the gunpowder. And then a voice tells me that I'm supposed to be in bed."

Sliding his fingers into her hair, Trick tugged her head back and said gently, "That doesn't mean that anyone else was there that night. I'm not saying you're wrong. I'm saying this could be your brain trying to put all the pieces together and mixing them into one dream."

She couldn't even argue with that. The human eyes on *The Face* hadn't been eyes that belonged to any of Clara's sons. The picture forming from the pieces she had didn't make sense. And she had to consider that just maybe she wanted to believe someone else had been there because she didn't want her father to be guilty. Since her wolf reacted so badly to the triplets' scent, they were convenient scapegoats, weren't they? Still . . . "I feel like my subconscious is trying to tell me something. I don't think I'm *remembering* what happened. Just that my subconscious has picked up on something that I've overlooked. Something important."

Trick rubbed his nose against hers. "I don't know what that could be," he whispered.

Neither did she.

CHAPTER FİFTEEN

As Frankie walked through the arched door of the underground nightclub a week later, her brows lifted in surprise. It was nothing like a usual club. The lighting was dim, and the dance floor was full, but there was no thumping overloud music, no stale hot air, and no flashing strobe lights. The club had both style and class. With the redbrick walls and the arched ceiling, she felt like she was in a large train tunnel or something.

The place belonged to the Mercury Pack and was allegedly run by its only margay wildcat, Harley. Apparently the females of the pack were anxious to meet Frankie, so Taryn had suggested that the females of both packs all meet up at the club for a girls' night. So they were having a girls' night. Only with Trick and Marcus. The males were there for "protection," they said—like the females weren't badass enough to protect themselves.

A few weeks back, Frankie might have been relieved to have Trick there. Now, though, she felt more settled in the pack. She wouldn't go as far as to say she'd *bonded* with her pack mates; Frankie didn't bond easily with anyone. But she'd grown to enjoy their company and feel more relaxed around them, especially Jaime and Makenna.

Trick put his mouth to her ear. "What do you think?"

"It's a nice place." Not everyone was dolled up in dresses. Like Frankie, some wore jeans, pretty shirts, and high heels.

Overhearing that, Jaime smiled. "It is, isn't it? Harley didn't make many changes when she took it over. She liked the look and feel of the place."

Trick stayed at Frankie's side as they all shouldered their way through the crowd, heading for the bar.

Taryn walked right up to the olive-skinned brunette tending the bar. "Hey, Ally, everything okay?"

The bartender grinned. "Great. Just give me a sec." She slid a tray of neon-colored drinks to a waitress and then turned back to them. "What about you guys? Please tell me you've brought Frankie. I've been dying to—" Ally spotted her and then smiled. "Well, hey. Aren't you just the cutest thing? I'm Ally, the Mercury Pack's Beta female."

Frankie knew her smile was a little on the shy side. "It's nice to meet you."

"You too. I have to say, I was *fascinated* to hear how you two figured out you were mates without any drama or near-death experiences to open your minds. You recognized her on sight, right?" she asked Trick.

"That's right," he confirmed, sliding his arm around her waist.

Frankie bit her lip, admitting, "It took me a couple of weeks to figure it out."

Ally sighed. "Yeah, it took me and Derren a little while, even though the signs were all there." She crossed her eyes as if annoyed with herself. She pointed to a group of people in the corner. "That's my mate over there. Derren's the dark-haired one. The guy he's standing next to is Zander, an enforcer, who's mated to the blonde human in the little shorts—she's Gwen. The redhead standing next to her is Shaya, our Alpha female . . . oh, and she's *just* spotted us." As Shaya took Gwen's hand and started pulling her through the throng of people, Ally asked, "So what are you all having?"

Taryn had just finished placing orders when Shaya sidled up to them. She threw her arms around Taryn, and it was clear just how close they were. According to Trick, they'd been friends since childhood.

After the females quickly exchanged greetings, Taryn turned to the newcomers. "Girls, this is Frankie. Frankie, this is Shaya and Gwen."

Shaya beamed at Frankie. "We've really wanted to go to Phoenix territory to meet you, but Taryn didn't want you feeling any more overwhelmed than you already do. Damn, you're so cute. Isn't she just adorable, Ally?"

"Utterly," said Ally, still preparing their drinks. "Even cuter than Jazz, and that's saying something."

"Jazz?" echoed Frankie.

"That's Harley's cousin," Gwen told her. "You'll see Harley in a second. She plays the electric violin. Totally awesome."

Ally clapped her hands. "Here you go, everyone. Beers, cosmos, tequila, and cocktails galore."

Riley was there first. She tossed back the tequila and then slammed the glass on the bar. "Needed that."

Makenna snickered and turned to Frankie. "Riley can do that for *hours* before she even nears the vicinity of drunk. I think it's a raven thing."

Trick grabbed two beers—one for Frankie, one for himself—and then propped her up on a bar stool. Situating himself between her legs, he splayed one hand on her back. "You sure you want to chance getting shit-faced again? I'd really rather not have to summon a priest."

She snorted. "I'll be sticking to water after this. I can't deal with two killer hangovers in one month."

A broad male wolf suddenly appeared at Trick's side and tipped his chin in greeting.

"Frankie, this is Jesse," said Trick. "Jesse, this is my mate."

Eyes so dark they were almost black studied Frankie carefully. Jesse then inclined his head, so she gave him a brief nod and said, "You're

Harley's mate, right?" Trick had told her plenty about the Mercury Pack.

Jesse's mouth softened at the mention of his mate. "I am. She'll be over to meet you after her set."

"Bracken doing any better?" Trick asked him.

Jesse's eyes dulled. "No. I'm just so fucking glad that Ally had a vision showing him injured and dying. He was bleeding out when we arrived on the scene. By that time the extremists had hightailed it out of there. Ally healed him, but I think part of him wishes she hadn't." Hearing clapping, Jesse looked at the stage. His pained expression smoothed out a little at the sight of his mate. "Looks like Harley's up now."

Frankie turned to the stage just as a dark-haired, golden-eyed female walked on holding a metallic-blue S-shaped electric violin. Casting Jesse a quick, intimate smile, Harley propped the instrument on her left collarbone and placed the left side of her jaw on the chin rest. She and the DJ played alongside each other, and the tune had the entire dance floor going wild.

Drawing out the final note, Harley gave the audience a beaming smile. They clapped and cheered as she left the stage.

"She's really talented," said Frankie.

Jesse's smile was one of pride. "I know, right?" His gaze was on the curtain that led backstage. Mere moments later, Harley appeared from behind the curtain and—smiling at each of the people who shouted compliments—made her way to the bar. Jesse pulled her into his arms and kissed her hard. "Amazing, as always."

Harley's mouth curved, her modesty clear. "Well, thank you."

Shaya spoke then. "Harley, this is Frankie." Leaning toward Frankie, she mock whispered, "Quick warning: our pretty kitty's not good at talking with strangers."

Harley rolled her eyes. "I heard about your mating," she told Frankie. "Congratulations."

Frankie smiled. "Thanks."

Harley looked at Shaya. "See, I can talk to people."

"You said six words," Jesse pointed out. "But that's actually progress."

Shaya turned to Trick. "Did Nick tell you that Morelli called us, asking for a meet?"

Trick nodded. "I can't say I'm surprised that Nick hung up on him without a word."

Shaya's nose wrinkled. "Yeah, my mate's not what you'd call social. A little like his sister, actually." She flicked a glance at Roni, who'd shoved a lollipop in her mouth and looked the height of uncomfortable.

Jaime turned to Makenna, sipping her cosmo, and then she frowned. "You're texting Grace, aren't you?"

Makenna didn't even look up from her cell phone. "I just want to check that Sienna's okay."

Jaime sighed. "She'll be fine. Relax. Enjoy yourself."

"Trick, thought I might find you here."

At those words Frankie's eyes snapped to the broad, Latin-looking guy who was fast shrugging his way through her pack mates, making a beeline for Trick. And going by Marcus's wince and Trick's sudden stillness, this was someone from Trick's past. Awesome.

"You haven't been to Enigma in a while and—" Rio paused, taking in Trick's proximity to Frankie and their claiming marks. "And you're mated," he sensed.

"That's right." Silently cursing, Trick tightened his hold on her as he said, "Frankie, this is Rio. Rio, this is my mate, Frankie." A mate who was currently staring at Rio, her face blank. Feeling her agitation through their bond, Trick soothingly rubbed her back and laid a possessive kiss on her temple, hoping to keep her and her wolf calm.

Rio was staring right back at her, clearly gobsmacked. Then he seemed to shake it off. "I didn't expect your mate to be female."

Frankie gave him a hard smile. "Funny old world, isn't it?" She took a long swig from her bottle, keeping her eyes on the male. *Black bear,* she sensed. Her wolf bared her teeth, wanting him gone. His very scent offended the wolf.

Marcus leaned toward Rio and spoke into his ear only loud enough for the bear to hear. Whatever he said made Rio bristle, and his eyes scanned their crowd. It was only then that Frankie realized that every Phoenix and Mercury member was glaring at the bear. He gave Trick one last look and then walked away. Smart.

Trick turned to her and rubbed his nose against hers. "Sorry about that."

"Why?" she asked. "You didn't do anything."

"I don't ever want you being touched by anything or anyone from my past, even though none of them were important to me."

While that was sweet . . . "There's no way you can guarantee that, just as I wasn't able to keep my past away from you. You handled Vance just fine, and I handled the bear—note that I didn't smash the bottle over his head, despite the temptation being so strong."

His mouth kicked up into a smile and he kissed her neck. "I like it when you get all possessive."

"Hmm."

"It's hot. My wolf likes it a fuck of a lot."

"Does he now?" She tilted her head slightly, giving him access to his claiming mark. Her eyes fell closed as he licked and nipped and traced it with his tongue. Feeling the weight of someone's glare, she opened her eyes and saw Rio watching them from the other end of the bar. It was instinct to possessively prick her claws into Trick's back.

Trick looked up, his gaze trapping hers, and kissed her hard and deep. "Mine."

She smiled. "Not gonna argue with that." At the sound of a low growl, Frankie looked in time to see Roni smack her mate's chest.

"No, no, no," said Roni. "There will be no dancing."

Marcus curled his arms around her. "But sweetheart—"

"No. You're not getting your way this time."

But he got his way after Roni had downed a few shots. They all gravitated to the dance floor, and Frankie wasn't surprised to find that Trick danced as smoothly and confidently as he did everything else. He also had her totally turned on.

Really, the entire group had a ball. They drank. They danced. They sang. They laughed.

When they were once again at the bar, Trick's cell phone rang. He fished it out of his pocket and told her, "It's Trey." Swiping his thumb over the screen, he answered, "Hello?" Trick knew that if it weren't for his enhanced shifter senses, he might not have heard his Alpha over the noise.

"We have Drake," said Trey. "Ryan tracked him. He's in the hut."

Trick went rigid as satisfaction and anger trickled through him. "Has Dante taken a shot at him yet?" The Beta was a damn good interrogator.

"No. We figured that you were owed that pleasure."

Grateful, Trick nodded. "I'll be there soon." He ended the call and looked at his mate, feeling like utter shit. She was relaxed, *truly* relaxed, with the females of his pack, and it was clear that she was even letting her guard halfway down for the Mercury Pack females. Now he was about to spoil her evening. "Baby . . ."

Frowning, she grabbed his arm. "Something's wrong. What is it?"

"Yeah, what the fuck put that dark look on your face?" asked Marcus, who'd been doing his best to eavesdrop on his conversation with Trey.

Trick scraped a hand over his jaw. "We have Drake in custody."

Frankie's brows flew up. "Drake?"

Trick nodded. "Ryan found him and brought him to our territory."

"You need to go," she understood.

"I can wait. You're enjoying yourself—"

"She'll be okay here with us, Trick," said Marcus. "Really. This place is safe. We won't let anything happen to her."

Trick curved his hand around her neck. It went against his instincts to leave her there, but he wasn't going to insist on her leaving when he had no intention of allowing her to join him in the hut to deal with Drake. "You can stay here and enjoy the rest of the night with the girls. They'll keep you safe and bring you home. Or you can come with me now back to our territory, but I can't let you come with me while I deal with Drake. I'm going to fuck him up, Frankie. I'm going to make him *hurt*. I don't want you there for that."

Frankie wanted to point out *yet again* that she wasn't freaking fragile. She also would rather enjoy watching the bastard suffer. But she could feel Trick's anxiety, and she knew how hard it would be for him to have her there. Despite how badly he'd wanted to get his hands on Drake, he hadn't left her that day when she was attacked. He'd stayed with her, knowing it was what she needed. In return she could give him what he needed now . . . on one condition.

"You might be better staying here than waiting in our room for me," Trick added. "I don't know how long I'll be in the hut, but I do know I won't be in the best mood when I'm done with that fucker."

Frankie rested her hands on his shoulders. "I'll stay here. But when you're done, you don't go running around pack territory to blow off steam. You come back to me. I should be in bed by then, waiting for you. If I'm not there, you wait for me. That's the deal."

"Deal." Trick kissed her hard, gliding his tongue against her own, needing her taste. "I love you. Stay safe." He turned to Marcus, face hard. "Anything happens to her, you pay for it."

"I wouldn't expect anything less," said Marcus.

As Trick stalked off, Frankie gaped at him. She spluttered, shooting a glare at his retreating back. "You can't tell someone you love them and then just leave." But Trick was too far away to hear her.

Marcus chuckled. "It's just like him to dump a bomb like that, casual as you please, and then walk off."

"Well, it wasn't fair."

"If he'd hung around, you'd have felt that you had to say it back. He probably wants you to say it when you're ready, not before."

Figuring Marcus was likely right, she sighed and felt her irritation slip away. "Do you think I did the right thing by staying behind?"

"Yes, I do. He needed the space to get his head ready to deal with Drake. He won't want you to see him that way."

Recalling how much he'd hated that she saw him fighting with Drake in the restroom, she nodded. "I just wanted to be sure he wouldn't feel like I'd left him alone while he was brooding. Why are you grinning?"

"You totally love him."

"And you're totally annoying."

"I can't argue with that."

Snorting, she returned to the dance floor. As the night went on, there was more drinking, more laughing, more singing, and more dancing. Later, when she was at the bar ordering herself another bottle of water, an offensive scent hit her nostrils. Her wolf lifted her head, instantly alert. *Dammit.*

Rio leaned against the bar. "I have to ask . . . how did you do it?"

Frankie gave him a bored, sideways glance. "Do what?"

"Convince a gay guy to imprint on you. How does that even work?"

"Trick isn't gay. Nor did we imprint on each other. We're true mates." Not that she owed the guy any explanations or anything.

"Not possible." He shook his head, adamant. "Let's not bullshit each other, okay? Life's too short for games."

She frowned. "Life is like the longest thing you will *ever* do. Once you're gone, you're gone." She had no idea why people said that.

He blinked, surprised, then gave a fast shake of his head. "You know what I'm getting at." He moved a little closer to her. "Look, I'm guessing you're not fully imprinted on each other yet. That's a good thing. It means you still have an out. You need to take it."

"Is that a fact?"

"Yes, it's very much a fact. Things might be going good for you and Trick *now*, but it won't work in the long run. Neither of you are what the other truly needs. On the sexuality spectrum, Trick is way, way, *way* more toward the gay end."

She snickered. "I'm pretty sure he's straighter than the pole you dance on every Saturday."

His face went rock hard. "You have a mouth on you. I'm actually trying to help here."

"No, you're being an asshole. A jealous, bitter one. I would have thought Trick had better taste. Now if I were you, I'd run along." She wiggled her fingers in the direction of the exit.

"Why? It's not like he can hurt me if I don't. He *left* you."

"Yeah, but, see, he left me with a ton of people—all of whom will leap on your skinny ass if you touch me. The fact that you're breathing my air will be enough to piss them off."

"I'm not going to hurt you. I don't rough up women. I do, however, like getting roughed up in bed." His mouth curled into a wicked, cruel smile. "Trick, well, he does like to play rough. I sure hope you're into anal. That's his thing. If you give him that, there's a chance he'll stick around awhile. A slight chance, anyway."

"You're mumbling. But then, I'll bet it's hard to sound coherent when you have a mouth full of bullshit. Just swallow it down. I'm sure you've had plenty of practice with swallowing."

His eyes flared. "Where Trick's concerned, I sure have. Tastes good, doesn't he?"

God, she really despised this asshole. She put her hand over his. "You know, I can only think that you asked a genie for a big cock but he turned you into one instead." She unsheathed her claws, stabbing them into his hand, scraping bone.

His eyes bulged and he cried out in pain—her wolf sure did love that sound.

Frankie gave him a mocking smile. "Why did the black bear cross the road? Because the she-wolf wanted to jerk him off with a pencil sharpener."

"You little bitch."

"I like to think of myself as more of a hemorrhoid. I mean, look how gifted I am at irritating assholes—you're practically steaming." She sheathed her claws, releasing him.

He cradled his hand. "Are you out of your fucking mind?"

"Depends what day it is."

He looked about to curse a blue streak, but then he froze as some of the Phoenix and Mercury Pack members appeared, including Derren and Zander. All of them radiated hostility as they glared at Rio. At the same time, Ally hurried down the bar to see what was happening.

"What did you say to her?" Marcus demanded.

Rio widened his eyes. "*Me?* She just stabbed my damn hand!"

"He just wanted me to be clear that Trick prefers guys to girls and it would be better for us both if I left Trick before we fully imprinted," Frankie told them. "I did explain that we're true mates and that Rio should just walk away, but he needed a little . . . convincing."

Marcus went toe to toe with him. "You tried to get between Trick and his mate? You actually fucking tried that?"

Rio swallowed. "She needed to hear the truth. You know as well as I do that he's g—"

"Mated," Marcus finished. "He's mated and *happy*. You saw that for yourself. That's why you came over here. You resent that she can make him happy when it was something you could *never* do. I told you long ago that pursuing him was pointless. There was only one person he'd ever commit to, but you didn't want to see that. Tonight, you *did*. And instead of being happy for the guy you've repeatedly claimed to care about, you're trying to plant seeds of doubt in his mate's head to spoil what they have."

"You're lucky all she did was stab your hand," said Taryn. "If she'd had a hammer nearby, things would have worked out very differently."

"Hammer?" echoed Ally.

"I'll tell you about it later," Taryn told her.

Derren clenched his fists, still glaring at Rio. "I'm thinking we should continue this *conversation* in the alley outside." Translation: he thought they should take the bear outside and pound into him a little.

"That's an idea I can get behind," said Zander.

Marcus fisted Rio's collar and began dragging him toward the rear of the club.

"Wait!" cried Rio, but they didn't.

Zander lingered long enough to shoot a look of warning at his mate. "Stay here with the others. Don't go off on your own."

He started to follow the other males when Gwen called out, "Wait, before you go, is it all right if I just . . ." Trailing off, she shook her head. "It's okay. Never mind."

Zander's eyes narrowed. "Gwen, spit it out."

She waved a hand. "Really, it doesn't matter."

"Tell me what you were going to say."

"But it doesn't matter," she insisted, eyes wide with innocence.

He swore. "Stop testing my sanity."

"But it's fun to watch you lose it a slice at a time."

With another curse, he strode off.

Smiling, Gwen said, "His protectiveness knows no boundaries."

Harley sighed. "I can relate. I'm pretty sure it's a dominant male thing."

"Yeah," agreed Shaya. "I feel sorry for them in a lot of ways. They never seem to realize that they're actually never going to get their own way all the time. They keep insisting on it. It's like watching people purposely bang their heads against a brick wall. Weird or what?"

Jesse cleared his throat. "I'm right here."

Shaya waved that away. "Ally, I'm still not drunk. Help me."

"You got it," said the Beta.

The hinges squealed as Trick pushed open the heavy wooden door. It scraped noisily against the plank floor. Unless there was a captive, no one set foot in the hut. They deliberately neglected it, wanting it to look as miserable and grubby as possible.

It stank of dirt, dust, and rot. It was bare apart from a hard chair, a torn mattress, and a red bucket. The windows were smudged with dirt, and there were stains on the floor thanks to the leaky roof. Dead flies dotted the windowsills, and there were some very elaborate spiderwebs in the corners of the ceiling. This far away from the cave dwelling, all that could be heard was the whine of mosquitoes and the tree branches scratching the outer walls.

Trick's gaze immediately went to Drake, whose arms and legs were tightly bound to a chair by a thick rope. Rope was also looped around his chest.

In short, Drake wasn't going anywhere. And he seemed very aware of it.

Rather than thrashing around, fighting his restraints, he sat very still. He wasn't sweating or breathing hard. Though his heartbeat was a little fast, it wasn't pounding with fear. Drake knew he wasn't getting out of this alive, and he'd apparently decided to accept that.

Trick's wolf *wanted* his fear. Wanted to see and smell it, just as he wanted to see and smell his blood.

The boards creaked with each step Trick took forward. Trey, Ryan, Dante, and Dominic fanned out behind him. Their captive didn't look good at all. His hair was greasy and unkempt, and his clothes were wrinkled and scruffy. Wherever the guy had been hiding, he clearly hadn't had access to clean clothes or a shower.

Drake glanced around Trick. "Your girlfriend isn't with you? Shame. I like her."

He seemed to genuinely mean it. "She broke your nose," Trick reminded him.

"*And* almost bashed my head in with a hammer. She's a fighter. I like that."

"She's not my girlfriend. She's my mate."

"Well, that explains a few things. Like why you had your pack mate run me down like a rabid dog." He flicked a look at Ryan.

Trick folded his arms across his chest. "From the things your Alpha said, that's pretty much what you are. He suspended you as Beta. And he claims to have cut you loose too."

Drake scoffed. "Nash is no Alpha."

"True. And you're no Beta."

"True," allowed Drake, unoffended. "So how is this gonna go? Execution? Brawl? Torture? In your position, I'd go the torture route. I would have tortured your mate if I could have. Well, not until I'd fucked every orifice in her body." He sighed when Trick didn't allow himself to be goaded. "Not easy to rattle, are ya?"

"It's hard to take that kind of stuff seriously when it's streaming out of the mouth of a guy who got his ass kicked by a girl."

"She didn't kick my ass."

"No, *you* did the kicking. Cracked a rib. You also bruised her jaw. Put a goose egg on her head. Fractured a bone in her leg. Pricked her neck with your claws. And almost dislocated her shoulder." Anger thrumming through his system, Trick took another step forward. "So tell me, Drake, what do you think I'm going to do to you?"

"Tit for tat," Drake guessed, his voice flat, his eyes dull.

"That's right. I'll revisit every injury you gave her right on back to you—only each wound will be ten times worse." And Trick would relish every fucking moment of it.

"If you hadn't knocked me down at the meeting, Nash wouldn't have sent me your way."

"You came after me in the restroom to get even."

"On Nash's say-so. He told me I'd lose the respect of the pack if I didn't retaliate. It wasn't until later, after my failed attempt to follow his order to kidnap your girlfriend, that I realized he was playing us all."

Trick lifted a brow. "You think he's playing us?"

"I'm not the brightest lamp on the street, but even I can see he was using me. If I'd killed you, what would your Alpha have done?"

"Demanded that Morelli hand you over for execution."

Drake gave a lazy nod. "That's right. And then your Alpha would have owed Nash. What do you think Nash would have asked for? An alliance, right?"

"It's a possibility. But it wouldn't explain why you tried to kidnap my mate."

"He wanted Trey to go to him for *help*. I told him it wouldn't work. I told him that your pack's tracker would be sent to find her. But Nash was sure that Trey would want his help, and then everyone could work together. Nash planned to call Trey to say he'd 'found' your girl. He said he wouldn't demand an alliance for handing her over. Said he wouldn't have to. He thinks you'd have felt like you owed him." Drake let out a long breath. "I wasn't convinced it would work out that way, but I followed orders."

"And you think that you should therefore be spared?"

"No." He released a dejected sigh. "I've done worse to others than what I've done to your girl. Karma comes for us all. But if I'm going down, Nash can sure as hell come down with me." His eyes twinkled as he added, "Bet you haven't been able to find out where he came from. On record, it's like he just sprang out of nowhere, isn't it?"

Dante came forward. "You know his real identity?"

"Well, that depends on how quick you intend to kill me."

Sighing, Dante shook his head. "Why do people always try to bargain for a quick death?"

"It's the only thing a captive has left to bargain with when they know they're not getting out of the situation alive," said Drake.

"That's true enough." Trick sliced out his claws, satisfied when their captive jerked. "Unfortunately for you, Drake, I really don't care where he's from."

For the first time, Drake's eyes flickered with panic. "You should care. Nash wants war."

"We sensed that much," said Dominic, sounding bored.

"But did you sense that he's not working alone?" asked Drake. "Someone picked him, gave him a new ID, helped him become an Alpha, and then set him on a new path."

"Who?" demanded Trey.

"I don't know who it was. He never called them by their name. But he did say that they're human. An extremist." Drake made a sound of disgust. "Those guys are nuts. I got no damn idea why Nash would be willing to work with one of them. But I know that they want war as badly as he does. They're planning to start it together."

"What you're saying is that Morelli and a human extremist are working together to then later destroy each other?" asked Trey, not bothering to hide his disbelief.

"No," replied Drake. "The agreement is that Nash and his closest alliances won't be attacked. But he'll give up the locations of those who are hiding. Like you, Trey. If you'd agreed to that alliance, he'd have placed all the vulnerable shifters here, taken your best fighters with him, and left you to die at the hands of extremists."

Trick twisted his mouth. "Well, that was a great story. Maybe there's some truth in it—we'll look into that. For now, my interest is purely in you. I really do hope you have a low pain threshold." Trick balled up his fist and slammed it into Drake's jaw.

CHAPTER SIXTEEN

S he was in bed when Trick walked into the room hours later. She looked young in her sleep, he thought. Especially with her hand tucked under her chin and the lines of her face smoothed into an expression of pure peace.

For a minute he stood near the bed, just watching her. Watching the slight rise and fall of her chest. He wanted to go to her. Touch her, wake her, slip inside her. But he couldn't. Not yet. Not until he was calmer. Not until he'd washed off the blood and violence.

In the bathroom he shed his clothes and stepped into the shower stall. He tipped back his head and closed his eyes as the hot spray pounded down on him. Even though Drake was literally dead and buried, Trick felt no real satisfaction. Not now that he knew Drake had been just a puppet. Nothing short of Nash Morelli's head on a pike would ease the lingering agitation that rode him.

His wolf wasn't even close to calming. Not while a threat to his mate still existed. Not when she still hadn't been fully avenged and—

There was a slight draft on his back as the shower door opened, and then soft hands slid around him. Trick let out a long breath. Fuck, he wanted her. Needed her. But he didn't want her to have to deal with this side of him. "Baby—"

"Shh." Frankie squirted some soap onto her hands and then lathered it into his shoulders. She didn't rush. Didn't talk. Just gave him the peace that she sensed he needed.

It hadn't been the sound of the water running that woke her. It had been the feel of his agitation pulsing down their mating bond. She figured he'd probably prefer to be alone, but she could no more ignore the need to soothe him than she could ignore the need to eat.

She soaped down his shoulders and back, digging her fingers into his skin just enough for it to feel good and push away the tension. Little by little, his muscles lost their stiffness, and the frustration buzzing down their bond simmered down to a slight hum.

"Turn around for me," she said. He did, and she washed his chest, abs, and arms. She'd meant to comfort him, not arouse him, but his cock was hard as steel and she could *feel* his need. It amplified her own, tightening her nipples and making her breasts ache. She ignored it as best she could—this here and now was about him.

Smoothing his hands down her back to palm her ass, Trick put his mouth to her ear. "I can smell how wet you are." The sweet scent of her need filled the stall, making his head spin and his cock throb. Nuzzling her neck, he scraped his teeth over the claiming mark. "Mine."

"Yours," agreed Frankie. He brought his mouth down hard on hers. Gripping his shoulders, she moaned. The kiss was hot, wet, and hungry. He plundered and dominated and demanded her submission.

"Your throat," he rumbled. "Give me your throat."

Oh, now, that was asking for a lot more submission than she was comfortable giving. Frankie didn't mind following his orders and letting him take the lead—it was often to her benefit, and she didn't get a kick out of controlling others anyway. But offering him her throat? Yeah, that was asking a lot. "Trick—"

"Give me your throat."

She lifted her chin. "No."

His eyes narrowed. "All right."

Unease pricked at her. Trick generally wasn't the type to back down when he wanted something, especially during sex. His mouth took hers again, tongue sinking inside and exploring every crevice as he backed her against the tiled wall. He raised one of her arms, and she felt something wrap around her wrist. He did the same thing with the other, and then her foggy brain remembered . . . *suction cup restraints.*

Well, fuck. She'd noticed them before. He'd taunted her that he'd use them one day, when she was least expecting it. Well, she sure hadn't seen it coming just now.

Trick hummed in satisfaction at the perfect picture she made right then. "Cuffed, helpless, and mine to play with."

The "helpless" part both pricked at her pride and fueled her need. Frankie might have fought him, if only for the fun of it, but she sensed that he needed this. Needed to lose himself in what they had. Needed the control that he'd no doubt shed tonight while he did what he had to do. So rather than fighting him, she remained still. And that earned her a lazy, lopsided grin.

Trick trailed his fingers down her neck, between the valley of her breasts, down to her stomach. "You look so fucking hot right now, Frankie." His cock was full and heavy, throbbing like a bitch. "*My* Frankie."

He kept his touch featherlight as he grazed his fingers over the plump lips of her pussy. He slipped his finger between her folds just enough to skim over her clit. Her hips jerked toward him, and he smiled. His mate had the most sensitive clit he'd ever come across in his life, and he loved to tease her endlessly. Loved pushing her as far as she could go. Which was why he said, "I think I'll come back to that later."

Ignoring her harsh curse, he closed his hands around her breasts and squeezed. "I fucking love your tits." He pushed them together as he licked from one nipple to the other. He sucked and licked and raked them with his teeth. With a choked moan, she arched into him as much as her restraints would allow. He thrust a finger into her hot little pussy

241

and groaned. She was already wet, but . . . "I want you dripping for me." He scooped out some of the slickness and spread it over her clit. "Is this what you want?"

"You know it is." Frankie gasped as he caught her clit between two fingers and squeezed just a little. He slid his fingers forward and backward, rubbing both sides of her clit with each glide. *Oh God.* She hooked one leg over his hip to lock him in place as the tension built inside her. Every part of her ached for him. Responded to him. Craved him.

"Frankie, give me your throat."

She hissed. "Why do you want it so bad?"

"I need to know you'll give me anything. *Everything.*" He sank his finger back into her pussy, scooped out more lube, and smeared it all over her clit. "There's only one thing I wouldn't do for you, Frankie— and that's let you go. I'll never give you freedom. But anything else? It's yours." He circled, rubbed, and pinched her clit. "Give me what I want."

Frankie squeezed her eyes shut. Even while she was out of her mind with need, her pride balked at his request. But the heart that he'd won and now totally owned wanted to give him whatever he needed. And the heart won out over her pride.

A growl rumbled out of Trick as she tipped her head back, giving him her throat. Like that, his control evaporated like mist. He tore open the Velcro cuffs to free her hands. "Hold on." He lifted her high and roughly dropped her on his cock. Her breath seemed to gust out of her lungs, but her pussy rippled around him. And he knew neither of them would last long.

He braced his hands against the wall, keeping his arms straight. "Ride me."

Frankie locked her legs around him as she gripped his shoulders and rode his cock like their survival depended on it. All the while, his mouth drove her insane—sucking on her neck, biting her earlobe, teasing her claiming bite, and whispering some seriously dirty fantasies down her ear.

"Come on, Frankie, fuck me." He slipped one wet finger inside the bud of her ass, and her pace faltered. "I didn't tell you to stop. Move." She resumed rising and falling, so that she was fucking both his cock and his finger. "Harder, Frankie, make yourself come."

And then it happened. White-hot pleasure blasted through Frankie like a hot wind, trapping a scream in her throat and making her pussy ripple around the cock that throbbed deep inside her. Just as it distantly occurred to her that he hadn't come, he lifted her off his cock and pushed on her shoulder.

"Get on your knees, Frankie," Trick growled. A little dazed, she did as she was told. "That's it. Open your mouth." The moment she parted those lips, he thrust inside. He wasn't careful or gentle. He gripped her hair as he fucked her mouth, frantically punching his hips. Then his release barreled into him and he exploded, blowing his load right down her throat.

He closed his eyes as it all drained out of him—the anger, the frustration, the thirst for vengeance. Slipping his hands under her arms, Trick pulled her to her feet. He held her to him, burying his face in her neck, rocking her loose body from side to side. "You always do that."

"What?" she slurred, weakly stroking his back.

"Bring me peace." He pressed a lingering kiss to her hair. "Missed you." Those few hours without her had felt a hell of a lot longer. Maybe because, for a while, he hadn't been himself.

"It was no fun going to bed without you. Let's not do that often."

He smiled. "Agreed." He breathed her in. His heart stuttered. "Our scents have mixed."

Frankie's nostrils flared, and she grinned. "That means the bond is strengthening, right?"

"Right. And now everyone will now you're mine just by your scent."

"I'd roll my eyes if I didn't get the same satisfaction from that idea." After they'd both washed their hair and rinsed away the suds, they stepped out of the shower and dried off. It wasn't until they were in bed—him on his back, her nestled against his side—that she spoke again. "I don't want to put a downer on the mood, and I know you'd rather not talk about it, but I'd like to know whether Drake—"

"He can never hurt you again."

Meaning he was dead, she thought. "Then what's troubling you?" She'd have expected him to feel better now that he'd had his vengeance. "You feel bad for killing him?"

"Fuck no." Sighing, Trick skimmed his fingers up and down her back. "He said that Morelli sent him to kidnap you." He relayed everything Drake had told him.

Frankie traced the lines and dips of his abs as she spoke. "He could be telling the truth. I mean, extremists have tried to provoke our kind into starting a war, but we formed The Movement instead. If they want the war bad enough, they need to try something else. And it would be smart to try to recruit a shifter they can work with. Not that I believe they wouldn't actually kill Morelli. He might not even believe that they'd let him live. They might simply be content on using each other."

"If he was telling the truth, Morelli planned to serve us to the extremists on a silver fucking platter." His wolf peeled back his upper lip.

"I'd say it's time for Trey to have a talk with him."

"Tried that. Morelli's number is no longer in use." That could mean a lot of things—none of which he wanted to explore right then. "Let's not talk anymore about that fucker." Trick caught her hand and kissed her palm. "How did the rest of your night go?"

"Good."

"No males were hanging around, trying to steal you from me?"

She chuckled. "No."

"No one gave you any problems?"

"No."

The slight hesitation before she spoke made him frown, especially since agitation briefly spiked down their bond. "What happened?"

She sighed. "I was going to tell you tomorrow. You have enough shit on your mind tonight."

"I want to know." He pulled her on top of him so he could better look her in the eye. "Tell me now."

She bit her lip, resting her chin on his chest. "Rio was a little . . . unfriendly."

Fucker. "Define *unfriendly*."

"He basically indicated that, as I don't have a dick, he believed I wasn't what you needed. He thinks you're gay—or at least mostly gay. And if what Marcus said is right, he's bitter that pursuing you never worked out for him."

Trick swore, pissed with both the motherfucker and himself. "I shouldn't have left you." He should have stayed at her side, protected her.

"I'm a big girl, you know."

"Tell me Marcus dealt with the bastard."

"He, Derren, *and* Zander took said bastard outside for a 'conversation.'"

"Good."

"Of course, that was after I stabbed his hand with my claws."

Trick blinked. "I shouldn't be surprised. You've proven over and over that behind your cuteness lies a mean little she-wolf." She just shrugged. "Tell me that you know Rio was chatting utter bullshit."

"I know," she assured him. "You want me, whatever package I come in."

"But the things he said hurt you."

"They stung a little, I'll admit that. No one likes to hear their mate's ex brag about how they know what he likes and what he tastes like. Not that I hadn't already figured out that you liked it rough and were a fan of anal. According to Rio, you'll stick around for a while if I give your dick access to my ass."

Trick cupped her face. "Hear me, Frankie. I *will* fuck your ass. I'll fill every inch of it and claim it as mine. Not because I like anal, but because it's *you*. Whatever we do, it's always about you."

Frankie lifted a brow. "Look, I don't mind you using a finger now and then." She'd grown to like that. "But your cock? No. That won't happen. Don't give me that indulgent smile, like I'm delusional or something."

"Oh, baby, I don't think you're delusional. I just think you're full of shit." He slid a hand down her back to cup one globe. "I *will* have this ass. I will fuck it and claim it and come deep inside it. And you know what? You'll love every moment of it." He narrowed his eyes. "You can wipe that indulgent smile right off your face."

"Annoying, isn't it?"

"Yeah, it damn well is."

She snickered. "We can argue about it tomorrow. I'm wiped." She rested her cheek on his chest and closed her eyes. She waited until she was on the verge of sleep before she said, "By the way, I love you too."

Trick went rigid. "You can't tell someone you love them and then just go to sleep."

"Watch me," she slurred. And then she drifted off.

The next day, Trick frowned as he stared at Ryan. "Say that again."

Standing in the center of Trey's office, the enforcer repeated, "Morelli is gone. The buildings on his land, including the pack house, were all burned to the ground. It was no forest fire or accident. Accelerant was used. Someone deliberately destroyed them. There wasn't a soul in sight."

Trey's chair creaked as he leaned forward and braced his elbows on his desk. "Any bodies?"

"Not that I could see," replied Ryan. "But I can't be sure that no one died in the fire."

"So either someone tried to kill the pack, or Morelli did the damage himself and then scampered." Trey tapped his chin. "Maybe he knew we had Drake. But how?"

Perched on the edge of the desk, Dominic said, "He could have someone watching our territory from a distance, or he could even have tagged Drake's body the way he tagged our SUVs."

"Both those scenarios are possible," agreed Trick. "Morelli might have worried that Drake would talk—or he wasn't prepared to take chances—so he did a runner. He could have burned down the buildings just so that no one else could claim them. He's spiteful that way."

Leaning against the wall, Marcus scratched at his stubbly jaw. "I didn't figure Morelli for someone to run."

"He's not a guy who's ruled by pride," Dante pointed out. "He's realistic enough to know that we have far more powerful alliances than he could dream of having. As we've said before, he has a plan."

Ryan grunted in agreement. "His mind is centered on that. If hiding means preserving that plan, he'll do it. But I think he'll adapt it to include us being wiped out—probably at his hand."

Trick turned to Trey. "You're my Alpha, I respect you, but if you wanted me to flee with you and hide somewhere, I'd expect there to be a damn good reason. Otherwise you'd lose a great deal of my respect. That makes me wonder if Morelli's pack is hiding with him. If they are, what reason would he give them?"

Dominic tossed a paperweight from one hand to the other. "I think we're right that Morelli burned down the buildings, but I don't think his pack knows it was him. I think he blamed it on someone else. Possibly us. His pack would leave with him and agree to hide if he gave them some spiel about lying low while they plotted revenge or some shit like that."

"It's probable," said Ryan. "Whatever the case, I think he'll launch an attack at some point. Not just because we messed up his plan, but because he truly wants our territory. His style is to take out the strongest members and try to recruit the others." He looked at Trey and Dante. "That means you two will be his main targets. But you'll need to watch out too, Trick. You and your mate both thwarted him. And in doing so, you made it impossible for his plan to work. Trey didn't come to him for help like Morelli wanted. You also ensured that Drake was hunted down, which lost Morelli one of his wolves. In other words, you'll be on his shit list."

The knock at the door made Trey frown. Still, he called out, "Come in."

Lydia took shy steps inside, teeth nibbling her lower lip. "Sorry to interrupt."

"Everything okay?" asked Dante.

She sighed. "Well, not really."

Trick narrowed his eyes. "What's wrong?"

"I was talking to Frankie at her studio. I just wanted to see her work and stuff. While I was there, she got a phone call. And then her face just went all weird. I asked what was wrong, but she blew me off and went back to work."

Trick checked her through their bond. She seemed calm enough, but he knew that she could throw herself so deeply into a project that her emotions took a back seat. His wolf urged Trick to find her, check on her.

"Go see your mate," Trey told him. "Make sure she's okay."

With a curt nod, Trick left the office and stalked out of the caves and through the woods. As he neared the studio, he heard rock music blasting out of her speakers. Honestly, he didn't know how the noise could possibly help her concentrate, but whatever worked.

In the studio she was bent over a huge, shapeless clump of clay. Slowly and cautiously he crossed to her and said, "Hey, baby. What's that going to be?"

"No idea." She flicked him a sideways glance. "Lydia went to see you, huh?" she guessed.

Taking her by the shoulders, Trick gently turned her to face him, taking in her pinched expression and pained stare. "Who called you, and what did they say to upset you?"

"It was my grandparents' housekeeper, Edna." She swallowed. "Geoffrey was admitted into the hospital this morning. He was shot in the shoulder outside the court building."

"Shot?" he echoed.

"He's okay. The shooter either had a shit aim or hadn't wanted to kill him." Frankie took in a shaky breath. "At first I was just shocked. I couldn't feel anything. I didn't know what to feel. It has to make me a shitty person that I went right back to my project like—"

"You're not a shitty person. You went back to your project the way someone else would have reached for a bottle of whiskey or a Valium. What you do here calms you and gives you an outlet. So now that the shock is subsiding, how do you feel?"

"Worried, even though he's okay. And . . . well, pissed." The moment she admitted to the emotion, her anger truly hit her. She hissed through her teeth. "They didn't even call to tell me about it, Trick. It's one thing to disapprove of me and need to make their point by giving me the cold shoulder. It's a whole other thing to not even call me when my grandfather is hurt."

Trick drew her against him and held her close, stroking her hair. "Breathe with me, Frankie. Nice and slow. That's it." When she seemed to have found her calm, he pulled back to meet her gaze. "Come on. We'll lock this place up and go back to our room so you can get changed."

"Changed for what?"

"I doubt you want to go to the hospital looking like that."

"I won't be welcome," she said, her voice low. "They'll just send me away. Going up there would make me a glutton for punishment."

"But if something went wrong and he didn't recover, you wouldn't forgive yourself for not at least trying to see him." That was the only reason Trick gave a damn about her going there. "You have every right to be at the hospital, Frankie. But if you really don't want to go, we won't go. It's that simple. I just don't want you to do something you might later regret."

"They'll chase me out of there."

"They might try." Trick wouldn't let them. "I'm coming with you. I know they won't like it, but I won't hang back. Not just because I don't trust them with you, but because they need to get used to the simple fact that I'm part of your life now."

Frankie gave a slow nod. "Okay."

"And if they behave like assholes, you can trust that I'll fuck your anger out of you later."

Her brow slowly lifted as amusement trickled through her. "How magnanimous of you."

An hour or so later, they walked through an automatic sliding door right into a hospital waiting room, where rows of plastic chairs lined the plain white walls. The only real color came from artificial plants, posters, and magazines. Her wolf's nose wrinkled at the scents of antiseptic, hand sanitizer, bleach, and coffee.

Marcia and Brad sat opposite each other, their postures stooped, looking lost in their own thoughts. Walking toward them, Frankie cleared her throat to be heard over the sounds of people muttering and the squeak of shoes as staff walked the halls in color-coded scrubs.

Marcia straightened in her seat, surprised. "Francesca." Emotion briefly glittered in her eyes, but it was gone too quickly for Frankie to identify it. "How did you find out?"

Tone dry, Frankie said, "I'm well, thanks, how are you?"

Brad raked a hand through his hair. "Frankie, I—"

"We'll pretend that you didn't meet with Trick to bribe him to leave my life and that you have no idea who he is," said Frankie, her voice even. This wasn't the time to let loose her anger. "Brad, Marcia—this is Trick, my mate. Trick, that's my uncle, Brad, and my grandmother, Marcia." Neither of them did more than cast Trick a brief look, but at least they hadn't scowled or attempted to send him away. "How is Geoffrey?"

Brad took a shaky breath. "The doctors said he'll be fine. The bullet went straight through and didn't hit any vital organs, but he lost a fair bit of blood. He's had a transfusion and . . ." Brad swallowed. "It was hard to see him like that. Pale. Weak."

"And the shooter?"

"She was arrested." He shifted in his seat. "I'd say, 'Sit down,' but these chairs will make your ass numb."

His attempt at humor didn't break the tension, but she appreciated the effort. She didn't sit—not simply because she didn't feel welcome, but also because too much tension rode her body. "Do the police know why the woman shot him?"

"It was someone from an old case," said Brad. "A custody battle."

Frankie's brow knitted. "Custody?"

"A couple wanted custody of their grandchildren. Their daughter joined one of those New Age cults after her husband died, and they didn't think it was a suitable environment for the children. Their daughter didn't want her parents to have visitation rights with the children, said her father used to . . . sexually abuse her. She said the cult was her sanctuary and that the children would be safe there. The battle was long and ugly."

"Geoffrey granted the grandparents custody," Frankie guessed.

"Yes." He looked down at his hands, seeming lost. "Recently, one of the children—she was thirteen—killed herself. She wrote a letter, claiming her grandfather abused her and she couldn't take it anymore."

And then Frankie understood. "The mother shot Geoffrey."

"She shot her father too," said Brad. "He's dead."

If they couldn't see the correlation to their own situation, they were blind. It was obvious that Geoffrey had seen Caroline and Francesca when he looked at that woman and her children. He'd seen the pack and Christopher when he looked at the cult. And he'd seen himself and Marcia when he looked at the grandparents. Which was why he should never have presided over that case, but there was little point in voicing what was so abundantly clear.

"He's speaking with the police at the moment," said Marcia, twirling her wedding band around her finger. "You can talk to him afterward, if you'd like."

Frankie nodded. "I'll wait."

Trick put his mouth to her ear. "Want coffee?"

"No, thanks. It'll either be weak or sludge." She rubbed her temple. The fluorescent lighting was giving her a headache.

No one spoke another word as they waited for the police to exit Geoffrey's hospital room. Once they finally did, Marcia jumped to her feet and pounded them with questions.

"He's in room 4A," Brad told Frankie.

Trick stayed close behind her as they walked down the hallway. Pushing open the door, Frankie saw Geoffrey propped up on pillows, watching the wall-mounted TV. She was surprised to see him hooked up to so many different machines that monitored his vitals, since he wasn't ill. She wasn't sure whether it was pain, blood loss, shock, or a combination of all three, but he looked pale even against the bright white linens.

As the door closed behind her and Trick, the noises of the waiting room were replaced by the soft drip of the saline, the reassuring steady beat of the heart monitor, and the low sounds coming from the TV.

He double-blinked at the sight of her. "Francesca." She half expected his heartbeat to pick up, but it remained steady. "I didn't think you would come."

She might feel pissed and let down, but . . . "I'm not heartless."

"No, but we've given that heart of yours a pounding lately."

The admission surprised her. "You remember Trick."

"I do." His head slightly moved in what could have been a weak, hesitant nod of greeting, but Frankie couldn't be sure.

She didn't take the plastic chair next to the bed. Instead, careful not to bump the IV stand, she went to his side and rested her hand on the metal side rail of the bed. "How are you feeling?"

"I'm fine. I don't need to stay here overnight and have all these extra tests done." He cast a glare at the admittance bracelet on his wrist. "Your grandmother insisted on it."

"She's feeling helpless. Using her pull is her way of doing something."

"Well, I'd be far more grateful if she brought me food that wasn't dry or tough." He sniffed at the table at the foot of the bed, on which rested a tray with a half-eaten meatloaf. "The way she's acting, you'd think I'd had a heart attack or was suffering from a mystery illness."

"At least you have a private room."

"The pain medication isn't up to much in this place."

"You're just complaining because you want to go home." She wanted to ask about the shooting, but she figured it was the last thing he'd want to talk about—especially when he'd no doubt just done that with the police.

He exhaled heavily, looking weary. "Believe it or not, Francesca, your grandmother and I have always wanted the best for you. Maybe we didn't always do what was best for you because of our own bias and guilt."

"Guilt?" she echoed, her brows furrowing.

"No one should have to bury their own child. Christopher might have killed her, but I let her down. If I hadn't agreed to set aside my reservations about her mating, if I had pressured her to leave him, she would be alive today. That's why I've been so immovable on this. I couldn't bear it if you were hurt when I could have prevented it. I didn't want to make that same mistake with you that I did with Caroline, but it would seem that I've made other mistakes."

"Your guilt is pointless," she told him. "She couldn't have left him. Mating bonds are metaphysical constructs that connect two people to the extent that they can't live without each other. You couldn't have convinced her to leave him—even if you had, she'd have died anyway because they needed each other."

He looked from her to Trick. "And you have that bond now?"

"I do. I'm sorry that you'll never be able to support that. But if your parents hadn't approved of Marcia, would it have made any difference to you?"

He averted his gaze. "No, I suppose it wouldn't have." He patted her hand, but he still didn't meet her eyes. "I was wrong to have said that you should get a real job. I hope you can forgive that, if nothing else."

Tears crept up on her, making her throat feel thick. Seeing that he was tiring, she said, "We have to go now. You take care." With that, she left the room.

Trick linked their fingers. "Let's go." At her nod, he led her down the hallway and through to the waiting room. Brad and Marcia looked up, but their expressions were unreadable. Trick guided her past them, straight to the door.

"Francesca," Marcia softly called out. As Frankie turned, the woman's eyes landed on the mark on Frankie's neck and then dulled. She knew it was a claiming bite. "I'll have Edna keep you updated."

In Trick's opinion, that wasn't fucking good enough, but it was better than nothing. He could see that Marcia desperately wanted to say something different, to extend an olive branch, but she just couldn't yet do it. He squeezed Frankie's hand. "Come on, baby."

It wasn't until they were in the SUV, buckling their seat belts, that Frankie spoke. "I didn't expect him to talk to me, let alone say those things. I didn't expect Marcia not to throw me out."

"She wants to reach out to you, but she doesn't know how. One thing you can say for her is that she didn't lash out with her pain. Just like you didn't lash out with yours when you were reunited with Lydia." Frankie and her grandmother were similar in some ways—cool, protective. It was a shame that an ocean of unsaid things lay between them.

Maybe Clara was right and the Newmans would one day soften, just as they had with Caroline. But Trick had a feeling that it would take a while for that to happen, if it ever did.

CHAPTER SEVENTEEN

*F*rankie's feet made no sound as she walked down the brightly lit corridor. It seemed like forever before she arrived at her grandfather's room. She pushed open the door. She frowned. Geoffrey was gone. There was no bed. No equipment. No TV. Only a red door at the other end of the room. Maybe there was a nurse in there.

Frankie turned the knob and walked inside. She was in her display room, surrounded by her sculptures. Chilled, she flexed her fingers and—

The chair was empty. The child was gone.

Frankie heard it then. Creaking. Like old, rickety bones trying to move. She turned, but it wasn't the child she saw. It was Marcia, Geoffrey, and Brad. They were looking at the sculptures, bored and unimpressed.

She called out their names, but they didn't answer. Didn't seem to hear or see her. She called out to them again, louder this time. But her grandparents turned their backs and walked away. Brad's body faded and morphed, and suddenly she was looking at Rio.

"You can't keep him," Rio told her. "Not in the long run. You're not what he needs."

Hearing the creak of bones, Frankie whirled on the spot. It was the child. She was crawling on the floor. She stopped. Slowly and stiffly lifted her head, making her hair part.

"Run," she whispered.

Frankie swallowed. "Why?"

"He hurt her. He'll hurt you."

The smell of gunpowder permeated the room. Blood dripped down the walls. A growl echoed in the small space—a space that seemed to be getting smaller and smaller by the second.

Another growl. "You're supposed to be in—"

Frankie's eyes snapped open, and her body jerked. *Jesus Christ.* Her wolf snarled and raked her claws, disturbed and anxious. The arm that was curled around Frankie from behind briefly tightened. She swallowed with a throat that was as dry as attic dust.

Trick kissed her hair. "Another nightmare?" His voice was rough with sleep.

Nodding, she struggled to sit upright and blew out a long breath. Trick sat up with her and grabbed the glass of water from the nightstand. She took it with a weak, grateful smile and sipped at the water. Her heart was pounding like crazy, and the beat seemed so loud in the quiet of the room.

Trick smoothed her hair away from her face. "What happened in the nightmare?"

Frankie handed him back the glass, and he returned it to the nightstand. "They're all so similar. I'm always in my display room. Always surrounded by my sculptures. At least one of them talks to me. And I always smell that scent mixed in with blood and gunpowder. And then there's that voice . . ."

"Come here." Trick scooped her up and cradled her on his lap. He did his best to remain calm, knowing it was what she needed, but seeing her this way pissed him the fuck off. She always looked drained after the nightmares, as if they took a lot out of her. His wolf snuggled up to her even as he growled in frustration—the thing that was hurting their mate wasn't something they could fight.

"What am I not seeing, Trick? What has my subconscious picked up that has gone right over my head?"

"I don't know," he said, rocking her gently. "I wish I did, if it meant these nightmares would go away."

Sensing that sleep wouldn't come easy, Frankie glanced at the clock. "It's just past six a.m. I think I'll go sit on the balcony for a while."

"Okay. Come on."

She frowned as he edged out of the bed with her still in his arms. "You don't have to—"

"Shut up, baby."

"Well, that's very nice," she muttered, though she was grateful that he'd be with her. He settled in one of the chairs with her on his lap, and she drank in the gorgeous view of the sun peeking over the mountains.

After a long silence, he asked, "You sure you're up to seeing Clara today?"

"If I could get out of it, I would. Packing up Iris's things isn't my idea of a good time. But Clara and Lydia really want me to be there. Apparently it's tradition for the women in the family to do it. And it's hard to say no to Lydia, especially when I know she needs the support. What will you be doing with yourself?"

"I'm going with Trey, Ryan, and Dominic to check out a spot where Morelli's rumored to be hiding. We've had plenty of tips since we put a price on his head. None of them have amounted to anything. He's deep underground. But he can't hide forever. It ain't over until the fat lady sings."

She frowned. "Who is this lady? What does it matter that she's fat? And why does her singing have such importance?"

Trick just shook his head. "Anyway . . . we got a tip that said Morelli was hiding near the landfill. He's probably not there either, but . . ."

"But you want to be there with Trey and the other enforcers in case Morelli is, because you want to be the one who kills him," she understood.

"Yes." Trick caught her gaze, wanting her to see the ruthless intent there. She needed to know he'd do it, and he'd do it without mercy or regret. "And I will be."

"Does this mean I'll end up cuffed to the shower wall again while you work off your brood?"

His lips twitched. "Probably. Marcus and Roni will escort you and Lydia to Bjorn Pack territory. It's unlikely that you'll run into any trouble there, but I want you protected."

Although she thought *two* bodyguards was overkill, Frankie said nothing. The last two times he'd left her, she'd been hurt. First by Drake, then by Rio. It made sense that he'd want her to be adequately protected.

"Onto a different subject, any news about Geoffrey?" he asked.

"I spoke to Edna just before I went to bed. According to her, he's fine." She'd thought about calling him to check in, but if they were going to make their way back to each other, it was something they should do in baby steps.

"Good. I wouldn't be surprised if he contacts you soon, inviting you for lunch. Your family thinks of shifters as monsters. The shooting reminded them that humans do bad things too."

She nestled closer to him. "Yeah, I guess it did."

Soon after breakfast, Marcus drove Frankie, Roni, Lydia, and Cam to Bjorn Pack territory. To give Clara, Lydia, and Frankie the emotional space to go through Iris's possessions, Cam went fishing with Cesar while Roni and Marcus relaxed on Clara's back porch.

As Clara was swathing one of Iris's many knickknacks in bubble wrap, she asked Frankie, "So how are things with you and Trick?"

"Great," replied Frankie, packing clothes into a box.

"Nothing can quite beat a mating bond, can it? It's a gift that most humans will sadly never experience. I've always pitied them that." Clara sighed, her smile nostalgic. "I was very young when I realized Cesar was my mate."

Lydia's brows lifted. "Really?"

"Fourteen. He was sixteen. It was too early for us to claim each other. Our parents wanted us to wait until I was seventeen, so we did. I didn't let him claim me straightaway, though. No, I insisted that he court me proper."

"Court you?" echoed Lydia, mouth twitching.

"Oh yes. I'd been reading a lot of Jane Austen novels at the time. I wanted romance. He gave it to me, bless his heart. Iris did the complete opposite when she realized Alfie was her mate. Like with Frankie, it took her a few months to see the truth. When she did, she wasted no time at all in stating that he was hers and demanding that they claim each other. The poor man was practically railroaded, but it was obvious that he was happy to be." Clara sealed a box with tape as she spoke. "Do the Newmans know that you're mated yet?"

"Yes," replied Frankie. "They saw my claiming bite when I spoke to them a week ago after Geoffrey was shot."

"Shot?"

"An old court case came back to haunt him."

"Ah." Clara began wrapping up another ornament with tissue paper. "How did they react to the bite?"

"They didn't, but they didn't chase me out of the hospital. Geoffrey admitted to making mistakes, but unless he's willing to accept Trick, it's neither here nor there to me. My grandparents and uncle have to know that Trick and I come as a package deal. I'm not saying they need to welcome him into the family, but they do need to accept that he's part of mine." The best and most important member of her family.

"It should be enough for them that Trick makes you happy," began Lydia, "but it won't give them any reassurance, because Christopher made Caroline happy, and yet . . ."

Frankie sighed. "And yet." She glanced out the window, catching sight of her old home. "I have something I need to do." She cut her gaze back to the other two females. "I want to go to the old cabin."

Lydia's eyes glinted with anxiety. "Frankie, I'm not sure that's the best idea."

"Maybe not, but I need to do it."

"Can you at least wait until Trick gets here?" begged Lydia. "You shouldn't do it alone."

"He'll try and talk me out of it. Josh granted permission for me to walk through it. I keep asking Trick to bring me here, and he keeps putting it off." She'd be an old woman before he finally let her do it. "If it was possible that I'd have flashbacks, I'd get why you're concerned. But whatever memories I have of that night are buried deep. For me, walking through the cabin will mean facing my past. Accepting what happened. Getting some closure."

Clara's eyes lit with understanding, but Lydia still seemed anxious.

"Trick once said to me that I need to accept my past and my heritage," said Frankie. "He's right. Our mating bond isn't complete yet. What if it won't fully snap into place until I do as Trick said and accept my past?" She lifted her chin. "I really do need to do this."

Lydia raked a hand through her hair. "I'll go with you. Please don't argue. I can't stand the thought of you doing it alone."

"It'll be hard for you," Frankie warned her. After all, the female's brother had died there.

"I didn't see anything that night. They didn't even let me near the cabin. The only memories I have of that place are good ones."

Frankie sighed. "All right. Clara, will you be okay here?"

260

"Of course," replied Clara with a wave of her hand. "Take whatever time you need. For what it's worth, I think this will be a good thing for you. I'll let Roni and Marcus know where you'll be."

"They'll probably follow us over there," said Lydia. "But they won't go inside—they'll give you the privacy you're due."

With Lydia at her side, Frankie walked out of the cabin and over to her childhood home. The place looked . . . sad. Boards covered the windows, panes of wood had been hammered into place across the door, and insults had been spray painted on the walls.

Hell, even its surroundings were bleak. There were overgrown weeds everywhere. On the cabin's right side was a dead tree that was somehow still standing. On its left was a pond that had long ago dried up.

A lone crow was perched on the rotted porch rail; it watched them as they clambered up the steps. The twigs and leaves littering the porch crunched under their feet as they crossed to the front door. Frankie and Lydia grunted and cursed as they worked to pull off the planks that obstructed the door. They probably would have had a harder time doing it if the wood hadn't gone soft with rain and rot.

Once the boards were gone, Frankie let out a long breath. The door had no knob, so she shoved it open with her elbow. The moment she stepped inside, she grimaced. The chilly air was stale and clouded with dust and smelled faintly of cigarette smoke and pot. Wrappers, empty bottles, beer cans, and cigarette butts were scattered around the floor.

Lydia sighed in disgust. "Looks like kids have hung out here over the years. I'm really hoping they didn't also use it as a make-out spot."

"That would be morbid, considering two people died here."

Their footsteps echoed as they walked over creaky boards, over-riding the sound of the wind whistling through broken windows. The cabin was empty of furniture. No pictures or paintings hung on the walls. The only items that had been left behind were light fixtures covered in cobwebs. Aside from the black splotches and graffiti on the walls, there was no hint of color. She could almost think that no one had ever lived there. It was a husk of a house, really.

"I expected to see some abandoned furniture."

"The cabin was stripped of all its belongings," said Lydia. "I think my mom and dad were worried that someone would set the place alight and everything would be destroyed. Emotions were running very high back then."

Silence fell between them as Frankie explored the downstairs space. "I didn't expect to have any flashbacks or sensory memories, but it's kind of gloomy that I can walk through my childhood home and find no comfort in it at all. Every inch of it feels unfamiliar to me."

They entered another bare room, and Lydia said, "This was, um, the kitchen. This was where it happened." She cleared her throat. "At first people panicked and thought that someone had taken you."

Frankie felt her brows snap together. "Why?"

"The people who first arrived at the scene called out your name, but you didn't answer. They followed your scent down to the basement. You were hiding there, ghost white and shaking."

"Really?" Frankie walked around, looking for another door, and . . . *There.* It was hanging on its hinges, so she carefully pushed it open, grimacing as it left the chalky feel of dust on her hands. At first the space looked like a large cupboard. But then she saw that there was another door. Frankie opened it, satisfied to find that it led to the basement.

Lydia made a pained sound in the back of her throat. "Frankie, don't do this to yourself."

"I'm not trying to torment myself. I can't explain it well, but I just need to do it."

Lydia flapped her arms. "All right."

The wooden steps groaned as they descended into the basement. Frankie's nose wrinkled. It didn't smell any better down there. *Must, mold, and damp concrete.* Even with the sunlight lancing through the wide window, it was as dark as it was cold, so it was a damn good thing that shifters could see well in the dark.

Her shoes scraped on the concrete floor as she explored the large basement. No boxes were stacked anywhere. Nothing stood on the shelves. The storage cupboard was completely bare. Aside from cobwebs and damp spots, the only things to see were the breaker box, a furnace, a water tank, and pipes.

"Well, I think it's safe to say that none of the kids who broke into the cabin over the years ever came down here." There was no litter or graffiti.

"Can't say I blame them." Lydia shuddered. "Basements are creepy."

"Where was I hiding that night?"

Turning, Lydia pointed to the far corner. "You were huddled behind the dryer, which they used to keep over there."

The idea of that made Frankie swallow hard. She *had* to have seen something. A child didn't hide in a spooky basement unless they were running from something much, much scarier.

Lydia rubbed at her upper arms. "Can we go now? I really do hate basements."

"Yeah." Frankie sighed. "We can head back."

"Good, because I'm about to freak out. Let's talk about something cheery."

"Okay. Did Jaime tell you that she passed out on girls' night?" The memory made Frankie's mouth twitch despite her sour mood.

"No, she didn't. She did tell me about Trick's ex-fling, Rio. You stabbed his hand, right?"

"Wouldn't you have done the same if Cam's ex insisted he wasn't your true mate?"

Lydia blinked, mouth falling open. "Rio said that? I thought he was just giving you grief out of spite."

"He did a little of that too. The way he sees it, I can't possibly be what Trick needs, since Rio is convinced that Trick is gay. Apparently he'd also hoped that Trick would one day treat him as more than a fling. He hates that I ended his hopes."

"Seeing you and Trick together will have made him *face* that Trick isn't gay, which means he also had to face that you're able to give Trick something he can't ever give him—not unless he's interested in a sex change, anyway."

Frankie stumbled to a halt as it hit her. Like a slap across the face. All this time, she hadn't seen it. Not even once.

"What?" asked Lydia.

"You're right. He probably hates me. He had it in his head, despite what the facts suggested, that he'd have Trick one day. Because of me, it'll never happen. But he also truly believes that Trick is gay. In Rio's head, I somehow duped Trick. I'm the bad guy." And just the same way, her mother had been the bad guy, she now realized.

"Pretty much, yeah. Honey, you've gone very pale. Is something— *oh my God*." She grabbed Frankie's arm, pulling her to an abrupt stop.

"What?" She tracked Lydia's gaze. "What the fuck?" On the floor someone had drawn a large pentagram. It was surrounded by candles and symbols. Worse, there was a huge reddish-brown stain that was quite clearly old blood.

"Oh my Jesus." Lydia put a hand to her chest. "It was probably just kids being stupid, fooling around and thinking they could summon spirits or demons. Right?"

"That's blood, Lydia. Look at what's in the center of the pentagram." Even though it was peppered with dust, Frankie could see it easily enough.

Lydia drew back, her heart now pounding as fast as Frankie's. "That's a photo of Christopher." Her fingers dug into Frankie's arm as she asked, "Do you think kids were trying to invoke his spirit or something weird like that?"

"I think someone wanted to talk to him." Someone crazy enough to not only sacrifice a living creature but think that it would actually work.

She jumped as the phone in her pocket rang. Taking a shaky breath, Frankie fished it out of her pocket. "It's Trick." She answered, "Hello."

"Baby, what's wrong? I can feel your anxiety. What is it?"

She licked her lower lip. "Well, I'm at the old cabin."

He sighed. "Frankie, you shouldn't have gone there without me. Look, I'm on my way to you now, okay—there was no sign of Morelli at the landfill. Just go back to Iris's house and wait for me."

A board creaked over their heads. And another. And another. Her gut dropped. "Someone's here."

"Probably Marcus or Roni," said Lydia.

"I don't think so," she said as another board softly creaked. Because the person above them was trying very hard to be quiet, like they hoped to sneak up on her. "I know who killed my parents."

"*What?*" both he and Lydia demanded at once.

"I know who it was." She listened as the footsteps crossed the floorboards, trying to determine which way the newcomer was heading. Even if she and Lydia hadn't left footprints in the dust that broadcast their location, the shifter would be able to follow their scents. "And I think they're here."

Trick swore. "I'll be fifteen minutes at most. Go back to Iris's cabin and wait for—*What the hell?*" She heard the roar of metal clashing, the screech of tires, and the shattering of glass.

"Trick? *Trick!*" Frankie looked at her phone, shell-shocked. "The line went dead," she told Lydia. "It sounded like the SUV crashed into something." Her wolf completely freaked out—raged, snarled, howled, battered at Frankie to go to him.

Panic punched Frankie right in the stomach, stealing her breath. The only thing that stopped her from joining her wolf in that crazed state was that she knew he wasn't dead; she could *feel* him. He was unconscious, but he was alive.

"Shit!" Lydia grabbed her arm. "We have to go *now*."

The hinges squealed as the basement door opened. Frankie's heart missed a beat, and her breaths started to come loud and quick.

Heavy footsteps creaked their way down the stairs. "I know you're down there, Frankie." Spoken like a taunt.

Lydia gasped as the male reached the bottom step. "Cruz?"

He grinned at her. "That would be me." His gaze cut to Frankie. "You don't look so surprised to see me."

Frankie swallowed. "I figured it out. Eventually." She remembered the photo albums, remembered how Cruz had often looked at Christopher, remembered seeing photos of them standing almost intimately close. She also remembered Cruz often glaring at Brad the same way Rio had stared at Frankie. But it wasn't Brad he'd been glaring at, she now realized. He'd been glaring at *Caroline*.

"You were supposed to be in bed that night," said Cruz, as though *she* were the one who'd done wrong. "You weren't supposed to hear or see anything."

Lydia's footsteps dragged as she shuffled backward, shaking her head in denial. But then he raised his hand and cocked the trigger of the pistol he held. Lydia froze, and every muscle in Frankie's body went rigid. *Fuck.*

"Hands up where I can see them, girls. That's good. Don't count on your bodyguards coming to help you." He smirked. "I paid some of the juveniles to lure them into the woods."

That wouldn't be enough, thought Frankie. No. Cam would feel Lydia's anxiety, just as Trick would feel Frankie's. *Someone* would come. They had to. Until then, she had to . . . what? She couldn't think. Couldn't reason. Not when she knew Trick was hurt and in danger. She needed to get to him.

Her eyes darted around the basement. The only exit other than the stairway was the grimy window behind Cruz. Getting out meant somehow getting past him and his pistol without getting shot. How the fuck were they supposed to do that? She had no idea.

Her wolf wanted to surface and rip the fucker limb from limb. Frankie would have shifted and given the animal the chance if she weren't so sure that Cruz would put a bullet through her head before she was able to finish the shift.

Hoping to distract him from thoughts of shooting her and Lydia, Frankie flicked a look at the pentagram and asked, "Is that your handiwork?"

Sadness briefly glittered in his eyes. "I missed him. I wanted to apologize for shooting him. I didn't go there that night to hurt him."

"You do know that making a blood sacrifice to try to speak to a ghost is pretty fucked up, right?"

"Depends on a person's definition of fucked up. My definition? Someone tricking a guy into believing she's their true mate—depriving him of what he truly needs and wants—is fucked up. Caroline trapped him into being with her."

Frankie clenched her fists. "So you killed her." *Bastard.*

"I hadn't planned to kill her. Just scare her. Make her *listen.* So I took the gun. That bullet should have killed *her,* not my Christopher."

Flicking a look at the pistol pointed at her, she said, "You sure like to use firearms, don't you?"

"It seems fitting that you'll die from a bullet, just like your mother should have done."

Her wolf peeled back her upper lip and lunged for him, but Frankie managed to retain control. "You were Christopher's lover for a while, before he met my mother."

His chin lifted. "I was more than that. Sure, we weren't exclusive. He needed to sow his oats first—I got that. I understood him. Not like Caroline. She didn't know him the way I did. She didn't get him like I did."

Frankie *felt* Trick regain consciousness. A pulse of his pain traveled down their bond. A lump of sheer terror clogged her throat. Fuck it all, *she needed to get to him.* Her heart was slamming so hard against her ribs that she wouldn't have been surprised if one cracked. But she didn't dare move. Not yet. There was no rationality in Cruz's eyes, and she *knew* that she was looking at somebody who was capable of absolutely anything in that moment.

She didn't want to die. She sure didn't want Trick to die, but it was unlikely that he'd survive the breaking of their mating bond, despite it not being fully formed. For that reason alone, she'd fight. But really, there was nothing she could do that didn't involve throwing herself in harm's way. There was nothing to hide behind. Nothing to throw at Cruz. Nothing to distract him with. He was bigger. Bulkier. Stronger. And motherfucking *armed*.

He dipped his free hand into his pocket and pulled out a small device that looked a little like an iPod. Without moving his gaze from Frankie and Lydia, he pressed the screen with his thumb and . . . and nothing. He gave them a wide, eerie smile. That was when something above them rumbled, shook, and roared as it collapsed. Shingles tumbled off the roof, and the cabin shuddered.

Frankie swallowed as her stomach bottomed. "What did you do?"

"Made sure that we wouldn't be disturbed. That's just parts of the porch roof collapsing near the front and back doors. Can't have anyone trying to get inside, now can we?" He returned the little device—which was obviously a remote—to his pocket. "I wired the place when I heard you'd asked Josh for permission to walk through the cabin."

Frankie gaped at him. Was he high? "The entire place could collapse."

"I know. That's why it's so perfect. My world collapsed when Christopher died. Now yours is going to collapse too." His grin dimmed as he looked at Lydia. "I'm sorry that you'll go down with us. I really am."

"Then let her go," said Frankie.

"It's too late for that."

"Why do this?" Lydia whispered. "Why, Cruz?"

"It's not *my* fault," he insisted, indignant. He jabbed a finger at Frankie. "It's *hers*." He sneered at Frankie. "I knew when I first saw you at Phoenix territory that either you or your wolf remembered something. I just wasn't sure what or how much. Then you started digging, asking questions, poking around in Iris's attic. I heard you wanted to walk through here too, and I knew it was only a matter of time before you worked it out. I had to do something."

A light shudder rocked the cabin walls. Things clattered and rolled along the floor above them, and she wondered if they were the glass bottles they'd found.

"See, I ain't gonna be executed. No. *I* control my fate. If I'm going to die, Frankie, it'll happen when and where *I* choose. Understand? And I choose to die in the same place my Christopher died. And since it's *your* fault that it's come to this, you're going to die with me. I've been waiting for you to finally come here—you sealed both our fates as soon as you walked through that front door. You know, I think Christopher will probably be happy that I'm sending his daughter to him, don't you?" He laughed, as if that were hilarious.

Frankie's gut twisted at the glitter of madness in his eyes. "You've been riding the crazy train for a long time, haven't you?"

"Yeah, I guess I have." And then he fired.

CHAPTER EIGHTEEN

Trick groaned. The god-awful ringing in his ears just wouldn't stop. He tried opening his eyes, but it didn't happen. The scents only aggravated his pounding headache. *Blood, gas, oil, and burned rubber.* He could taste blood, and he realized he'd bitten his tongue. Even with adrenaline pumping through him, he started to feel the ache of several injuries. What the hell had—

Images flashed before him, and his eyes snapped open. *A black car hitting the passenger side. His neck snapping sideways. The SUV tipping. His head smacking into the window as they rolled and tumbled down, down, down.*

Apparently the SUV had righted itself when it finally stopped rolling. Trick glanced out the broken window. They were in a vast, dry pit among high mounds of sand and rubble. As he saw the tall, stairlike sloped walls, he cursed. The fuckers had sent them crashing to the bottom of a goddamn quarry.

Unmanned machinery was nearby, including bulldozers, cranes, tractors, and pumps to remove pooling water. It was no doubt thanks to those pumps that the bed of the quarry was dry.

Trick winced as he tried to move. The seat belt had snapped taut in front of him and *fuck* his chest hurt. He was pretty sure that at least

one rib was fractured, if not broken. Others were badly bruised. "Knew
we should have gone for the model with the side airbags," he muttered.
Clawing open the belt, he took a deep painful breath. His neck
hurt like a bitch from the way it had snapped from side to side as they'd
rolled. He'd definitely cut his head on the window, because he could feel
the burning slice of pain and smell his blood.

He had a concussion for sure, but he couldn't let that matter. His
injuries probably would have been a damn sight worse if he'd been
human. Shifters were hard to hurt. Half the bruises would be gone
within the hour, but that didn't mean Morelli wouldn't pay for every
single one of them.

Someone moaned behind him while another cursed.

Trick tried to glance over his shoulder, but pain shot through his
neck and he swore. "Any of you dead?"

Beside him, Ryan grunted.

"Feels like it," rasped Dominic. "What the hell just happened?"

"It was a trap," said Trey, voice strained with pain. "Morelli lured us
out here, and then he or one of his friends crashed into us."

Eyes narrowed, Ryan peered out the window. "Said 'friends' are outside in their wolf forms, pacing on the wide stairs. I count eleven. Don't
know if that includes Morelli—I've never seen him in his wolf form."

"His pack was a lot bigger," said Dominic. "Either it split after they
abandoned their territory or the others are nearby."

"I think it's the first," said Trey. "His pack was made up of lone
shifters and people whose Alphas and pack mates he destroyed. I doubt
many of them would have felt a burning need to stick by his side—
especially when he's made an enemy of us and, by extension, our allies.
These wolves here are likely his only loyal followers."

"Why haven't they just pounced on us already?" asked Dominic.

"They're playing with us," said Trick, carefully brushing shards of
glass from his hair. "They want us to see that we're no safer outside than
we are in here. Doesn't matter either way. We've got to get out." Smoke

hissed out from under the slightly raised hood. That couldn't be good. "Anyone have their phone handy? I dropped mine somewhere."

Ryan grunted, unzipped his jacket pocket, dug out his cell, and pressed what Trick knew was the panic button. It would send an alert and their GPS coordinates to each of their pack mates. "The cavalry should arrive soon."

Carefully twisting in his seat, Trick got a good look at each of his pack mates. Bruised, bleeding, and rumpled, they didn't look any better than he did. But they were alive, and the need to *hurt* practically shone from their eyes. "Ready to get out there?"

"*Raring* to get out there," Dominic ground out.

As his wolf raked at him, wanting his attention, Trick pressed his fingers to his aching temple. There was something . . . something he needed to do. Someone who—

Frankie. Trick gripped the edge of his seat. "I need to get to Frankie." He told them about their phone call. "If she's right and the person in that cabin killed her parents, she's in danger."

"We'll get to her," Trey assured him in a "Keep the fuck calm" voice, "but we have to get out of this shit first. She has Roni and Marcus; they'll protect her."

They'd better, Trick thought. He checked on her through their bond. Fear was a living thing inside her. The drive to get to her pounded through him, *but he couldn't answer it because of that damn bastard out there.*

Trick hissed out a breath. "*Fuck.* I'm going to enjoy killing this motherfucker and his sorry excuse for a pack." He used his sleeve to wipe at the blood dripping down his face and then shoved open the dented door, leaving bloody fingerprints. Glass tinkled as it dropped from his lap to the ground.

The others slid out of the SUV too, but Trick kept his eyes on the wolves glaring at them from the wide, rising steps. The air was bone-dry and smelled of rock and dirt.

A gray wolf let out a low howl, as if calling for his Alpha. Morelli appeared at the top of the quarry moments later, a wide grin on his face. Descending the steps, he clapped. "Damn, I wasn't sure if you'd survive." He said it with admiration, like they'd crashed for the thrill. "That's one hell of a drop." He stopped halfway down the wall and petted the head of the closest wolf.

"Hiding behind your pack, Morelli?" taunted Trey. "Is that what Alphas do now?"

Dominic snickered. "You're forgetting, Trey—this guy's no Alpha."

Trey's lips pursed. "Valid point."

Morelli's face tightened, but then he smiled. "Must we really resort to insults?"

"No," said Trey. "You could fight me, Alpha to *supposed* Alpha."

Trick's wolf growled, not liking that idea. *He* wanted to be the one to end the bastard.

"Prove to me and your wolves here that you're what you claim to be," continued Trey. "Prove to them that you're worth following. Prove to them that you're worth *dying* for. Because they *will* die if they come at us. Come on, show them that you're willing to protect them from that and let's settle this, one to one."

Morelli's smile hardened at the edges. "But that would be depriving them of the luxury of killing the people who burned down their homes."

"You blamed it on us?" Ryan grunted. "We thought you might."

"It was a good idea," said Trick. "Burn the buildings down, pin it on us, and then propose to the others that you all lay low and come up with a plan. Well, it's not like you could tell them you wanted to *hide*. I'm curious, though, have you told them all that you work with an extremist?"

Morelli froze, and his wolves became edgy and restless. Trick knew why. The animals wouldn't understand the words, but the people within them would. The human emotions would bleed out onto the wolves, making them agitated and confused.

"Drake had plenty to say before he died," Trick told him.

Morelli snorted. "And I'll bet he found delight in talking bullshit to you—it was really the only way to fuck with you at that point."

"He was telling the truth," said Trey. "You know it. We know it. By working with an extremist, you've betrayed your kind. You deserve to die for that alone."

"Such bravery from someone who's outnumbered, weakened by injury, and has no chance of a rescue." Morelli sighed, pulled out a cigar, and lit it. "I gotta hand it to you, Trey, you really do have balls. I honestly do like you. It saddens me that you have to die tonight. We could have been allies."

"We would *never* have been allies."

"But if you'd just agreed to give it a shot, you wouldn't be about to die, your territory wouldn't soon be invaded, and your other pack mates wouldn't be given the option of joining me or dying." Morelli shrugged. "You only have yourself to blame. But while your death will sadden me, I really am looking forward to taking over that territory of yours."

A growl rumbled out of Trick. "We won't be the ones who die here tonight," he warned as he and his pack mates shed their clothes, ready to shift. Sure, they were outnumbered and injured. But they were also filled with the need for vengeance. For Trick and his wolf, this fight was personal. And now that the motherfucker effectively stood between Trick and his mate when she needed him, there wasn't a chance in hell that Morelli would survive this fight.

Morelli took another drag on his cigar and then sat on the step, settling to watch the show. Wolves sat on either side of him like sentries. "Can't say I agree with you on that one, Trick. It really was nice knowing you all." He signaled the waiting wolves, and then they were scrabbling down the walls.

Trick shifted. With his pack mates around him, the wolf charged at the other pack, paws thudding into the dirt. Colliding, the packs brutally slashed at each other.

There was growling, snarling, and yelping as they battled. Claws scored deep. Teeth bit hard. Blood sprayed and splattered. Dust and dirt clouded the air, causing eyes to itch and nostrils to tingle.

Adrenaline pumped through Trick's wolf, helping him ignore the injuries from the crash. He raged as one enemy clawed at his flank while another attacked from the front. The wolf fought them both—lashed out with his big paws, snapped his powerful jaws, slammed his large body into theirs.

One attacker toppled over. The wolf pounced and tore into his throat, letting blood gush into his mouth. He didn't take time to enjoy the victory. He whirled and lunged at his other opponent with a snarl.

The enemies were strong. Sneaky. Agile. But they hadn't been trained to fight. Lacked the stamina and speed that the wolf and his pack mates had. Still they fought, determined. The Phoenix wolves showed no mercy. Never hesitated.

The scents of fear and rage fed the wolf's bloodlust. As he took down yet another enemy, a heavy weight barreled into the wolf's side, sending him crashing into a stone slab. His vision blurred. The world tilted.

His opponent was on him in a flash. The wolf swiped out his paw, clawing at his attacker's muzzle, sinking his claws deep. Warm blood spurted. The enemy jerked back with a yelp. Taking advantage, the wolf quickly righted himself. They both pounced.

The wolf *hurt*. Claws and teeth ripped through skin, tore muscle, and scraped bone. His opponent was brutal. He fought just as brutally. Each yelp of pain and spray of blood from his enemy spurred the wolf on. Paws repeatedly attempted to grab the wolf's neck and wrestle him to the ground. The wolf fought every attempt.

It was hard not to be distracted by his mate's fear—and his fear *for* her. But he had to shelve it, just as he shelved his pain. His focus needed to be on the enemy in front of him, who tore yet another strip out of the wolf's side.

With a snarl of rage, the wolf lunged. He wrestled the enemy to the ground and used a rear paw to slice open his belly while he bit down on his throat. Under him the body went lax and the heart thudded to a stop.

Triumph flooded the wolf. He leaped to his feet in time to watch his Alpha pin an enemy flat on its back and clamp his jaws around a throat he quickly he tore out. The wolf growled his approval.

He took a moment to look around. Through the dust clouds, he saw the savaged bodies sprawled on the ground, throats torn out, bellies slashed open. None belonged to his pack mates. They—

He heard a familiar yelp. Turned to see his pack mate, "Ryan," being savagely raked by two enemies. One of the scents wrenched a snarl out of him. *Morelli.*

Laughing hysterically, Cruz said, "I fired at your feet on purpose, in case you're wondering. I didn't miss."

Frankie's wolf bared her teeth. "Then why bother shooting at all?"

"Once I kill you, it's over. I'm enjoying your fear. There's power in causing such fear in another person."

"Christopher wouldn't have wanted this," Lydia said, shaking her head sadly.

"But he'll forgive it," said Cruz. "He loved me, like I loved him."

Frankie snickered, an angry flush marking her cheeks. "You can stop with this bullshit about how much you loved Christopher. You *killed* him, and then you framed him for my mother's murder."

His eyes hardened. "I wouldn't have had to if Caroline had just left like she was supposed to," he snapped, defensive. "She didn't care that she was making him live a lie. Didn't care that he wouldn't have been happy with her in the long run." He shook his head madly. "She fooled him into thinking they were true mates. But I knew that wasn't true. I told her that. I tried to reason with her, tried to make her see that she didn't belong here, just like her parents and her brother did. She said I was crazy and that Christopher would never be mine. Before I even thought about it, I'd pulled out the gun."

As Frankie looked down the barrel of *this* gun, muscles tight with fear, she had a pretty good idea of how Caroline had felt.

"Oh, she changed her tune then," he went on with a chuckle. "Promised she'd leave and take you with her if I'd just put the gun down. I believed her. I was going to lower it. But then she dived at me with that damn knife, knocking the gun out of my hand. The next thing I knew, I was stabbing her in the chest with her own knife. But she was making too much noise, so I had to shut the bitch up."

Frankie's chest went tight as she pictured it—her mother bleeding, struggling, gasping for breath, scared out of her mind as big hands squeezed her throat. Frankie wanted to kill this motherfucker *so* bad. "Why kill him? Why?"

"He must have felt her pain through their bond, because he barged inside. She was dead by then, and he was weaving all over the place— the breaking of the mating bond hit him so hard, he could barely walk, let alone think straight. I talked to him, told him that her death was for the best, but it was like he couldn't even see me. He just kept sobbing her name, begging her to wake up. He thought he could save her. Pulled the knife out of her chest and tried CP fucking R."

And in doing so, thought Frankie, he'd gotten Caroline's blood all over him.

"Then he seemed to snap out of it. He twisted and grabbed the gun I'd dropped on the floor. I knew he'd shoot me. He wasn't thinking straight, you see. I came up behind him and gripped the hand holding the gun. I tried wrestling it from him. He might have overpowered me if he wasn't weak and disoriented from the breaking of the bond.

"He wasn't supposed to die. You hear me? *He wasn't.* I just twisted his hand so that he was pointing the gun at his own temple. I did it to get his attention. To make him stop, think, and *listen.* To make him realize that he didn't want to hurt me. But he kept on struggling and . . . it just went off. And then he was dead."

Lydia whimpered, and Frankie risked a quick glance at her. The female's body was trembling, and her breathing was quick and shallow. God, they needed to get out of there. Frankie's muscles twitched with the need to act—to fight, run, hide, lunge, *anything.*

An ominous groan of wood made her stomach churn. The cabin shuddered, and dust sifted down through the cracks in the wooden beams of the ceiling, hitting her face and creeping down her collar. She couldn't even bat at it. If she moved her hands, he'd fire.

The building was becoming more and more unstable by the minute. Every now and then she'd hear something twist, crack, or splinter. It was going to collapse, and then they'd all be trapped down there—that was, if they weren't immediately killed by the impact.

There were other noises too. She could hear people outside—running around, shouting, and hopefully doing fucking something. Wanting to keep Cruz distracted, she said, "And you were heartbroken by Christopher's death. So damn heartbroken that you confessed to the crimes. Oh no, wait, you blamed it all on him." She ignored his growl. "Why didn't you kill me too?"

"I would have," he said. "I didn't realize you were there at first. But then I turned and found you standing in the doorway. I wasn't sure how much you'd seen, so I told you that your daddy killed her and himself and that I was here to get help. But then you ran, and I knew you'd seen something. People crashed inside—they'd heard the gunshot. I didn't have time to go after you." He tilted his head. "I don't know why you never said my name and told people what you saw. Maybe your little mind just wanted to block it out. Maybe you didn't know which of the triplets I was."

Maybe she'd been experiencing the same choking, incapacitating, logic-stealing fear that was riding her now. It wasn't just fear for herself and Lydia, it was fear for Trick. Frankie took a deep, controlled breath. God, she needed to *think*, plan, and—

Frankie heard the scrape of wood and a muffled curse. Someone was trying to clear the mess blocking the door, she thought. Hope briefly sparked in her belly . . . until she realized that Cruz had heard it too.

He roared. *"If anyone tries to come in here to save these bitches, I'll shoot their fucking faces off!"*

Silence.

More dust slipped through the cracks in the ceiling and poured down on them. Squinting, he coughed, putting a fist to his mouth, lowering his hand for just a moment. It was the opening Frankie needed. She leaped at him and reached for the gun.

Flattening his ears, the wolf sprang at "Morelli." With a renewed vigor, he slashed and bit as he fought. By now blood matted his fur, just as dirt muddied it. His rake wounds burned. His ravaged ear stung. His ribs—still sore from the crash—hurt with each heave of his chest.

Pain and blood loss were slowing him down. He didn't care. His opponent *would* die. He *would* howl in agony. He *would*—

Something thudded into the wolf's stomach. No. His *mate's* stomach. An echo of her pain rippled through him. The wolf's heart jumped. Panicked, he froze. His opponent took advantage and slammed into him. The wolf crashed to the ground, vulnerable, and—

Howls rang through the air, and then a number of wolves were running down the sloped walls. Not his pack mates, the wolf quickly realized. Their allies.

His enemy fled, taking him by surprise. The wolf jumped to his feet and pursued him, who scrambled over piles of rubble, kicking up dust. The wolf sneezed and growled, eyes itchy with the dust. He didn't let it stop him.

He kept chasing his opponent. Wove through the construction cones. Ducked under the ropes. Leaped over wooden pallets. Hopped over wires. Almost crashed into scaffolding.

Pebbles and gravel dug into his paws. He ignored the pain and the wooziness. Kept running and running. His enemy slipped on a loose piece of shale, lost his footing. That was all the wolf needed. He lunged, maneuvered the other wolf onto his back, and—

Jaws clamped around the wolf's leg and heaved him aside, allowing his opponent to leap to his feet and race away. Growling, the wolf spun and tackled the interferer onto his back. He delivered the killing bite, tasted blood. Dark satisfaction would have filled the wolf, but panic for his mate was still riding him.

He backed off the corpse, breaths sawing in and out of his heaving chest. He glanced around, searching for "Morelli." Most of the other enemies had been taken down. He shook his fur, ridding himself of dust and dirt.

A sudden rumble filled the air, followed by the heavy scent of exhaust. The wolf whirled, narrowed his eyes. His opponent, back in his human form, was inside a truck. The engine revved. Something beeped. And then the truck charged him.

The wolf ran with the truck hot on his heels. He made a sharp turn. Tires screeched as the truck tried to follow. "Morelli" made the turn, but it slowed him down.

The wolf repeated the pattern. Ran. Sharply turned. Evaded and slowed the truck. On the third run, the truck didn't turn fast enough.

It clipped a crane. The large piece of equipment shook. Wobbled. Then toppled on top of the truck.

Trick leaped to the surface, wincing as every injury on his body blazed with agony. He hobbled to the truck, dragged a dazed Morelli out of the driver's seat, and tossed him on the ground. The other shifters gathered around Morelli, some still in their wolf forms. All were breathing hard and covered in bites, rake marks, and blood. And all were glaring at the bastard with hatred and lethal intent in their eyes.

"I wanted to be the one to kill you," Trick told him. He'd dreamed of it, fantasized about it, planned just how much pain he'd exact on Morelli. But right then, vengeance didn't seem so important. Not when the pull to be with Frankie was so much more powerful.

"Is that so?" Morelli didn't try to rise. He shot nervous glances at the growling wolves, eyes hard, chest heaving.

"Yeah. I wanted to take my time with you, make you suffer long and hard. But I don't have the time for that, and there's no fucking way I'll give you a swift execution. Tonight, three of my pack mates and several of my allies could have died. Our mates would probably have died along with us. You would have killed other members of my pack—including the pups—and then stolen our territory. So I'd say all these wolves here have the right to make you bleed." As one, the wolves leaped at him.

Trick turned his back as Morelli screamed and gargled while the wolves growled and snarled. He had something much more important on his mind. "I gotta get out of here," he told Trey, who was currently being healed by Ally. "Frankie's been shot."

"*Shot?*" echoed Trey.

Not giving a shit that he'd be leaving them an SUV short, Trick hiked up the rough, sloped walls. Each step he took hurt like a bitch, pulling on his rake wounds and sending pain blazing up and down his fractured leg.

"Wait!" Ally called out. He didn't stop, but—uninjured—she easily caught up to him and put a hand on his arm, sending healing energy trickling through him as she spoke. "Taryn should be with her by now, Trick."

"Taryn?"

"Yes. She called us after she got Ryan's alert—our territory was closer to your location, so she asked us to go to you. She wanted to get to Frankie. Apparently Cam called Taryn to tell her that Cruz was keeping Frankie and Lydia trapped in the basement of her old cabin. If she's been shot, Taryn will heal her."

Reaching the top of the incline, Trick made a beeline for the nearest vehicle. "She's hurt and she's scared. Taryn hasn't healed her, which means Cruz still has her at what I'm assuming is fucking gunpoint, considering she's been *shot*." Trick spit on the ground, grimacing at the tastes of sand and blood. At least his pain had lessened. "I need a phone so I can call Taryn."

Just as Ally handed him her phone, the others joined them.

"If Frankie's been shot, we're *all* going," declared Trey, chucking Trick's clothes at him—it was only then that Trick realized he was naked.

Quickly, he dragged on his shirt and jeans, and then everyone packed themselves into the two SUVs. The badly injured went in one SUV with Ally to be healed; the rest of them hopped into the other.

Riding shotgun while Zander drove like a madman, Trick used Ally's cell to phone Taryn. He put the phone to his ear and waited. And waited. He frowned. "She's not answering."

"Try Cam," Trey advised.

He dialed the wolf's number and then waited, fists clenched. When Cam answered, Trick immediately asked, "Cam, what's going on? Where's Frankie?"

"She's still trapped in the basement with Lydia," Cam said, distress in every word. "We can't get inside. Cruz rigged the front and back porches; both collapsed and blocked the doors. The explosions weakened the cabin, and I don't think it'll stay standing for much longer. Marcus tried to get inside, but Cruz lost his shit and threatened to shoot Lydia and Frankie if we try. Then . . . I don't know what happened. We heard a gunshot."

"He shot Frankie in the stomach," Trick managed to grit out. Her pain pulsed down their bond, and his wolf raged inside him.

"Oh Jesus. Trick, we can't get in there." There was muttering in the background, and then another voice came on the phone.

"Trick, it's Marcus. Man, I'm so fucking sorry. Cruz paid some juveniles to distract us; they didn't know why he did it, they thought he just wanted to yank our chains, but—" He swore. "God, Trick, I really am so fucking sorry."

He didn't blame Marcus, he didn't, but he also didn't have any words of reassurance to give him while panic and anger were clawing at him. "I'm on my way. I'll be there soon. Do whatever you have to do, Marcus, but get in there and *get her out.*"

Crouched on the floor beside Frankie, Lydia pressed her hands on the wound on Frankie's stomach and let out a sob. "Oh God, Frankie, I don't know what to do."

"There's nothing you can do," said Cruz. "That was the whole point of me shooting the bitch." He smiled down at Frankie. "I've heard that a gut shot hurts like holy hell."

It did. The pain was unlike anything Frankie had ever felt in her life—it was as if something molten had exploded in her stomach. She didn't know whether Lydia's efforts were paying off or not, but warm blood had soaked her shirt and dripped onto the concrete below.

The wound throbbed with every breath until it was like one giant, aching pulse. Tears filled her eyes, and her lips trembled. Deep inside her, her wolf panicked.

Above them wood creaked and moaned. It sounded like frames were scraping against each other. The walls were becoming weaker and weaker. She heard a hissing sound. A broken pipe? She wasn't sure.

Morbid glee dancing in his eyes, Cruz taunted, "That bullet tore through your stomach, which means all the acid and bile is loose."

Bastard. She winced as Lydia's hands pressed harder on her wound, and he seemed to absolutely relish the sound of Frankie's pain. Her wolf sneered, wanting out, wanting the taste of his blood in her mouth.

"Cruz?" a voice called out. "Cruz?"

It was Clara. The glee cleared from his eyes, and for a single moment he looked lost and sad. But then his cheeks flushed and he shook his head. "You're not here!" he bellowed.

"Son, please come out here," Clara begged, sounding heartbroken. "Come on, everything will be fine."

The hand holding the gun twitched. "No, it won't! Nothing's been fine for a long time!"

"Cruz, we can fix whatever is wrong. We can. Just come out. *Please.*"

He shook his head again. "It can't be fixed! You can't bring Christopher back! No one can!"

"Let the girls go, Cruz. They haven't done anything to hurt you." She paused. "Let me come in and talk to you."

With a roar Cruz fired at the ceiling. "No one comes in here!" He fired again and again and again. Debris rained down on them, stinging Frankie's eyes and pounding at her skin—

A loud crack split the air.

The basement window shattered.

Cruz roared again as his body jerked forward like he'd been shoved.

Frankie could only stare at him, completely stunned. Eyes wide in disbelief, he dropped to his knees. He blinked rapidly, let out an animalistic grunt. And then he slumped forward. That was when she noticed the blood blooming on the back of his T-shirt, and she understood he'd been shot.

Marcus appeared at the window and elbowed the rest of the broken glass away. "Come on, we have to get you out *now*."

Frankie hissed as Lydia carefully pulled her to her feet. Wooziness slammed into her head, making her knees buckle.

Lydia bit her lip. "I'm sorry, Frankie, I'm so sorry."

"It's okay," she said through gritted teeth. *Lie.* The room was spinning, and her head felt . . . fuzzy. "Get to the window." She blinked rapidly, trying to focus on Marcus, trying to fight the darkness heading her way. She would *not* pass out. Not when they were so close to freedom. Not when the cabin was still creaking, and bits of debris were still falling.

Reaching the window, Lydia made a sound of frustration. "Marcus, there's nothing for us to stand on. You'll have to pull us up." He hung over and reached out with both hands. Lydia gestured for Frankie to go first, but she shook her head.

"Not leaving you," mumbled Frankie. "We go *together.* The window's wide enough for us both to fit through."

"She's right," said Marcus. "Now move."

Lydia slung Frankie's arm around her neck, and then they each grabbed one of his hands. At Marcus's direction they tried to "walk" up the wall with the tips of their shoes. The whole time, darkness beckoned to Frankie. It just hurt so fucking bad.

Finally their heads slid out the damn window. Frankie would have laughed in relief if Marcus hadn't planted a chaste "Thank fucking God you're okay and Trick won't have to kill me" kiss on her mouth. Behind him Roni chuckled.

Cam appeared and literally hauled Lydia out the rest of the way. Marcus moved more carefully, mindful of Frankie's wound and—

A hand locked on her ankle and yanked hard. She slipped, face grazing the wall, but she didn't hit the floor. Marcus grabbed at her hands, and she latched on tight. Her fingers heated and stung from how tight his grip was, but she held on to him desperately.

Glancing down, she saw that Cruz had somehow crawled her way, and his long arm had stretched out just enough to reach her. She kicked at the hand seizing her ankle until, with a curse, he let go. Elation filled her—

The cabin again shuddered, creaking louder than before, and the ceiling above her cracked. Marcus's eyes widened with realization. He tried pulling her up, but it was too late. Just as she let go of his hands and hit the concrete mere inches away from Cruz, someone yanked Marcus out of the way.

Frankie curled into a protective ball on the floor, shielding her head, as the world seemed to fall on top of her. Pain slammed into her arms, shoulders, legs, hands, feet—even the head she tried to protect.

Every part of her seemed to hurt, but that wasn't what made her want to scream. She couldn't move. Not even an inch. She was stuck. Trapped. In the dark. Her breath stuttered out of her just as her heart began racing like a wild horse. Panic choked her, squeezing her chest so tight she couldn't seem to get enough oxygen. Her wolf let loose a primal howl.

Frankie told herself to calm down, but she couldn't. Her breaths kept coming faster and faster. Her heart kept beating like crazy. Lights flashed before her eyes as her head swam. Then her body flushed and heat rushed to her head. *Oh God, oh God, oh God.*

"Frankie!"

Her heart skipped a beat at the sound of Trick's voice. She clung to it, using it as an anchor to calm herself.

"Frankie, talk to me!"

"Trick?" Her voice was weak and raspy, but she *felt* his relief down their bond.

More wood groaned and shuddered. That was when she realized that the whole building hadn't collapsed yet, only the ceiling.

"Get out of the way, Marcus. She'll be crushed if I don't get her out!"

"*We'll* get her out," insisted Marcus.

"Baby, I need to hear your voice again so I can work out exactly where you are."

"You'll find me under a mound of debris," she quipped, using humor to keep the panic at bay. "Cruz is only a few inches away, but I can't see or hear him."

"Okay, I think she's directly beneath the window," Trick said, voice muted. "It's going to be hard not to stand on her. Be careful and try sliding to the side."

"Got it," Marcus agreed.

"Frankie, we're coming in. Don't move. Stay still."

She did as he asked, listening as they slid through the window, hearing the debris rattle as their feet hit the floor. "You were hurt," she said. "Are you okay?"

"I'm fine, Frankie. Ally healed me. Let's just worry about you."

The weight on top of her jangled and shook and cracked. She waited and waited, silently praying that they'd find her. Soon a shaft of light shone through a small gap in the boards, and her heart leaped. Moments later a plank of wood was slid aside, and then Trick's face was staring down at her.

Relief flashed in his eyes, and he squeezed them shut. "Christ." He blew out a breath. "Don't move."

"Hurry." Because the wooden walls were creaking and splintering again. He and Marcus swiftly cleared the rest of the weight from her body, and then Trick snatched her up. A sob slipped out of her, and she tucked her face into his chest.

"Shh, baby, I got you. You're okay." He kissed her head. "We have to go. Look up and reach for Trey."

She fisted his shirt. "No, you can't stay here. You have to come. You'll get crushed."

"I'll be right behind you, baby, I swear it. Now reach for Trey."

Not wanting to waste time arguing, she did as he asked. The Alpha carefully pulled her the rest of the way out. The fresh air hit her face, and a tremor ran through her body. Lying on the ground, she greedily inhaled, gasping in huge gulps of air. Every gasp made the wound on her stomach throb and burn, but she couldn't quite stop.

"Breathe slow or you'll pass out." With Marcus at his side, Trick scooped her up and moved her far away from the cabin to where the others waited anxiously. "Taryn—"

A roar split the air as wood came crashing down—snapping, splitting, cracking, and thudding. The cabin literally caved in on itself, sending debris and dust everywhere.

"Well, fuck," muttered Marcus.

"Lay her down, Trick. I'll heal her." Taryn smiled at Frankie when he rested her on the grass. "Good to have you back. We were losing our minds out here, thinking we might not get to you in time. Did the bullet go straight through?" she asked Trick.

He nodded, having already checked. Taking Frankie's hand, Trick slid up her T-shirt enough to see her bullet wound. He needed to watch as it closed, needed to *see* that she'd be okay. Impatiently he waited as his Alpha female healed her—all the while conscious that if his mate had been human, she might have been dead by now.

The moment she was fully healed, Trick cradled her on his lap. Shit, her heart was beating too fast and her breathing was now too damn shallow. He rocked her. "Breathe with me, Frankie." She looked up at him, eyes wide and glassy. Her face was pale and clammy and made him want to punch something. His wolf paced, still edgy with panic.

"Who shot Cruz?" asked Frankie.

"Josh," said Marcus, hovering. "He's a crack shot."

Trick recalled Cesar telling them that the Alpha kept a rifle as a keepsake. He made a mental note to thank Josh. Right then his only concern was his mate.

He smelled a familiar scent just before his mother crouched beside them. Her soft smile was all for Frankie as she held out a glass of water. "Here, baby girl, drink this."

Trick took the glass and lifted Frankie just enough for her to sip at the drink. That was when Uma lightly smacked his head. He flinched. "Ow. What the fuck?"

"Don't curse at me," reprimanded Uma, her voice shaky. "My heart almost burst right out of my chest when you went through that window. I know you had to get to your mate, I understand you couldn't leave her in there, and I'm glad that you didn't. But that doesn't mean you didn't just put me through hell."

Completely stunned that she'd break down that way in public, Trick glanced at his father, who was standing beside her. Michael gave Trick a look that said "See, she loves you."

Trick simply told her, "I'm okay."

"I know. That's why I'm not a sobbing wreck."

Michael offered Frankie an affectionate smile. "Glad to see you're all right."

Uma took the glass back from Trick and stood, almost bumping Trey as she backed up. She lightly touched his arm. "Sorry, Trey."

His Alpha blinked, clearly surprised that he hadn't gotten his usual scowl. His brow creased as he said, "Um . . . no problem."

People gathered around, checking on Frankie, gently petting her. When they finally cleared, Trick looked down at his mate and noticed that her eyelids were drooping. "Let's get you home."

"You got me out," she whispered.

He frowned. "Of course I did. I'm sorry I didn't get here sooner," he added, kissing a spot on her forehead that was free of dust and blood.

"You shouldn't have come in after me. You could have been killed."

He spoke against her mouth. "Frankie, you have to know there isn't a damn thing I wouldn't do for you. Get that through your head."

Her eyes suddenly filled. "Cruz killed them. He killed my parents. He was Christopher's lover for a while."

Trick's brows lifted. "I would never have guessed."

"Cruz believed my mother tricked Christopher into thinking they were mates. It was like the Rio situation magnified by a thousand." Nose tingling, she sniffled. "I'm so fucking angry at Cruz, but a part of me is also relieved."

"Because now you know the truth."

"Yeah. And now I know that I really wasn't holding back from you or the bond. I just hadn't accepted my past because it would have meant accepting that my father was guilty. I so badly wanted it to have all been some big mistake." That inner turmoil had felt like an elastic band around her chest for so long. "Now that I know it was, I can make my peace with everything. So you'd better brace yourself." And the elastic band snapped.

"Brace for—?" A sharp impact slammed into Trick's head and chest. His world briefly shook and dimmed, but there was no pain. And suddenly it was like she was *inside* him. Their bond had clicked fully into place, and a relieved breath shuddered out of his wolf. "About fucking time."

She chuckled weakly. "Yeah, it is." Her wolf pushed against her skin to rub up against him, soaking up his warmth.

"Home. We're going home." Keeping her in his arms, Trick stood just as Josh approached them. "I heard what you did. I'm in your debt."

"You're my brother's pack mate—there's no debt." Josh cast the wrecked cabin a look. "I think it's safe to say that Cruz didn't survive that. If he did, he's all yours."

CHAPTER NINETEEN

Trick buried his face in her neck as he slammed his cock deep and erupted inside his mate, filling her with everything he had. Even as that familiar peace stole over him, the panic didn't entirely abate. It didn't matter that she'd been fully healed for over twenty-four hours. Didn't matter that he had her right there in their bed, all soft and warm and relaxed. Anxiety still had a firm grip on him.

Maybe she sensed that, because she wrapped him up tight, curling her arms around his neck and locking her legs around his hips. He kissed her neck, taking her scent inside him to soothe both him and his wolf.

"Let go of the guilt, Trick," she whispered. "It's senseless."

No, it wasn't. She'd been scared, and he hadn't been there. Hadn't helped. Hadn't protected her. Hell, he'd barely gotten there in time to save her from being crushed by a fucking building.

She'd firmly assured him again and again that she wasn't upset with him for not getting there sooner. In fact, she'd ordered him to "give yourself a fucking break." She didn't feel that he'd failed her or even that he could have been much help if he *had* gotten there earlier. Though intellectually he knew that it wasn't his fault that she'd gone through that shit alone, he couldn't help feeling like a bastard.

"You have to stop torturing yourself sometime, Trick."

He softly snorted. "Says the person who won't stop torturing herself for not bringing Cruz to justice twenty-four years ago."

She sighed. "I just don't get why I didn't tell people what happened."

Bracing himself on his elbows, he lifted his head and tucked her hair around her ear. "You were traumatized."

"I just had to say his name. That's all. Why didn't I do that?"

"You are not allowed to feel guilty about this. If I told you that a three-year-old pup didn't name her parents' killer because she was shocked and terrified, would you blame her?"

"No."

"Then you don't get to blame you." He kissed her softly, sipping from her mouth. "You need to forgive your three-year-old self, Frankie. You need to let it go. Okay?"

She exhaled heavily. "Okay." She skimmed her fingers along his jaw. "I love you."

"I know you do. And I love you." He kissed her again. "And I love that our bond is now complete."

"Me too." Her cell phone rang, pulling them out of their own little world.

Trick grabbed her cell from the nightstand and glanced at the screen. "It's your agent."

Frankie took the phone and answered, "Hi, Abigail."

"Hi, how are things?" she asked.

"Good, thanks. How about you?"

"Oh, I'm fine. I'm calling because I managed to find out who purchased the sculpture you told me about. The gallery kept the records."

"It's okay," said Frankie. "I already know who it was."

"You do?"

"Yeah. Cruz Stewart, right?"

There was a pause. "Um . . . no. Sweetie, the name I have here is . . . Well, the buyer was Brad Newman. Isn't that your uncle?"

Frankie's stomach plummeted, and her smile faded. "Yes. Yes, it is. I have to go, Abigail."

"You call me later."

"I will." Ending the call, she asked, "Did you hear that?"

Trick nodded. "Brad bought the sculpture that you found at Iris's cabin." His brow furrowed. "That makes no fucking sense, baby. Iris wouldn't have accepted anything from him."

"No, she wouldn't have. Yet, it somehow ended up in her hands. I suppose she could have received it from an anonymous sender, but that's the kind of thing you tell people, isn't it? Clara said nobody seems to know where Iris got it."

"She wouldn't have taken anything from Brad." Trick was sure of that much. "Maybe he asked someone to give it to her as a gift from them, but I can't think who—" He frowned at the odd look on her face. "What?"

"I need to speak to Lydia. I have to ask her something."

"So call her."

Frankie did so, drumming her fingers on Trick's back. Her stomach fluttered and her heart pounded, because she was quite sure that she already knew what Lydia's answer would be.

"Hello," Lydia softly greeted her.

"Lydia, hi. How are you feeling?"

A long sigh. "Better, thanks. But I'm not the one who was shot. How are you?"

"I'm okay. Listen, remember I went exploring in your mom's attic? Well, there was a box of my mother's things there, but it was empty. Someone had ripped open the tape and took whatever was in it."

"Really?" Lydia puffed out a breath. "Well, I remember your grandparents demanded all your mother's belongings. Like they were trying to erase her from our lives. Mom was mad about it, but she cooperated because she was hoping they'd let us see you if we kept everything civil."

"Do you know if there was anything that Iris held back?"

"She only kept two things, and that was because she was positive that your grandparents would destroy them. She kept the dress your mother wore for her mating ceremony, and a ring that Christopher gave her."

Heart pounding even harder, Frankie asked, "Can you describe the ring?" But she already knew, because she could see it in her head; she remembered it from the photos she'd seen of her mother in Iris's albums.

"It was white gold studded with diamonds, and it had a gorgeous gray pearl in the center."

Frankie closed her eyes. "Thanks, Lydia. That was a great help." When Trick put her phone back on the nightstand, she said, "I know what it was now."

He frowned. "What?"

"I know what I overlooked. I saw pictures of my mother, but only my subconscious seemed to notice the ring. I get it now." She bit her lip. "There's someone I need to talk to."

His eyes narrowed. "Who?"

A little while later, Frankie was sitting on the curb in a busy parking lot, near a very familiar car. A car she'd ridden in many times, completely unaware that its owner had betrayed her family in too many ways to count.

It wasn't long before said owner came along. Even with the sounds of traffic, she'd heard his shoes ticking on the asphalt before she saw him. She knew what hours he worked, had known what time he'd leave his office.

Rising, she waited for him to stop fumbling with his car keys and look up. Finally he did. Her wolf snarled, flexing her unsheathed claws.

Brad stilled and blinked. "Frankie, hey." His face split into a grin that quickly faded. "Is everything okay? You don't look so good. You have shadows under your eyes."

"I'm fine," she lied. She inhaled deeply, searching for calm, and instead ended up with a lungful of the annoying scents of exhaust, motor oil, and hot pavement. "I wouldn't be fine if it weren't for Trick. He got to me in time."

"In time?" Brad crossed to her, the picture of concern. "What does that mean? Honey, what happened?"

She kept her tone even. "I was held at gunpoint in the basement of my old home."

His mouth fell open. "*What?* By who? And please tell me they've been arrested."

"It was the person who killed my parents."

He sighed, pinching his nose. "Frankie . . . it was Christopher who—"

"Who Cruz framed, I know," she finished. "He made a full confession when he pointed that gun at my face. A *full* confession."

Brad's eyes flickered nervously.

"I remember when I was a kid, I was helping you pick cuff links to wear out of that big box you have. I found a ring. A ring with a gray pearl. I picked it up and asked if I could have it. You freaked out. Snatched it out of my hands, shoved it in a drawer, and told me to never ask about it again. Cruz got the ring and her dress for you, didn't he?"

Brad glanced around. There was one other person in the lot, but he was chatting away on his cell phone, not paying them a lick of attention. "Okay, yes, he agreed to get me Caroline's things," Brad admitted in a low voice. "They didn't deserve to have anything of hers, Frankie."

"And he agreed to give Iris the sculpture too."

That comment surprised him. "I liked the idea of her having one of your pieces without even knowing it."

Frankie narrowed her eyes. "You sensed that Cruz was jealous of my parents' mating. You saw an ally. You used him."

"I encouraged him to push her to leave the pack, sure, but that's all."

Frankie shook her head. "You gave him the gun."

"Frankie—"

"You gave it to him," she insisted. "You've fed me enough lies over the years. No more."

Brad closed his eyes for a moment. "He was only supposed to drive Caroline out of the pack. If anything, she became more determined to stay. I told Cruz to be patient, but he wouldn't. He asked for a gun. Said if he couldn't have Christopher, then no one would have him."

Her wolf swiped out her claws. "And the idea of him shooting my father suited you just fine."

"No, it didn't."

"Really?" Frankie shrugged one shoulder as she asked, "Why not? You hated him. He was a shifter. An animal. What would be so bad about putting him down?"

Brad let out a ragged sigh. "There are things you don't know."

"Explain them to me, then."

"Christopher planned to take you and your mother to Canada!" he burst out.

She lifted a brow. "Canada?"

"Yes. He didn't like that we were in her life. He wanted to switch packs, to take her and you far away."

"Far away from you and your 'You need to leave the pack' bullshit, you mean? He was tired of you trying to make her leave him. Tired of seeing her so unhappy about the way you were acting." Like Trick had been unhappy with how the Newmans treated Frankie. "He wanted to put distance between you."

"I'd have rarely seen her, Frankie. I wouldn't have been able to watch you grow up. I'd have been a damn *stranger* to you. I wasn't going to allow that. I wasn't going to allow him to take her away from me."

A disturbing amount of possessiveness coated his latter words, and Frankie stilled as the truth hit her. "Did she know?"

"Know what?"

"That you loved her a little *too* much?" It explained why he'd never been in a relationship and didn't have a family of his own. All he'd wanted was Caroline. It even explained why he thought of Frankie as a daughter. "I'll bet my father sensed it. No wonder he wanted her far away from you."

Brad swallowed. "I was never going to allow him to keep her from me."

"So you gave Cruz a gun, even knowing that if Christopher died, *she'd* die."

He scoffed. "That's what shifters say, but it's not true. The bond isn't some magical thing." He paused at the beep of a remote car lock, but the owner of the car didn't even look their way as they hopped into their vehicle. "She was convinced that the bond was unbreakable. Convinced that she couldn't live without him. I knew that when he was dead, she'd see the truth. See that he'd fooled her, lied to her, manipulated her." He swallowed. "If I'd known that Cruz really meant to kill Caroline, I would *never* have given him that gun. I would never have urged him on. You have to believe that, Frankie."

"Do I?" She sneered. "You say you hate that pack because they stole Caroline from you. But you knew *exactly* who killed her. You knew . . . and you didn't tell anyone. You protected his identity to save your own skin and because it suited you just fine that I was taken from the pack. And then you used him in other ways—maybe even threatened to expose his secret if he didn't do things like steal her belongings, pass the sculpture to Iris, and God knows what else you asked him to do. By that point you'd truly convinced yourself that you played no part in my mother's death."

"If she hadn't mated with him and joined that pack—"

"Oh, everyone else is to blame but you, aren't they? The person who you should be angry at is yourself. *You* played Cruz. *You* armed him. You, you, *you*. If you'd have exposed Cruz for what he was, I wouldn't have almost *died* yesterday. That's right, I almost died. That's on you."

"And you deserve to be dead for that alone," Trick rumbled.

Brad swerved to face him, eyes widening as he noted that both Ryan and Marcus were closing in on him. Brad turned to her. "You wouldn't let them hurt me, Frankie. I'm your uncle. Hell, I've been a father to you all these years—"

"Because you helped Cruz murder mine," she snapped. "And now you're going to pay for it."

Fear flashed across Brad's face, but he jutted out his chin. "You can't prove that I did anything. There's no evidence. If you go to the police—"

"There would be no point in handing you over to the police, although I did record your confession on the cell phone in my pocket. See, the crimes occurred on pack territory, which is out of the police's jurisdiction. Even if there was some way they could charge you for something like conspiracy to commit murder, a good lawyer would get you off—especially since recent events prove that Cruz wasn't entirely stable. No, the human authorities wouldn't make you pay for what you did. But someone has to."

Sweat beaded on his forehead. "I'm not responsible for Cruz's actions. He was the one who stabbed and strangled your mother. He was the one who fired the bullet that killed Christopher. If Cruz really wanted them dead so badly, he'd have done it regardless."

"Maybe Cruz would still have killed my parents without you feeding his anger and giving him that gun—I guess we'll never know. But you gave him that gun *knowing* he intended to kill my father. You say you loved Caroline, but it sure didn't bother you that her killer wasn't brought to justice. No, you protected his identity and let my father take the blame for something he never did. Heartbreakingly, both his parents died believing he was truly guilty of it.

"Because of you, I lost my parents and was taken from my mate, my paternal family, and my pack. Call me a bitch, but I can't let any of that go. I don't think either of my parents would want me to—not after all the pain you caused, not after I almost died. And I really can't expect Trick to let it go. Not when we've been apart all these years because of what you did, and not when you betrayed me and my mother the way you did—he's my mate, he'll never be able to overlook that someone hurt me that way." She cut her gaze to Trick. "I'm done."

Brad's eyes bulged as Trick grabbed him by the scruff of his neck. "Wait! What are you doing?"

"Like I said, you need to pay for what you did," Frankie told him, astonished she could sound so very calm.

"They'll kill me!"

"Maybe. To be honest, I don't want to know what they'll do to you. All I've asked is that they make you . . . disappear. They've assured me they can stage things so that it looks like you packed your shit and left. People will certainly believe that when they hear the recorded confession and I tell them how I assured you that I'd be sharing it."

Fear blazed in his eyes. "This will destroy Marcia and Geoffrey."

"You should have thought about that before you gave Cruz that gun," said Frankie. "But I think it's been a very long time since you've thought of anyone but yourself." With that, she turned her back on Brad and strode over to the SUV.

CHAPTER TWENTY

Four months later

Frankie carefully swiped the fine paintbrush over the clay fang, making it a dull white to match the others. It was the last unpainted tooth within the ugly, prehistoric dire wolf's mouth. She hadn't yet decided whether to add drops of red paint to the jaws. She probably should, since she'd streaked it over his lower legs—as if he'd trampled through a river of blood during his travels. His claws were thick and long, but one was sharper and longer than the others; it looked more like a knife, and she'd painted it bloodred.

Yes, she was well aware that the creature symbolized Cruz in some way. He'd been metaphorically knee-deep in blood. He'd killed her mother with a knife. And if anyone were to look beneath the large paws of the sculpted wolf, they would see black spots resembling the gun residue that should have been on *his* hands. Christopher's finger might have been on the trigger, but he *never* would have shot himself. His death was on Cruz.

After clearing the rubble and unearthing Cruz's body, the Bjorn wolves had confirmed that he was in fact killed by the cabin's collapse. His family was naturally devastated by everything. They were mourning him while also hating what he'd done and feeling ashamed for being blind to it all. Clara felt particularly guilty, knowing the pain her son had caused her best friend. So guilty, in fact, that she hadn't felt she deserved to attend Frankie and Trick's mating ceremony—nothing they'd said had managed to convince her otherwise.

Putting down the paintbrush, Frankie took a swig from her water bottle. The mating ceremony had gone exactly how Iris had told Frankie it would. The whole thing had still felt almost magical. Her wolf had loved every second of it.

The after-party had been a blast. Taryn had tried getting Greta rotten drunk, but she'd had no luck. The old woman apparently wasn't going to take any chances that she'd pour out any more of her true feelings.

By unspoken mutual consent, Frankie and Greta had decided never to speak of the karaoke incident. Trick thought it occasionally amusing to hum "Greased Lightning" under his breath when she and Greta were in the same room, but Frankie didn't find anything funny about it.

With the exception of Bracken, who was still deep in grief, the Mercury Pack had attended the ceremony. There had also been some other outsiders, such as Trick's parents, Makenna's coworkers, and even Abigail.

During the after-party, Frankie had asked Uma why she'd suddenly been able to push aside her anger with Trey. She'd said, *"When Trick went into the basement to rescue you, I saw the same panic on Trey's face that I knew was on mine. He shoved everyone out of the way, determined to be the one who pulled you, Trick, and Marcus out of there. How can I be angry with someone who would risk themselves for my son that way?"*

Her change of behavior toward Trey hadn't relaxed Trick. In fact, it seemed to Frankie that he was waiting for the other shoe to drop. But so far, so good.

Frankie hadn't invited her grandparents to the ceremony, since she'd known it would be as hard for Trick as it would be for them. He was still tremendously pissed at them, and she suspected that he always would be, purely for keeping him and Frankie apart for so long.

After Brad "disappeared," she'd gone to her grandparents' house and played the recording of his confession. At first they'd been outraged and insisted that the voice didn't belong to Brad. She'd expected their reaction, though, so she'd simply left. A week later, Geoffrey called and told her they'd found her mother's ring and dress among Brad's possessions.

They still weren't yet ready to come to terms with Brad's involvement in the murders, but they were no longer accusing Frankie of lying. They were also struggling to accept Christopher's innocence. They'd spent so long hating him that they couldn't quite shake it off. Still, they were no longer insisting that she shouldn't have any involvement with her pack. In fact, they occasionally asked how things were going with Trick.

Frankie doubted they would ever visit pack territory or be *happy* that she was part of a pack, but they seemed to have lost their bitterness about it. They'd even hinted that she and Trick could one day go to their house for lunch. None of them were ready for that yet, but it was enough that they were making progress.

Geoffrey had asked if she knew what had happened to Brad, and she'd replied, "No." Whether he believed her or not, she couldn't be sure. But she'd never asked what had been done to Brad; she didn't want to know, and that seemed to suit Trick just fine.

A few weeks after the ceremony, Frankie visited Christopher's grave with Trick, who didn't release her hand even once—as if to remind her that she wasn't alone. And as she'd stared down at her father's grave, a lump had formed in her throat. Not just at what he'd been through and the years with him she'd lost, but at the fact that he hadn't even been able to be buried alongside his mate. Such a thing seemed cruel, but she doubted she'd be able to convince her grandparents to relocate Caroline's body. That just made the whole thing even sadder.

WILD HUNGER

Her nightmares had stopped, which had relieved Trick. She'd forgiven herself for not speaking up as a kid. But Marcus hadn't yet forgiven himself for being drawn away from her on Bjorn territory that night. Roni also felt sincerely bad about it. In addition, Ally was bummed that she hadn't foreseen the hostage situation, and she'd needlessly apologized to Frankie and Trick for it numerous times.

After screwing the cap back on her bottle, Frankie set it down. She then lifted the paintbrush and dabbed it in the white paint. She gave the fang yet another coat, keeping her hand steady and—

Arms snaked around her waist just as a familiar scent cocooned her, making her feel safe and cared for . . . and freaking annoyed. She sighed. "You said you'd just sit and sketch."

Trick brushed his nose along her neck, inhaling her scent. "I did sit. I did sketch."

"Well, either go do it a little longer or head back to the caves."

"Why?" He pressed a kiss to the hollow beneath her ear. "I'm comfortable right here."

"You can't be this close to me while I'm trying to work." How was she supposed to concentrate when he was eating her space, stirring up her hormones? It had been hard enough just having him in the studio. The heat from his gaze had made it difficult for her to get into the flow at first. Whenever she'd flicked him a brief look, she'd seen his hand moving fast, drawing in short, light strokes. "I mean it, Trick, you're too distracting."

His arms flexed around her. "Sorry, baby, I don't want to distract you."

She snorted. "Yes, you do."

"Yes, I do."

As he pressed his solid body closer to hers, she felt his cock digging into her back. "How can you be hard right now?" She was dressed in baggy overalls that were not the least bit alluring. Her hair was styled in a messy ponytail, and she was wearing zero makeup.

303

Trick nuzzled her. "You have no idea how hot you are when you work," he said. His breath, warm on her neck, sent a light tremor down the length of her spine.

"Hot?"

"Hmm." Trick scraped his teeth over her claiming mark and then laved it with a swipe of his tongue. "You're competent and confident. Your focus is solely on what you're doing. Seeing you like that reminds me what it's like to be the center of that focus." Especially of the times she sucked his cock, when she seemed totally absorbed in what was doing, devoting every bit of her attention to him—just as she had that morning. And as he'd sat there recalling each of those times, his cock had gotten harder and heavier, until he simply couldn't take it anymore.

Trick whispered into her ear, "I want to fuck you. Right here."

She swallowed, too easily caught up in his spell. "I'm not done."

"It's my birthday," he reminded her, pulling out her hair tie. He sank his hands into the silky curls, loving the feel of them. "You're supposed to let me have my way on my birthday."

"I did let you have your way—hence why you were in here, sketching, in the first place."

His mouth curved. "I want to be in my happy place."

She would have laughed at that, but then he grabbed a fistful of her curls and snatched her head back.

His lips grazed her ear, tickling the tiny little hairs there. "I wasn't *asking* to fuck you, baby," he said, soft and low. "I *am* going to fuck you. This body is mine. I can have it and mark it and use it whenever and however I want."

Frankie shivered. That calm, dominant, confident voice seemed to seep through her skin and sink into her bones. Her blood thickened. Her nipples tightened. She felt herself go damp.

"Put your hands on the bench. Don't move them unless I tell you to. Good girl."

Her eyes fluttered shut as he kissed, licked, and sucked at her neck. She melted into him, nipples tingling, pussy throbbing as a slow burn started deep in her core. Using his grip on her hair, he forced her head forward and then left a trail of warm, wet kisses along her sensitive nape.

Trick flicked out his tongue to trace the shell of her ear. "I can smell how much you want me." She couldn't have any idea just what the heady scent of her need did to him and his wolf. They both greedily inhaled it. It was better than any perfume, any flower, any other fragrance that existed. "Fucking love that smell. Almost as much as I love you."

He very slowly tugged down the front zipper of her overalls, thinking it a shame that she wasn't naked beneath them. He slid them over her shoulders and down her arms, letting them puddle at her feet. After peeling off her tank top, he pushed down her shorts. "Kick them and your shoes aside, baby. Good girl."

Standing in only her underwear, Frankie waited, expecting him to tear them off. He didn't. Didn't touch her at all. In fact, he took a step back. She could almost *feel* his gaze raking over her. Everything in her seemed to be holding its breath in anticipation, waiting for him to do something. *Anything.* "Trick—" She almost jumped as his hand landed on her nape and then softly swept down her back.

He palmed her ass and gave it a little squeeze. "You have the hottest ass." Trick skimmed his hands down her arms, smoothing the little goose bumps on her skin and easing the prickle. Reaching around her, he unclipped the front clasp of her bra. He almost groaned as her breasts spilled into his hands. He squeezed and shaped them, loving how soft and creamy they were. He traced circles around her taut nipples with his thumbs. "Mouth, Frankie."

She turned her face to his. His clever mouth was hot and greedy on hers as he took complete possession of it. The whole time, he pinched and twisted her nipples. She felt each pinch and twist in her pussy. Low in her stomach, the tension built and built until the ache was so bad she wanted to cry.

Tossing her bra on the pile of clothes at their feet, Trick slipped his hand into her panties and pushed up with his palm. *So hot and wet.* He growled, low and deep, in her ear. "All mine." He dipped his thumb between her folds and swirled it around her clit. "I remember eating this pussy this morning. I remember sweeping my tongue right through here." His thumb slid between her slit. "I remember sinking my tongue in here." He drove two fingers inside her, groaning as her walls quivered around them. "So warm and slick and snug."

As he pumped his fingers, just as he'd earlier pumped his tongue inside her, Frankie's head fell back on his shoulder. She rocked against his hand, moaning each time the heel of his palm ground against her clit. She felt hot. Needy. Like her skin was too tight. Every sane thought in her head had long ago scattered—she was totally caught up in Trick and what he was doing to her.

"You want me to let you come?" asked Trick, knowing she was close. Her response was a broken moan. "Once, baby, I'll make you come once with my fingers. Then I'm getting in that pussy." He picked up the pace, thrusting his fingers even deeper. All the while he pinched and tugged on her hard little nipples. Soon her thighs were shaking and her pussy began to quake. He sank his teeth into her shoulder, growling as her pussy tightened around his fingers and she came with a raspy moan that fisted his fingers. And he was done waiting for her.

Frankie had so many feel-good chemicals racing through her, she felt like she was floating. Weightless. Deep inside, she still ached for Trick to fill her. But while her orgasm—

She gasped as he roughly gripped her nape, bent her over the bench, and then kicked her legs apart. Her nipples scraped cotton, and she realized he'd grabbed her overalls and laid them over the bench in front of her, protecting her skin from the wood. She'd been so caught up in her postorgasm buzz she hadn't even noticed. Her wolf bucked a little at the extremely dominant move, but Frankie was too damn turned on to care.

"Stay still, Frankie."

Hearing his zipper lower, she almost moaned. Yes, this was what she needed. Him inside her. He didn't remove her panties; he roughly shoved them aside. She sucked in a breath as she felt his thick cock began to sink inside her. He stretched her until it stung, and the pressure was amazing—

His cock sliced through her as he slammed home with a shocking, brutal force that sent the breath gusting out of her lungs. Mouth slack, she blinked. In one fluid move, he'd stuffed her full. "Fuck," she rasped.

Trick did what he'd been imagining doing for the past hour—he hammered into his mate, digging his fingers into the globes of her ass. Her pussy was blazing hot and so gorgeously fucking slick he thought he might lose his mind. Even with the music blaring, he could hear every cock-hardening moan and the sound of flesh smacking flesh.

When she tried throwing back her hips to counter his thrusts, he landed a sharp slap on her ass. "No, baby, *I'm* fucking *you*," he gritted out, clawing off her panties, scraping her skin just enough to make her moan. His wolf loved the sound, wanted to hear more.

Using the finger still wet from her pussy, Trick circled the bud of her ass. "You know what's coming, Frankie, don't you?" He pushed the finger knuckle-deep. "The moment you're done coming around my cock, I'm going to plunge inside this tight ass."

Frankie fisted the overalls as he drove deeper into her pussy, jackhammering into her like just the thought of being inside her ass made him lose control. She'd let him take her there several times before and liked it more than she'd expected. Still, she shook her head just to tease him. "Not today, I'm—" He gave her another sharp spank.

"Did it sound like I was asking for permission, Frankie?" He added a second finger and scissored them, stretching her. Every time she'd bent over to grab something, sticking her pert little ass in the air, he'd wanted nothing more than to fuck it. And he would. But first he needed to feel her inferno-hot pussy ripple greedily around his cock. He slammed into her harder. Faster. "Come, baby. Do it now." He used the fingers of his free hand to part her folds, exposing her clit to the cool air, and then he thumbed it hard.

Blinding white-hot pleasure tore through Frankie, making her spine snap straight and wrenching a scream out of her throat. Trick pulled out of her lightning-fast, and then she felt him lodge the thick head of his cock in her ass. Her eyes snapped open as he inched his way inside. "Fuck." Halfway in, he punched his hips forward and flexed his cock, stretching the walls of her ass. She gasped. He was so thick, but it didn't hurt anymore. She'd gotten used to the slight burn. Liked it.

Balls-deep in her ass, Trick groaned. It was just as tight and scorching hot as her pussy. He eased his body over hers, giving her his weight, and spoke into her ear. "Come whenever you're ready." Because he knew he wouldn't last long. He bit into her nape, pinning her in place, and then pounded her. There was nothing gentle about it. It was raw and primal and territorial. And he knew through their bond that she was loving every moment of it.

When he felt the telling tingle at the base of his spine, Trick swatted her ass hard. That was all it took. She came again, clamping down on his dick and groaning his name. He swore viciously and jammed his cock deep as he exploded, filling her with his come.

For a short while, they stayed where they were, panting and shaking with aftershocks. Trick pressed a kiss to the dip between her shoulder blades and then slowly pulled out of her. He straightened, but she didn't move. Mouth curving, he rubbed one of the globes that were a pretty pink from his hands. His wolf growled in satisfaction at the sight. "You okay, baby?"

"Hmm."

"Sore?"

"You like it when I'm sore, so don't bother trying to sound concerned."

Chuckling, he lifted her and carried her into the little bathroom. After cleaning up, they dragged on their clothes and he drew her to him. "Love you, baby."

Frankie smiled at the way his brown eyes drifted over her face, warm and possessive. Her wolf basked in that possessiveness. It wasn't an emotion that was constricting or hurtful; it made her feel safe and cosseted. "And I love you." She kissed him, licking at his tongue and sipping from his mouth. "Did you actually finish your sketch?"

"Yep."

"I want to see." She leaned into him when he slid an arm around her waist and then guided her to the chair where he'd left his pad. As she got a good look at his sketch, she smiled. "Hey, that's really good." He'd somehow captured her energy. He'd even mastered the intense "Don't bother me" expression she subconsciously wore when working. She could see his confidence in each of those strokes and the clever use of shade.

Handing him the pad, she said, "I'm seriously impressed."

"Thank you." He dabbed a kiss on her mouth. "You done for the day?"

She glanced at the sculpture. "I have a little more to do, but I could really use a shower right now."

His voice dropped an octave as he said, "A shower sounds good."

Hearing the sexual intention there, she frowned. "You had me this morning, and then again just now."

"Yes. And?"

Frankie just shook her head. "I'm still a little sore, so you'll have to wait until later."

Trick pursed his lips. Wait? Nah. At the very least, he'd eat her out in the shower. But he didn't say that. "I can wait. But I'm getting back in that pussy tonight."

She snapped her teeth. He was *such* a bossy bastard. And totally spoiled. "Fine. But tonight, instead of you taking over, can we do what *I* want to do?"

"It depends on what you want to do."

"Well, if it 'depends,' we're not doing what *I* want to do because you're in control of what happens."

"It's good that you get that. It's like one mind."

She splayed her palm over his face and turned away. "You're not here. You're really not. I don't know why I let you sketch me."

Chuckling, Trick grabbed her hand. "It was only fair that you let me sketch you, since you started working on a sculpture of my head." He'd seen it tucked under one of her benches.

Frankie narrowed her eyes at him. "How do you know about that?"

"A little bird told me."

"Well, since I don't have a parrot that could sell me out, I'm guessing that you're lying."

"Oh my God. It's just a turn of phrase."

"It's a proverb, and they're dumb."

He sighed. "You're always going to make me crazy, aren't you?"

"You say that like it's a bad thing."

Acknowledgments

I 'm very conscious of how super lucky I am to have so many awesome and incredibly supportive people around me. My family, my assistant, and the fabulous Montlake Romance team are my own personal angels sent from heaven. Thank you all for everything you have done and continue to do. Also, a massive thanks to each and every reader who has taken a chance on one or more of my books—I will adore you all forever.

Website: www.suzannewright.co.uk

Blog: www.suzannewrightsblog.blogspot.co.uk

Twitter: twitter.com/suz_wright

Facebook: www.facebook.com/suzannewrightfanpage

About the Author

Suzanne Wright can't remember a time when she wasn't creating characters and telling their tales. Even as a child in England, she loved writing poems, plays, and stories. As an adult, Wright has published sixteen novels: *From Rags, Burn, Blaze, Ashes,* five Deep in Your Veins novels, six books in the Phoenix Pack series, and two books in the Mercury Pack series. Wright lives in Liverpool with her husband and two children. Visit her online at www.suzannewright.co.uk.

Made in the USA
Columbia, SC
07 March 2018